Nick Amies

she's electric

She's Electric
by **Nick Amies**

Copyright © 2012 Nick Amies
Cover Design by Benita Lipps

Ordering Information:
Quantity sales. Special discounts are available on quantity purchases by corporations, associations, and others. For details, contact the author at the following address:

www.shes−electric.info

Printed in the United States of America
2nd Edition: 10 June 2013

she's electric

*a britpop love story**

*...sort of

Chapters

one

Slide Away

November 1994

There are those moments in life which define you as a fully paid up member of the male gender - the moment you lose your virginity, the moment you first set eyes on your progeny, the moment you realise that beer makes you superhuman - and then there are those which define you as a big poof. Sitting in my parents' living room, cradling an oversized, luminous blue Care Bear while crying over the closing scene in *St. Elmo's Fire* where Rob Lowe leaves his friends behind, I realise this is probably one of the least masculine moments I am ever likely to experience in my adult life.

If I was fourteen and a girl, this may be remembered in time as one of those tender moments of sentimentality which become so few and far between as the responsibilities of being a grown-up take over. But I'm not a teenage girl. I'm a twenty two year old man whose three year relationship has just ended in a short, ten minute break-up visit. The Care Bear on my lap should have been going home with her tonight, not sitting uncomfortably in front of a Brat Pack sob-fest, waiting for the film to end and the right time to leave. If I was the bear, I'd be out of here like a shot because this is not a pretty scene and is unlikely to get any more attractive once my mum and dad get back from their tactically arranged visit to the cinema. While I appreciated the gesture of giving us some space, especially since this was supposed to be a reunion with some long-time-coming missed-you shagging, I now half wish that they had stuck around. She may not have dumped me if my bodyguards had been here to back me up. See? This is why I deserve to wear a t-shirt with BIG POOF printed on the front for all time. I even wish my mummy and daddy had been here to make everything all right like they used to. I sicken myself. I loathe what I have become. The credits roll and the Care Bear calls a cab, leaving me searching my abstinent parents' cupboards for anything alcoholic. Banana liquor...Advocaat...Sambuca? Interesting. I'd like to see my mother explain that one away as a cooking ingredient or Christmas treat. Failing to imagine mum secretly knocking back flaming shots while dad's down the snooker club, I presume it's a long forgotten gift from one of Auntie Val's trips to Como. Dislodging the thick wad of despair from my throat, I toast my dad's sister and start necking it. This will teach the bitch...

I'm halfway through the bottle and my mind is slipping between thoughts like a drunk trying to find his way out of a pissy alleyway; recollections slide between synapses on a greasy path of inebriation. Sloppily I stumble and bump into painful memories which were, until a mere couple of hours ago, happy snapshots of a life with Anna. Skidding away from these tinted views of former bliss, I crash into walls of reality and smash through the window of the here and now. I feel the pain as real as if I had shards of glass stabbing me in the heart, the injuries of my car-crash life. The sickness comes quickly afterwards; sour bile and poisonous hate replaces the fleeting soma of drunken numbness. I'm then staggering back into *St. Elmo's Fire* - there's Judd Nelson yelling "wasted love!" at Ally Sheedy as they bitterly argue over the post break-up record collection: "No Springsteen leaves this house!" Judd's a dick. He brought it on himself. He has no reason to deliberately mutate his love into loathing. He was the one who shagged a shop girl in front of a three-way mirror. It was the hot sex with a leggy blonde sales assistant in a changing room cubicle which brought an end to his relationship. He has no defence. I, on the other hand, did nothing to bring this on. I did everything for Anna. I tried to be everything she wanted. I adored her and made sure she knew it at every opportunity. There was no lingerie shop bunk-up for me. No infidelity, no sales girl offering to model a lacy gift for the girlfriend I was about to cheat on. There was no-one else. Just Anna.

As Judd throws his football through a glass wall, I step aside and stand in a fresh pile of self-pity before careening into a spontaneous explosion of pathetic tears. Why did she do this to me? What did I do wrong? I was sensitive. I was caring. I even tried to talk about my feelings. I wanted to be a 90s man - a New Man - the kind that women were supposed to be falling over themselves to find. What good did it do me?

My mind trips back into the living room to find that the television is still on and has been ever since Rob Lowe skipped town and the giant Care Bear left me for the nearest strip club. A re-run of *The Sweeney* is half-way through. Detective Inspector Jack Regan, tie askew and suit crumpled, bellows at some tart in a fur coat in some dingy interrogation room. The bloke from *Minder* stands in the shadows, sweating in an acrylic shirt. Jack stops barking at the prostitute and looks through the screen at me with a look of disdain on his face.

"Look at yourself. You're a disgrace."

"She broke my heart, Jack," I slur.

"She stole your knackers more like," Regan spits. I can almost smell the stale scotch on his breath. Carter chuckles derisively behind him, mocking me. "You should be ashamed of yourself...the way you behaved. Call yourself a man?"

"I'm a New Man," I belligerently assert.

Regan bangs his fist on the table. "Bollocks! There's no such thing. You're either a man or you're not. What's it going to be, sunshine?"

"What about you?" I ask. "What kind of man are you?"

"We're The Sweeney, love," Jack says, turning his attention back to the tart. "And we haven't had any dinner."

The Sambuca makes its last push for supremacy over my senses. My defences are shot to pieces. It's a slaughter. "Whatever you say, Jack. Whatever you say..."

The next day I wake up in my childhood bedroom with a bastard of a headache splitting my skull in two and a throat which seems to have been sandblasted. My one working eye slowly scans the room and sends back signals of vague recognition to my damaged brain: Stone Roses poster, Liverpool scarf, mother standing with a mop and bucket.

"Have a good night did we?" I can't remember them coming home so I presume I was already in this kind of state by the time they got back. Her face suggests that she made an unpleasant discovery sometime this morning, probably behind the sofa or somewhere else where flushing wouldn't have been an option, and that she has no idea that Anna chucked me. Anna. Oh, man... "I hope if you were both drinking that stuff you called Anna a cab before you passed out." Great. They came back to find me comatose on the floor, probably, with an empty bottle of Italian liquor rolling around beside me. Hang on...I painfully stretch an arm down the length of my body. I touch only bare skin and, eventually, boxer shorts. "And when did you get that tattoo? I don't think I approve." Ugh. Undressed and put to bed. Is there no end to the indignity? "Anyway, your grandparents are here so hurry up." Apparently not.

"Morning, boy." My father looks up from his *Daily Mirror* and gives me a knowing smile. I don't really know this man. I mean, I know about what he's been up to for the past twenty two years but before that? It's a part of his story that rarely even gets hinted at, let alone told. Plus, you can never really tell what he's thinking, which is unnerving. He seems entirely at ease with his surroundings but I'm guessing that calm comes from an earlier lifetime spent experiencing much of what that world had to offer. I'm sure a truly innocent man would not have described *The Clangers* as being like a bad acid trip if he had not experienced said psychedelic experience himself.

"Cool sunglasses," my mother chimes in, sarcastically. Mothers of a certain age shouldn't say things like cool - and mine knows this, which is why a sly smile of satisfaction spreads across her face as I wince behind my protective eyewear and my shoulders contract at hearing the word. She gives me a peace sign and my defeat is assured. I slump down at the table across from my grandparents and my brain rattles down my spine before shooting out my arse. They never see me like this which explains why they are looking at me like I've just beamed down from Outer Space.

"Is he ill?" Gran whispers to my dad.

"He was," says the voice behind the sports section. "But it's all cleared up now."

"What's been wrong with you, dear?" Gran asks. I can't answer. Someone is currently using a corkscrew to pull my eyes from their sockets. I instead reach for the orange juice and hope someone with tact and diplomacy can answer for me. Unfortunately, my mother steps in before that person can speak up.

"He's hung-over. He and Anna went through a bottle of Val's Sambuca last night. And then he passed out and was sick on that expensive rug Keith bought us last year." I'm surprised you noticed, I want to say, considering my brother's extreme lack of taste. But I have no strength to drag the Golden Child into these painful proceedings and no desire to roll out my usual line of abuse concerning that dreadful IKEA rag he had the audacity to try and pass off as a Persian floor covering.

"How old are you now, Daniel?" Granddad takes out his cigarettes but sheepishly replaces them in his jacket pocket when two identical looks are shot at him from wife and daughter.

"He's twenty two, Dad," says mum. "Old enough to know better."

"I'm not sure if there's ever an age when you stop making mistakes," he replies, and winks at me. Cheers, Granddad. An ally at last.

"Well, he's not a child anymore and I don't expect to have to come home to find my youngest son paralytic on the floor and his vomit everywhere. Keith was never like that." Fucking Keith. Of course he was never like that. He's never done anything remotely exciting or life-affirming in his whole sorry existence. So he has a steady job, a good income, a wife and two beautiful children who will no doubt grow up to be Nobel Prize winners or diplomats at the UN. He's still a boring twat with no personality. The most outrageous thing my older brother has ever done is have sex with his wife. Twice. Probably in the missionary position with the lights out after a glass or two of Chardonnay on the sofa with Simply fucking Red turned down low on his expensively assembled Bang and Olufsen hi-fi. "I'm surprised Anna let you get in such a state," Mother continues. "She's such a lovely, responsible girl. How she copes with you sometimes, I don't know." Well, mother, she doesn't have to cope anymore. In fact, if she had stuck around for the Sambuca-tasting part of the evening I'm sure she would have just sat back and let me drink myself to death because, you know what, she doesn't give a fuck anymore. She's met some guy called Steve at university and, while it breaks her heart - yeah, right - she couldn't see our relationship going any further. It had apparently run its course and it was time for a new beginning. At least she came and told me to my face, the lovely, responsible girl that she is. Now will you all please shut the fuck up and leave me alone for ever.

"Can you give me a lift to the station, dad?" I eventually mumble.

The bone-shaking, livestock class journey back to the city seems to take an eternity rather than the usual half an hour. Every minute is stretched out to accommodate the full scope of my mental and physical torment. The cigarette I cadged off my granddad before taking the short trip to the station is proving to be another in the long list of bad ideas I've been compiling over the last few months. The initial rush of head-swimming nicotine has passed and now I want to spray my fellow travellers with projectile Minute Maid. I try and stave off the reflex by feeling sorry for myself and reliving the moments which got me into this mess.

I should have just accepted it as the end when it seemed most obvious but like a dog with a battered and long since satisfying chew toy, I just wouldn't let it go. It was such a beautiful full-stop. We had gone away to Brighton for a week, just the two of us for the first time in ages, and had a really nice time. The weather had been great and we had managed to rent a tiny apartment not far from the beach for a steal. A friend of Anna's dad lived nearby and knew the owner. Our week away had been planned to fill the only free period the flat was available before high season really kicked in and the geezer was happy to get a fair price for it before he began raking it in. Despite the certainty in the air that Anna would be leaving for university at the end of the summer - something I'd been dreading since we both decided to return to education - neither of us wanted to dwell on that. I felt strong during that week. Whatever was coming our way, we could handle. I had eventually got my arse into gear and earned enough to support myself once I was back at college. I was looking forward to starting in the city after the summer while Anna was preparing to move to Loughborough. We would both be working towards an exciting life in our chosen careers together; she a Physical Education teacher and me? I dunno...something to do with media. I hadn't chosen a speciality yet.

This belief in the certainty of our future swept away the paranoia which had been dogging me since Anna had been accepted at university. I'd been a right pain in the arse; mooning around wondering if she would still love me, a humble college student stuck in his home town, living with his parents, while she was training and working out with all these buff PE types. I'd been insufferable at times, I could admit that. But during that week, with the sun shining and with our own place in which to do lots of naughty, dirty things to each other, everything felt like it was going to be fine.

Fast forward to September and Danny Paranoia was back in full effect. We both had so many new things going on in our lives but all I could think about was Anna. She had only been away for a week when I started to lose the plot. If I didn't get a daily phone call from her, I'd have these visions of her being spit-roasted by a couple of rugger buggers while the football team jizzed on her back - and she was loving it. At weekends, I went insane wondering why she hadn't made the journey home to see me. She was obviously enjoying too many orgies to consider spending twenty quid on the fare to get a portion of non-kinky, one-on-one lovemaking with her actual boyfriend.

In October, I decided that I couldn't live at home anymore and moved in with Ellis, a friend I'd made on my course. Now, living in the city, with my independence, things would be better. She'd come and stay and we could rekindle things. But she didn't and I found that the annoyance of my family had actually helped to keep my demons at bay. Now I was alone with them. That's when the manic letter writing phase began. At my craziest I was churning out two or three multi-paged declarations of love a day. My hand was permanently deformed into a misshapen claw and my fingers had angry, red indentations in them from gripping the pen like my life depended on it and yet I carried on. But the letters weren't enough. That's when the Care Bear obsession reared its sparkly, Made in Hong Kong head. It was my mum's fault to start with.

She'd seen a tiny, cute version in the local newsagent and had bought it for Sally, one of my nieces, for her birthday. It was garish yellow, with cheap plastic gossamer fairy wings stuck on its back and a huge red heart on its chest. She'd shown it to me on one of my now rare weekend visits home. Suddenly, nothing said "I Love You" more sincerely than mass manufactured tacky merchandising crap from the Far East. I started off small. I bought a red, sportier version of Sally's and sent it to Anna in an old Cadbury's Roses box. The next two increased in size, both needing a shoe box each. The Fourth? Well, the fourth never made it to its intended, as you now know, and would have cost me a fucking fortune to post anyway.

This inundation of bears seemed to be the final furry nail in our relationship's coffin. The phone calls, which were sporadic at best, stopped completely in late October. It was two weeks before I heard from Anna again. In a call from a phone box, she told me that she would be back for a couple of days at the end of the first week of November. She would be staying with her parents and didn't want to come into the city. Could we meet at my folks' house? Sure, I said, no problem. At this point, my insanity was such that I was so far away from seeing what was actually coming that I actually started getting excited.

Now, as I sit on this rickety train, trundling through the arse end of nowhere to somewhere of no particular importance to the majority of the human race, I suddenly have a moment of clarity. Jack Regan was right. All the longing, all the insecurity, all the...bears, have robbed me of an integral part of who I am, what I am. What am I? Am I an empty, devastated broken hearted bloke who spent the previous night with a cuddly toy, a terrible 80s movie and a bottle raided from his parents' kitchen cabinet? Well, yes but that's not the whole story. I am a person who has spent the last eight months of his life worrying about what it would feel like to be alone, to be unloved, to be single. Someone for whom being without a girlfriend means the end of life itself. I was someone who was living for someone else, trying to be the person I thought she wanted me to be. But I am not that person, not deep down. I was becoming that person - that despicable, weak shell of a person - but that's history. What am I? I am a man. I'm The Sweeney and I haven't had any dinner. And things are going to change around here.

she's electric

The voice on the other end of the line tries to remain professional but the tone still suggests that a certain amount of piss is being taken.

"You'd like to reserve a table for four people, sir? We may have carpet on the floor these days but we're still a pub. I'm afraid we still do things the old fashioned way, even in 2010 - first come, first served."

Listen, dickhead, do you want my custom or not? At least two of us are borderline alcoholics and we intend to drink very heavily. Are you sure you want to blow the chance of making a week's profit in one night? "I'd really appreciate it if you could make an exception," I diplomatically choose to say instead. "It's a very special occasion and we've chosen your establishment as it comes highly recommended. We'd hate to arrive and find there was no seating available." Failing that, I could abuse my position as a member of the Fourth Estate and roundly slag of your divey little shithole, bringing scorn and bankruptcy down upon you in the form of some fabricated article about white slavery and semen samples in the soup of the day. "I'd really be grateful if you could help us out. Most of us are flying in especially."

The cocky bar manager considers my insincere platitudes and lies for a moment. "As it's a special occasion, sir, I'm sure we can make an exception for you. Seven o'clock, table for four. But I'm afraid that if you haven't claimed the table by quarter past, I'll have to make it available."

"Seven o'clock will be perfect," I reply. "And don't worry; we'll be there on the dot." Cock. Instead of a short conversation with a satisfactory ending completed in a matter of seconds, that unnecessary little exchange ran into minutes. In hotel phone bill time, that amounts to your tip, matey. I check the time on the phone against my watch. The others won't be arriving for a good few hours. I look out of the window at the rain and start regretting my decision to take the early flight. I wanted to reacquaint myself with the place, maybe revisit some old haunts. I was also champing at the bit to escape the daily drudgery and growing pressure of my increasingly adult life so I arrived well in advance of the others to get some respite and an early start. Freedom and opportunities to cut loose are so few and far between these days. But it's pissing down as usual and the city looks uninvitingly morbid and grey. I briefly consider getting my head down for a couple of hours but the short hop from Dublin is hardly reason enough to act like I'm jet-lagged. It took me longer to drive from home to the airport this morning than it did to actually fly here. Besides, despite the shitty weather, I'm actually quite keen on getting out of this room as soon as possible. There are too many contrasting floral patterns doing battle in here and the combination of fluorescent rainforest wallpaper and fuchsia-coloured furniture is threatening to bring on an acid flashback. While I'm game for anything this weekend, I was hoping to wait until much later in the festivities before having any hallucinations. I grab my jacket, wallet and room key and leave the LSD suite behind.

"Hi. I wonder if you could help me. I came totally unprepared. Do you have an umbrella I could borrow?"

The pretty receptionist smiles sweetly but in an apologetic way. "Sorry, sir. We have umbrellas but I'm afraid they're for sale, not for hire." Who said anything about hire? I just wondered if you had one I could use for the afternoon. "If you'd like a Heighton Hotel umbrella, I can put the cost of one on your room bill."

"How much will a Heighton Hotel umbrella set me back then?"

"Five pounds, sir."

I look out of the reception doors just as the persistent rain turns into a violent downpour. It suddenly becomes a no-brainer. "I'll see if it eases up and I'll get back to you on that. Could you point me in the direction of the bar?"

I resist the temptation of ordering a familiar Guinness and invest the fiver I could have spent on a brolly on a pint of Gamekeeper's Satchel, whatever that may be. I have a strange tradition of making sure the first drink I have at a travel destination is locally brewed. It proves to be an inspired idea in places like Brussels and Munich but during an assignment in Uzbekistan I ended up consigned to bed for a week after downing a litre of a brew which had no vowels in its name. I feel pretty safe in England, even with a cloudy pint of Gamekeeper's in front of me. I suppose it could contain a few pheasant droppings or a dab of salmon slime but nothing that'll kill me. It could be worse. The locals could have brewed an ale called Fishwife's Gusset or something equally off-putting. I take my Gamekeeper's Satchel over to a battered old Chesterfield armchair by the fire and take a welcome seat with a view of both the main bar area and the reception. I'm about to ease myself into a spot of people-watching when my mobile phone starts vibrating in my jacket. It's the Scotsman.

"Get the beers in!"

"Uncanny," I laugh. "I've just sat down with one. Where are you?"

"Amsterdam."

Oh no. Memories of previous visits to Sin City with McKinley come flooding back. "You are going to make it here tonight, right? You're not blowing this off for a peepshow and a suck'n'fuck?"

"No worries big man," the jovial voice assures me. "I'm at the airport. My connecting flight leaves in a couple of hours. I'll be in the city by three. Where are you?"

"I'm in the Heighton already, having a pint of Gamekeeper's Satchel."

"A fucking what?" McKinley doesn't share my interest in supporting local brewers round the world. He's a confirmed lager drinker, wherever he is on the planet. "What are you doing there so early?"

"Keeping out of the rain."

"Excellent. Heard anything from wee man or The Ponce?"

"Not a word but they both know we're meeting at that place Ellis recommended, the Korova, down the Riverside at seven."

"Okay, I'm going to see if I can get a happy finish before my plane leaves. I saw a massage parlour signposted in departures. See yer later."

The 'wee man' is still at work when I call him to find out what time he'll be knocking off. He doesn't sound in the best of moods. "I'll have to meet you there," he moans. "Some bastard has just dropped a week's worth of case files on my desk. I'll at least have to look through them before I get out of here."

Ah, the burden of a social conscience. Something I rarely have to deal with in my profession. "Mate, it's your stag do for fucks sake. They'll all still be on parole on Monday morning, you know? Knock off at five and meet me and the Scotsman at the hotel." Ellis takes his work very seriously so I know he won't, even on his last official bash as a single man.

"No can do, geezer. So you've heard from the Jock? What about The Ponce? Nothing, I bet." Ellis is sparing with his use of real names, especially when he's pissy about something or other. "That's typical. It's all about him, isn't it? It always has been." Ellis is not wrong but it is a little unfair. Rob is an actor. It's almost mandatory to be conceited and self-obsessed. But fair play, Ellis has known The Ponce for as many years as I have and we both know that he was up his own arse long before he started making a living from stage and screen. "I bet if he does come, he won't take the subtle approach. I hope you asked the Korova to provide a red carpet and an extra seat for his ego."

"Settle down, man. You're getting in a state," I say, attempting to cool his boots. "I spoke to Rob a couple of weeks ago and he knows the score. He knows not to this fuck up. He'll be there."

I didn't exactly lie to Ellis but I did shield him from some of my own concerns. It's true that I did speak to Rob a couple of weeks ago (after I called his agent so many times I was nearly served with a restraining order). And I did emphasise the importance of this get-together in a way which left little doubt as to what would happen if he didn't show - "I still have the photos from the tarts and vicars party, Rob, and I'm not afraid to use them" - so that much was true. But when I told Ellis, in my most assertive and reassuring voice, that Rob would be there, I was mentally crossing every finger and toe. Back in the day, Rob very rarely arrived when he said he would and quite often failed to show up at all. These days, he's much the same only there's more at stake for him now. It's a miracle that he still manages to get work in the industry after pissing off a fair percentage of the West End's producers and a number of the country's more prominent film directors. Maybe that's the reason he's currently starring in a mid-afternoon soap and not in some edgy Brit flick. Luckily for someone who is such an unreliable egomaniac, Rob's actually a bloody good actor. Without that talent, he'd just be one of a thousand insufferable arseholes with unfounded pretensions of being the next Gielgud. The fact that he's such a good actor makes me wonder why he can't just pretend to be conscientious and humble. Maybe that's what we need to do. We should write a fake screenplay in which Rob plays a down-to-earth guy who always keeps his promises and arrives on time. Given his dedication to method acting, we could get a good few months of reliability out of the bastard. Maybe I should have come up with this idea six months ago when Ellis first announced he was getting married. Oh well...The rain's stopped.

I shrug apologetically at the pretty receptionist in a way that suggests I'm actually sad I didn't have to buy one of her umbrellas and step out into the struggling sunlight. The weak rays battle to shine through the still stubborn clouds but their effort is a winning one. Soon the pavement will smell warm and musty as the April deluge becomes vapour, much like the pint of Gamekeeper's Satchel which is already starting to manifest itself in the form of rancid beer farts. My pace quickens from time to time to escape the miasma I'm intermittently leaving behind as I walk into the city.

The city. My city. Our city. Or at least it was. I deliberately follow a convoluted route, taking in sights and areas which hold special memories. I'm saddened but not surprised by the rapacious nature of the progress which has swallowed many of our personal landmarks since we went our separate ways. The Pulse nightclub, the site of many an evening of post-pub debauchery, is now a swanky eatery. I wonder if they still have the strippers poles in place. And those dark corners where lovers now share candlelit suppers could tell a few stories too. I stand across the road and watch a young family enjoying the 2 for 1 kids menu deal by a first floor window and wonder if either of the blonde-headed cherubs eating fish fingers and chips were conceived there or after hours in the dingy alleys of the surrounding clubland. Their parents look around the right age. A floor above, an older couple enjoy a view of the clearing sky from their seats while sipping continental beers. He is heavily tanned and laden with chunky gold; she is all fake blonde mane and leopard skin. They share a joke, possibly about the times she used to slap his hands away from her arse when she used to dance for him in that very room before the old knocking shop became a classy discotheque. The tenners he used to stuff in her g-string may have even paid for that facelift. Ah, the good old days...

Pulse was the best of a bad bunch, in all honesty. The lesser of multiple evils. On the whole, the city's clubland pandered to the masses and their gaudy, populist ideas of having a good time. Cheesy Euro-disco always comes with white stilettos as standard. Out of the few mainstream clubs we actually frequented, Pulse was the least offensive. It appealed to us because of its failures as a traditional club. There was no central or main dance floor, just tiny spaces under flashing lights on each of its claustrophobic levels. Stretched vertically over six floors, Pulse never suffered from the obvious over-crowding which made a night at Chrome Dreams feel like exercise time at Wormwood Scrubs and never seemed as full of hags and arseholes as the cavernous Speakeasy's. At least the clientele at Pulse was well distributed, meaning that you could actually bump into someone you wanted to avoid on one floor and then never actually see them again for the rest of the night. It also played relatively decent music – relatively being the operative word. While Speakeasy's was the last sanctuary on earth for fans of Rick Astley and Milli Vanilli, and Chrome Dreams throbbed with the happiest of happy House, Pulse would at least play host to some edgier DJs at times. Unfortunately, it also had a penchant for ABBA and the Village People – which made having more than one dance floor a Godsend. It also had all those little nooks and crannies in which you could hide or cop off away from prying eyes; private rooms from its bordello days which allowed flirtatious encounters in preciously dark corners. It's no surprise that most of us have fond memories of girls we picked up in Pulse. They were usually nice enough to get hot and sweaty with on the premises – unlike those acquired in the other clubs. Making a pick-up in Speakeasy's usually led to a frantic search for a cab in an attempt to escape the ridicule of your peers.

Leaving the building formerly known as Pulse behind, I wander into a familiar side street but here again something has changed. I stand and try and place what it is which makes it so different. I smell the air and my memory contradicts my senses. Where is the smell of hot fat and burnt lamb? I turn my head in an attempt to hone in on another recollection. Nope. No sickly sweet mixture of detergent and vomit. It's then that my eyes join the search. There, where Amir's Kebab Emporium should be, is an estate agent's office. I walk to the window and look in. A young man is sat at a desk in a shirt and tie, typing on a computer with one finger from each hand. The interior is spotless and glaringly white. I'm tempted to go in on some fabricated property mission just to see if they really did manage to shift ten years of animal grease from the walls and ceilings. But part of me doesn't want to know for sure whether Amir's long service to our community has been sanitised and white-washed from memory. My mind replays scenes of Friday night chaos; fights over ketchup not far from where that young man now works, secretive hands straying into moist panties in the queue for burgers not far from where the water cooler now sits, Rob shouting abuse at Ellis, the Scotsman and I as beers stolen from the Orchard get thrown all over the floor he'll be mopping until four in the morning, right about where a display of expensive country villas now stands. It may be Granger's Real Estate now but it will forever be Fatty Amir's Botulism Factory as far as I'm concerned.

Thinking of the Orchard brings me to my next diversion. Despite the unsettling nature of the Gamekeeper's, I'm about ready for a proper drink and after staying true to my tradition, I'm now up for a pint of something less specialized. I take an almost subconscious detour through the alleyways behind Fatty Amir's and come out beside the Orchard. The place looks a bit tatty these days, ignored by the developers who must have snapped up the ancient Tudor properties on the Haymarket opposite without even a glance at the old girl's finery. Inside the beams are still coated in that fire-hazard pitch, the furniture, an Antiques Roadshow buff's wet dream, remains gloriously unpreserved and the hardy bar which stretches to eternity on the upper floor still stands strong. The paint is flaking in some corners and the jukebox is playing the Pussycat Dolls but for the most part, it's like the good old days have been preserved in at least one of my old haunts. Steroid, the legendary Orchard bouncer, is even in attendance, although he must have stopped doping a few years back as he now looks about twenty stone of pure whale blubber. I order a Guinness and sidle up to where his girth is blocking the route to the backroom.

"Alright, Steroid? How you doing?"

Steroid squints at me and clenches a fist. Luckily his mind appears not to have gone to seed even if his body has. It takes a sphincter-tightening moment for him to recognise me but recognise me he eventually does. "Fackin' 'ell, Danny Boy? Danny Jones!" Forgetting that a good fifteen years have passed since he last did the same thing, and that I'm no longer one of the twenty-something rowdies who used to keep him busy on a Thursday night, Steroid slaps one of his gargantuan hands down on my head and starts squeezing my skull like a gala melon. "Where have you been, son? It's been fackin' years."

"You know, moved away...got a job...can you let go of my swede, Steroid, I think I heard something crack."

Steroid releases his grip and punches me on the shoulder, nearly knocking my arm out of its socket. "Sorry, son. Force of habit. Where are the rest of the boys then? I never see any of them about? What about that lanky streak of piss you used to hang around with? He was fackin' trouble he was after a few beers."

"Ellis? He's still in the city, actually. The last one to leave. I'm seeing him tonight. We're throwing him a bachelor party."

"Yeah? Getting hitched, is he? I thought he was a poofter." Steroid smiles and the corners of his mouth join up with the two ends of the crescent scar that runs from ear to ear over the top of his bald head. "Well, give the groom one of these from me." With that he raps me on the forehead with a monkey knuckle and wanders off chuckling to himself. "Fackin' Danny Boy Jones. Fack me..." Yeah, not much has changed at the Orchard.

It never struck any of us as strange that we considered the Orchard to be our local even though it was a good half an hour walk from all our houses. Ellis and I had the Castle round the corner from our student digs at Calvin Road, while McKinley's nearest pub was in fact the rather dubious Potter's Wheel where even a swift lunchtime half came with the threat of ultra-violence. (Rob's local was the bar closest to wherever he was spending that particular night). We patronised these other places more frequently but the Orchard was always our 'event' pub. On nights when the lads were expecting to fly, this was the launch pad. It was the city's main Britpop pub and catered for the clientele accordingly. The jukebox was stacked with Oasis, Blur, Pulp, Verve, Elastica and most of the also-rans. There was no dress code other than that which we brought with us, making it a showroom for Ben Sherman, Fred Perry, Adidas and Puma. Lads would wet their Beatle cuts down in the bathrooms while Ladettes would adjust their mod girl styling in anything which gave a reflection. It would all be in vain, however, because the cheap piss on offer at the bar meant that even the most fastidious Liam Gallagher wannabe would be covered in Fosters by the end of the night. The Orchard wasn't just about Britpop – it was also Lad central. Bad behaviour was not only tolerated (to a certain degree) but mandatory. Steroid would always stop things going too far but the Orchard's limits were a lot more flexible than other city pubs. All in all, it was the beating heart of our scene, pumping us up for nights exploring the city's soul.

Sitting here now, in the early afternoon lull, it's hard to imagine this place being the hub of anything. An old geezer sits by the fruit machine, reading the tabloids while an overweight Labrador struggles to lick its balls clean at his feet. A couple of lunchtime stragglers slowly finish up their ill-advised 'quick ones before heading back to the office' by the roaring open fire. Some out-of-towners quietly debate whether or not to stay, considering the kitchen is now closed and they were actually really only here for the food. I wonder if it was always like this before the city's Lads and Ladettes rolled in for evenings of cut-price mayhem or if the thief of change has also robbed the Orchard of its essence. After a few minutes of sipping thoughtfully, reminiscing and hoping for some injection of life, I speed up my drinking and make the decision to move on. If this is what the Orchard is like these days, it's best I leave with my warm memories unsullied. If it is still a venue for raucous entertainment, we'll find out later when the sun goes down. But for now I have places to go and people to see.

While a few shops have moved on to be replaced by new businesses, the city centre remains pretty much as I remember it as I make my way to the Hartington. I don't know what or who I expect to find there but I'm drawn to my former place of employment out of curiosity and sentimentality. If the Orchard was our final tether to reality before being cut loose to float among the stars, the Hartington was often Mission Control, a solid base of operations where plans for hedonism were hatched in the company of the misfits and lunatics we called colleagues.

Thinking back, our time as 'The Kitchen Staff' as we were collectively known was a strange one really. Ellis, the Scotsman and I all worked there to bring in a little extra while on our respective college courses but it never really felt like work. Of course, the washing of dishes, the preparation of starters and main courses and the endless final duties before indulging in the bar's seemingly bottomless hospitality welcomed us back into the outside world could be considered toil. Those mornings spent preparing fry-ups for sleepy guests on Sunday mornings were certainly hard work, more because of the hangovers we usually carried with us than the actual act of cooking bacon and eggs ever was. But everything else seemed to drift by in the background. Our minds were always filled with plans: where the night would lead, what adventures would we be pursuing next, which waitress would we try and fuck this week. The actual work we got paid for was secondary to the work we put into getting pissed, stoned and laid in the crumbling, grand old walls of the Hartington.

As I veer off the main street and take the long, rising driveway through towering firs towards the old Georgian mansion, I'm filled with more than a little trepidation. If anyone from the good old days is still there, will they even remember me? I mean, The Kitchen Staff worked there for a good two years and spent on average three nights a week there in its employ. But that's almost a decade and a half in the past now and surely the number of part-time and full-time staff members who have passed through the heavy double doors have made three former chefs from a 24-month spell back in the mid-90s a very distant memory. And even if we are remembered - that might not be a good thing and could present its own set of uncomfortable problems. If we do continue to stand out, it won't be because of our sterling work rate. I take a deep breath and walk in through that ominous entrance, hoping that I won't get saddled with the mammoth bar bill we never paid - plus interest.

On entering it's clear that some things haven't changed. It's dead. The reception is deserted, there's no one on duty at the bar and Robbie Williams is serenading an empty dining room. I crane my neck towards the staff entrance to the kitchen in an attempt to hear any of the tell-tale sounds of pre-service preparations. Again, nothing. I take a right at reception and cautiously make my way down the long glass corridor which links the main house to the East Wing in the hope of at least finding a dozing guest in the adjoining sun lounge. Not a soul. I check a menu which has been left by a wicker chair to make sure I have the right place. Yeah, it's the Hartington alright. I haven't stumbled into the Overlook Hotel out of *The Shining*. I mumble "redrum" to myself - and then shit my pants as someone behind me calls out my name.

"Danny?"

Danny's not here, Mrs. Torrance... I turn quickly, half-expecting to see two ghostly twins asking me to 'come play with us' or a tsunami of blood flowing down the corridor. I'm relieved in more ways than I can say to see Barry the Barman standing by the back entrance to the snug. "Alright Bazza? I see business is still booming."

"Danny Jones. What the bloody hell are you doing here? You're not after your old job, are you?" Barry's voice is a mixture of surprise and hope, his question already tinged with the knowledge that it's a stupid one but carrying with it a tiny amount of longing. It tells me in an instant that Barry missed an opportunity to leave a few years ago and has regretted not taking it every day since. I suspect everyone else grabbed their ticket out of here when it was offered. He looks his age now. A fifty-something stalwart of that age-old profession; the barman-stroke-counsellor. Cursed with a friendly ear but never afforded his own shoulder to cry on, Bazza has heard it all but has never said a word. You can see the troubles of a thousand customers etched into his face, the burdens of the drunken heaped on his slightly humped back. I was on the verge of turning round and walking out before he called. Now I almost feel honour-bound to provide this familiar old servant with the courtesy he has offered me on countless occasions.

"Come on then, old son," I smile as I make my way to his outstretched hand. "Let's see if you still pull the best pint...I'll warn you though, I've seen the competition. You'll have to be on top of your game." I shake his pudgy hand warmly and his face lights up. "It's good to see you, man. You're looking well." He actually looks ready for the scrapheap. He looks exactly how he should look: a middle-aged man who never married and who spent his life behind the bar of a hotel which lost stars faster than *Strictly Come Dancing*. Barry puts extra effort into pouring me the perfect pint of Stella, as if I am actually here to test him on the skills which he still seems to take great pride in. The pumps haven't changed since my days as a regular but even so, I'm slightly touched that he remembers what I used to drink. He places the crisp, misty cold glass of Artois in front of me and steps back to admire his work. I take a sip with both eyes fixed on Bazza's over the lip of my pint. I take an authentically appreciative gulp and let out a satisfied sigh as the hoppy liquid passes over my tongue and down my throat. "Perfection, Baz. Perfection."

Bazza winks. "So what are you doing back here, Danny Boy? Last thing I heard you'd upped sticks and moved to Dublin."

Well, someone has been keeping tabs. I can't remember telling anyone from the hotel other than the other members of the notorious Kitchen Staff circa 94-96 about my relocation. In fact, I haven't seen anyone other than McKinley and Ellis from the hotel since 1997. "How did you know about that?"

"McKinley dropped in a couple of years ago," Barry says, pouring himself a cola. "He was here selling his house. Told me all about it. Says you're a journalist or something these days."

I remember hearing the story of the Scotsman's last appearance in the city, from McKinley's own skewed perspective of course. The most illuminating part of that particular conversation was not what he told me but what he was obviously leaving out. The recollection of how cagey he was when telling me about it reminds me to grill the Scotsman on the details of what actually happened during that visit when he arrives. There's definitely more to that story than what he originally told me. "Yeah, I work for a number of magazines and papers these days," I say. "It's alright. It pays the rent."

"Must have seen a few places in a trade like that, eh? Travelled a bit? Not like me. The world comes to old Bazza, not the other way round."

"Is it just you who's left then, Baz? From the old crew?"

"Yeah," Barry says sadly. "Even Gerry and Angela moved on...Sold up about a year ago. They hung on for as long as they could but Gerry isn't long for this world so they thought it was the right time to say goodbye to the old place. Cancer, poor bugger...Looks a shadow of his old self. Shocked the life out of her. Angie turned white overnight when she heard, admitted all the affairs and everything. I was surprised the poor old fucker didn't keel over there and then. She must have been there for hours, admitting all those indiscretions. She used to put it about, did our Ange." He grins and then winks at me. "Well, you know."

"Yeah, she was never the most subtle of adulterous wives," I chuckle.

"But you sorted her out, right?"

I choke on my next mouthful of Stella, causing Barry to expertly step out of the potential firing line, mostly out of an instinct borne of a career spent avoiding projectile vomit. "Sorry? I never did. Who told you that little gem?" Realisation dawns on me as I get my breath back. "I bet it was the Scotsman who told you. Bastard..."

"McKinley says you had her bent over in the gazebo out back during the Lord Mayor's procession one summer night," Barry looks confused as his mental timeline tries to realign itself. "Gerry was away with his mother, if I remember correctly."

"That was him!" I laugh. "He got her pissed up and abused her with a courgette." McKinley drew the line at shagging Angela but he didn't see anything wrong about juicing her up with a vegetable. "And the bastard told you it was me?"

Barry continues to look baffled. "Come to think of it, I did think it was a bit out of character but he insisted it was you. I always thought you were too into that little blonde lass to mess about with the boss's wife."

That little blonde lass. Kate. Of course. The lovely Kate. I was into her, that's true, and was very nearly *into* her too - but my favourite waitress wasn't the only reason why I didn't shag Angela. Her being old, minging and clearly insane topped the charts there. Bastard Scotsman. Just you wait until later... "Speaking of Kate, the blonde lass," I add, to ease the latest puzzled look settling on Barry's face, "Is she still around?"

"I see her sometimes in the city," Barry says. "Still a lovely looking girl...well, woman now. Married her childhood sweetheart in the end. Got two little kiddies, spitting image of her. Little blonde angels the pair of them. She left here with the rest of the waitresses from that time, as soon as their catering training at the college was over...that would have been the summer of 1998, I s'pose."

"And everyone else?" I ask, slightly gutted that Kate didn't immediately retreat to a convent after I walked out of her life and even more pissed off that she stayed with that sad fucker she was seeing.

Barry's face softens with the recollection of bygone days. "As you know, Dennis left to run that dodgy club in the city, the Attic. I only saw him once after that, maybe ten years ago now...or even more. It's hard to say. Anyway, he just strolled back in here that day as if he'd never left the place, shouting around that he wanted to buy the hotel. I think he was on drugs because he looked even thinner than ever and had a crazy eye...you know, like Tony Blair...Like it didn't belong to him, like it had a life of its own. Very strange. It got a bit tasty and I ended up having to throw the bugger out. He wouldn't take no for an answer, had a wad of cash and everything, waving it about like fucking Loadsamoney."

Of course - Dennis the Menace. The former manager of the Hartington and notoriously unstable pervert. If I ever make it to the Pearly Gates, that is one long conversation me and St. Peter are going to have. While I'm not entirely to blame for turning the previously humble and naïve man into a sexually aggressive, drug addicted gangster, I will have my fair share of explaining to do. McKinley and Ellis will have to take a seat in line - except the Scotsman will probably be accepting warmer hospitality in the other place considering the list of crimes he will have to atone for. Telling Barry that I took Angela up the gazebo being one of them. "Is he still here in the city?" Curiosity may get the better of me in the coming hours, especially if the drugs and alcohol have any say in the matter.

"Actually, someone who was in here the other day told me he's running a new place just off the Haymarket. No idea what kind of club it is, probably something shonky knowing that bloke. Hang on..." Barry starts hunting in a pile of scruffy papers by the till and soon finds the scrap he's looking for. He takes a biro out of his back pocket and scribbles an address on a beer mat. "There you go. You know him as well as I do so mind yourself. He's an unpredictable one. Tread lightly, Danny Boy."

I drain my pint and tell Barry a well-meant lie. "I'm here for a couple of days, meeting with Ellis and the Scotsman for a bit of bash. I'll drag them over here one night and we'll have a session, just like old times. Will you be here?"

"I've always been here," says Bazza, giving off that unsettling Overlook vibe again. He stops short of telling me that I've always been here too but it doesn't stop me casting a nervous eye over the old photographs behind the bar, hoping that my grimacing face doesn't stare back from the pictures of the Hartington in 1928. As I get up to leave, Barry stops me, reaches into a hidden drawer and then slips a tatty brown envelope across the bar. Is this the bill I've been dreading? Two years of taking the piss, both literally and metaphorically? I wince...

"Just in case you don't make it back, for any reason," he says, adding a fresh coat of black to my soul by seeing through my lie. "I want you to have these. I don't need them anymore and I certainly don't get any pleasure out of them. Maybe you and the boys can have a laugh." I go to open the envelope. Baz stops me again, placing a swollen mitt over my hand. "Open it when you're altogether," he winks. "It'll be better that way, believe me." I put the envelope in the inside pocket of my jacket and salute before slapping a fiver on the counter, hoping this will go some way to paying off my lifetime of debt.

"Take care, Barry. Look after yourself."

"Will do, Danny Boy...Will do."

Long-held fantasies involving Kate evaporate, filling my mind with acrid smog as I slouch down the driveway and back into the real world. What was I thinking? That I was going to come back after all this time and make up for the mistake I sometimes feel I made when I turned my back on her? That she'd still be pining for the one that walked away? Of course she's moved on. She probably dismissed what we had in the moment I denied it. And what if she hadn't? Did I really believe that I could put everything that has happened since that day in a hermetically sealed box until I'd finished satisfying those urges from fifteen years ago? Could I have ignored everything which makes up my life, just to touch the past for a few brief illicit moments?

Part of the plan I've been concocting for the past year or so crumbles to dust as I realise that pursuing Kate this weekend was never going to be the route back to myself. The dissatisfaction and unhappiness that currently dogs me will never be solved by a shag-for-old-times-sake. Besides, she's a mother, a wife. I'll never find what I'm looking for by destroying the lives of her family - or my own. My salvation lies elsewhere.

My head is still recalibrating when I catch a road sign out of the corner of my eye. I almost walk straight past the turn off to the cul-de-sac known as Calvin Road such is my preoccupation with my internal struggle. I shake the last remnants of thought I had regarding the possible saving grace of infidelity from my mind and stand at the entrance to Calvin Road as the 22-year-old Danny Jones walks past me, rucksack bulging on his back, on his way to his first home away from the family nest. He's got a cocky swagger despite the obvious weight of his worldly possessions on his shoulders. He's walking towards an unknown future but one which is already filling him with excitement. I stroll down the street in his wake and watch him proudly take his first house keys out and open the door to his new student digs. I lean on the wall outside and smile as he crosses that threshold for the first time, breathing in that house for the very first time. He loves the smell of mould in the morning...smells like...freedom. With Danny safely inside, presumably laughing loudly at the surreal thrill of independence and shouting his welcome to the house which will be his sanctuary for two years, I turn and embrace the scene: It's an arena of tightly-packed terrace houses with one open side leading to a busy road where traffic zooms past indifferently; each house tells a story of those inside - the proud family-owned homes sitting snugly with neglected rentals, the ostentatious renovations shoulder-to-shoulder with the decaying post-war originals. The parked cars mirror the diversity of humanity forced to dwell so closely together in this dead-end street; sensible family models vie for space with the SUVs of affluent bachelors and clapped-out hatchbacks of the down-at-heel. It's a pleasingly familiar vision.

I'm also pleased to see that the local wildlife hasn't been eradicated as two wiry street toms enter the arena from opposite corners and stop to stare at each other across the pot-holed tarmac, oblivious of the human interloper viewing their confrontation with amusement. The cats assess the level of threat each other poses before choosing to avoid a confrontation. Their fight for dominance can wait until sundown. The person sleeping in my old room will get a ringside seat, I know that from experience. I chuckle at the memory of Mr. Sifter's arrival on the scene and the fucking racket his own championship bout generated outside my window one night. (I sometimes wake up in my bed back home, hundreds of miles away from the one in Calvin Road, and swear I can hear those wails, like a soul in torment.) The following morning, the previous dominant tom was nowhere to be seen. Only Mr. Sifter was in attendance that day. It was a new dawn in every sense. I remember how he looked up from cleaning his paws when I stepped out of the house to get a paper. I sneered at him, knowing he'd been the noisy fucker scrapping on the flat roof outside my room. He just held my stare before going back to checking his weaponry. When I got back from the corner shop, he was sat on our doorstep. My pathetic attempt at shooing him away was met with an equally nonplussed expression, one bordering on disdain. We weighed each other up for a moment and through his amber eyes, I eventually got the message. "You look a bit of a knob but you'll do." He didn't rush in when I opened the door as some opportunistic cats may have done. He sauntered in as if he'd always lived there. Perhaps he had. No-one ever knew where he came from or where he went. We only knew that Mr. Sifter had chosen to live with us - or, more likely, he was allowing us to live with him.

A tinge of fond sadness rolls from stomach to brain and back again, turning into a hunger pang when it completes its return journey to my gut. Time for one more stop before the Flying Scotsman rolls back into town. A stop which will have to include food - I'm starving. Economy class peanuts and three pints of ale is not the breakfast of champions in anyone's books so I head for a nearby hostelry which I know serves up hearty fare - or at least used to.

"What can I get you, love?"

Maybe the phone number of my local MP - if I was still local - or perhaps a shotgun with which I could go after the heartless bastard who turned the Castle into a fucking theme pub. This isn't some tourist haunt or even a city centre bar which finds itself in a battle for custom. This is the Castle. This is this centre of the surrounding universe. Or was until it was transformed into Dracula's Castle. And I'm not being sarcastic here. This is what the pub is *actually* called these days.

Fucking Dracula's Castle. The large Goth behind the bar smiles a heavily pierced, dark grin and cocks her head as if to ask her original question again without actually speaking. I'm worried that she might be checking out my jugular. "I'm actually after some food," I say. "Are you serving?"

"Open all day for food, darling." She pronounces it daaahlink. She's either Transylvanian or she's been watching Gary Oldman murder the already quite dead Prince of Darkness. Oh, ze children of ze night....what sweet mewsic thy maike...

"Err...okay. I'll have the steak sandwich," I say without checking the heavy, leather bound menu on the bar. Pubs, even vampiric ones, always serve steak sandwiches.

"How would you like that," Elvira asks. "Well done? Or extra bloody?"

Burnt. Charcoaled. Like coal. Leave the blood out if it. "Well done would be good, thanks. And I'll have a pint of..." O-Positive? "John Smiths...bitter." Not blood.

"Thank you," Elvira says before shouting my order to whatever dark entity lurks in the kitchen. "Oi, Terry, give us a steak sarnie will yer? Well done. Cheers sweets!" Okay, she's more East End than Eastern Europe. That makes me feel a bit better. However, it's not enough to ease my overwhelming discomfort over what the fans of *Twilight* have done to our pub.

It wasn't just the proximity to Calvin Road which made the Castle our pub. If we were basing our allegiance on the shortest walking distance, we would have spent two years shocking the life out of the pensioners in the Stanley Arms. The Castle had the vibe we were looking for and all the Lad accessories needed should the apocalypse come and we found ourselves barricaded into our local; pool tables, big screen TVs, a former sportsman as a landlord, fully paid-up satellite football channels, fit female clientele - and perhaps more importantly (even, whisper it, more important than the beer) a cracking jukebox filled with exquisite tunes.

The Castle didn't just accept us either. It didn't just become our pub - we had to earn it and the privileges which came from being regulars. It took a lot of man hours to get to that level. In fact, it took almost an entire autumn term of bunking off college to get known as more than just passing guests. Such was our determination to conquer the Castle that Ellis and I would sit and plan our lessons around times we could go to the pub, not the other way round. If there was a particular lecture one of us couldn't miss, the other would go to the pub to put in some face time with Kirsty the barmaid or Bob the Bastard, our miserable host. If a particular lecturer got wind that something was going on, one of us would go in with news of some nasty bug which was laying the other low - while the patient in question would hold court on one of the more prominent pool tables, hustling the lunchtime trade and hogging the jukebox. Even after we were grudgingly welcomed into the fold (and we're also talking gaining the acceptance of the old guard customers too, not just the staff), it was a while after that before McKinley and Rob were afforded the same status. But when we were all in, when the Castle became a home-from-home, it was like *Cheers* - everybody knew our names.

Looking at the sad, empty corners and the sporadic groups of PVC-clad students sat in faux church pews sipping snakebite and black, it becomes painfully obvious to me that it isn't just the original décor which has been ripped out but the heart and soul of the place too. And whoever thought Nine Inch Nails at high volume is conducive to a pleasurable eating and drinking experience is next on my list of shotgun victims.

A squat waiter - presumably called Igor or something - ducks under the Habitat-meets-Hammer Horror hanging cages above me to serve a rubbery looking sandwich and a warm pint. He unceremoniously fills my table with unnecessary condiments and an extra set of cutlery, presumably in case I need to fight off an invasion of zombies. Igor prepares to depart without a word.

"Excuse me," I ask, expecting a 'yes, massssster?' in response. "Is Bob still the landlord here?" Looking at the amount of steel skewered through the skin of Igor's face, I realise what an utterly preposterous question this is. Bob wouldn't have even served this kid let alone given him a job interacting with other humans. Bob would never have hired Elvira behind the bar either. In fact, Bob would never have gone for any of this shitty Goth shtick. He would have probably resigned his tenure rather than have some spotty brewery dickhead force this marketing nightmare on him. It's quite likely that this is what actually happened. Bob was a bastard - but he was our bastard and a bastard with integrity.

"Bob who?" slobbers Igor.

"Never mind," I smile. "Can I have the bill?"

"Aren't you going to have another drink?" asks Igor.

"I don't think so."

It's pissing down again when I finally manage to pay my debt with the cast of *Vampyros Lesbos* and escape Dracula's Castle. I'm zipping my coat up to the neck when my phone goes off in a yet undesignated pocket. I fight to find it and answer it in time and thankfully get it just before it goes to voicemail. It's McKinley again, this time from the road. He's in a taxi heading straight to the hotel, which is a good thirty minutes' walk across the city for me. He tells me he'll meet me in the hotel bar and asks if there is any saucy female staff at the Heighton. I tell him the receptionist is cute in a girl-next-door kinda way and that appeases him. I hear him tell the cabbie to step on it and the line goes dead. I zip up my jacket again and prepare to battle through the returning rain and wind. I'm half tempted to get a taxi myself but as usual in this city during daylight hours, there are never any to be found unless you're at the train station or airport. Head down into the gathering deluge, I plot the fastest route back, taking into consideration all opportunities to make progress under shelter.

Thunder is rumbling overhead as I dash into reception out of the pelting monsoon. The pretty receptionist watches as I rub a hand through my drenched hair and shake the rain off my jacket. She stops herself reminding me about the very reasonably priced umbrellas available but gives me a smile which suggests she has at least thought about it. My look in return acknowledges my foolish optimism. "Oh, Mr. Jones, your friend has arrived. He's in the bar waiting for you."

"Thanks."

"He's very...attentive, isn't he?" she adds, somewhat nervously.

I smile to myself and move to reassure her that McKinley is mostly harmless. "He's been in the Far East for the past thirteen years. White women fascinate him."

"Really? He's not very tanned."

"He's from Glasgow."

"Oh."

As expected, the Scotsman has turned his nose up at the Gamekeeper's Satchel along with the Adders Ale, Pastor's Best and Finest Old Wallop. He is staring myopically over a pint of Carlsberg at a middle-aged businesswoman's cleavage when I eventually track him down in the quiet snug. "Being attentive again, are we?" Few things can tear McKinley's stare away from a pair of breasts but gladly the arrival of an old friend is one of them. He cheers enthusiastically, causing the businesswoman to frown over her important iPhone conversation, and comes to meet me in the middle of the room. We hug in that masculine way where the genitals are kept safely at a distance before retiring to the sofa in the corner. McKinley has already generously bought me another pint of Gamekeeper's. Oh well. I'll keep the windows open tonight. We toast. "I think she likes you," I grin, spotting the expression of annoyance which has now taken up residence on the face of the businesswoman.

"She loves it," the Scotsman says with conviction. "Get a few gin and tonics in her and she'll be sitting on my face."

"She'll have to get in line by all accounts. I think you've made quite an impression on the receptionist."

He cheers loudly again and laughs. "She fucking loves it too. That innocent look isn't fooling anyone." The businesswoman snorts loudly, gathers her coat and briefcase together and stomps out of the snug. McKinley waves sarcastically. "Yeah, bye!" This is the usual banter which goes on whenever we meet up. We've long since abandoned the usual small talk about the flight, the weather, the state of each other's health. Email and Facebook have kept us informed on the ins and outs of our surface lives. When your best friends are scattered across the face of the earth, time in their company is too precious to waste. It should be about the here and now, which usually means the preparation and execution of a few days drinking, drugging and generally not acting our age. That's what I'm hoping for. "So what's the plan?" he asks. "I heard a new lap dancing bar has opened in the city...The Camel Club. I'm definitely up for a bit of toe action."

"Ellis has booked us a table for dinner at 9.30. Given Rob's reputation for lateness, that gives us a good couple of hours of drinking and waiting for him at the Riverside. After the food, the city will be our oyster."

"Very civilised. I bet we're going somewhere flashy with added security because of The Ponce, right? No chance of going down the Indian for a curry with fucking Bonnie Langford in tow."

"Actually, I think Ellis has booked us in at the Passage."

McKinley laughs and raises his glass again. "A night in the back Passage - top stuff! Just what the doctor ordered."

The Scotsman's slightly predictable Passage joke reminds me I must take him to task before things go any further. "Oh yeah, I have a bone to pick with you," I scold, playfully kicking him in the shin. "I popped into the Hartington earlier..." McKinley stops theatrically rubbing his leg and suddenly looks sheepish. "Barry was tending bar and, you know, we got chatting about old times...and how I was supposed to have shagged the boss's wife."

McKinley cracks up before a fake apologetic expression settles on his face. "Big man, I could hardly tell him that it was me, could I?"

"Why did you have to tell him anything in the first place?"

"He gave me beer!" McKinley switches from pleading to a look of coy innocence. "Did you tell him it was me?"

"Of course."

"Did you tell him about the courgette?"

"Of course."

"Excellent," he beams. "She was gagging for it. Was the mad old bint there?"

"No, Gerry's got cancer and so they sold up about a year ago."

"Bummer." McKinley pauses for a moment. "She might have been up for a sympathy shag..."

"Fuck's sake, man..." I kick him in the shin again. "Where did that courgette end up, by the way?"

"Dunno, exactly," the Scotsman ponders. "Table three, perhaps?"

I can never stay angry at McKinley for long, especially when the anger is only the comedy version. He's a rogue and we love him for it, which is why he has always gotten away with things that mere mortals would have been hung, drawn and quartered over. Like serving paying guests with a courgette which has been rammed up a middle-aged woman's private parts.

"Bazza also told me that Dennis the Menace is running a new place just round the corner from here. If you're game, we can go and look him up. See what the beast is up to these days."

"I'm going to need a few more pints before I'm ready to reconnect with that deviant," says McKinley with conviction. "But I'm definitely up for seeing what kind of fucking mess the mad bastard's got himself in. Aye, why not?"

We spend the next hour filling in the gaps of information that occur in sporadic email and social networking exchanges; jobs, sex, more sex, other people's jobs, other people having sex. We're onto pints of Thresher's Girth or something equally random with the conversation ticking over nicely when McKinley tries to enquire about life in Dublin. "How are things back home? Any better?"

As I was driving to the airport this morning, I made a pact with myself not to talk about or even think about Dublin while I was here. This weekend is all about forgetting about Dublin. Reality can begin again when I'm sat in my seat on the tarmac awaiting take-off on the Monday red-eye. Until then, real life is suspended. "No change," I say, crossing my arms across my chest and hoping my body language and clipped response is enough to kill the topic of conversation stone dead. No such luck. This is the Scotsman after all; the man who has been my confidante and relationship counsellor from day one, the most unlikely bastion of common sense throughout the misogynistic Lad era and beyond. Even when I haven't wanted to open up, McKinley has had a cat burglar's talent for breaking and entering.

"You know you'll probably find yourself closer to a solution if you talk about what's going on. Have you spoken to your woman about how you feel?"

Bastard. He's done it again. "I'm not sure telling her that I feel like I'm living the wrong life is going to make things better," I mumble grudgingly. "It's just going to kick up a shitstorm I don't see any way out of. She'll want to know what life I really want and the truth is, I haven't got a fucking clue. I'm just not feeling the one I have. Besides, she's happy while she doesn't know and I prefer to keep it that way until I've figured things out."

"So she hasn't picked up on the brooding yet?"

"I don't brood."

"Big man, you're the fucking brood-master," McKinley says. "Brood of Brood Hall."

"Bollocks," I reply, sulkily...before going into a brooding silence.

"There you go - right there."

I try to force some lightness into my face but the scowl has settled. McKinley starts to smirk and slowly the corners of my mouth unclench and my forehead returns to its natural space above by eyebrows. "Anyway, I don't want to talk about Dublin this weekend."

"Aye, that's fucking crystal." The Scotsman levels one of his prompting stares at me. I relent one last time.

"I'm hoping a bit of time with the boys will clear things up. Maybe get a new perspective on things." Or rediscover the joys of an old one.

"Yeah, that's worked out well in the past, hasn't it?"

"It worked for you, right?"

"When?"

"When you came back to sell your house."

McKinley's slightly thrown by my change in direction. He's now the one facing an intrusive line of questioning he seems keen to avoid. "Fucking hell, Danny...Err...What did I tell you before?"

"You just told me that you bumped into an old friend while you were here during that visit and that by the time you flew back, you had a completely different perspective on your relationship with your bird. What happened to change things for you?" Before I can put the Scotsman further on the spot, my phone goes again. This time it's Ellis. "This conversation isn't over," I tell McKinley before answering. "Alright, man? What's happening?"

"How hammered are you?"

"We've had a few but we're still on top. McKinley's here." The Scotsman cheers down the phone and shouts 'get down the pub, you sad fucker' before handing control of the call back to me. "Are you still at work?"

"I'm on my way out of the door as we speak," Ellis says. "And guess what? I just got a call from Rob's agent. His fucking agent! Can't call me himself but can manage to phone his agent to do it. He's running late due to traffic but he'll be at the Riverside before eight."

"Traffic? He isn't taking the private jet?" McKinley frowns at me and I mouth 'the Ponce' back at him. He raises his eyes to the ceiling and slumps back into the sofa.

"Anyway," Ellis continues. "He's on his way. We should be thankful for small mercies."

"Are you coming here or going straight to the pub?"

"I gotta change, man. I've been knee deep in car thieves and granny bashers all day. I've got to wash the scum off." Ellis restrains himself from launching into full *Taxi Driver* mode which must be hard because if there's a particular quote in my head, I'm sure the same one's on his tongue. He keeps his inner Travis Bickle at bay and continues: "I'll be at the Riverside by seven, half past at the latest. I need to make a stop on the way, if you know what mean." With that, he's gone.

"The Modfather is loose," I tell McKinley. "He's going to score some gear and then meet as at the pub in an hour."

"Great. I'm going to need something to keep me going tonight. I was on a plane for fifteen hours so it better be good."

"Ellis doesn't usually disappoint," I smile before a void in my memory starts to bug me. "What were we talking about before he called?"

"No idea, man," lies McKinley. "Right, I need a shower if I'm going to socialise with other humans." He gets up and rearranges himself. "Do you think sweet-and-innocent at reception is up for conserving water?"

two

Girls & Boys

December 1994 – January 1995

It would be fair to say that, when it comes to employment, I hate the work but I love the money. I learnt very early on in my life that if I wanted something then, more often than not, I would have to work for it. I tried stealing but it didn't work out. It's not like I was rubbish at the actual thieving - I was a dab hand at shoplifting as an innocent-looking little kid - but I'm cursed with a very choosy conscience. Nicking stuff turned out to be a real talent of mine but the devil on one shoulder decided to sit it out once the angel on the other started making a fuss. That's when I started a potted career in the crap job sector.

As a kid, I had the usual paperboy job - an after-school round which lasted until a colleague got hold of some of his dad's ales and convinced me it would be more fun to do our job pissed. When I turned fourteen, I started working in a small electrical store on Saturdays; first on the video rental desk (which allowed me access to such risqué titles as *The Blue Lagoon* and *Emmanuelle*), and then on the shop floor where I developed a previously unexplored talent for selling TVs while wearing a satin piano tie. When school ended and all my friends left for various colleges, I stupidly fought for my independence by refusing to follow the route through life which society - by which I mean my mother - had plotted out for me. So while my contemporaries learnt how to become computer programmers, social workers and teachers, I dug holes in the ground and clung on for dear life on precarious scaffolding in high winds.

Despite the fact that I had money in my pocket and felt as though I was contributing to the world in ways my freeloading friends were currently not, my dissatisfaction with my life would grow and seethe whenever someone returned from their outrageously full life in higher education. When they talked about their latest exam results, the most I could offer in return was to point out the new guttering on the local supermarket. I did that, I did.

Eventually, I grew tired of the labouring life and jacked it in. It felt good not to have to climb vertiginous ladders or wallow in the shit like a hard-hatted sow in the middle of winter. It would have been even better had I thought it through beforehand and had another, better job to go to after I quit. I didn't and as a result I added a period of the limbo most people call unemployment to my increasingly unimpressive curriculum vitae.

Being on the dole, as anyone who has ever done it knows, is like being a ghost. You move and operate in a realm between worlds. You have nothing to do with the world of work and, after the first month, it becomes glaringly obvious that this is no holiday. In the stage of feeling sorry for yourself, you drift through the streets unnoticed as people rush around in their busy lives, with places to go, things to do, people to see. You have no place to go, except the job centre, nothing to do, except sign on, and no-one to see, except fellow dole moles and your benefits officer. After the bitter acceptance period, during which you watch a lot of day-time television, there comes a time when you have to kick your own arse and really make good on the lie you've been telling for the past few months that "yes, I have been actively seeking work." It's then that you find out that there are actually jobs out there. Careers, however, are almost impossible to find.

And so, I became the proud owner of a hairnet and a pair of white wellies. The only redeeming aspects of factory work, especially on the night shift, is that normal, sane people won't do it and the company has to pay the mental ones a lot more to get the work done. At this point, I barely had a social life anyway. Anna was studying for her A-levels with the dedication of a Tibetan monk, my school friends were now mere acquaintances who lived away and the people I knew from the building sites worked all day and boozed all night. So when I took the job of a machine operator at the local cannery on the 10 p.m. to 6 a.m. shift, I wasn't really denying myself any quality time with anyone. Plus I was raking it in - which was all part of my new plan to get my life back on track.

The money was so good that it made getting covered in tomato sauce every night and spending the wee hours in the company of the living dead more than worth it. Even so, listening to the earthy banter between women who had not spent a night in the same bed with their husbands for the past ten years due to their nocturnal employment can take its toll - as can being splattered by exploding baked beans every night for six months.

Eventually I had enough cash to support my next project - going back to college. Although my choices and decisions up to this point may suggest otherwise, I'm not an unintelligent human being. It may have taken me a while but it eventually dawned on me that if I wanted more than this shadowy, hand-to-mouth existence, I needed some guidance and training. If I eventually wanted a career and not just a series of part-time jobs, I needed to be taught new skills. That's why I was going back to college to study media.

So how come, as I arrange a salad in the shape of a rosette, am I currently working as a starter chef for six quid an hour? Why am I back where I started? Why do I drag myself to a hotel kitchen three nights a week after listening to some dusty old fart bang on about paradigm shifts and the hierarchy of needs? Because the money I earned working for the George A. Romero Canned Goods Empire two summers ago may be enough to pay half the rent on a small, dilapidated, two-bedroom terrace house but it won't stretch far enough to actually allow me to live in it. This is the reality of the existence my old school friends were living while I was having my balls sprayed with bitumen by tattooed Irishmen on some embryonic housing estate. You don't get rich at college. You leech or you work. And I'm no bloodsucker.

I look up from the artistry I have just created - and which will soon be destroyed by the engorged pensioner on Table Four - and catch McKinley having a moment. I'm not the only one living the dream. Here's a man, five years older than me, who has returned to his first skill to make ends meet as he pursues self-improvement. He is also pursuing cash, and sometimes young girls, but essentially he has picked up the knife and spatula again to get himself through hard times as he plans the future. The similarities in our situations are striking and yet the Scotsman is a lot further down his path than I am. In just under two years, he'll have an economics degree and will be on the first plane out of here to save the developing world. That's if he doesn't drink himself to death or get murdered by the deranged father of some teenage prick-tease.

Usually, his taut yet craggy face is creased in a mischievous leer. Dark but exciting fantasies of sexual adventure dance behind those glasses; his mind a blank page in the new issue of Men Only, his thoughts the pornographic text being spewed out by a deviant genius of the erotic word. The nubile waitresses make his eyes burn, his brain race and his crotch twitch. But in this moment, standing motionless behind the hot plates, McKinley is not on the hunt. His gaze is distant, the lustful smirk a listless line. The lovely Kate swishes in, all shiny blonde tresses and teenage promise, but the Scotsman doesn't even check out her arse. He's somewhere else entirely, with someone who is a big part of his life but no part of ours. Kate waits for a smutty remark and the salad I've created. She stands there for a second and gets neither as my stare continues to rest on McKinley in thought.

44

"Should I leave you two alone?" She eventually says and the moment is gone. My eyes turn to Kate and the Scotsman comes back from distant lands. I hand her the salad which she acknowledges with a cheeky smile before breezing out of the kitchen. I look up at the Scotsman again and now he's waggling his tongue at me, a lecherous fire behind his eyes. You're back. But I know you were just with her.

When it first became clear that I was going to have to work as well as study, I gave myself a list of conditions. I would not work in a factory. I would not work far from home. The money should be enough to live on but the emphasis would be on the fact that I would actually enjoy the job - as much as possible, at least - and that it would not encroach on my social life should I have one. After meeting Ellis on the first week of the BTEC Media course, and bonding over our shared love of the Stone Roses, I found out through our regular pub lunch discussions that he worked at the local Tesco on Saturdays and part-time at the Hartington Hotel during the week. The chef at the time was a cock and had flounced out of the kitchen a week previous to our discussion, taking his loyal starter chef with him to some fancy London gaff where he probably went on to become some highly-paid, frying-eggs-on-the-telly tosspot. Gerry the Boss was covering in the kitchen until a new head chef could be found and the word was out that the hotel needed a new starter chef. Ellis had progressed from washing dishes to filling in on starters a couple of nights a week and they were looking for someone else to do the same - no qualifications or training necessary. Ellis described the job as a piece of piss - "cut up some tomatoes, throw some dim sum in the fryer...kid's stuff." Shortly after that I made one of my ill-conceived decisions and found a house in the city, convinced Ellis to share the rent, and filled the vacancy.

The new head chef and I started on the same night, which should have given me some indication of what a thoroughly chaotic establishment the dear old Hartington would turn out to be. Here was a novice starter chef starting work on the same night as a new cook - neither of whom had any idea how this hotel worked. (I actually had no idea how *any* hotel worked). The utter insanity of the place, the situation and members of the established staff only made it easier for McKinley and me to get on as soon as we were thrown together. We had little time to get to know each but the ridiculousness of that first night gave us all we needed to strike up an affinity.

When we actually managed to get time to talk, it turned out that - far from being the tyrannical control freak I feared a head chef would be - McKinley barely gave a shit. He was committed enough not to get fired but would not be overstretching himself by any means. This attitude included my tutelage. We made a pact that we would do the necessary and do it as well as possible but no-one was going to be breaking their backs or getting into a state about things.

There were other rules agreed too. The hotel would get fleeced within our set boundaries. Stealing - as in hotel items actually leaving the premises - was forbidden. The secret consumption of food and alcohol, however, while on site was okay - within reason. For example, one steak sandwich was acceptable, while cooking a whole Sunday roast on the side was not. In addition, all senior staff were fair game for ridicule (in the cases of Dennis the hotel manager, Barry the Barman, and Gerry the Boss) and shags (waitresses, chamber maids, the owner's wife - added to the list by McKinley). These house rules were then extended to Ellis when he shared his first shift with the Scotsman later that week.

A shared love of drinking, illicit substances, excellent music and the opposite sex cemented us as a trio of kindred spirits and the relationship between the three of us moved out of the kitchen into everyday life. Our little world expanded when McKinley arrived on the scene. Ellis and I now had his house to hang out at as well as our own. His university contacts and campus parties sometimes took us out of our provincial college scene from time to time. When Rob started hanging around - and sleeping on our sofa when things got tough at home - we had a gang. The city suddenly became a wider expanse, a honking vista full of new possibilities.

Being closer in age, McKinley and I slowly opened up another front in our kinship. While the madness of going on the pull or on the piss was enjoyed by all, away from the group dynamic we shared a personal openness which would have been ridiculed as too serious or even poofy had we attempted to talk this way in the larger round. It soon became clear that both of us had things we needed to talk about, things the younger and less experienced of our gang would have little knowledge of.

It wasn't long after I moved to the city that my relationship with Anna ended and I was a wreck. Ellis and I had been sharing the house for just over six weeks and he was still in the transitional phase of weaning himself off the cushy security of family life. This meant that he was rarely there. So while he wrung the last drops of coddling and cooked meals out of his doting parents, I wallowed in our rickety student digs alone. I was rattling around the house one afternoon when the doorbell rang. I opened it to find McKinley on the step. "Alright, big man? Fancy a pint? I'm fucking gasping."

After moving in, Ellis and I had tried out most of the pubs closest to home in a quest to find 'our local'. After extensive research, we'd settled on the Castle, a lively two-floored establishment run by a former rugby player and local celebrity known affectionately as Bob the Bastard. It seemed the natural choice for my first real heart-to heart, the only place where I felt relatively comfortable enough to talk about my pain. Still, it wasn't easy getting started. This was still very early in our friendship and I didn't know whether there was another side to McKinley's sometimes brash, Glaswegian machismo. It was a risk but one I eventually had no real choice in taking. Once settled with pints, it all came out, aided and abetted by that collection of heart-breaking ballads that every pub has on its jukebox and which miraculously starts playing when you're drowning your sorrows after a break-up. McKinley sat and listened intently as I spewed out my feelings. There didn't seem to be any awkwardness or desire to make for the exit. He created an atmosphere where I felt comfortable talking about the pain I was experiencing. When it was all out in the open, he finally spoke.

"Sounds like it just ran its course, man," he said, leaning back and fixing me with a serious look. "She has a new life, you have a new life and they're moving in different directions away from each other. Of course it hurts like a bastard, but you knew it would happen from the sound of it. You're sad that it's over, and rightly so, and you should mourn it. But you should also try and accept it. See it as an end of a chapter and look forward to the next one." There was no 'you big Jessie' or 'sort it out you sad fucker'. Just a considered answer and sound advice. I was taken aback. "Listen, if it was supposed to work, it would have done," he continued. "Both of you would have found a way. But if one person doesn't want it, however much the other one does, it won't happen." It was then that McKinley explained that there was a better half somewhere in the world, a long-term partner he'd been with since his late teens. Her work took her far away for long periods and they rarely saw each other but they'd found a way. They both wanted it.

"So, what's with all the skirt chasing?"

"I'm a bad bastard," the Scotsman smiled. "I'll never dip my wick...well, never is a strong word...but I'll definitely try not to. The other stuff is just messing around. See, you have to get it straight in your head...what it means. If you understand what you're doing and how it fits in the big plan, then..." He raised his glass and winked over it without ending his sentence. That was when I started understanding the Scotsman.

"So, fancy a few sherries after work, old bean?"

I come back out of my thoughts to find McKinley standing beside me with a chip sandwich in his hand and another on a plate. The usual sign that our work here is nearly done. The clatter of plates and cutlery from the washing area tells me that the underage slave we have doing the dishes tonight is taking the strain while our duties wind down. Time to look ahead to the rest of the evening.

"What do you have in mind?"

McKinley always talks a good shag but in reality, due to his extraordinary circumstances, he has never been known to actually put his penis where his mouth is. He has, however, been known to put it where someone else's mouth is. But as far as any of us can say, when it comes to keeping his distinct brand of fidelity intact, the Scotsman has kept true to his belief that while a shag breaks the rules, all other options are forever on the table. Or under it.

The current permissive state of society and the fact that a new battle of the sexes is being waged in pubs and clubs the length and breadth of the nation plays merry hell with the Scotsman's self-control. Everywhere you go, there are birds willing and capable of drinking each and every one of us under the table, before hitching up their microskirts, mounting our inebriated bodies and riding themselves to orgasm without a care for the manhood underneath. They demand satisfaction and then belch clouds of Southern Comfort-tinged farewells as they hop off in search of fresh meat and laughs. Men are not superior in this new paradigm; men are not even equals. Men are competition and sport. These women, these 'Ladettes', are doing what men have been doing since the beginning of time: getting what they need and not giving a shit about how they get it. Not everyone is pleased with that.

The ironic thing is, these Ladettes are a male creation. Why, when it suddenly became okay for men to behave badly, did we think that we would be the only ones to take advantage of this new attitude? We created this blueprint for the New Lad but got too pissed one night and left it lying on the kitchen table. Our womenfolk, coming home to find us passed out in front of Match of the Day again, only had to pick up the instructions and follow the easy steps to empowerment. 1) Drink loads. 2) Drink loads more. 3) Act outrageously and obnoxiously - but with mischievous charm. 4) Pursue sex in the style of a rabid hyena. 5) Drink some more. 6) Puke.

We brought it on ourselves.

So right now, it's a real headfuck for the mid-90s man. He is both lord and slave in the kingdom of his own making. He is both having his cake and starving to death while some woman greedily consumes the last slice. He is getting exactly what he wants only to find out it is more than he can handle. We should have listened to the advice of those who said: be careful what you wish for. You might just have to drink yourself blind before you can get her tits out.

And so, for a man who absolutely adores women for the pleasures they can offer him, it must be hell to be stuck on the sidelines when the game you've loved playing all your life suddenly gets a new set of very interesting rules.

As for me, this isn't just a new set of rules; it's a whole new fucking sport. I sometimes wondered if I was missing out on something being with Anna but I never thought it would be like this out in the single world. Apparently it wasn't, which in one way means that my newly acquired bachelor status is perfectly timed. Of course, coming out of a relationship and into a sexual free-for-all is proving to be a bit of a shock. What's not helping is the continuing, underlying feeling of rejection and bitterness which I'm managing to keep under wraps as I find my feet in this new Lad culture and deal with the concept of Ladette emancipation. I need guidance which is why McKinley is sat beside me at the bar of a city pub explaining how his new doctrine - known as 'the Proxy Fuck' - is going to make me a player.

"It's quite simple," he says. "We identify the fit birds we both fancy, then we work on them together, setting them up - and then you shag them."

Long pause of comprehension. "Let me get this straight," I say, somewhat suspiciously. "You're going to help me screw girls that you like but you're not getting anything out if it?"

"Aye." He pauses. "Well...sort of."

"What's the catch?"

"Big man, I can get a slapper to nosh me off or give me a tug. That's no problem. But the tasty ones? I can't get involved. On the one hand, I'd want more than just a wank off someone like Kate and, you know my situation, I can't go shagging around. Plus, if I did, I'd want more. Could you screw Little Miss Perky Tits just the once?" I'd take that over nothing right now. "I just need to know what it's like, that's all," he says, wistfully. "I can imagine it...believe me, I've imagined it loads...but it's time that I really know. And you're going to tell me."

So this is what it comes down to. The Scotsman would prefer to beat off over my real-life tales of conquest than imagined erotic episodes in which he is always the star. "So, you want me to fuck Kate and then give you the details."

"Not yet," he smiles. "She's a work-in-progress. I've got someone else in mind for our first mission."

Ominous doesn't do justice to the pause that follows. The Scotsman's eyes widen and his wicked smile spreads. I make a mental list of all the women he's been lusting over for the past few months and by the time I get to the last name, he's nodding at me as if he's been watching me climb down the ladder in my mind to the murky depths of that particular barrel. As it dawns on me who he's thinking of, my face drops and McKinley laughs.

"You don't mean...Julia?"

"Fucking right, man," McKinley grins. "Lovely jubbly."

It's Sod's Law that out of all the waitresses at the hotel, the one who will actually let me have sex with her turns out to be the ugliest of the lot. It's kind of unfair to call Julia ugly. I should be charitable and upgrade her to plain. It's just...when you compare her to the platinum cuteness of Kate and even the porn star-in-waiting poutiness of Jailbait Alex, Julia is a bit of a pig. But the way I see it, after receiving endless pep talks, is that you have to work your way through the sluggers to get a shot at the title. I've got to fight my weight at the start and that means dealing with street brawlers like Julia. Only then can I work up to challenge for the WBF belt (...that's World's Best Fuck, if you're wondering).

Maybe it's the endless encouragement coming from my mentor and guru but the Scotsman's plan makes perfect sense to me. To others though, it probably seems a very strange set-up, this Proxy Fuck arrangement. Most people wouldn't even entertain the idea but right now - in my current situation - I don't have a problem with it. If the Scotsman is willing to devote his time to getting me laid just so he can have some second-hand experiences to keep him warm at night, then who am I to argue? It isn't like I'm doing so well on my own and besides, there's no contract saying I have to go through with any of McKinley's nefarious plans. Even if I do agree, there is a safety phrase which allows me to get out of any deal at any point should things get nasty. It goes something like this: "Piss off and shag her yourself." It's generally understood that this means I want out.

In the few days it actually takes to get to the point of no return, I consider the usefulness of this phrase while McKinley prepares and bastes the plump Julia, getting her ready for stuffing. I question the wisdom of every part of this plan; from whether or not it will spoil my future chances with the lovely Kate who I hope to have more than just a fling with, to whether or not I'll have to quit my job and/or flee the country in the small hours after the deed is done. There is also the voice of my conscience in the background, enquiring about my morality. Thankfully, both the devil on my shoulder and the penis in my trousers combine to drown this out. All the while, Cupid's evil twin is charming and smarming poor Julia while hinting that someone - he won't name names - has a secret crush on her.

The part I'm supposed to play is easy. I'm the secret admirer and as such I am required to no longer treat her with the usual polite indifference but engage with her in small talk and banter, trying my best to show the endearing qualities she clearly believes I have. Poor, deluded girl. I have a black heart, Julia Kennedy, and an optioned soul ready for collection at the fiery gates of Hades. But I'm not allowed to show my dark side, not if I'm going to get into her pants. The fact is that part of me actually wants to shag her. While she's built for comfort rather than speed and with no striking features to speak of, Julia does give off the faint aura of someone who could be quite fun in the sack. She has a slightly devious smile which hints at mucky hidden depths and the breasts which constantly keep the Scotsman enthralled could be quite spectacular once unbound. Besides, I have to start somewhere and if I'm going to start racking up conquests and getting my moves honed in this new arena, someone is going to have to be the first. And it helps if it's someone who would actually entertain the idea of sleeping with me without too much coercion. However, as my desperation increases, so does the feeling that this is someone who actually likes me and someone who may take any physical intimacy as meaning more than just a casual poke. While I'm sure McKinley doesn't intend to personalise Julia when he tells me "fat birds need love too," he just adds to the growing assertion that this is exactly what she is looking for and is as far removed as possible from what she is likely to get. And what about what I want? Is this what I am really looking for? Does that even matter? This tactical pursuit of females for our own pleasure is so in tune with the times that, on the surface at least, it doesn't seem wrong and in the end, I get to have sex - which is the ultimate target at the moment. Everyone's a winner. Right? Besides, it's also a source of amusement and camaraderie between the boys. We're a fledgling band; a tribe at the beginning of everything, creating our own legends and writing the early stories of the Gods of Lad. This exercise fills drunken conversations and lifts the spirits. It drives us on in our hedonistic, excessive quest. No-one admits to having reservations. Why should we? We are the Lads, and the Lads want it all - at any price.

It is this mentality, plus the usual diet of Thursday night pound-a-pints, which brings us to the neon-lit hell of Speakeasy's. The best way to describe this most populist of city clubs would be to imagine an abattoir and then hang a glitterball in the middle of it. You wouldn't even have to remove the cows and carcasses from this vision, just dress them in skin-tight Lycra and get them to shuffle around by zapping them with the musical equivalent of a cattle prod. At the far end of the abattoir is a lengthy bar where most of the bulls spend their time getting appropriately slaughtered while the heifers stumble about with their bottles of cheap piss to the likes of the heinous Whigfield. Why oh why do we come here? I'll tell you why. Because just like every abattoir, Speakeasy's employs a number of Judas goats to lure the unsuspecting to their deaths. And despite knowing that the fit birds we followed in here will either miraculously disappear or turn into wizened hags once Ace of Base kicks in, we still succumb to their empty promises.

Tonight is no exception. The Orchard ends up as a mass of heaving, seething testosterone as per usual and after picking our way through the gashed punters and over-enthusiastic coppers, we leave the bright blue flashing lights behind to venture into the radioactive wasteland of Beaumont Park, the urban development that civilisation long since abandoned. The fifteen-minute walk from the throbbing heart of the city to its cankerous liver might as well by a 650-year journey back through time. As you get closer to the concrete monstrosity, all signs of normal life start to disappear. Shapes stir in the shadows and crippled forms lurch out of the darkness. You expect to hear a cry of "bring out yer dead!" or dodge a bucket of human faeces chucked from a window above. One of the reasons for Speakeasy's popularity may be that this cavernous ballroom tacked onto a closed down multiplex is the only sanctuary for miles around; a refuge from the Black Death that stalks this part of the city every night of its accursed life.

As ever, we have stumbled into the Dark Ages in careless ignorance, following a bunch of boozed-up birds out on a hen night. Their behaviour in the Orchard even exceeded ours for obnoxiousness. Rarely, if ever, have any of us bared our arses through the front windows at passers-by or given drunken lap dances on request. These girls are out for a good time and that is more than an admirable reason to forget we all have early lectures in the morning and should really know better.

Once the hen party has evaporated on entry, we're stuck with the usual crowd. Housewives with black eyes and white stilettos hot-step in the eerie half-light of the dance floor while local brutes exude malevolence from the shaded sidelines. Ladies men of a certain age strut around with their mullets and moustaches hoping to find a game divorcee while a gang of shirtless skinheads on ecstasy sweat themselves towards deadly dehydration. Mingling between the misfits are those who are there just because it's open and they're not ready to go home yet. This is the category we fit into. We could have gone to a number of other after-hours establishments, some definitely more salubrious than this, but we were chasing skirt and the pursuit led us to Speakeasy's. Plus, McKinley has discovered that Julia sometimes drops in for a dance on occasion. Something he reveals to me when it's far too late to do anything about it.

"You set me up, you bastard," I slur at him as Julia spots us from the other side of the club.

"That's the whole point, big man." McKinley waves Julia over. "Time the great white hunter made his kill."

Julia teeters across the dance floor on heels which would give a steeplejack vertigo. As she negotiates the pill'eads, she narrowly avoids being floored by Rob and Ellis who have quickly entered into the spirit of proceedings before making it gingerly to where the Scotsman and I are standing. On closer inspection, her whole outfit pegs her as a regular: short white skirt stretched over her ample thighs, a flimsy satin blouse seemingly at the mercy of her unrestrained melons and a faux-fur jacket which looks more moggy than mink. She is also quite pissed.

"Alright, darling?" asks McKinley, lasciviously. "You're looking lovely tonight. I see the puppies are out to play. Good girl." Julia giggles a shy, tipsy laugh which makes the puppies sit up and beg before turning her heavy-lidded gaze to me.

"Hello Danny." She blinks at me in slow motion, which could be her way of making bedroom eyes at me or just the fact that the ton of mascara she's wearing is starting to weigh heavily. "I've never seen you in here before." McKinley subtly moves towards the bar and makes the universal hand gesture for screwing over Julia's head before giving me the thumbs up, grinning and fading away like the Cheshire cat from Alice in Wonderland.

"Yeah, well...It's the other side of the city from our house," I offer as way of explanation, rather than the truth which is 'I only come here when I'm utterly wankered or when I've been stitched up.' "Do you live nearby?" This polite question without any true desire for an answer gives Julia the opportunity to give me a ten minute verbal tour of the streets around Beaumont Park. I lose her pretty much after she takes a left out of the door as my mind starts to quickly weigh up the pros and cons of this plan for perhaps the final time before execution. On the pro side, I'm very close to being too pissed to care about the cons. The mesmerizing qualities of her heaving chest and slutty ensemble blow the rest of my doubts out of the water. Fuck it, let the knickers fall where they may. "Look, Julia. Do you want to get out of here?" She hesitates for a second, biting her lip in a slightly nervous way before taking my hand and leading me towards the stairs. Above the constipated strains of Shaggy's 'Oh Carolina', I'm sure I hear a loud hurrah.

I know I daydreamed through the guided tour section of our spoken foreplay but I'm sure Julia's place doesn't need the assistance of a taxi to get there. And yet, I'm suddenly sitting in a cab, speeding across the city with nervous excitement and confusion mixing with the awkward silence between us on the back seat. I was again going over the implications of the coming shag when we got in so I missed the address Julia gave the driver but as the urban devastation makes way for more familiar surroundings, it dawns on me that we're heading to Calvin Road and my gaff. An unusual choice, I must say. Most girls feel more comfortable on their own turf in situations like this. It's also easier to kick the other person out when it's your place. She's either hoping to make it until the morning or has something to hide. Neither option really makes this whole situation any less dubious. There's no contact between us, not even any of the eye variety. The only fingering going on is the nervous sort which focuses on items of clothing and hair.

Things remain strange when we get to the house. From my experience with Anna in situations like this, the crazed tearing off of clothes normally began in the hallway just after the front door slammed shut behind us. Shoes and jackets were quickly discarded, perhaps followed by some quick, slightly uncomfortable, foreplay on the stairs. The insane urges then normally led us to my room where more frantic stripping and clumsy probing took place before all mental cognition gave way to animalistic rutting. But not tonight. All the spontaneous and passionate abandon I would expect from a one-night stand is missing.

Julia asks where the bathroom is; I point her in its direction, adding a warning about the broken flush and an enquiry about whether she'd like a cup of tea. She politely accepts my advice and refuses the offer of tea. It's hardly the stuff of porn movies...not even those bad 70s ones where a scantily-clad housewife with Farrah Fawcett hair always needs her TV repaired. While Julia's either relieving herself or looking to escape through the toilet window, I hang around the living room like a spare prick at a wedding. As I'm cursing the Scotsman for his fucked-up plan, Julia shyly comes out of the bathroom in her underwear (which is weird if you think about it - she's obviously made the decision to get things started with a very clear indication that I can have her body and yet she appears very self-conscious about her own choice. I, of course, don't consider this until later because I have a near naked woman in the house and, well...you know).

"It's cold," she says with a nervous smile, hugging herself and shivering. She comes up to me, hoping for comfort and warmth. There's no going back now - unless I'm to be an even bigger bastard than I already am and reject her in all her vulnerability. So I hug her and any thoughts I still have of whether this is a bad or good idea go out the window. As she snuggles closer into my chest, I feel her heartbeat going ten to the dozen. My hand strokes the small of her back and she shivers again. I take an exploratory pass of her backside - which is firmer and smaller than I thought it would be - and do the decent thing (sort of, in the circumstances).

"Let's go to bed."

The sex is passionless and functional. Once naked and under the covers, Julia relaxes a little but I'm still forced to do all the work. Not once does she touch my cock, which may actually be a good thing as this is the first shag I've had in a good few months and the old chap rarely needs any encouragement to go off at the best of times. But there's no fear of that happening here. I'm so focused on trying to get her involved that it becomes more like a science project than a fuck. I go through the biology textbook checklist of how to get a bird damp with no help from the subject herself. She lies there and lets me stroke, probe, lick and suck with barely any audible encouragement. I'm no slouch, believe me. I've been known to get a girl wetter than an otter's pocket with the minimum of effort but this is becoming hard work. Hoping to get her at least out of neutral, I go down on her and set up camp for a good ten minutes. It gets her into first gear at least but even though things below are now sloppy enough for action, she goes back to ticking over, saying in a matter-of-fact voice as I come up for air: "I haven't been with many blokes who like doing that." Well, love, maybe they all quickly came to the conclusion that muffing you out just prolongs the agony. I reach for the rubbers on the night stand and after a brief moment where I hope she'll offer to help me on with it, I roll off onto my back beside her, unceremoniously sheath my neglected penis and resume my position on top.

I wake up with breath which could solder iron and a head the size of Venezuela. The curtains are wide open and as I open a pained eye, my retina is scorched by a piercing laser beam of sunlight. Through the red pain I can make out the form of another human in my bed. This body is turned away from me, its back towards me, its shoulder-length hair splayed across the pillow beside my head. For a short, sweet moment, I have no recollection of the night before. Oh heavenly amnesia! But then, as my natural chemicals fight through all the artificial ones I imbibed the night before, dreaded realisation swamps my consciousness. Shit. Julia. I lay there for a moment, hoping not to wake her. By a cruel twist of fate, I have ended up on the side of the bed next to the wall. There is no easy way out; no Slinky-esque slither to the floor, no silent SAS roll, no escape. Any manoeuvre will wake this woman and precipitate the painful small-talk and awkward negotiations involved in parting with what's left of our self-esteem. Luckily my limbs are with me and not sandwiched between conquest and bed. There's no need for me to take drastic action because, believe me, Julia is definitely an arm-biter - the kind of girl you'll willingly chew through your arm to avoid waking up. I sit up like The Mummy slowly rising from its sarcophagus; a controlled action which is difficult at the best of times, let alone when you have a fucking killer hangover and an unwanted bed partner beside you. I'm halfway through the hardest stomach crunch in history when a person with no desire to live starts hammering on the door. The banging undoes all my efforts in an instant. Julia is now awake and confronting her own slowly-dawning regrets.

"Danny, if you're coming..." Ellis bursts in. "Oh...I see you already have. Alright Julia?" He beams at me from the doorway and through my embarrassment and dull torture I plead with him to get me out of this.

"Are we late?" I hopefully enquire, my expression passing on my hope in no uncertain terms. Ellis takes a moment too long to react.

"Nah, man. We've got ages." The daggers I'm willing into him are nothing compared to the ones he's jabbing in my back. "Tea or coffee, Julia?" Et tu, Bastard? Once Ellis has his breakfast order, he slopes off down the stairs merrily singing Oasis to himself at just the right volume to be heard: "Round are way...the birds are minging..." Inside the inescapable hell of my room, Julia and I begin the unpleasant task of dealing with our night of joyless humping while coping with the sight of each other naked in daylight. Neither is something that either of us is happy about.

"Morning," she mumbles.

"Hi," I reply with my back to her as I search for a pair of boxer shorts. "Sleep okay?" I look round to see the full extent of her naked arse as she bends over to reclaim her knickers. It seems to have doubled in size from last night. My head swims - from the sight before my eyes or the effects of alcohol, I'm not sure which.

"Not really," she mumbles. "You snore."

Let's get this over with for fuck's sake. "I'm going to grab a quick shower. Should I call you a cab?"

As I stand under the piping hot water, relishing the warmth and the solitude, I try to gather my thoughts. Once I get Julia out of the house and ease the pressured atmosphere which has been building since our ill-advised sexual encounter came to an unspectacular end, I can start thinking about dealing with the fall-out. I have a day before I have to see her again. She's doing evening service at the hotel on Saturday night. That gives me the rest of the day to get my head straight and find that fucking Scotsman. He got me into this and now he's going to get me out of it. I don't have to wait long before I can hold him personally responsible. I come out of the bathroom to find that Julia has gone (thank God) but has been replaced by McKinley. Ellis is ready to leave the house and taps his watch at me.

"Get your arse into gear. We're going to be late."

I look at the Scotsman who's nursing what I assume is Julia's untouched coffee. He looks at me sheepishly. "I'll meet you in the canteen later," I reply. Ellis tuts and strides out of the house, slamming the front door behind him. I slump down in the armchair opposite McKinley and fix him with a mock-stern glare. "So, the puppet master shows his face at last. I suppose you want your gory details."

"I take it you sorted her out," McKinley grins. "She looked very self-conscious when I saw her. Nothing says 'I'm a dirty stop-out slut' like standing in your glad-rags at a bus stop at eight-thirty in the morning, looking shagged through."

"It was fucking pitiful, man," I start rubbing a towel gingerly over my head. "She lay there like a slab of meat and, okay, so I wasn't totally into it but I was more enthusiastic than she was...and she was the one who supposedly wanted it."

"What are the jugs like?"

"You know what? You don't get any details from this one. I don't even want to think about last night and I certainly don't want you thinking about it."

"I could improve it," he offers. "Make you look better."

"Then why don't you just make the whole thing up from the start? Save me from having to live through nights like that." I'm only marginally joking. "I'm not looking forward to having to face her again. It would be fair to say it rates as an all-time low."

"Leave it with me," he concedes, sensing real strife below my faux-offended demeanour. "I'll make sure she knows the score." McKinley pauses over Julia's coffee. "Did you keep her panties?" I throw my towel at him and any remaining tension promptly dissipates. "The next one will be better, big man, I promise. This was just a test run." He leans back and raises his mug. "I can guarantee you're going to be into this one."

Girls like Natalie are the epitome of pleasure and pain. When you're high as a kite, plastered on beer and spiritualised by the tunes, a girl like Natalie can be the icing on the cake. They're always there and willing; wonderfully unattached and yet exclusively yours whenever you're in attendance. These girls are few and far between, each one a gem if you can find one and hang onto her. But as I said, there is pain as well as pleasure with these girls. Their affection only ever lasts until lights-up. You can hook up for a month of Saturdays but you very rarely get the chance to end one of those nights with the screw the evening of flirtation has been promising you. In the cold light of day, your regular dalliances don't carry the same heat. There are never any plans to meet up for a drink, never a chance to take things further in the sober quiet of a midweek night-in. Luckily, just as the pleasure is fleeting, so is the pain. Soon Saturday comes round again and for another night at least, none of the normal rules apply.

This strange connection with Natalie began two months ago. We were standing beside each other at the bar in the Warehouse, fruitlessly waving tenners in the direction of the overwhelmed bar staff when the futility of the exercise became a common bond. The conversation was easy and there was an instant attraction. It helped that Natalie was blonde and had huge tits. The rest was kind of a blur. Her boobs, however, almost ended our connection before it began. Actually, Rob's reaction to her boobs almost ended our connection before it began. It's generally understood that if one of the lads is making progress on a shag, none of the others should do anything to jeopardise that chance. Rob, however, can be a dick at times and this was one of those times. After muscling into our conversation, Rob stood there drunkenly ogling Natalie's chest before shouting "Wazza jugs, love!" in her face. I didn't blame her at all for walking off. I did blame Rob though and if it hadn't been for the fact that my apology on his behalf eventually led to Natalie giving me a wank at the end of the night, I would have kicked the bastard in the bollocks for his troubles.

Ever since that first night, Natalie has been a regular pull down the Warehouse. But our fumbling has never amounted to more than damp underwear for either of us. This, so I'm told, is all about to change. This week, Natalie and I are going to stop with all the messing about and get serious. And, according to McKinley, he's going to be in the closet with his camcorder to consign the historic moment to celluloid.

I decide to bunk-off the entire day of college and spend it wandering from bar to bar with the Scotsman, who has also decided that there are more pressing matters to deal with than macroeconomics. Neither of us are on at the hotel this evening (Ellis is alone with Dennis, which should do nothing to improve his mood) so, with no work commitments to consider, we spend our Friday drinking beer and smoking pot.

"Big man, it's simple," says McKinley, striding around his spare bedroom, checking angles and lighting like a slightly off-his-face, and less portly Alfred Hitchcock. "You get her back here tomorrow night...I'm thinking you strip her off about here..." He waves a wand-like spliff around to mark where the X would be on the stage floor. "I'll be in there," he turns and points to the stable door wall cupboard, "and if you shag her on a chair about here or bend her over there, I should be able to get it all on film."

"You're serious," I chuckle, taking the joint. "You really think this is going to work?"

"Oh yeah, no problem." The Scotsman tries out his hiding place for size. Behind the winter coats, with the bottom half of the door closed, he is completely invisible. "See? Smile, you're on Candid Camera!"

"Okay, but this is going to happen on one condition," I say sternly to a rustling duffle coat. "No masturbating. This is weird enough as it is without you whacking off in there."

An evil grin leers out from the darkness. "Maybe, when you're taking her from behind, I creep out and get a few lengths in without her knowing."

"I'm sure that's illegal and no fucking way."

The Scotsman comes out of hiding and picks up the camcorder. "I wonder if I can get a live feed down to the living room...get the boys round for a few beers while the show's on."

"No."

The idea of making a secret porn movie has helped to keep the dread of seeing Julia again at bay for a good few hours. Even if this all turns out to be the beer and weed talking, it has been a laugh and no small amount of sweet relief. When Ellis arrives later in the evening and finally stops pissing and moaning about how he spent the day as a slave to both education and then employment while we gave in purely to pleasure, he starts getting enthused too. There is a brief moment where McKinley and Ellis argue over who is better qualified to handle the camera:

"I'm studying film, for fuck's sake!"

Versus...

"It's my house, my closet and my camera. And my idea."

After which McKubrick remains in control of the camera while Ellis C. DeMille settles for the role of creative assistant. When Rob turns up and offers to be my body double, the distasteful events of the night before are forgotten - for the time being.

In the cold sober clarity that follows the next day, I begin to question my involvement in this low-rent skin flick and the actual reasons behind the whole sordid plan. As my cornflakes become soggy mush and my morning coffee becomes tepid tar, I drift into the half-conscious realm of post-hedonistic analysis. On the one hand, the result of tonight's experiment will be a positive one regardless of whether there is any sex and whether that sex is filmed by my pervert mate hiding in the closet. This is essentially about the laugh, the thrill and the buzz - and all these things can be achieved through the build-up, the pursuit and the attempted execution. If I get Natalie to come back, it will be an added bonus which will take the evening closer towards the legendary status it deserves. If she does a runner again, then the story ends there with the hilarious, ill-fated attempt the four of us made one night to get some slapper to make a secret porno movie.

On the other hand, there's the reality of being drunk, naked and (hopefully) erect on video forever, at the mercy of unscrupulous types who may dig out the evidence at a moment's notice, either for humiliation purposes or possibly something even darker. There I'll be, indulging in the sex act with a girl who'll no doubt be a sloppy mess by then. My moves will be studied, my body critiqued and my staying power monitored with the help of the in-screen timer. Maybe if I spend the rest of the day pumping weights and then drop some E, I won't look quite as much like a slightly doughy premature ejaculator for the future generations who'll watch me sweatily ploughing some nightclub pick-up in the years to come.

Then there's McKinley's enthusiasm for the project. On the surface, this isn't a big surprise. The Scotsman has no hang-ups about his or anyone else's body and probably doesn't care that I'll be the bloke waving his wanger about in front of him. It could be anyone because it has been anyone for as long as he can remember. It's just more sex to him; another dimly-lit live show to add to the memories of a thousand others, or a contribution to the stacks of diverse and disturbing VHS tapes he has by the TV in his room. What he plans to do with the tape afterwards unsettles me though. Using my stories from the proxy fucks to help him get off when he's alone is one thing, but using moving images of me in the act is completely different - and while he won't see it that way, I find it very creepy.

And then there's the Lad thing. Everyone is fair game. The laugh is everything. No-one is safe from being exposed and ridiculed for the benefit of all the others. I could be playing into their hands, quite literally in the Scotsman's case.

My mind starts drifting away from the moment of decision as another, more dread-inspiring thought muscles in and shouts through a megaphone: "EIGHT HOURS BEFORE YOU SEE JULIA AT WORK!" I abandon the cornflake mulch and reach for the weed and bong before staggering back to bed in search of sweet oblivion.

I brace myself for my first shift with Julia after our night together only to discover on my arrival that she has inexplicably quit her job at the hotel and won't be coming back. Dennis offers no explanation, meaning she either didn't give him the real reason or the one she did give him had nothing to do with me. My relief is tinged with something else which could be guilt. I never wanted her to quit working at the hotel - or did

I? I'm sure at some point over the last two days I must have hoped that something would happen which would prevent me from ever having to see her again, but I was putting my money on her being a figment of my imagination which never existed in the first place. I never meant for her to give up a source of income just to avoid ever having contact with me again. Hang on...She resigned because of me? Was it that bad? What's so awful about me that she could never face me again? "I beat myself into a stupor last night, thinking about Julia Jugs on all fours," the Scotsman beams, as he ambles into the kitchen for the start of the shift. "Good lad...did it for the boys." There's the answer right there.

In a sensible, model world where morals are at the heart of every decision, I would have learnt a lesson from the Julia episode. But what fun would that be? Besides, from careful probing, I manage to find out that none of the other staff members know about my misdemeanour and that none of the waitresses are a bit surprised that Julia just quit. "She hated it here anyway," Kate says in passing as I'm trying to get an ounce of truth out of the pathological liar that is Jailbait Alex. "I'm glad she's gone. Miserable cow." I'm in the middle of an egocentric fantasy where Kate knows about the proxy fuck and is pissed off because it wasn't with her when Alex offers some fabricated insight.

"She was shagging Dennis, that's why she left. But he fell in love with her and it got too much." At hearing this, McKinley appears from the meat locker and raises his eyes to the heaven while shaking his head. "They used to do heroin together," Alex says. It seems my secret is safe under the comforting warmth of the Hartington's in-built insanity blanket. Once the coast is clear of deranged and perky waitresses, and the talk of Julia has died down to a few lewd asides from the Scotsman, our attention turns to the filming of *Drunken Sluts Part Two*.

"You've got to give us at least fifteen minutes warning, big man," says the director. "When she's agreed to come back with you, give us the nod and we'll take off. Everything will be ready by the time you get her back and then it's lights, camera, get her tits out for the lads."

"Okay, who is this 'we' you're talking about?"

That worryingly sheepish grin spreads slowly across the Scotsman's face. "I found out the microphone on the camera is a bit shit..."

"So?"

"We need a sound man." McKinley beams demonically. "Ellis will be under the bed."

I stare at him in stunned silence for a moment. "Can't we just put some acid jazz over the top? Maybe JTQ...or Corduroy?" He laughs and slaps me manfully on the shoulder. I guess not.

It seems a little strange coming from a bloke who has agreed to shag some tart on video for the titillation of his friends but the idea of two of my mates being in the room at the same time is now bringing on a bit of stage fright. I'd managed to get over the fact that not only will the chosen few see me naked in the film but also with a hard-on while sorting out some bird (no doubt leading to a blunt analysis of both my tackle and technique). This, in itself, is quite a big deal. We're British after all. We're not usually that comfortable with exposing our naked bodies to each other, unlike the Germans and Swedes who walk around starkers all the time, throwing beach balls to each other while their bollocks and breasts swing pendulously. We Brits prefer each other to be clothed at all times and when not, the lights should be off to prevent any inadvertent naked flesh being seen. So agreeing to star in what amounts to an enduring record of the sex act should not be underappreciated. I'd even got used to the fact that the Scotsman would be there in the wardrobe and, despite his promises, probably having a tug while he was at it...or while I was at it, more like. Now Ellis is going to be hiding under the bed with a boom mike like some stranded window cleaner in a 'Carry On...' movie. The Scotsman's assertions that "nothing could possibly go wrong" continue to have an increasing ring of ominous inevitability about them. Despite all this, nothing can deter me from the ultimate goal. Camera crew or not, I'm out to get into Natalie's pants tonight.

The night progresses in its regular Saturday pattern; complete with depressingly familiar non-committal noises from Natalie over whether she'll let me get inside her for once. The all-inclusive japery I was expecting is also failing to materialise. Ellis and Rob seem to be treating the evening as any other and only rarely break free of the dance floor for long enough to get another pint or piss out the previous one. McKinley appears not to be a fan of the foreplay and is eager for the deal to be sealed. He sporadically looms out of the darkness to slur enquiries on my progress before slithering away unsated, leaving me to increasingly shark the Warehouse waters alone and in desperation. When the opening drum beats of 'I am the Resurrection' boom out I know time is running out. If they play the extended album version, I have just over eight minutes to get Natalie to agree to come home with me. If the DJ commits the heinous act of cutting the Stone Roses short, I've got approximately two-and-a-half minutes less to cast my leading lady. I scan the sea of hands and glistening, blissed-out faces for Natalie but only manage to spot Ellis in full Christ pose, gurning like a constipated mental patient by a speaker, and a serious-looking Scotsman tapping his watch at me from the wings. It's then that an arm snakes round my waist from behind, unzips my fly and slides a warm hand inside my jeans.

"There you are," purrs the inebriated voice in my ear, "So are you going to fuck me tonight?"

Before agreeing, I check this is Natalie. It's a female voice so in truth it doesn't really matter but considering the mission I'm on, it would be better if it was. "You only have to ask, Nat."

Natalie's hand grips my shaft and gives it a rough, fast stroke before the rest of her appears in front of me, smiling the droopy-lidded grin of the overly-refreshed. "How did you know it was me?" she giggles. She doesn't wait for an answer. Her face suddenly takes on an out-of-focus intensity before she plants two very wet and rubbery lips over my mouth and invades my throat with a serpentine tongue. Out of the corner of my eye, I see McKinley fighting his way through the crowd towards the exit, dragging Ellis behind him like a chemically-challenged rag doll. From the state of the pair of them I quickly ascertain that this is not going to rival *Out of Africa* for cinematography.

Giving the film crew time to get in position (and probably take on more narcotics) I break up the short stagger back to McKinley's with a few impromptu al fresco fumblings. By the third alleyway, Natalie is actually growling and trying to shin up my front like a nymphomaniac squirrel. This, and the fact that her eyes are no longer a coordinated team, suggests that I'm not going to have any problem getting her up for what's to come. Now if I can just shake the image of my two best friends in the room with us as we fuck, I'll be there too.

Natalie is so plastered that the loud shuffling and barely stifled laughter I hear as we stumble up the stairs barely registers with her. I lead her into the bedroom, quickly surveying the area for any trailing feet or visible lenses. I have to suppress my own giggles as I spot a raised thumbs-up protruding from the wardrobe as we enter. Any worries about how I would manoeuvre the previously uncoordinated and rubbery Nat into position are soon obliterated as she suddenly becomes very focussed on getting me out of my clothes. My shirt loses at least three buttons as she tears it off and is soon ripping my jeans undone. Quickly realising that I have more than just an acting role in making this a box-office success, I take control and turn her to face the closet. Burying my head in her neck, I then lift her t-shirt over her head, exposing her barely restrained melons to the presumably ecstatic Scotsman. I cup them from behind and then pull her bra up over them, letting them find their natural balance after some firm wobbling. There is a loud bang from the wardrobe but again Natalie doesn't notice. Turning her around and guiding her to her knees, I give the camera team a nice profile shot as she enthusiastically goes to work on mouth duty. Between savouring the moment, I look down from time to time, and on one occasion I see a microphone on a boom slowly protruding from under the bed. Not taking the risk of being caught, I stand Natalie up and, as we passionately kiss, I turn her to face away from the wardrobe, lifting her short skirt up with both hands before sliding her panties off, giving her peachy arse its Oscar moment. Much to my amusement, her thong comes with the legend ALL YOU CAN EAT emblazoned on the front. After picking it up from the floor, I show this with glee to the wardrobe and then get started on the buffet.

I've watched enough porn to know some of the standard moves but now I'm starring in one I suddenly find out that I'm not comfortable performing additional crowd pleasers like the meat slap (the act of hitting a kneeling blower across the cheek or forehead with your cock) or the fish hook (the currently popular and slightly baffling practice of hooking a finger in the woman's mouth while pounding her from behind). Strangely, considering what else I'm willing to do, I find these to be a little bit disrespectful.

The actual sex lasts longer than I ever thought it would due to the fact that, despite it being one of the best shags of my life, I'm also concerned about getting good camera angles. The curse of the media-student-turned-amateur-porn-star I suppose. This preoccupation with aesthetics certainly helps with my staying power (and hopefully makes me look like a raging stud at the same time). There is a scary moment where I can't find a condom but after some frantic naked searching - which I want edited out - I find an old flavoured rubber which is nearing its use-by date. Once things get rocking, we put on quite a show. I'm particularly pleased with the reverse cowgirl to camera while sitting on a chair, and the final doggy-style pay-off during which I can't appear to be anything other than a blur. I decide against the money shot because full penetration is one thing but no-one wants to see a mate shoot his load, right? Instead, I go for the balls-deep orgasm and freeze-frame peace sign to camera. That one will probably end up on the cover. We collapse to a standing ovation somewhere in my imagination. After packing Natalie off home in a cab, the crew resurface and meet me in the kitchen.

"Fucking hell, big man," beams the Scotsman, almost beside himself with joy. "Top stuff."

"I thought she'd never leave," I sigh happily, mainly through relief of it all being over but also through the satisfaction of a job well done. "If she had wanted to sleep over, you boys would have been stuck there all night."

"You didn't say much," Ellis pipes up. "I was hoping for some filthy dialogue."

"I called her a dirty bitch a couple of times," I add in my defence.

"So did I," says McKinley.

"Did you shuffle one off in there, you pervy git?" Ellis adds. "I bet you did."

"Nah, man. I made a promise."

I catch him looking apologetically to the heavens and punch his arm. "Bastard. You're going to edit the comedy condom search out, right? I must have looked a right tit shuffling about like a fucking Dalek." McKinley nods and winks in a way that suggests that scene will end up in the bloopers at the end of the main feature, along with the series of loud fanny farts that came during the awkward legs-round-my-neck-on-the-desk manoeuvre.

"At least you found one," says Ellis. "Would you have gone through with it bareback?"

"Who knows? There was a lot of pressure to perform, you know," I muse. I had my doubts from the start about Natalie's sexual history and despite the amount of alcohol in my system, I was still aware throughout the entire evening that I needed some johnnies. However, once things got going, I became more and more casual about it. "Thank God for that old fruit-flavoured one."

"Lemon-entry, my dear Watson," McKinley grins, prompting huge laughs. He turns to the well-stocked fridge. "Beer?"

"Beer," comes the joint reply.

McKinley and I stand in the street outside the building where Dennis the Menace is supposed to be holed up these days and swap suspicious looks. I check the address on the Hartington beer mat again and squint at Bazza's spider-scrawl handwriting. Not for the first time, I pass the coaster to the Scotsman for verification. He refuses to take it, instead offering me a slightly pissy look which says "it's still the same fucking address as last time, big man." We survey the establishment in front of us one more time, take a few more deep breaths and then finally enter.

I've been in a few dives in my time, and on many occasions with McKinley at my side but I can't remember feeling as uncomfortable walking into a place as I do right now. Even the Scotsman, a survivor of Govan's mean streets, looks nervous. We look for a table, preferably one near the door, but have to settle for two stools at the bar. With every pair of eyes in the place burning holes in our backs we take our seats and smile wanly at the barman as he approaches.

"What can I get you, gents?"

"What have you got?" asks McKinley, bravely.

"It's a wine bar, sir. The clue's in the title."

I can't stand fucking wine bars, the type of staff who work in them or the people who frequent them. Just being here puts me on edge. I love wine and will drink wine willingly in all manner of places which serve it but bars which specifically set out not only to serve the grape but also promote the image of the wine drinker as some kind of *übermensch* really piss me off. It's an elitist concept that should have died out long before its heydays were over. Sadly, those who were supposed to save us from the conservative ideologues who dreamt up wine bars were actually yuppie wolves in socialist sheep's clothing - which means that we're now pretty much back where we started. We're in a recession, the Tories are in power, everyone's doing cocaine and wearing day-glo clothes - and wine bars are back in. It's the fucking 1980s all over again. Tony Blair has a lot to answer for.

After ordering two glasses of pinot noir, McKinley cautiously turns to survey the terrain. All the office workers and bright young things in their blazers and novelty ties have lost interest in us and have gone back to talking about how they protected their portfolios from the financial crisis. "What a bunch of bankers," he mutters. "I hated yuppies when they were first about and I hate this new breed even more. At least when it was privileged tossers   bleeding us dry, we could depend on the working classes to fight back. These cunts are straight off the housing estates. There's no distinction anymore. No solidarity. Everyone's a greedy bastard. Give them a mobile phone and a subscription to Forbes and suddenly they're Gordon fucking Gecko."

"Robbing the poor to feed the rich," I sigh. "Where did it all go wrong?"

"When everything seemed to be going right, big man." McKinley takes receipt of our wine from the barman, pays the man and passes me my glass. "We walked straight into it. Slap a big pair of tits on a pig and it's still a pig - only with jugs, you know what I mean?"

"Not really but go on." Knowing McKinley's strong political views and the story of his upbringing, I know he will.

"Everyone was blinded by the tits. They didn't see the pig until everyone was bored of the tits."

"Okay..."

McKinley puts down his untouched wine and spins in his stool to face me. Some of the eyes begin to turn back to us as the Scotsman's rant increases in volume. "The Labour Party was the pig, okay - and history has shown that it doesn't matter how fucking heinous the Tories are at any time, no one if going to elect the pig. Look at Neil Kinnock. He was Labour leader at the height of the nastiest Tory government ever and he still couldn't win. When Blair came along, he understood that the Tories had ground everyone down. No one gave a shit about the politics anymore so he gave us all what we wanted. He slapped a great big pair of Dolly Parton tits on the pig and won a landslide. He tarted it all up and sold it to us as fucking Cool Britannia, not four years of Labour. No-one knew what that meant anyway. Most of the people he was targeting were too young to remember the last left-wing government. He must have shot his load when Britpop came along. Suddenly he had a tight, hairless teenage vadge to add to the swinging jugs and practically overnight his pig became the one bitch everyone wanted to shag." Just over McKinley's shoulder I spy a middle-aged stockbroker type having a word with the barman and pointing in our direction. "We should have known it was doomed when Noel Gallagher went to Downing Street but instead of seeing it for what it was – Blair cosying up to the real power in the country – we saw it as our breakthrough, not his. Coup de fucking ta very much, our kid. Have a glass of champers and a line, shut the fuck up and leave us to get on with lining our pockets."

"So Noel shagged the pig?" I ask, still a little unsure if I'm using the analogy correctly.

"Not just him. They all took a shot," McKinley sneers. "Roll up your note and rock the vote. Fucking bunch of cocaine socialists, man, all blinded by a blizzard of spin and snow. Couldn't see the wood...

"...For the tits?"

"Now you're getting it."

The barman nervously approaches and leans over the maple counter. "I'm sorry sir, would you mind toning down the language and the volume, please? We're starting to get a few complaints."

"Aye, big man," says McKinley, genuinely apologetic now that most of his spleen has been vented. "Not a problem. We'll be as good as gold. Scout's honour." The barman smiles, happy that he now won't have to try and have us forcibly removed from the premises, and retreats to the far end of the counter where he assures the stockbroker with another relieved smile. "Saucy cunt," whispers the Scotsman with a nefarious smirk.

I raise my glass and McKinley does likewise. We toast. "Viva la revolution!" We each take a sip and the irony of the situation begins to dawn. Two old socialists dreaming of the welfare state while spending some of their inflated salaries on expensive wine at a chrome and oak altar to capitalism. How easily we were turned. What a fucked up world we live in. "Can you remember that thrill everyone had when Blair got in?" I ask after savouring the vino for a moment. "We had that party at yours on election night, remember? Everyone was so buzzed about the future. I can remember being on a massive high for weeks after that, what with the combination of the music and the optimism. It really felt like we'd won our future back. How wrong could one generation be?"

"You were off your fucking rocker that night if I remember so I'm not surprised you were high for weeks," says McKinley, winking at me over his glass. "That's why it all worked out so well for Blair. We were all off our tits - for years. Lagered-up lambs to the slaughter."

"That party summed it all up for me," I smile, replaying some hazy memories in my head. "The hedonism, the vibe, the music...the hope. It was supposed to be like that every day after that."

"It's a good job it wasn't, if you think about it. It was carnage. I knew things were going to get out of order when Dirty Den turned up with that big bag of E...Speaking of which..." The Scotsman catches the barman's eye and waves him over. "Big man, we want to see the boss."

"Is there a problem, sir?"

"Is your boss called Dennis Edmunds?"

"Yes."

"Then you're the one with the fucking problem, pal. Just tell him a couple of old friends want a word." The barman, obviously not a fan of the boys, grumpily turns away from us and angrily slaps a few digits into the phone by the till. He grumbles a few words into the receiver while staring daggers at us. McKinley smiles sweetly at him but again mutters insults under his breath: "There you go, not that fucking hard is it, you saucy cunt."

"Mr Edmunds will be with you in a few minutes." With that he walks over to a female member of staff and has a word. He'll not be dealing with us anymore tonight. He's brought his seniority into play. His reasonably cute underling will be attending to our needs from now on. Fine by us.

"So what do you make of all this?" I ask the Scotsman who is already assessing the vital statistics of our new hostess. "When Bazza told me that Dennis had left the Hartington to manage The Attic, I expected him to either be dead or feeding a skag habit by toilet trading down Beaumont Park by now, not running a swanky wine bar." Long before I actually met anyone who'd been brave (or drunk) enough to go to the Attic, I'd been willing to believe the rumours that it was just a front for some nefarious underworld enterprise. I'd heard that people had seen bodies being carried out of there and loaded into 4x4s under the cover of darkness. It never seemed to be open and even on busy Friday and Saturday nights there was never any music coming from it or any sign of life behind its matt black facade. Eventually I heard from an eye-witness (or perhaps a complete bullshitter) about what went on there. According to the source, it was a grimy, industrial goth venue with a strong sado-masochistic vibe. It wasn't a full-on gay club but a number of dark rooms were available for those wanting to fist any of the passing Gary Numan lookalikes should the desire arise. Drugs were rife and as long as you didn't take the piss, dealing and using was tolerated. The underworld connotations allegedly came from the policy of the management taking a cut of any deal going down on the premises. It was also suggested that a number of dealers were actually in the employ of the club. When I heard Dennis had taken over as the boss, I feared his all-or-nothing attitude may have led to the mad bastard being found dead after doing a Michael Hutchence in the cloakroom. To then find out that he's actually alive and well and running a wine bar kinda messes with my whole perception of a man whose catchphrase in the mid-90s was "I love cock."

McKinley also seems to be having a hard job equating our current surroundings with his own memories of Dennis the Menace. "Maybe it's not him," he muses, sipping thoughtfully on his wine while staring unblinkingly at the barmaid's arse. "Dennis Edmunds is quite a common name...probably."

At that moment, a familiar stick-thin, considerably beaked figure minces into the bar through a door marked PRIVATE. The sickly pallor is more deathly than before and the widow's peak has been reduced to a thin pencil line of hair down the centre of the forehead but it's definitely him. Jesus, he looks like someone just dug him up. He narrows his bulbous eyes and purses that paper-cut mouth of his as he scans the bar for potential ghosts from the past. I kick McKinley in the back of the leg and point a fully extended arm over his shoulder at the squinting Dennis. "No doubt about it, geezer. That's our man." McKinley hones in on the vision at the end of my finger tip. It takes a moment for them both to register and understand what they're seeing. They seem to come to the same conclusion at precisely the same moment but the reaction is completely different. McKinley cheers and starts laughing. Dennis frowns and appears to growl. "Did you bring a stake or a crucifix?" I whisper as he begins to cross the room. "The Prince of Darkness looks more than a little pissed off."

"Alright, big man? How you doing?"

Dennis stands with his hands on his hips, peering down his pointed nose at us. He has that feint whiff of death about him that sometimes follows junkies around; that over-ripe sourness which precludes a premature end. In the awkward seconds of silence, I notice his suit is jet black Armani and he's wearing an open neck purple Yves St. Laurent silk shirt underneath. Vlad the Impaler meets *GQ*. Very nice. He's obviously doing alright. "Where did you two degenerates spring from?" he drawls disdainfully.

"Simon Le Bon said he'd meet us in here...something to do with a Duran Duran reunion party," I grin. "We forgot our headscarves but he said you could sort us out." Dennis sneers and narrows his bloodshot eyes to snake-like slits. It appears he still doesn't appreciate my brand of humour. A part of me is glad that not everything has changed.

"You don't seem too happy to see us, man." The Scotsman adopts a fake expression of hurt.

"I've left a lot of lives behind," Dennis wheezes. I'm hoping he's referring to his own and not to the victims of some soon-to-be revealed bloodlust. "And you were in one of them. I've moved on. I'm not that Dennis anymore. This Dennis was born in the year 2000 and as a result does not share a history with you."

The still clearly insane Dennis is reliably incomprehensible as ever. Whatever the lunatic's banging on about, McKinley's not having it. "Big man, we're 15 years older. We both have kids...if you can believe that. We're not here to drag you down the Warehouse, nick your wallet and force you to get your dick out on some bird...unless you want to 'cause we're probably going down there later..." I kick the Scotsman again and he gets back on track. "What I mean is, we're different too - like you wouldn't believe." He sounds almost miserable when he says this. "Look, we're back for a get-together with Ellis and the Ponce and wanted to see what you're up to, man. Have a drink with us. Just a drink and a catch-up. Then we'll walk out of this life if you want. We just thought it would good to stop by and see how you are."

Dennis' facade seems slightly shaken by the Scotsman's genuine honesty. He's not the only one. I thought we were just dropping in for a piss-take. Now I'm ready to play nice and properly re-establish contact with an old acquaintance. We shared a lot of good times even though Den was never a fully-fledged member of the Lads. But he was there for Amsterdam. He was there for Knebworth. He was there - or at least somewhere nearby - for Election Night 97. (Come to think of it, he was actually there for more of the memorable events than Rob.) McKinley's right. He does deserve to be visited with respect. But he also needs to accept that time has moved on and that while we may share certain memories of wild times gone by, that doesn't necessarily mean we're here to recreate them. He can at least share another glass with us before we head off. "Come on Dennis, have a drink with us," I say, following the Scotsman's tone. "Tell us what's been happening with you."

The softening of those razor-edged features suggests Dennis can sense a more mature atmosphere around us and a certain warmth begins to emanate. A slight smile flickers on his lips. "What are you lowlifes drinking?" He sniffs my glass. "That's filth." He turns to our hostess. "Caroline? Bring a bottle of the Château Corton Grancey Grand Cru '99 to my table in the restaurant, will you please? And no interruptions. If anyone calls, tell Adrian to take it." He leans over and pours our 'filth' in the sink. "Come through," he says, relaxing considerably. "We won't be disturbed in here. Service doesn't start for another couple of hours."

The restaurant is in an adjoining building to the bar through a covered atrium at the rear. Its pristine white decor is in glaring contrast to the muted lighting and dark wood shades of the bar. It's silent apart from the now self-conscious table arranging of the few staff members preparing for dinner on its fringes. McKinley, a man with a lot of experience and appreciation of such places, nods approvingly. "Nice gaff. You've landed on your feet here." Dennis guides us to a table by the floor-to-ceiling windows which look out onto a walled garden and indicates for us to sit in that flamboyant yet sincere way that only a man with considerable experience in the hospitality trade can get away with.

"It cost me every penny I had," he smiles, taking his own seat and leaning back with satisfaction. "And it was all worth it."

"Wait. You own this? I thought you were just the manager."

The Menace digs out a very familiar smug look from the repertoire, completing the slow transformation into the Dennis we all know and strangely love. "Not a chance. What do you think I did with all the money I earned at the Hartington? There was a reason I barely went out...until you lot came along. I was planning for the big time."

"Is that why you ended up off your tits running an S&M club and pretending to be something out of fucking *Goodfellas*?" asks the Scotsman, somewhat uncharitably.

Dennis' bonhomie takes a slap. "Who told you about that?" He already knows the answer. "You went to the Hartington, didn't you?"

"I did," I admit. "Bazza filled me in."

A waitress appears at the restaurant entrance and takes what seems an age to reach us through the pristine white landscape. She takes a dusty bottle and three crystal glasses from the silver tray she is expertly carrying and arranges them in front of us without a word. She departs in silence, crossing the white expanse again like a lonely character from some winter fable. "I always go for the '99 with old friends," muses Dennis, easing the already opened cork from the slender neck. "It marks the year when I started getting my memory back."

The next half hour is spent in the void of events missing from our version of Dennis' story. The last time any of us actually saw him was Election Night 97. He already seemed lost by then, a far cry from the well-mannered, simple man we first encountered when starting work at the hotel three years before. He was using a lot of different drugs by 1997, his sexual appetite ranged from young fast food boys to the gourmet abandon of orgies, and his grip on reality had become overly greased and tenuous. He was on the precipice and yet, because of the times and the way we behaved, he didn't appear to be that out of control. We were all pushing it. Den was just pushing it a little further and in different directions. What we didn't consider was that his starting point was a lot further away from ours, which meant he was way more fucked up than any of us could ever get. "You boys already knew the illicit joys of life back in 94," he says. "I knew nothing of that. When my eyes were opened, the world became a completely different planet. I think seeing it for the first time with new eyes damaged me more than anything I smoked or snorted in the years that followed. I wanted it all."

"You used to say that all the time," McKinley reminds him. "And that you loved sucking dick."

Dennis cackles. "I still do, sweetie!" Just as it always used to, his laugh becomes a hacking cough which takes a few seconds to subside. When he recovers, his tone has a tinge of regret. "I didn't just want it all, I took it all and fucked everyone. But by 1997, I wasn't making sense...life made no sense. It suddenly just became a haze. The next thing I knew, it was the end of the century. I woke up and everything was different. I'd lost two years in a black hole. Everyone was back to feeling shite about themselves, the whole country seemed to have a hangover...Blur were making music about heroin and Oasis weren't doing anything. I completely missed *Be Here Now*."

"So it wasn't all bad then," deadpans McKinley. I let that one slide. For now.

"No, not all bad..." Dennis suddenly looks haunted. He takes a sip of wine and holds the taste in his mouth for a moment before swallowing hard. His voice is less assured when he finally speaks. "I've never told anyone this but the reason I cleaned up..." He hesitates in a bid to find a modicum of composure, not for dramatic effect as he would in the past. "There was an incident at the club." The memories of anecdotes referring to the removal of corpses from the Attic come flooding back and send a chill down my spine. "I thought I had that place under control but it was *never* under control. I was never under control. It was dark chaos from day one. Extreme stuff..." Dennis raises his glass towards the faint light coming from the window and peers into it as if watching a particular a scene from the past in the shimmering crimson of the wine. "One night after hours, the party continued with some of the hardcore punters. I was doing a little smack back then...Maybe more than a little..." His voice drifts off. McKinley and I share concerned glances. "I came to and there was panic in the club. The lights were blazing...it was never light in there...always murky...but this time it was glaring. People were running everywhere; some screaming in fucked-up hysteria, others barging through the frozen bodies, heading for the exits. During my black out, one of the leather boys who'd been hog-tied in the back rooms had choked. Some young thing... Maybe only just 21. He was full of ecstasy, ketamine, you name it. By the time I had any idea what was going on most of the party had run off, leaving me and the staff to deal with the police. Of course, they shut us down and brought us in. Luckily no criminal charges were brought against us, God knows how because he'd bought the drugs on site and had been severely buggered while trussed up in a harness on the premises. The judge ruled death by misadventure..." Despite the No Smoking signs on the tables, Dennis lights up. He draws deeply on his Marlboro as McKinley and I absorb his story. Dennis had a reputation as a fantasist back in the day but his stories were always told to enhance his reputation. Never did he tell us anything which would have been such a blight on his soul or character. His demeanour today also suggests that this is no fabricated anecdote. Before he would be all puffed-up bravado. Today he looks fragile and barely repaired. "The club was finished. The party was over. There were no more reasons to celebrate. It would have been disrespectful and inappropriate to continue living it large after that. I'd been given a huge opportunity to change so..." His voice trails off again. He waves his cigarette in one hand and holds his wine glass up in the other. "These are my only vices now. Oh, and a little treat called Clive who lives with me upstairs." He winks and a little of the old Menace spirit shines through the pain and regret.

After briefly filling in our own gaps and finishing the excellent '99, we extend an invitation for Dennis to join us later and I give him my mobile phone number just in case he reverses his initial decision to decline. The number of staff busying themselves around the fringes of the restaurant increases as does their industry and Dennis prepares to welcome his diners as the genial host. It's highly unlikely that anyone crossing his latest threshold will know of the lives he has left behind. He seems more than happy with that and I can see how this has liberated him from many of his personal demons. Some, of course, will never leave him in peace but for the most part, Dennis is a free man. I feel a hint of admiration for him - a slight pang of envy.

We hug awkwardly and bid him farewell. The Scotsman and I step out into the early evening sunshine, somewhat shocked by the nature of the revelations. After taking a moment to gather ourselves, we start walking silently in thought in the direction of our next rendezvous with the past.

three

Star Shaped

February 1995

Rituals are central to any tribe's culture. Most ancient civilizations filled their social calendars around worshipping some god or other or giving thanks for their crops not failing. Some just liked to sacrifice the odd virgin for no particular reason other than that's what they usually did on a Monday. We normally reserve that little ritual for a Thursday or Saturday night.

Saturday nights are Warehouse nights – almost without fail. Something drastic needs to happen to stop us hitting our spiritual home for cheap beers, cheap women and fantastic tunes after slaving in the hotel kitchen on a Saturday night. We even made it down there in the middle of a hurricane warning one time; dodging flying garden furniture and potentially decapitating roof tiles only to find out that the lightweights had not bothered to open the place just because it was a bit windy. The following week we made the point of insulting all the door staff for their lack of belief. That was another of the few nights we didn't make it into the Warehouse on a Saturday night.

The ritual usually begins at the end of dinner service. I usually work the weekend shifts with McKinley as Ellis is otherwise engaged on the delicatessen counter at the local Tesco until seven on a Saturday and then incapable of getting out of bed to handle breakfast on Sunday. Saturday service is one of the best shifts to work as everyone at the

Hartington seems to be in that weekend mode. Gerry the Boss is at his most affable, probably because he knows that Angela will be hammered on Courvoisier by six which means he'll have a bit of peace for once and the opportunity to indulge in a bit of flirting with the female clientele without his harpy missus screaming at him. Dennis will be full of himself as usual when his role as second-in-command isn't being questioned by the boss's wife so instead of being the humourless arsehole he usually is, there'll often be an air of humanity about him. Barry the Barman tends to be a lot more open to our pleading on a Saturday. We're normally allowed a gratis pint after service but at weekends, with Gerry trying his luck with some tarty sales rep in the lounge, Bazza indulges us with all manner of free alcohol. As a tee-totaller himself, and a man with no life away from the Hartington's impressive oak bar, getting us pissed up amounts to the most entertainment he gets all week. And we're all too happy to oblige in the role of performing chimps. Even the waitresses, who can normally forget about having any kind of Saturday night due to their long hours, are more cheerful than usual. This is mostly because the ones who have to spend half the night clearing dinner, setting up for breakfast and then serving in the bar and lounge until the last guest stumbles off to bed rarely have to come in for work on Sunday. I usually spend most of the night trying to get the lovely Kate - our own air-headed but sweet 17-year old little Barbie - to come out on the town with us. I fail every time but at least her excuses change each week. The one time she agreed to come out with us, she made the condition that we went to this tacky theme bar where she was meeting her mates. That was the last time me and the Scotsman passed on the Warehouse. My excuse was obvious, his less so. McKinley is the closest you can be to being married without actually having a band of gold and a certificate filed at City Hall. He's been with his bird for about ten years but because she lives and works overseas, they hardly ever see each other. But they have a plan and once the Scotsman actually gets his degree, he'll be Mr. Impoverished Third World Nation. He's committed to that, and I respect him for it. But he is only human and quite large pervert to boot. Which is why he was tagging along that night. He was wondering if the Julia incident and the Natalie porn shoot had put me off the idea of the Proxy Fuck and whether I had grown a big enough set of balls to go after the major prize all on my own.

As it happened, Kate's fella turned up which led to about an hour of insecurity on the poor lad's part and intense boredom on ours. I think we ended up back at McKinley's where a lot of ganja was then consumed. The ultimate goal of shagging Kate - for both our pleasures - would have to wait.

Anyway, after getting my regular Saturday night knock back from Kate, we'll convene in the bar and wait until Ellis and Rob roll up, usually around nine. Then, after getting overly refreshed and contributing to the hotel's rising debt, we'll head to the Scotsman's for a quick smoke or a crafty line or two before heading for the main event.

It doesn't get any better than this. Seriously. It doesn't. The Warehouse is the only decent place in the city as far as anyone with any music taste is concerned. The tunes are always sublime, the beer cheap and on the right side of horse piss, and the females are top form. It's Britpop and Madchester all the way, served with lashings of knock-off Heineken Export and a large helping of the finest local indie babes on the side. Unlike the townie clubs in the city centre, everyone's here for the music and the dance floor is always packed with blokes frugging like gibbons and birds flailing in hedonistic abandon. Everyone's up for it, out of it and looking to get on it. Being here without fail every week has its advantages and disadvantages. On the one hand, we're known and can play the crowd. If the regulars are one big happy family, then we're the slightly raffish, black sheep uncles who show up for every party or wedding. We're the catalysts and when we're in residence, the night will surely be one to remember. On the other hand, however, regular attendance gets you noticed in other ways and nothing cements a face in the mind of a bouncer than like having to deal with a repeat offender.

While we arrive together as a gang, more often than not we'll spend most of the night operating in smaller cells or as lone wolves. After stocking up at the bar and getting the lay of the land, it won't take long for a tune to entice Ellis and myself onto the dance floor. It's usually one of the warm-up songs before the real heavy-hitters start rolling off the decks, something like Ride's 'Twisterella'. Rarely, if ever, do I use the dance floor as an arena for the pursuit of women. The dance floor is for just that - dancing. I lose myself in the music; feeling its unearthly power in my body and seeing the swimming psychedelia of sound behind my closed eyes. Without looking, I know Ellis is seriously churning up the crowd around him with his arms and legs spread spider-like from his lanky frame. A study of seriousness and purpose, he'll fight with the music, pushing himself into it and against it. The music challenges him to respond and he normally does so with all his might. While we're working up a sweat, McKinley and Rob will drink heavily at the bar for a while and eye up the birds. Rob is terrible at chatting up women and the Scotsman will soon realise that he stands a much better chance on his own and will choose an opportune moment to extricate himself from Rob's painful attempts at conversation to join us on the dance floor. (Rob never dances before his body is actually at the stage of being incapable of standing up, which presents an obvious set of problems once he does make it onto the dance floor). McKinley will often spot a gazelle - or more times out of ten, a wildebeest - which has strayed from the herd and will subtly make his way out of the heaving mass of bodies like a slightly inebriated cheetah circling its next kill. This will leave Ellis and I thrashing around until the DJ puts on something which doesn't quite come up to scratch, at which point we'll find Rob and end any small chance he has of getting his end away.

The night will progress along these same lines with each of us swapping roles depending on whether a potential shag presents itself to any of us. Usually, if we don't get thrown out before lights up, we'll all get wildly connected to the cosmos during the finale of 'I am the Resurrection' and then stagger out into the cold night in search of the rank bird who promised the hand-job, a kebab or both. Sated by a pita of dubious meat - and maybe a rough tug round the back of the chip van - it's back to McKinley's for drugs and improvised cocktails. Saturday never ends until you wake up the next day and have to fight the urge to vomit for the next six hours as you cook and serve English breakfasts after forgetting that you again stupidly agreed to do the Sunday morning shift. Unless you're Ellis of course.

With such a large dose of substance-fuelled hedonism inked in permanent marker on our weekly schedule, you would think that Thursday's down the Orchard would be a more sedate affair. But what fun would that be? As Michelle Pfeiffer reminds Al Pacino in *Scarface*, nothing exceeds like excess. And no period in recent memory has given us more belief in ourselves and our invincibility than this one. Britain is on the rise; our music is back in fashion, our *fashion* is back in fashion, we're back in fashion. We're rocking 'n' rolling towards something huge. Everyone can feel it. There's a party coming and we're all going to get an invite. And everyone knows the best way to enjoy a party is to get into the spirit of things beforehand.

While the Saturday ritual is about celebrating the music which drives us on, Thursdays are all about attitude. It's about 1995. It's about having a laugh. It's about having the time of your life. It's about pushing yourself to experience it all, drinking what you like, taking what you like, working enough to get the cash to blow it over the bar and piss it up the wall. Thursday night is pound-a-pint craziness at the Orchard, where bad behaviour comes as standard. You throw cheap beer over each other; you throw cheap beer over yourself. You down pint after pint of watered down lager. You sway out belligerently into the street to the next bar, the next club. You roll around in your designer shirts, your retro trainers, you smoke, you sing your songs, you blag your way past the bouncers who will sell you amphetamines in the club's toilets later in the night. You flirt with housewives, you cheer couples having public sex in the seedy corners, you hold self-made score cards up at the birds, hoping they find it either charming enough to blow you at the end of the night or outrageous enough to give you an angry reaction which will drive you into the embrace of further chaos. You're out of control but it's okay - because everyone is. Sing after me: "I'm free...to say whatever I like, if it's wrong or right...it's alright..."

This Thursday starts and progresses like any - every - other. We meet at the bar; all dressed in our best drinking finery, knowing by the end of the night it'll be soaked through with lager and sweat and reeking of cigarette smoke. A number of the faces are already in attendance and a few casual acquaintances stop by for a word, usually to enquire about whether we know if there's any speed around or if we're heading onto one of the possible club nights after chucking out time. It's too early to tell what will happen but there are always possibilities. Depending on how nasty the evening gets, we could end up in one of the meat markets such as Chrome Dreams or the even more heinous Speakeasy's, the club that time and taste forgot in a part of the city left to die of urban cancer. The other option is Pulse, a former strip club with newly acquired pretensions of grandeur but with the old lap dancing décor still intact. But, like I said, we'll see how things pan out.

Rob is on form tonight. He's been off the radar for a few days and his patronage tonight gives him the chance to explain why. "She's a stunner, mate, for her age," he says with a sloshing pint held to his puffed out chest as we crush together at the crowded bar. "Mature women are the way to go. Fuck all these young tarts and their brainless crap. Jane knows the score and believe me, I'm not against being taught a lesson or two."

She's a stunner - *for her age*. If he hadn't added that caveat then maybe McKinley, Ellis and I would not now be sharing secret raised eyebrows and knowing smirks behind Rob's back. By adding that caveat, he has also set himself up for a dousing in cheap beer and a chorus of "granny fucker" later in the evening. But for now, we play along.

"So where did you pick up this Jane, then?" asks Ellis, not really caring about the answer.

"Probably when he helped her across the road," mutters the Scotsman in my ear as he turns and orders three more pints over the heads of the masses.

"I was down Speakeasy's after work the other night with Amir and met her in there. I ended up back at her place," Rob beams. The fact that he went straight from his three-times-a-week stint in Amir's Kebab Emporium to one of the cheesiest clubs in the city, while presumably still smelling of lamb and chip fat, doesn't do anything for our developing opinion of this Jane. "She's fucking wild," he giggles.

Rob's chances of avoiding getting soaked in Carlsberg diminish as he rattles off the last three nights spent in Jane's company in what feels like real time. Ellis is drinking pints faster than it takes to get to the bar while McKinley is getting that tell-tale 'I'm on the verge of axe-murdering this bastard' look in his eyes. I take the opportunity afforded me by Rob's changing of sexual positions in his latest tale to fight my way to the toilet. The pub has filled to almost bursting point and despite that fact that it's February, many drinkers have spilled out onto the street to avoid suffocation. The popularity of pound-a-pint night has also contributed to the men's toilet being crowded and for once the women's is not the only pisser with a queue stretching out of the door. I'm contemplating using the alley beside the pub when a husky voice grabs my attention. I turn round and see a familiar face, although one which is older than the memory I eventually match it with. I forget about my near critical bladder situation and squeeze myself over.

"Karen?"

Karen Anderson - the slightly puppyish little cousin of a class mate at high school, now a curvy, gorgeous young woman - breaks off from her loud exchange with a girlfriend and looks at me questioningly. After a moment, a look of realisation flickers in her deep brown eyes and a heart-breaking smile creeps across her face. "Danny?"

Daniel Jones - the scrawny, mulleted fifth-former who she once had a schoolgirl crush on, now a slightly heavier, shaggy-haired beer monster - smiles back, thankful that his compromised eyesight has not just helped to make a tit of himself. "Wow, you look great. It's been a long time."

"It has," she smiles, in a genuine way and not in that pained 'oh God, how long do I have to talk to this wanker before I can make a run for it?' way that some girls do. "My, haven't you grown?" The sarcastic tone is not hurtful but it reminds me not to state the bloody obvious again if I want this conversation to progress.

"Are you just visiting or are you in the city now?" Location, location, location. Is she still an out-of-towner or someone who I could bump into from time to time? It's a good question and one which is less creepy than 'where do you live?'

"I moved here just before Christmas. I couldn't handle it out in the sticks anymore. Plus I work in the city now, I'm a vet's assistant."

"Really? Don't you need some kind of medical degree for that?" She may have one, Danny, give her some credit. They don't normally let you cut living things open without qualifications. "I mean, you know, you're, what...20? Those courses take ages, right?"

"I'm studying part-time at the university. What about you?"

"I'm back at college now..." Which normally prompts the question as to what I was doing before returning to education so I speed things up. "I'm doing a media course there. So, animals, eh?"

"Yeah. I love them," Karen replies with a slightly quizzical look. "Do you have any?"

A commotion in the direction of the bar catches my attention. The Scotsman has cracked under pressure and has just thrown a full pint in Rob's face. Much cheering and copy-cat behaviour is ensuing. "Yeah...sometimes." At that point, Karen's slightly more rotund friend returns from the toilet and gives me a look which suggests she's going to punch me in the face. Please don't tell me this is her lesbian lover.

"Danny, this is Amanda. My flat mate." Phew.

"We're late, Karen." Amanda's stare never leaves my face.

"Right. Hey, it was great to catch up, Danny. Maybe we'll bump into each other again." Bump. Grind. Slide. Whatever. I'm flexible.

"Wait!" Much too urgent, Daniel. Foot off the gas...That's better. Breathe. Try again. "Where are you heading? Maybe I can buy you a drink in...wherever it is you'll be later."

Amanda sighs audibly and angrily. Karen hesitates and thinks, looking to the ceiling in a totally cute way which suggests she's waiting for an answer from God himself. "Err...Pulse, maybe?"

"Maybe I'll see you there." I stand there long enough to watch Karen's arse wave goodbye through the flimsy satin of her short party dress before fighting my way frantically back to the war-zone at the bar. "Boys, we're going to Pulse," I gasp to my soaked comrades. "But first I really need a slash."

Pulse is a fucking nightmare to find anyone in at the best of times. Dragged out over four floors in one of the thinnest buildings in the northern hemisphere, getting around the place is like trying to slide up a fireman's pole while someone fires strobe lights and lasers at you. It's a cross between Studio 56, the Death Star and a neon-lit mine shaft. In the centre of each level is a small round dance floor with a metal bar stretching from floor to ceiling, a remnant of the club's more naked past. Climbing between each level through the spine of the club is a silver, circular staircase which, if you're unfortunate enough to fall down it, spills you out onto the middle of the dancing area like the victim of a tacky helter skelter. If that doesn't mess with your head, each level has mirrored walls and is randomly dissected into smaller rooms which used to serve as VIP areas back in the day. The whole effect, when pissed out of your skull and high on drugs, is like being inside a child's tubular kaleidoscope. As the night slips on, it begins to feel like the little bastard is manically twisting the whole thing like its life depended on it.

Trying to find someone who may not even be in there is something I wouldn't normally recommend. All the cave-like booths and dark antechambers start to look the same after thirty minutes of searching. You forget which floor you're on or which ones you've already been to, and you soon start catching the eye of someone you're sure you know - only to find out its your own face reflected in those fucking mirrored walls. But this is no normal quest and I am quite willing to lose my mind in this twisted Danny in Wonderland nightmare if it gives me the brief opportunity to see Karen Anderson again. As I stumble further down the rabbit hole, I ask myself why. Karen was always the cherubic little face which would beam shyly at me whenever I hung out with her cousin Andy. Theirs was a close family and the cousins would quite often be visiting during school holidays and weekends. At school, Andy always looked out for his little cousin and so she sometimes hung around with her own friends within earshot. I always thought she was pretty in a much-too-young for me kinda way. Three years younger at high school was always a really big deal. Fancying someone from that many years below you was going to get you the nickname 'cradle-snatcher' or worse. When we left school, I lost contact with Andy. He joined the army and ended up in Germany I think. But I saw Karen around from time to time, and noticed how fit she became as she grew into her late teens. By then, of course, her crush on me had vanished and, forgetting the stigma of those forbidden school days, I kicked myself that I hadn't taken advantage of it while she still had it. Now, three years after I last saw her, I see her again with new eyes. In those brief moments we shared earlier in the night, something I can't explain happened to me. As I descend these life-threateningly ridiculous stairs for the umpteenth time, I realise that I'm as nervous about actually finding her as I am excited at the prospect. It's clear that her pubescent shyness is a thing of the distant past and that, during our brief exchange back in the Orchard, she exuded a sexy calm and confidence unseen in my most recent awkward exchanges with women. The more I think about how she handled herself and how I dealt with the situation, the more I come to realise that she was in control. I'm beginning to wonder if this pursuit is such a good idea and whether I'm actually ready for such a challenge when I exit the helter skelter on level three and walk straight into her.

"There you are. I've been looking for you." She's been looking for me? "You promised me a drink and now I'm thirsty."

See? All shyness out of the window. The new Karen Anderson is quite a proposition. Am I up to the task? "Well, if you've been able to find a bar on your travels, lead me to it and I'll gladly make good on that promise." My mouth takes the advantage before my brain can answer. My legs appear to be in league with my gob as I'm suddenly following that gloriously animated arse into a dark, distant catacomb. At a bar I have never seen before Karen orders a vodka and tonic and I ask for a beer, getting some poncey Spanish bottle with a lime in the top which costs almost four quid in return. I'm about to ask her about her cousin when she comes straight to the point

"Why didn't you ever ask me out in school? You knew I fancied you." Because, Karen, I was a stupid, stupid boy who was afraid of being called names by other stupid, stupid boys. And now I'm hoping that I don't turn out to be a stupid, stupid man.

"The only thing stopping me back then was the age difference," I admit. "It was a big deal then, remember? Would you have gone out with a second-year when you were in the fifth?"

Karen does that heaven-gazing pause for thought again. "Second-year boys wouldn't have had the equipment necessary," she smiles. "Fifth-years on the other hand..." She moves closer and presses herself against me. It's like someone has attached small electrodes all over my body. My cock immediately pulses and swells. She tilts her face towards mine. "Is the age difference a problem for you now?" My hand, throwing its lot in with my mouth and legs, ignores the maelstrom in my head and gently strokes a stray curl from her face, pushing it behind her ear.

"There's no problem here at all."

After about ten minutes of passionate kissing, during which it's made very clear that the most daring place my hand can go is on her backside, Karen breaks off and steps back. She smiles sweetly at me. "I have to find Amanda. I have the only key."

I snake an arm around her waist in preparation for pulling her back towards me only to find that she's remarkably sturdy for one so petite. Again, the message here is that I'm not going to get what I want. "Are you going to come back?"

"I'll be here somewhere...around." With that, she's gone. I stand gobsmacked for a second until legs and brain make their peace and I'm surging out of the darkness into the fluorescent chaos again. But she's definitely gone. What the hell was that all about? Was that revenge for not making my move almost a decade ago? Am I supposed to now foster a unrequited longing just like she did when we were barely adolescents? What the fuck? The sound of a collapsing table and the smashing of multiple glasses snaps me out of my head and back into club around me.

There in the wreckage lie Rob and Ellis, wrapped around each other, laughing hysterically. A couple of black-clad bouncers emerge from the disapproving bystanders and haul my friends to their feet. As Rob and Ellis are dragged to the exit, I sadly decide that there is no better time to end this night than right now.

Outside in the car park, Ellis has got a tenuous grip of himself while Rob sits on a dustbin giggling to himself and swaying; his eyes rolling around in his head, totally independent of each other. He's a mess. I, for some reason, am now almost straight as a die and sober as a judge - and the only one to realise that we're a man down. "Where's the Scotsman?"

"Och, aye, ya bastard! See you Jimmy!" screams Rob, almost falling off his bin. Both Ellis and I ignore him.

"Last time I saw him he had his tongue down some tart's throat and his hand up her shirt." Ellis slurs, his demeanour more serious now but no less unstable. "She was minging as usual."

"You cheeky cunt." A familiar Glaswegian brogue comes into earshot as a satisfied-looking McKinley saunters out of the club like he's going for a Sunday afternoon stroll. "She wasn't that bad...A bit chunky but a lovely a set of jugs."

"So why are you here with us and not somewhere else?" asks Ellis.

"Because she had to find her flat mate. Something about only having one key or some bollocks like that."

"Hang on. Was her name Amanda?" The chances that there are other scenarios like Karen and Amanda's going on in that club tonight could be quite high but then again...

"Aye, fucking Amanda, that's her," McKinley says, his face lighting up. "Do you know her?"

"I don't. But I was getting off with her mate until she did one too."

"A-MAN-da..." cries Rob, teetering precariously while pointing an accusing finger at McKinley. "A fucking man! Manimal!" The Scotsman pushes Rob off the dustbin and he crumples in a heap on the tarmac.

"That bastard's been twisting my melon all night. I'm off."

"Wait," I stop him. "Did you get an address?"

"Big man, I'm going home alone with only the prospect of a wank to keep me warm. What do you think?" With that McKinley strolls off, aiming a kick at the prone Rob as he passes. "See yers later."

Ellis helps Rob up and props him up against a tree. "Have we got enough cash for a cab?" It turns out we're all skint. With Rob slung between us, Ellis and I start the long walk home.

Rather than attending lectures like I should be, I spend the next day scoffing paracetemol like they're Smarties and scouring the phone book for Anderson, K. I harass the five total strangers who have never heard of Karen before trying the Yellow Pages for veterinarians. After being told by three stroppy receptionists that they won't divulge any personal information regarding their staff, I consider pestering Karen's parents. Surely I'll get a result there. Our little one-horse town can't have too many Anderson families and one of them will certainly be her folks - unless they moved too. It's then that the headache behind my eyes and the growing sense of my own desperation combine to convince me that she left without giving me her number for a reason and that I should stop this needless telephoning and lie down in a dark room. Before I succumb, I make one last call.

"Ugh?"

"It's me. Can you remember Amanda's last name?"

"Ugh?"

"Manimal. The fat bird with great jugs? Last night?"

"Ugh?"

"Forget it."

While the subtle - and not so subtle - changes to familiar old places in the city centre stand as a testament to the passage of time, the Riverside development screams of unbridled progress. A former wasteland of abandoned warehouses and barge houses, the only life which used to inhabit this disintegrating concrete expanse around the football ground were the homeless who dossed in its crumbling buildings and the furtive clients who would avoid the main road by scooting across its cracked tarmac to get to the nearby red-light district around Allerton Square. Now the asphalt desert is a neon strip of gastro-pubs, faux-Western saloons and equally tacky nightclubs dominated by the huge multiplex-slash-entertainment monstrosity which almost dwarfs the nearby stadium. It has become the city's very own Vegas.

The Riverside's creation and subsequent promotion as the place-to-be has had a number of effects on the city; none more disturbing than the one which appeared so glaringly obvious to me earlier in the day when taking my nostalgia tour. The Haymarket area, with its clubs, pubs and theatre, used to be the throbbing heart of the city - for what it was worth. Just as the Haymarket had sucked the life out of Beaumont Park, the previous holder of that title, so the Riverside has slowly cut the oxygen off from the Haymarket's brain in much the same way. By moving the city's entertainment focus from the centre, the local council may have injected new life into this previously barren landscape but in doing so it has ensured that the urban decay which turned Beaumont Park into a cancerous tumour will eventually spread to terminally infect the Haymarket. Coupled with the policy of building new shopping malls and warehouse outlets on the boundaries, consecutive councils have effectively signed the city centre's death warrant.

Of course, this means little to those who profit from this outward and upward expansion. People will still flock to the city's flashy entertainment paradise, which is more Nevada than nirvana, and will spend, spend, spend. Those people for whom the Riverside is the pinnacle of cool probably can't even remember the heydays of the Haymarket, just as I can only vaguely recall Beaumont Park being anything other than a shithole you passed through to get to the nice parts of the city. They come from miles around; shipped in on cheap trains to the nearby station where they pile out in their hundreds to mix with the thousands of locals, all crowding to see and be seen in drinking holes and eateries the length and breadth of this sleazy mile. How anyone can stand to watch is beyond me. It's painful to the eyes to witness this maelstrom of large-logo fashion victims clashing in their G-Star Denim, Juicy Couture and fake Versace. If the glad-rags aren't blinding enough, everyone looks like they've spent the last six months on a beach in Marbella when in fact they're just glowing from the last three sessions at one of the city's Chernobyl-inspired tanning studios. Fake'n'Bake then out on the make. For these fun-seekers, dragging their outrageously attired carcasses down the Riverside every weekend is what it's all about. It's about dressing like a lap dancer, caking yourself in cosmetics and dancing to Usher - and that's just the blokes. It's also about the binge-drinking, cheap coke and after-hours stabbings but this is nothing new. We never drank in moderation, in fact it was more of a sport than a pastime for us. Cocaine wasn't widely available but we could get it - but it didn't matter if we couldn't because there was a speed dealer in every toilet. It wasn't like it is now - speed was being consumed by everyone. It wasn't a sad fucker's charlie substitute, it was what kept you going every night. Knives may be the weapon du jour but people were regularly getting slashed down the Haymarket back in our day. The violence was not as indiscriminate as it is now. No one got shivved over a crappy pay-as-you-go phone back then. You had to earn your pain. There were often stories of Chelsea Grins being handed out as revenge for crossing some local maniac and a night rarely ended without someone getting glassed somewhere after putting the moves on an off-limits girlfriend. Those not looking for trouble rarely stumbled into it.

Compared to what's beginning to take shape around us as McKinley and I wander towards the Riverside strip, it just seems that we approached our own brand of hedonism with a bit more class and style - which should leave the casual observer in no doubt as to how unpleasant the current situation is.

Feeling like outcasts from the mainstream is nothing new to us either. There have always been cheesy city wankers and cheaply-attired sluts in direct opposition to every underground or edgy youth culture and Britpop was no exception. Even before what we were doing and wearing became the mainstream, our slowly building movement remained on the fringes of popularity. Mass market entertainment, lowest common denominator pop music and high-street fashion was as dominant then as it is now. Back then we revelled in the fact that we were beginning to wear clothes that no-one had thought about for 20 years or more; digging out stuff from the mod and skins revivals from the 1970s and adding a Nineties casuals twist. The same went for the music. To start with, the bands we would come to love and champion were not producing material quick enough so we rehabilitated sounds from the 60s, music our parents would have been into, and made it cool again. All of which went against the majority of trends. Now, though, McKinley and I could probably be dated by the way we look, not only in the way we dress but also by how we hold ourselves. We're products of that era and the contrast between us and those people already out on the piss around us is hard to ignore.

"Jesus, look at the state of them," says McKinley, slowing to ogle disbelievingly at a gaggle of barely-clad teenage girls knocking back pitchers of Long Island Ice Tea on the terrace of the Hog's Head. "I see three options for these lassies tonight; in the river, down the nick or date-raped behind the cinema." He looks at his watch and then back at the group as they down tall glasses of potent cocktail. "It's not even seven yet." A lecherous smile develops. "Maybe we should stop off here for a swift one before meeting up with the wee man." One of the girls laughs so hard at spilling half her drink down her cleavage that she falls out of her seat. The others scream hysterically, sending a flock of nearby ducks into the air in panic. In days gone by, this would have been a target rich environment and I would have taken the Scotsman's suggestion to join these girls as the green light for our own pursuit of abandon. But we both know that we no longer feature on the radar of girls like this. We're not even the type of older guys they could go for. We're literally from another age. McKinley's smile fades as this same realisation puts the brakes on his ardour. "Bitches," he mutters before tearing his eyes off a scene which - if it was taking place about fifteen years previously - would now be featuring the two of us flirting outrageously with these girls.

"Does it make you feel old?" I ask as we veer off from the main path in search of the partially hidden Korova Bar. "Those birds...They must have been half our age."

"Half *my* fucking age, definitely," McKinley replies. "And more. Not a 20-year-old among them, I bet."

"So does it make you feel like an old fart?"

"I feel like a dirty old man, more like," he says. "Because birds keep getting younger and fitter, and I still feel exactly the same way towards them as I always have. I have to tell myself sometimes when I'm having a perv that it's not okay for me to look at young girls in that way because I could be their dad. It worries me. I sometimes forget that I'm not that Lad anymore. Thankfully birds like that tend to run a mile from me now so temptation tends to keep its own distance." A rueful look flashes across his face. "What about you?"

I didn't want to have to answer my own question. In recent years, what I'd hoped would be a face which could continue to hold some of its boyish charm until it was replaced by a more distinguished look has settled into a transitional, haggard phase. I no longer look like the younger me and I'm not close enough to be being the older Danny Jones of my coming middle-age to be happy with what I see. I'm stuck in this moment where my face is telling all the stories I'm trying to keep secret. In the distinguished phase, a man's face shows his experience and knowledge of the world without giving away specifics. It's what gives the older man his charm and mystery. Right now, my dark-rimmed eyes tell the story of years without proper sleep; the flesh barely hanging onto my bones broadcasts news reports from a life spent in excess, the early flecks of grey in my beard and hair tell of the shock of experiencing what life had in store for me once the party was over. Until recently, I didn't feel inside how I looked on the outside. Now, it's hard not to look in the mirror and be that person I see rather than a young soul peering out onto an ageing face it doesn't recognise. "I still have contact with the old me," I finally reply. "But it's getting harder to stay in touch."

McKinley nods sagely. "Aye. Well put, big man. That's it, right fucking there."

The Korova, much like its current clientele, doesn't feature on the radar of the Riverside's main demographic. Off the beaten and puked-upon path of the main strip, it's an anomaly of sorts; a more sedate establishment which has more in common with the pubs of our youth than the Ibiza-styled, three storey monstrosities now filling with gelled-hair pricks and foul-mouthed tarts at the water's edge. But it's still false. It may be a more traditional looking bar with a jukebox at the mercy of the customers and not the other way round, but it has been made this way. There's nothing organic about it. Every hint of character and age is part of some cynical marketing plan. Just as those pubs filled with legless kidults have been designed to draw them in with two-for-one offers and Ministry of Sound CD compilations on repeat, the Korova has been set up to cater for people like us. We could have gone to some city centre alehouse and sat with the grizzled locals but we wanted to feel the pulse; we wanted to feel that we were still mad for it, that we could still survive in that after-dark netherworld of alcoholic excess and abandon - but at the same time, we wanted to feel safe and comfortable. That's what Korova is all about. It gives you the illusion you're in the middle of it all while being wrapped in nostalgic cotton wool.

McKinley is counting the meagre change from a tenner after shelling out for two bottles of Peroni Nastro Azzuri when a waft of the past blows through the pub, blowing a recollection my way. "Did you mean it when you said that Dennis was lucky to have missed out on *Be Here Now*?" I ask as 'Stand By Me' by Oasis strums out of the jukebox. "I like that album, well...most of it."

"I can't listen to it anymore, man," McKinley replies, sinking into his chair after pocketing his shrapnel. "It's bloated and overproduced. 'Magic Pie'? Magic bag o'shite more like. They jumped the fucking shark with that one, man. It took the piss. I haven't bought an Oasis album since."

"Seriously?" I'm incredulous. Okay, so the third Oasis album was, as Noel himself said, the sound of five guys on coke not giving a fuck and it's true the Gallaghers took longer than most of their peers to accept that the tide had turned after Britpop but they still managed to make some great music, albeit sporadically, throughout the Noughties. "You didn't get into *Heathen Chemistry* or *Don't Believe the Truth*? They came out with some top stuff in the last decade, man. Even *Standing on the Shoulder of Giants* has some tunes. 'Go Let it Out', 'Who Feels Love'...'Sunday Morning Call'? You've gotta love those songs, man. They're ace."

The Scotsman takes a swig of his beer. "I didn't hate everything they put out," he clarifies. "I've liked a few of the songs since *Morning Glory* but Oasis were a product of the times as far as I'm concerned. They should have left it with the first two albums. They were always trying to recreate the good times with what followed but it got to be a bit sad at times. When it's over, it's over. They outstayed their welcome if you ask me."

I choose not to pursue the argument further even though I disagree with McKinley. The idea of a bunch of blokes, stuck in a period of time and painfully reliving their past glories is a bit too close to home right now. This is a secret fear I hold deep down, one that nags me whenever the four of us reunite these days. I choose instead to make a shallow toast in a bid to avoid facing that worrying possibility and embrace the journey ahead - here's to oblivion. "To the good times." McKinley raises his glass to mine and the debate is officially closed.

We're halfway through our second bottle of exorbitantly-priced, imported Italian lager when Ellis makes his entrance. To the casual observer, it probably looks natural and nonchalant but McKinley and I know that this has been meticulously planned. Ellis has probably been watching and re-watching Scorsese's *Mean Streets* for weeks as part of his preparation. He swaggers into the pub like De Niro's Johnny Boy. The only thing missing is the girl on each arm. The Verve's 'Bittersweet Symphony' may be on the jukebox but 'Jumping Jack Flash' is playing in Ellis' head as he weaves his way to our reserved table at the back. It's been a year since I last saw him and maybe two-and-a-half since the Scotsman last laid eyes on the wee man. Regardless of how much time has passed, he looks remarkably similar to how he did fifteen years ago in both demeanour and fashion. Always a lanky streak of piss - as Steroid quite accurately described him earlier in the day - Ellis is still thin but his bony frame has seen some extra muscle packed on in the passing years, probably from heaving that heavy-as-fuck old parka around. The mod staple is in effect today, its lustre dimmed from countless winters, its faux-fur hood lining showing signs of mange. He suppresses a smile that threatens to break out and spoil the aura of cool detachment he's going for and raises his shades. "Alright?"

"Looking good, wee man," McKinley says, getting up and hugging him. "Can't afford to buy another fucking jacket yet? You should get a proper job."

I wait my turn and embrace my friend and former flat mate. "Hard day at the office dear?" Ellis shrugs off the parka and takes his seat, blowing out his cheeks as he eases into his chair. He allows a smirk to creep into the corners of his mouth and a sparkle fires in his tiny bloodshot eyes. "Are you okay?"

"Yeah, man." He exhales again. "I just had a joint in the car. It's good stuff."

"I hope you got some uppers as well or I'm going to be in my bed by eleven," McKinley says, somewhat sulkily. "I'm almost nodding off now."

Ellis taps an imaginary breast pocket and winks at the Scotsman. "It's sorted, man. Don't worry." McKinley mimes a gesture of encouragement across the table but Ellis is having none of it. "All in good time," he replies with a smile. "I know what you're like. If I get it out now, it'll be gone in two snorts. You can have a line when your eyelids start drooping."

"Cheeky bastard," mumbles the Scotsman. I laugh.

"That goes for you too," Ellis adds, waving a long ET finger at me. "You're just as bad. You two weren't known as the Dyson brothers for nothing." Fair point, well put. "Now, who's getting the beers in?"

The time passes between us as comfortably as always and the volume of our conversation increases in line with the bar tab. As ever, it doesn't take long for us to find our collective wavelength and the banter soon begins to flow in line with the beers. It finally begins to feel like home for me even though this place hasn't been mine for a long time now. But these people always feel like home. My friends give me that feeling of belonging, wherever we may be. They make me feel at ease. This is exactly what I've been looking forward to and what I've been missing. The boys: reunited and happily on the piss once again. A proper *Leon* weekender. No women, no kids.

"So are you going to let us strip you naked and tie you to a roundabout, or what?" McKinley grabs Ellis' knee and pinches it hard, causing the groom-to-be to wince. "Don't be a big poof. It's tradition."

"Yeah, that's exactly what's not going to happen," Ellis shoots back. "This is why I'm in charge tonight, not you."

McKinley feigns a broken heart. "Wee man, I'm truly hurt. After all I've done for you the least you can do is let us put you on stage at a donkey show or something."

"All you've done for me?"

"If it wasn't for me, we wouldn't be here and you wouldn't be getting..." Ellis holds his hand up. There are rules and the Scotsman is close to breaking them. "I never said it...All I'm saying is that you and your other half wouldn't even be together if it wasn't for my intervention in your sad excuse for a love life. I set you up."

"Yeah, but we also nearly got chopped up and dumped in a ditch because of you, if you remember," I add, dredging up the memory of a deeply-suppressed and traumatic episode involving a blind date with a couple of mental patients.

"Ungrateful bastards. I sorted you out with loads of shags. What about Julia Jugs? How could you forget her?"

"Somehow I had...until now."

"You're welcome."

"Look, we're getting very close to breaking the rules here," says a nervous looking Ellis. "Can someone change the subject?"

"How are things with your brother?" I ask after a moment of consideration. The bubble of euphoria which has been slowly deflating ever since the impending nuptials became a topic of conversation suffers a fatal puncture as my enquiry pricks its fragile skin and I feel a pang of guilt for completely harshing the mellow. Ellis takes a thoughtful quaff of ale and slowly retreats into the secure embrace of his armchair while the Scotsman leans in with the smell of blood in his nostrils. For all his affection for affable jousting, McKinley loves a serious verbal tangle. Even more so when it means he can push Ellis' buttons. It's the only sport he has any true affinity for.

Breaching the subject of Ellis' brother has always been a delicate operation but in recent years, the sore point has become increasingly tender and inflamed. Ellis is the younger of the two and - in much the way as I've lived my life in the shadow of the deity known as my brother Keith - he's always had a lot to live up to in the eyes of his parents. As a precocious teenager, this was less of a problem for Ellis as he had the drive and naïve ambition to set his sights on bettering Saint Sean and eclipsing his achievements. During our time at Calvin Road, Ellis' brother was less of a rival and more of an idol. Sean - then a successful advertising executive in Manchester - had escaped the clutches of their sometimes smothering mother and made his way in the world through hard graft and determination. While his brother's chosen occupation wasn't what Ellis had in mind for himself, the way Sean achieved his success was something to aspire to, replicate and then surpass in Ellis' own field of dreams - film-making. Looking at the slightly bitter parole officer sulking in the armchair across from me, it's clear that the on-going failure to achieve that plan is still eating away at Ellis somewhere behind his cool exterior.

The fact that Ellis still hasn't managed to emulate Sean's success, let alone that of his other idol Martin Scorsese, isn't the real reason why the relationship between the two brothers has soured in recent years. As far as I can ascertain by reading between the lines of the sad stories of self-sabotage that Ellis periodically emails me, until quite recently Sean had continued to be his little brother's biggest supporter and benefactor. However, the last incident between them had effectively tested the patience of the Saint to breaking point. Analysing the evidence available, it's not surprising.

"I heard about Paris," smirks the Scotsman. "That has to be one of the best fuck-ups you've managed to date." Ellis gives me a resigned look, unsurprised that the events he relayed to me in a dingy bar in the Marais last summer would make it to Jakarta before his Eurostar arrived back in St. Pancras. I was on an assignment in the French capital, covering the Kasabian tour for one of my music press clients and as luck would have it, Ellis was also in Paris that same weekend. Sean was getting married to his Parisian sweetheart and Ellis - in his role as family charity case and wedding videographer - had been given the job of documenting the nuptials. I'd met Ellis in a bar across the road from Gare du Nord on the Friday and it soon became quite a session. I'd managed to wangle a couple of press passes for the concert at Le Bataclan that night and despite being under strict instructions from his brother to stay sober for the service the next day, Ellis gladly accepted my invitation and wasted no time in getting in the mood for the show. Now, a casual observer may raise the issue at this point that I should take a certain amount of responsibility for what happened next but I will defend myself vehemently by saying that I advised Ellis - on numerous occasions during the afternoon and evening, I may add - that he should take it easy. You see, casual observers won't know that you can't tell Ellis to do anything. You can't even subtly advise him to do anything. If he wants to do something - he'll do it. And on that night, he wanted to drink heavily and score some magic mushrooms off some African dude on the Metro.

I know I felt like crap the next day, and I didn't even drop any of the shrooms. I had a breakfast appointment with the band at their hotel and barely made it in time for my interview slot at 8.30. Ellis had to get to the house of the bride's parents in Montmartre by nine. He was still in a coma when I left our digs an hour before that. I scrawled a reminder of our plans to meet the next day on a sheet of hotel stationary and left him to his fate. Again, casual observer, I did try to rouse him. Waking up is also something Ellis only ever does when Ellis wants to.

I'd been sitting in a smoky cafe nursing the same cup of overpriced coffee for about an hour and was considering settling the bill and bailing on Ellis when he eventually shuffled into our pre-arranged meeting place on Sunday with a pale, sheepish face and his tail dangling balefully between his telescopic legs. The story he then told - and now repeats for McKinley's enjoyment - explains fully why his relationship with his brother is now on life support.

"When I woke up, I had absolutely no fucking idea where I was," he begins, now wearing a similarly shifty expression to the one he displayed when he turned up in the Marais that afternoon. "I only remembered that I was in France when I stepped out of the hotel and into the cycle path. Even then it took me a while to understand why that bitch in a crash helmet was swearing at me in French. Anyway, it took me a good couple of hours to get to Marie's place and by that time, everything was completely nuts; crazy garlic munchers everywhere; bridesmaids, hairdressers, wedding planners - the whole deal. Sean's bird is the only one in the whole mad lot who can speak English, he's on the phone calling me every five minutes demanding to know where I am, and on top of that I'm constantly fighting the urge to puke. So I finally get it together to start filming the preparations - which I almost missed completely - and then suddenly I'm being bundled towards a car.

Everyone's flapping around, zooming off to the church...and then I have to throw up. So I dash round the side of the house to vom, almost slipping over in my tux in this swampy rose garden and start chucking up. I've got the cold sweats, a banging head and the possibility of a nasty case of the shits brewing. Marie starts calling for me and so I run back towards the car - and step on the fucking wedding dress."

"Excellent!" beams the Scotsman. "Comedy gold."

"It wasn't funny, man. It was a huge fucking muddy skid mark right across the train." Ellis looks more gaunt than usual as the memory takes on a horrific lucidity. "It gets worse. No-one noticed, at least not then. And I didn't say anything. Maybe they could have done something about it if I had but I got in the car and just concentrated on not adding my undigested breakfast to the mess. So we get to the church and I run off to start filming things from my brother's perspective, right? He is right fucked off and starts having a go at me..."

"What a bastard," giggles McKinley. "How dare he?"

Ellis ignores him. "Anyway, I get the shots I need of the groom and his best man, shoot the families sat in the church yadda yadda yadda, and then the wedding march begins. I find a nice angle to get the entrance and the long aisle to the altar, right? Then the bride comes in - crying her eyes out. The train is stretched out behind her and it looks like a baby with diarrhoea has wiped its arse all over it. There's this green-brown slimy stripe, about two feet long, right in the middle of it. It also looks like it's a bit ripped near where it joins the actual dress. It looks a right fucking state. My brother clocks this and immediately searches me out. Man, if looks could kill... So he's on the war path. During the service, I make the decision to keep out of his way but as this is his wedding day - and I'm supposed to be capturing the happy event on video - it's not going to be easy. So I decide to film everything in long shot...from behind pillars, tables, flower arrangements - anything I can hide behind to keep out of his way while at least getting something on camera. It was like a scene out of a fucking *Pink Panther* movie. All I needed was Kato to jump out of a cupboard and start throttling me and it would have been perfect."

"So I take it he hasn't forgiven you yet," I ask, searching for the answer to my original question.

"He may have done had I actually finished the video and got it off to him. It's been about a year now and I still haven't edited it," Ellis says glumly. "That's not the worst part... They announced that they're getting a divorce a month ago." McKinley bursts out into hysterical laughter. I look at Ellis in shocked amusement. This is a development I didn't know about.

"You don't think it had anything to do with your skid mark, do you?"

Ellis frowns at me while contemplating the possibility. "I do now!"

"Wee man," McKinley says, finally regaining composure. "You're a legend. Thank fuck you're not filming your own wedding."

"Oi! You said the W word," scolds Ellis. "That's a forfeit. Your round."

"What goes on in your head, man?" I grin. "Something always happens with you." This isn't an isolated incident, although it is the worst to date. As well as helping convicted criminals to keep on the straight and narrow once they get out of prison, Ellis also attempts to build a better life for himself by providing a full video production package to those who need it; weddings, theatre productions, corporate events. You name it, he'll film it. He'll also ultimately have a story of fucking it up to go with it which is why he hasn't been able to quit his job yet and make a living from the movie business.

"You obviously don't give a shit," says McKinley, coming up for air from a rapidly drained glass of lager. "You don't care enough about what you're doing to avoid situations like getting hammered with Danny

Boy and tripping your bollocks off before you have to film your brother's wedding. Subconsciously, you're fucking it up because you resent having to do these shitty video jobs when you want to be making proper films."

Ellis gets that familiar defensive look he digs out whenever someone tries to get to the source of his problems. "Okay, Dr. Phil, why would I even bother making these videos if I hated doing them so much?"

"Because, wee man," the Scotsman replies, softening his tone, "you can't let go of the dream. You have to film something - anything. You just sabotage these things because you hate the fact that instead of being the next Tarantino, you're a second-rate contributor to *You've Been Framed.*"

Ellis knows McKinley has a point and is only making it in his own acerbic way in an attempt to help him face facts but he still looks gutted. The truth hurts - and even more so when put to you by the Scotsman. Each time we meet it becomes increasingly obvious that this particular door of opportunity for Ellis is edging closed and that he's watching it creak shut without sticking his foot in it.

"So are you going to stick with the video side-line then?" I ask.

"Actually," Ellis says, coming out of his moment of regretful reflection, "I've got a gig filming the local primary school's end of term play. I reckon I can get the parents to pay a fiver each for a copy and make a tidy little sum."

"They'll probably end up getting the 25th anniversary edition the way you go about things," deadpans the Scotsman. "Maybe they can hand it out to the kids when they graduate from university." Ellis flicks him the Vs and the mood lightens once again.

Credit where credit is due: Ellis started out at college wanting to make films - and, technically, that's what he's doing. I'm know he still harbours distant dreams of winning at Cannes or Sundance and as such, documenting King's Bridge Elementary's production of *Little Red Riding Hood* must batter his resolve but he's still out there with a camera in his hand. Until he gives up on that, he's still a parole office-slash-movie director. "So the dream of getting out of this place and making the next great British gangster flick is still as far away as ever then?" adds McKinley, somewhat heavy-handedly. He immediately realises that even in jest, this is a bit unfair and moves quickly to prevent the mood dipping any further. "You could still make it here, though. We always said we had everything we needed close to home: the director, the writer, the actor and the producer...even though, these days, only the director lives here."

This is true - and while it's a courageous attempt at injecting positive vibes into this unfortunate segue, a feeling of opportunities lost briefly passes through each of us. We did have a chance to make something together in the dying days of our halcyon period in this city. Before the party ended and we went our separate ways, the zeitgeist was with us. When Britannia was still cool, we had the chance to surf the artistic waves she ruled. But we blew it - or rather inhaled it. We embraced the wrong aspects of it. Instead of capturing that energy from those heady days and channelling it into something creative, we immersed ourselves in the dark side. However, in spite of all the drugs - actually, because of all the drugs - we did manage to make one movie.

"That reminds me," I squeak, the sudden recollection taking me by surprise and strangling my vocal chords. I clear my throat in the hope I sound a bit more masculine when I continue. "Whatever happened to that skin flick we made?" McKinley and I shoot back in our seats as Ellis sprays the table with expelled beer.

"Fuck me," he finally says, spluttering slightly. "I'd totally forgotten about that." The Scotsman remains ominously quiet as Ellis recovers from almost choking to death.

"What happened to that tape, McKinley? You were the last one to have it if I remember correctly." Watching the Scotsman squirm in his seat slightly, it suddenly dawns on me that it's possible that I have a secret career as an adult film performer in the Far East and that the dubious job that the Scotsman has held on the other side of the world for the last decade and a half has nothing to do with financial consulting and all to do with being a porn baron. "You still have it...right?"

"Big man," he soothes, somewhat unconvincingly. "That tape's a national treasure. Would I let it out of my sight?" He looks shifty - or at least shiftier than usual. "Don't worry, man. It's under lock and key." I remain unconvinced.

Somewhere near the entrance of the pub, in the bar area, a minor kerfuffle erupts. A group of middle-aged women begin squawking excitedly, forming a slightly obese scrum around a tall dark figure who appears to be doing little to avoid the attention. The lighting and distance prevent us from getting a decent view of events but it's clear to the three of us what's going on.

"The Ponce has arrived."

four

Do You Remember the First Time?

March & April 1995

In the league table of smug bastards, the newly coupled male is Manchester United. After enduring the wilderness years where the odd FA Cup or second-rate European trophy has kept him in the national consciousness, once he gets himself the Premiership trophy of a girlfriend, the newly coupled male can start to enjoy a period of dominance over his less successful rivals. This elevation to the top of the heap allows the newly coupled male to constantly direct envious glances to the trophy cabinet which sustains his level of flashy smugness and belief in his God-given right to be considered the champion. Rob is currently Man United and is despised as such. Meanwhile, Ellis and I are locked in a relegation battle; two minnows holding onto the memories of their last successes which are now gathering dust in the annals of history. We are Coventry City and West Bromwich Albion. At best.

I, at least, have had two nasty shags and a top snog in the last two months. With real life girls. How much longer I'll be able to bring that up in our battle to avoid the drop is a matter of debate. While I'm willing to forget the Julia fiasco and skin-flick Natalie, I still hold up the brief yet passionate tryst with Karen Anderson as a result worthy of reference. She was well fit after all. However, as that moment drifts further into the past, it becomes increasingly difficult to display it as a trophy marking my superiority over Ellis. Thankfully, our shared bitterness towards the

117

currently successful Rob has forced our own inner-house rivalry onto the back burner. While we don't begrudge him his sudden promotion (he has, after all been competing in the lower reaches of the Beezer Homes League for some time now) we are united in our resentment of his constant crowing. As a result, we have joined forces and have vowed to make a combined effort to challenge him for the title.

(It must be mentioned here that Ellis is relatively new to all this. Until the start of this year, he had no real interest in getting his leg over as it would have distracted him from precious drinking time. The added complications arising from trying to get a shag would just use up energy reserves which would be better served knocking back pints or throwing himself around to extremely loud music. That changed in early January. Funnily enough, it seemed to coincide with the end of his annual subscription to Penthouse.)

The phone rings. It's Rob.

"Yeah, I won't be able to make it tonight," he barks, as if the essence of the telephone's invention has yet to make its mark on his consciousness. "Jane has gotten hold of some really hot porn so we're going to stay at hers." The receiver would normally have gone down at this point but I make the mistake of hesitating to sneer bitterly at Ellis who is sat opposite me, making wanking gestures at the phone. Rob sounds like he also expected to be cut off. "Err...yeah, so...we'll probably be drinking and screwing all night, y'know...Jane gets really wet watching filth so..."

Click. "Rob's called off. He's ploughing the troll again."

Another away win for the league leader. Meanwhile, we're heading for a scoreless draw round at the Scotsman's.

"So the smelly cunt is getting his cheesy bell-end away, so what? It's hardly what I would call a result," McKinley says, adding the final touches to his famous mushroom risotto (non-hallucinogenic version). "She's well fucking nasty and I would have to question whether in fact she is female at all. If she is in fact some old tranny as I suspect, then it's null and void."

Ellis finishes rolling the last of the post-meal joints and lays it with the others in the special cigar box McKinley keeps for such occasions. "Lady-boy or not, he's still getting some and we're not which, considering the state of him, is pretty hard to take."

"But what are you doing to change the fact, eh? Danny Boy shagged a couple tarts at the start of the year and got a snog about a month ago but you...I haven't even seen you near a bird since Jailbait's birthday in January and if I remember correctly, you vommed on her shoe. Not exactly the stuff of romantic novels, wee man."

Ellis concedes the point with a rueful nod. I set the table for our weekly update dinner and crack open three icy brews. Despite the dubious successes of the Scotsman's ill-fated Proxy Fuck doctrine - which led to the Julia Situation and our subsequently infamous foray into the porn industry - both Ellis and I agreed before coming round that we need McKinley's help, even if it could potentially lead to further distasteful liaisons. "We were thinking you may know a couple of women at university who would be up for some."

McKinley stops stirring and levels an extremely nonplussed look at the pair of us. "Yeah, right. I'm going to set you two up with birds I have to see every day. I don't think so."

"What's that supposed to mean?"

"Let me think...the fucking Puke Master and the Boy Wonder. I'd have to apologise for the pair of you every day until graduation. That's a year of having to say sorry for setting them up with a couple of bastards."

"Look, we'll be on our best behaviour," I promise. "If it'll get us laid, then we're not going to blow it, are we?"

"And they don't even have to be that fit," Ellis chips in. This isn't something that has been agreed between us but as it seems to have turned the Scotsman's mood slightly in our favour, I go with it. "They just have to be desperate."

"In that case," McKinley says with an ominous smile, "I think I know just the birds."

For me, to be honest, this is less about keeping up with the Rob-ses and more to do with getting my own ball(s) rolling again. Since Anna and I split over a year ago, I've been happy to spend my newly acquired independence in the pursuit of my own pleasure but that has mainly consisted of excessive drinking and drugging with the odd flirt, finger or futile fuck on the side. The worrying bouts of conscience and self-loathing which followed my nights with Julia and Natalie have proved that, despite resolving to be more of a man after breaking up with Anna in the style of a brutalised puppy, I've yet to find my feet as a Lad when it comes to women. The booze and gear aren't a problem. It's the birds that are holding me back.

The truth is, I'm confused. I want to change and to shed the conscience and morals that stop me from embracing this moment in time in its entirety. But at the same time I want more than just the passing thrill of casual sex. The philosophy of this movement I've bought into dictates that this thrill is at the centre of what it means to be a Lad. It's the thrill of misbehaving, the thrill of excess, the thrill of the chase and ultimately the kill. When it comes to sex, once that excitement has been achieved and enjoyed, you're told that you aren't going to get the same buzz from repeat performances with the same partner. The only way you can keep the high going is to keep things fresh. We're told that this is the pinnacle of the permissive society, that it's a target-rich environment, and that everything and everyone is there for the taking - so why limit your choice. One side of me wants that primal urge to be the energy that powers me. The other needs more. That side of me wants connection.

Shagging Natalie on film - and sorting out Julia to a much lesser extent - gave me an unbelievable buzz. I was wild and free, I was indulging in pure, detached personal pleasure. It was all about me, what I wanted and how it felt to get it. It felt fucking great. That is until the cold light of day shone a beam of conscience into the dark corners of my heart. Julia wanted more from me than just an awkward, biological process that failed to satisfy either of us. She wanted me to want her, not just to want her body. She certainly didn't want to be part of a game or a marker on a check sheet. She was hoping for a connection too.

Natalie got what she wanted as much as I did - except while she giving in to the alcoholic horniness and chemically induced desires which she'd chosen to embrace, she was secretly being abused and exploited. This was all part of my pleasure. I enjoyed her body and it was great, messy animal sex but the great thrill came from the fact that she didn't know that her most intimate surrender was being filmed for the amusement of the Lads.

This sexual schizophrenia is twisting my melon.

Who do I want to be? Do I want to be the Lad who doesn't care who he hurts as long as he gets the shag or do I want to be a bloke who enjoys the flesh but also wants to see into the soul? Can't I be both? I suppose if I spend time actually getting to know my conquest before sealing the deal, I could satisfy both the need to connect and the urge to screw indiscriminately. Maybe if the interaction leads to a couple of shags before it fizzles out, I could have the best of both worlds; the fleeting buzz and the human connection. I could have my minge and eat it. What better opportunity could I have to try this out than the coming double-blind-date with Ellis and the two women McKinley has set us up with.

I tag along with my house mate as he heads into the hotel for work after hearing that the Scotsman has news for us. Three days of the hard-sell around campus has apparently paid dividends. Ellis gets his whites on as McKinley begins his sales pitch. He really doesn't have to try that hard because it's more of a commission job and we've already agreed to the deal but it quickly becomes obvious that he is actually quite excited about how his negotiations have paid off. And who are we to deny him his big moment as a potential match-maker?

"Right, Danny Boy, have I got a little raver for you? Her name's Faye, she's 29 and she's totally fucking sexy. Tall, long dark hair...little tits but they go well with the rest of her as she's quite slim. I reckon she's a bit of a goer, actually. A bit of a wild one on the side...I'd definitely do her." That means nothing as the Scotsman is the least choosy bloke I know but I appreciate the personal seal of approval. "Wee man, yours is a definite shag. She's 27 and mad for it. She's half Indian...beautiful skin, mega set of jugs and she's well into tall, skinny freaks like you. It's a match made in McKinley heaven."

"So you went for the more mature end of the age scale."

"Big man, these are single birds in their late twenties. This is the demographic horny young blokes are going for these days. Plus, they're gagging for it."

"What's wrong with them?" Ellis asks. "Why are they single at their age?"

"Just go on the date and don't worry about it," the Scotsman scolds. "You wanted some action with the possibility of it lasting more than just a couple of shags, and I come up with the goods so don't question the master. Besides, you should be the last person to worry about whether they're damaged goods or not. Now chop some fucking carrots."

I thank McKinley for his good work and head for the bar.

"What are you doing here? You're not working today," says the ever astute Barry the Barman as I pull up a barstool.

"You have to get up early to catch you out, eh Bazza."

"You need to stay up all night, my son. Pint?"

"You're a gentleman and a scholar."

Barry pulls a glistening pint of Stella and puts it on the bar as Dennis strides past on his way to the dining area. "He's paying for that."

"He already has," Barry shouts back as Dennis disappears into the restaurant. "So what are you doing here on your night off?"

"The Scotsman has set me and Ellis up with a couple of birds. He was just giving us the details."

Barry's eyebrows head up the difficult north face of his unfeasibly high forehead in surprise. "Good luck with that." He disappears out of the bar, shaking his conical head slowly, leaving me with my beer and some new doubts for company. So this is actually going to happen. I am going to be in a social situation with a woman (who isn't Anna) where there will be conversation and the shared nervous expectation of casual sex hanging in the air. This isn't some pull in the pub or a nightclub grope, this is going to be a date - an extended period of time spent in someone's company with romantic overtones. After hooking up with (and getting dumped by) my one and only real girlfriend while in my late teens, this means that this is going to be my first ever real adult experience of this mythical event that you hear so much about. When Anna and I started seeing each other, it came about because her friend told my friend that she liked me. As soon as my friend told her friend I liked her too, we suddenly became a couple without ever having to deal with each other face-to-face. There was no need for any negotiations or stating of terms. I liked her, she liked me - bosh. Sorted. If only it was always that easy. Adult shag quests appear to be a lot more complicated. Now I'm going to have to hold down a conversation with a woman six years older than me and be charming and funny for as long as it takes to get her into the sack. It's a very, very different kettle of fish. I glug down a third of my pint to steady the rising nerves. In addition to this new and terrifying concept, I have never met the woman and I'm basing the fact that she could be compatible on the information provided to me by a well-known, indiscriminate pervert whose blood is 70 percent proof and who has been known to consume enough narcotics to kill a donkey. I down the last two-thirds of my pint and go in search of a dark room to lie down in.

Date night. As neither Ellis nor I have ever been through an experience like this before, it's lost on both of us that we are prancing around the house in the stereotypical pre-date flap. There are frantic knocks on the bathroom door as allotted tarting-up time is exceeded; there is loud, courage-affirming music belting from the stereo (Radiohead's *The Bends* until the mood-dipping 'Fake Plastic Trees' comes on, then the more consistently upbeat entirety of *In The City* by The Jam), and both bedrooms are strewn with discarded items from long since abandoned outfits. Ellis is again swapping his Adidas Gazelles for his bowling shoes when the telephone rings. It's Rob.

"What's happening tonight? Fancy going to Speakeasy's?"

"Rob, I never fancy going to Speakeasy's. And anyway, we have plans."

"That's cool. I'm flexible. What are we up to then?"

"Well, Ellis and I have dates and the Scotsman's working. No Kama sutra classes tonight?"

He ignores the jibe. "Dates? Who with?"

"A couple of university babes."

"Bollocks. I'm coming over."

"Fine. We won't be here. We'll be out knobbing. Have a good one."

Click.

Ellis shouts down the stairs. "Who was that?"

"The granny fucker," I shout back. "I told him we'd be out shagging all night."

"Nice one. That's a six-pointer."

I'm in the middle of trying to get my unruly Barnet under control when the phone rings again. This time it's McKinley.

"How's things? Ready for the off?"

"Yeah, you know, just chilling with a jay before heading out." He doesn't need to know that for the past hour we've been flitting around the house like the Pink Ladies in *Grease*. "Got anything to report?"

"I saw Faye this afternoon and all I can say is that you better have a good supply of johnnies with you. She was so excited she was almost leaving oil spills behind her." Okay, maybe there won't be any need for me to break into my fabricated anecdotes about exciting travels around the world before she spreads. Sounds like I just need to turn up.

"What about Ellis' bird? Is she a pig? You can tell me."

"Big man, what would be the fun in that? Have a nice time. I'll pop round tomorrow for the juicy details."

Ellis bounds down the stairs after finally deciding to go with his trainers. "Right. Let's do this."

Being university students, our two blind daters are housed in the arse-end of nowhere on the city limits near the sprawling campus. One of the concessions made in McKinley's sales patter was that we would meet them at a pub of their choice which is why we're sat on the number

21 bus heading in the vague direction of the Boundary pub, a good twenty minutes away from home. Fair play to the Scotsman though, should this go well for both of us, neither Ellis nor I will have to do much extra travelling before the wick can get wet. Our dates are flat mates and they live just round the corner from the pub. However, it'll be a long bus ride of shame should only one of us score. But we're not thinking in those terms. Due to a crafty snifter of some nasty speed Ellis had knocking about, both of us have a little extra confidence and the mood is optimistic.

"So we'll play it cool, build up the whole media thing...but not too wanky...mention a few independent projects we're working on, some film scripts..."

"That's all bollocks though, right?" Ellis suddenly gets nervous as though he's missed out on an important piece of information.

"Of course but we've talked about doing stuff like that before," I assure him. "Just run with it. We'll bounce off each other. It'll give us an edge."

As the bus moves out of the city centre and begins its direct route to the outer ring, Ellis turns a little pale. "I have a confession to make," he whispers, even though we're at the back of the bus and some way away from the old couple and young mum with kid who make up the other passengers. "I've never done it before."

"What, go on a blind date? Nor have I, geezer. But how hard can it be?"

"No, man. *It*."

"*It*?"

"Sex."

"You're a virgin?" I whisper back, but with surprised force. Ellis fixes me with a hard stare and nods slowly. I had misgivings about double-dating with Ellis when we first started talking about the possibility but

126

these concerns were based purely on his overly boisterous and often obnoxious behaviour whenever he comes into contact with alcohol. I thought he might blow it for me by coming on too strong with his date. Never coming at all with any date failed to make it onto my list of worries. I have to admit, in the year or so that we have shared the house, I have never heard him once shaking the head board, at least not with a person who wasn't spread out on a glossy centrefold. But I thought that it may have happened on occasions when I wasn't there or at the girl's house maybe. I mean, he had opportunities, I'm sure of that. "I thought you and Jailbait Alex..."

"Not once, man. She's one too, by the way..." That I'm not surprised about. Alex is only just sixteen and is well known for talking a good shag but never coming across with the goods. The heavy petting Ellis and the waitress had enjoyed on sporadic occasions, including the one where he was sick on her, were widely accepted as the closest she had ever come to bleeding on the sheets. Now it seems that this goes for both of them. Excessive nerves tend to have the same effect on Ellis as a half bottle of vodka so instead of making a big deal about his cherry status, I opt for calm and deliberate advice. "Right. It's not a big deal. As far as this bird knows, you're a stud. That's what you have to think too, mind. That you...are...a...stud. When we get there, the first thing you do is head for the bogs, crank one off and then do the whole Mr. Orange thing, okay? Super cool."

"Mr. Orange?"

"Mr. Orange."

"You know about that?"

"Mate, the walls are very thin."

"It's just a psyching up thing, you know."

"Whatever works, man. But you need Mr. Orange tonight so do your thing."

The Boundary is a popular student haunt and is therefore not as seedy and threatening as some of the other pubs on the periphery of the city. Some are downright dangerous and many a fresher has been fucked up after straying into the wrong bar, despite the ready advice available through the Students Union on campus. The housing estates on the outskirts are the main breeding grounds for social unrest in our seething little metropolis and with many of the inhabitants living off benefits and crime, the close proximity to the privileged and educated leads to a certain amount of animosity. The badly-lit but thankfully short walk to the pub from the bus stop is therefore taken at a fast-paced march.

Once inside, Ellis heads off to the toilets to flush a load and get into character. The whole Mr. Orange thing became known to me shortly after we moved in together. I knew Ellis liked his gangster movies and one of the first films we sat and watched together in our shared living room was his favourite, *Reservoir Dogs*. Being a media student, Ellis had not only watched the film countless times but studied and analysed it inside out. It was also no surprise to me that he knew the dialogue almost off by heart. On one occasion, before a big night out, I went looking for him to hurry him up and discovered him reciting a short scene from the film in front of his bedroom mirror. The scene, in which Tim Roth as Mr. Orange psyches himself up before meeting members of the diamond heist gang, seemed to do the job. Ellis bounded out with a newly found confidence. I never told him - until now - that I had heard him on numerous occasions running through the dialogue in readiness for a challenging situation: "Don't pussy out on me now. They don't know. They don't know shit. You're not gonna get hurt. You're fucking Baretta and they believe every word...because you're super cool."

As I wait by the toilets for Mr. Orange to come out, I survey the pub for our dates with McKinley's vague descriptions in mind, which means I'm looking for a tall, skinny, small-titted brunette with a puddle under her seat and a short, half–Indian shag monster with big breasts and flawless skin. I'm making another scan of the main room when two women who display some of these qualities enter the pub. From my vantage point by the cigarette machine, both look quite nice. The one which could be Faye is dressed casually in slim jeans which compliment her long legs and peachy arse, and a tightly fitted jumper which clings to her small but firm mounds. The Indian shag monster looks buxom in a short mini–dress which hitches even higher than it should do due to the demands of her expansive chest. Any slight movement of her arms in an upward direction gives brief flashes of a considerable backside. If the virginal Mr. Orange is going to become a man tonight, he'll be reaching that milestone with a bird who is definitely all woman.

"So are they here yet?" Ellis comes out of the bogs and gets himself twenty Marlboro from the fag machine.

"I think we have just established contact," I reply. "Did you shake one off like I told you?"

"Yeah, but the old boy is still rock hard. I don't think it'll ever go down."

"Tell her that a little later and you'll be golden. Let's go."

The pub is quite busy and noisy enough to have a good atmosphere. The student–orientated jukebox is playing 'Here Comes a Soul Saver' by the Charlatans (always a soothing and inspirational tune during times of duress) as we make our way through the tables to where our dates are nervously standing by the bar. Just as we make eye contact, Ellis frantically whispers in my ear. "What's mine called again?"

"No idea. He never said?"

"Bastard Scotsman."

I smile warmly and hope for the best. "Hi, I hope you're Faye because if not, my date is going to be really upset when she turns up."

Faye's face lights up. She has a wide smile full of insanely white teeth and her sapphire blue eyes glint even in the dim light of the bar area. But the spark in the irises is more disconcerting than appealing. "Are you Danny? Your friend made it sound like you'd be taller." Okay... "This is Sheena," she quickly adds, helping us out of our name dilemma.

"Like Easton, the singer?" Ellis asks, offering an outstretched hand.

"Good one. I've never heard that before," the alleged Indian shag monster grins through gritted teeth. "Should we find a table while you get the drinks? Mine's a pint and Faye will have a vodka tonic." I agree with a nod as Ellis curses himself under his breath. Faye and Sheena head for a small free table in the cosy lounge area, whispering as they go, as I order at the bar.

"Sheena fucking Easton. Of course she's heard that before." Ellis is still kicking himself.

"You could have asked her if she was a punk rocker."

Ellis, not the biggest Ramones fan, ignores my attempt at humour. "Yours sounds like a bit of a head case."

"Why? She just said she thought I would be taller." The barmaid passes over the drinks and I pay. I act as though the comment didn't bother me. It did. As did the eyes. I shiver a little, unnoticed.

"Yeah, but it sounded as though it may be a problem."

I take my beer and Faye's vodka, leaving Ellis to follow with matching his-and-hers pints of Carling. "You're just projecting. It's cool. Just try not to mention any more Eighties pop singers."

"Funny."

We take our seats and pass the drinks round. After a cautious toast, we all take a few nervous sips and prepare for the games to truly begin. I start by throwing the obvious ice breaker into the mix. "So, tell us about yourselves."

"Isn't that a little intrusive?" Faye asks, somewhat defensively. The sapphire's flash again. "Maybe a little personal for the first question of the night? I could ask you why you're not as tall as your friend said you would be. Would you feel comfortable with that?"

"I'm hardly a dwarf," I offer from behind a stunned and forced smile. Ellis is ominously onto the last third of his pint already. "How tall did McKinley say I was anyway?"

"Six foot. Do you have all your own teeth too?"

"Why? Did he say I was a midget with dentures or something?" My response raises a nervous titter from Sheena as Ellis drains the last of his lager. Faye remains cool.

"We didn't get into teeth. I like your hair," she says, sitting up slightly to survey the top and back. "Any pattern baldness in your family?"

"I'm going to get another drink. Anyone else? Sheena?" Ellis is already out of his seat.

"No thanks, I still have a good seven-eighths of mine." Ellis doesn't bother waiting for any other requests. "Is he an alcoholic because if he is I'm so not in the right space right now to be in such a damaging co-dependent relationship."

I'm suddenly very aware that I've been abandoned in this *Twilight Zone* episode with the Riddler's more psychotic sister and her presumptuous mate. "No, he just drinks too quickly when he gets nervous." I turn back to Faye who's sizing me up from her chair. "Faye, did you just ask me about baldness in my family? I think I may have misheard you."

"Why, are you deaf?" she asks, shocked. "That can be a hereditary problem too."

"Okay, what is this all about? I know we're getting to know each other here but this is a little more in-depth than I'm comfortable with."

Faye necks her vodka and tonic in one. "Your friend said you were interested in having sex with me. If this is the case then I want to know what kind of genetic material our child is likely to be created from."

"If he's a nervous drinker then maybe there are a lot of unresolved personal problems we'll have to deal with first and, you know, therapy can play havoc with emotional bonds," Sheena muses in a concerned tone.

Right. Time out. One lunatic at a time, please. "Faye, firstly, what's all this about a child? We've only just met. And Sheena, Ellis is probably the most stable person at this table."

"He just seems unable to make a connection without alcohol."

Faye becomes a little more aggressive. "The only reason for having sex is to make a child and as your Scottish friend insisted that you would be more than willing to ejaculate inside me, I think it only responsible of me as the mother to consider the stock our baby would be coming from."

I look from one of these basket cases to the other, my jaw almost scraping the floor. Coming out of my shock, I make a judgment call. "Goodnight ladies, it's been...fucking insane."

I catch up with Ellis at the bar where he is taking an absolutely - and deliberately - inhuman amount of time to make his way back to the table. "Drink up, we're out of here."

"Thank fuck for that."

We sit at the bus stop in stunned silence. Is that what dating is? Are we destined to spend our search for companionship being interviewed for vacancies as sperm donors and emotional crutches by mentally unstable females? If so, this is not what I signed up for. In fact, if this is the allegedly civilised and socially acceptable way of finding a partner then I'll be very happy going back to the frowned-upon version of getting paralytically drunk and groping the nearest inebriated slapper. I was hoping for the door to open on a new world of interaction, where I could move away from the fart-arsing about and get myself back into the game. I was supposed to finally lay the ghost of Anna to rest by finding that I could be with someone else, maybe not forever but for long enough to realise that my first real girlfriend was not my one and only, that Anna was not The One, that there are many, many options out there and that it would be okay to try out my share in the hope of hitting the bull's-eye one day. But if they're all going to be mad, desperate bitches who want my semen to sate their insane baby urges, then I'm better off keeping it on the most base level. Anna will be consigned to the history books in time and maybe lots of meaningless, casual sex off the cuff will be the way of making that happen. Spending time getting to know people is just asking for trouble. Knowing someone, specifically Anna, was what led to so much pain and heartbreak in the first place. Fuck that. Love 'em and leave 'em. It's less complicated that way.

"What just happened?" asks Ellis, offering me a cigarette.

"We just had a lucky escape, Mr. Orange."

The next day, McKinley swings by for his mission update. After he finally manages to coerce me out from under my duvet, he discovers that he may have been better off leaving me there. I'm not in the best of moods, and not just because the bastard has spent the last ten minutes ringing the bell and pounding on the door. As I pull on a t-shirt and tracksuit bottoms, McKinley creeps off to make the coffee he hopes will calm me down.

After a large intake of some much-needed caffeine, my pissiness subsides enough to make my case. I explain to McKinley that I agreed to this dating lark because I was under the impression that I could actually meet someone nice who might stick around for a bit, not some psychotic bint with a biological clock which resembles the timer on car bomb. "She just wanted me for a fuck," I complain.

The Scotsman looks back at me as if he doesn't know what the problem is. "Aye, so how you managed to avoid getting one is beyond me."

I thought explaining that she was madder than a sack of badgers would have cleared this up but obviously having sex with lunatics is something normal in McKinley World so I offer a little more information. "Maybe I wanted more than that. Maybe I was hoping to actually date her. The date part of the blind date thing led me to believe that there was a chance that we might end up going out together." "Why the fuck would you want that?" The Scotsman is again at a loss. "I thought I was setting you up with a shag, not helping you find a wife."

"It wasn't about getting coupled up, man," I say, somewhat exasperatedly. "I just wanted to find a bird I could spend more than a night with."

The Scotsman takes on his guru persona and injects a sense of calm into proceedings. "Danny, you're free," he soothes. "Enjoy it. You're like one of these criminals who can't face life on the outside so they reoffend as soon as they're let out of jail. Don't go looking for another life sentence, big man."

"What if my head's wired that way? What if I can't just love 'em and leave 'em?"

"You've been listening too much to fucking Rob banging on about his pensioner project. He's getting it as wrong as you. It's not about getting yourself coupled up. Look around. The world is suddenly full of birds up for a shag. Make the most of it, Jesus. It's not going to last."

It's my turn to look confused. "What about you? You're attached."

"Aye...well..." He looks wistful. "That all happened before this so it rules me out. You don't think I'd be at it like a fucking jack hammer if I was in your position? You have the choice. I don't. Why do you think I started this whole Proxy Fuck thing? So I could whack off to you shagging the birds I fancy? I don't fucking think so. It's because you can still be saved, man. You're damaged, you're broken but you can still be mended – and the best glue is plenty of fanny batter, liberally applied."

"This is all for my benefit?" I ask, suspiciously.

"Exactly. I love a challenge."

"Why didn't you pick on Rob then? He's more of an emotional fuck-up than I am."

"True. But he's too far gone. He's a lost cause. You, on the other hand...You have potential."
I narrow my eyes at him over the lip of my coffee cup. "So what now?"
He winks and smiles knowingly. "Leave it to your Uncle McKinley"

You would have thought that it would have taken more than a month to get over that utter fiasco. Coming as close as we did to getting murdered and chopped up by the two escaped mental patients that McKinley set us up with (which, is not that close at all in reality, but it was scary all the same), no-one would have blamed Ellis and I for fleeing to the nearest monastery. At the very least one would have expected the complete avoidance of arranged meetings with previously unseen women.

Do you see where I'm going with this?

The Orchard. Thursday night. The pints are, as ever, a pound a go. It's 10pm. Ellis and I are leathered and screaming along to Suede's *We are the Pigs*. The surrounding pub is a blur of orange light and fuzzy dark figures as we hang off each other, glasses and voices raised in brutalised song. Neither of us notices Rob arguing with Mutton Jane by the jukebox or McKinley conspiring with Peruvian Tony, the midget hairdresser from the Arcade. This particular scene would have caused confusion in already addled minds. The Scotsman and the Peruvian are sworn enemies. The two of them usually only trade insults from a distance. They never get as close as they are now and never speak in such hushed tones. The last time they were in such close proximity, the incident which forever set them against each other occurred. All I'll say right now is that it involved a slip from a step ladder, a pair of electric hair clippers and a grazed testicle. Actually, I don't think any more needs to be said. Ever.

McKinley swaggers over to where Ellis and I are now spilling half our drinks down each other as we try and stay upright after the exertions of our duet. "Boys, good news. I've found you a couple of birds."

"Where?" I raise my head on an elasticated neck and then lose control of it. "I can't see any birds," I slur as my loaf dangles near my feet.

"Fucking liar!" Ellis crossed the boundary into belligerence about four pints back. He's already had two verbal warnings from Steroid, the pub's chief bouncer. "Where are the birds?" McKinley knows the score. Anyone else would have taken the lanky streak of piss out into the alley and given him a good kicking as a lesson in respect. But the Scotsman is wise, and marginally less drunk.

"Wee man, sort it out for fuck's sake. They're not here tonight. Next week...you'll be thanking me next week."

"Give me the fucking birds! Oi, birds, get on this!" Ellis climbs unsteadily onto a chair and starts to unbutton his fly. Steroid moves fast for a big bloke and within the blink of a lazy eye throws Ellis over his shoulder in a fireman's lift before he can start waving his pork sword about. The half-man, half-chemically-enhanced-bear strides through the pub with Ellis draped over his shoulder like a sleepy five year old after a long drive home. And so ends another night.

Neither of us manages to get to college the next day. Friday's are usually either faced in a haze of pain or not at all. We both opt for the second option. I surface a good five hours before Ellis struggles out of his pit to find the Scotsman and Rob in the living room playing on the Sega while Mr. Sifter points his weighty gonads at them in protest at having his sofa commandeered.

"What are you two doing here?"

"It's lunchtime." Rob motions to the huge plate of sandwiches he has beside him without taking his eyes off the computerised football action he's absorbed in.

"How did you get in?"

"The door was wide open," McKinley says, before slamming a shot beyond Rob's keeper to make it 5-0. "You're so shit. I don't know why I bother."

I can't be arsed to follow up on the info about the wide open door. It's obvious Ellis and I both expected the other one to shut it when we rolled home last night. I head for the kitchen in search of aspirin and caffeine in that order. The final whistle blows and after flicking the V's at his gutted opponent, McKinley follows. "So, these birds, right..."

"Remind me again...I'm sure I had a bad pint last night."

"Hmm...one bad pint," McKinley deadpans. "That must have been it." I raise a cup at him in an offer of a coffee which he accepts with a nod. "These birds, man...top stuff and mad for it."

"Mad probably being the operative word. If they're anything like those badgers you set us up with last month, I'm not having any of it." Faye the Sperm Stealer's stare still haunts me in the dark, lonely hours of the night. I shudder and set up the espresso machine.

"Not this time. We're talking quality. Peruvian Tony..." I blink in shock and my wide-eyed horror prompts further explanation. "We've called in a truce - for now. I called in a favour with the midget...He fucking owes me big time." McKinley curses under his breath at the memory and absent-mindedly covers the left side of his crotch with a protective hand. "Anyway, have you ever seen that tart who works for him?"

"The blonde? She's a bit of a Tracey." I was never a fan of the corkscrew perm, denim mini-skirt and white stilettos look even when it was fashionable in the Eighties.

"Debbie, actually," the Scotsman corrects. "And she's gagging for it."

"Does she expect me to father her child as well?"

"Are you ever going to let that go?"

"Never."

McKinley presses on. "Tony says Debbie and her mate are game for a fuck and are always talking dirty in the salon. He has to beat off at least twice when they're there...and he's a bender so they must be filthy." I chuckle and the movement reminds me that I wanted to get a pill for the crushing pain behind my eyes. "So, are you in?"

"This is just for a fuck, right? I'm done with the whole dating thing."

"Big man, have you seen her? She looks like the bird they modelled those blow-up dolls on. She's purely a pleasure model and definitely not a keeper. So?"

It may be the remnants of last night's binge or the desire to get the Scotsman off my case but for whatever reason I blank my better judgment and agree. "Okay but this time you have to tell me about Ellis's bird - just in case I want to swap."

"I don't think that's gonna happen," McKinley grins. "Unless your idea of female perfection is Tessa Sanderson." As I'm more into the lithe Mary Decker long distance runner type than chunky Jamaican-born heptathletes and javelin throwers I choose to pass on the option to swap. I'm intrigued though, on Ellis's behalf.

"Who are we talking about?"

138

McKinley gets that Luciferian smirk of his. "DJ Sonique."

"MC Steak Hammer? Jesus..." The Warehouse's turntable spinner on hip-hop nights has quite a reputation for being sexually aggressive, one that has saddled her with a nickname which strikes fear into many a penis. "God save him."

We fast forward a fortnight. After a week of walking around in a silent huff, I eventually manage to get Ellis to tell me what's been bugging him. While the comedy value of what he has to say has the potential to be immense if it falls into the wrong hands, I find it difficult to use his revelation as a cheap gag at his expense. Whatever it is it has, after all, kept the gobbiest person on the planet quiet for a full seven days. Besides that, the issue in question - when it is revealed - actually disturbs me greatly and strikes at the very vulnerability that most men prefer to keep deeply hidden. However, once he tells me, I know I won't be able to keep it to myself.

I know it's not going to be the usual gripe about Rob using up the last of his shower gel or McKinley sticking the pages of his newest Mayfair together when Ellis suggests we give the Orchard a miss and have a few Stella's at the much quieter, and - it has to be said - much gayer, Golden Star. Just his choice of chosen location already gets me fearing the worst. If Ellis is going to come out to me, that I can handle. I have no problem with homosexuality as long as it's kept at a safe distance and doesn't try to touch me. If this is his secret, then it actually explains a lot. Taking me for a pint down the Brown Star, as it's more commonly known, would be a very subtle way of pushing the closet door open in readiness for his Dale Winton-esque arrival on the local gay scene. What I'm worried about is what it has to do with me and me alone. Could he be in love with me?

"What? Fuck off!" Ellis almost loses half a mouthful of Artois down the front of his best Ben Sherman drinking shirt. "Is that what you thought the problem was?"

"I dunno, do I? You've been sulking ever since the double date. And then when you suggested the Brown Star of all places...What else was I supposed to think?"

"Anything but that! And anyway, get over yourself. If I was going to shag any of the boys, it wouldn't be you."

"Why not? What's wrong with me?"

"You're just not my type, okay." Ellis looks over to the bar where a couple of leather queens are taking an interest in the overheard discussion. "Look, can we not have a hypothetical conversation about this right here and now."

"I didn't want one at all, mate. You brought it up."

"You asked me if I was in love with you!" The queens at the bar unsubtly lean further in the direction of our table. Ellis lowers his indignant voice to a whisper. "I suggested we come here because there is no way we would run into any of the lads in this place. And I wanted this to be between the two of us...okay?" I nod, relaxing slightly now the conversation appears to be steering a course away from unrequited homosexual love. "Hang on...do you think I'm gay?"

I sigh. "Ellis, just tell me what's on your mind."

I'm right about one thing. All this started on the night of the double date. We'd decided on meeting Debbie and Steak Hammer at the Potter's Wheel where Bad Reputation, a Thin Lizzy tribute band, had been booked to be bottled off stage later that night. After the initial weirdness, things started to go well from my perspective. Debbie was mildly intelligent despite the fact that she felt that she had already reached the pinnacle of her hairdressing career by becoming senior stylist at Peruvian Tony's. Contrary to what might have been expected, she'd abandoned her usual Pepsi and Shirley look in favour of a tight black vest and jeans to match. She was also less irritating than I thought she'd be, given her reputation for sounding like a four-year old with a helium addiction. The conversation was light and as the drink flowed, the whole bizarre set-up became more comfortable. I'd been tuning in from time to time to check on Ellis and Sonique, just to make sure he wasn't being a dick. Nothing would have ended my chances at this delicate stage of shag negotiations than Deb's mate throwing a wobbly because the Mouth of the South had called her a fat tart or something equally charmless. After half an hour of shared small-talk, we'd split into two separate parties, both chatting across the pub table. Ellis seemed to have loosened up (after three pints of rapidly quaffed lager and what I suspect was a visit to the gents for a crafty line) and he and the MC had become immersed in a discussion about music. With one ear switched on to their natter, I became more confident that nothing disastrous would develop which would scupper my chances of banging the hairdresser. In fact, when it came to the end of the very alcoholic and increasingly raucous night, things had gone so well between the two pairs that we both tumbled into separate cabs and sped off into different directions for the much-hoped for and planned sexual relations.

The extent of my knowledge on what went on with Ellis and the MC stops there. Back at Calvin Road, Deb treated me to a rather amateurish blowjob before she rushed to the lavatory to spew up twenty quid's worth of Hooch. When I'd imagined holding her hair back, this had not been what I'd had in mind.

What Ellis is now telling me about the hours between last seeing him shoving Steak Hammer's ample arse into the back seat of a mini-cab and the subsequent week of silence is best heard from the man himself.

"So we're in the cab, right, and we're both really messy...y'know...really, sloppy drunk...hands everywhere. I'm thinking this is probably leading to a quick bit of doggy in the living room before I make my excuses about working early and then leave. She has other ideas..." At this point, his face loses its colour and he visibly shivers. "I thought things were getting a bit out of control before the cab pulled up at the flat. She was really strong, you know? I mean she's a big girl...not just a bit tubby but like Schwarzenegger strong, muscles on muscles. So she basically drags me up the stairs and has my jeans off before I even have time to have a fumble myself. Next thing I know, she's starkers, I've got wood...God knows how, the old boy was probably scared rigid...and she's fucking rocking back and forth on me like a mad woman. It was like the porn version of that scene in Fantasia where all the hippos are going nuts. Anyway...that's when Vernon arrived."

"Vernon? Her ex-bloke?" Word has it that the marriage is not officially over. It's common knowledge in Warehouse circles. Plus Peruvian Tony can't keep his trap shut. The papers haven't been signed, sealed and delivered to the divorce lawyer due to the fact that Vern is reluctant to let his wife cut the nuptial ties. Maybe he'd come round for another attempt at reconciliation...

"Not the geezer," Ellis whispers. "Something worse. Much worse...I would've gladly taken a beating from her husband than what happened next. Vernon," he gulps, "...is a foot long, black rubber cock." Okay..."Just thinking about it makes me go cold. Now, you know me...I don't do anything I don't want to do but this was something else. I had no choice in the matter. She's fucking mental, man. I couldn't even get off the bed, let alone out of the room. Then she starts...using it. I...I'm biting the pillow trying not to scream." He looks up at the bar and the queens are now thankfully engrossed in their own conversation. "Twelve inches, geezer. It's like having the biggest dump you've ever had...in reverse. And she wasn't gentle, oh no. She was hammering on it like she was getting the last bit of ketchup out onto her chips." He doesn't need to but he mimes the act of slapping the base of a sauce bottle all the same. "It was so far up there I thought I could taste plastic."

My mind is reeling. It's like that scene in *A Clockwork Orange* when Alex has his eyes clamped open and he's forced to watch endless atrocities. Except it's my mind's eye which is clamped open and my brain is the screen. I try to focus on the one thing that blocks the mental image of my best mate being tunnelled out by a massive ebony dildo flashing across my imagination in glorious Technicolor. "Why did she name it after her husband?"

"I forgot to ask, Danny," Ellis replies, somewhat incredulously. "Next time she's auditioning for Dyno-Rod I'll turn round and ask her!"

"The next time?"

Ellis takes a sip of his beer and looks sheepishly at me over his glass. "We're going for a drink next week."

"Jesus Christ. Top bird!" McKinley's face beams like the stereotypical man-in-the moon, complete with slightly disturbing lunar landscape grin. "And he's going back for more?"

"Maybe he's a glutton for punishment," I say, checking the kitchen door for signs of ear-wigging waitresses.

"Glutton for a fuckin' large amount of anal massage more like!"

"This is between us though, right? He trusted me with this."

"Aye," McKinley levels one of his most witheringly sarcastic looks in my direction. "And he was obviously right to do so."

"Promise me you won't say anything."

"Say anything about what?" Kate sashays into the kitchen with her arms full of dirty plates. The restaurant outside is heaving and she looks stressed; her blonde hair escaping its clips at either side of her flushed face, the strands encircling her pretty features like a golden frame.

"About how Danny's gonna get you lagered up on Saturday night so he can take advantage of you while I watch," the Scotsman jokes, while his face and tone suggest - to me at least - that he's deadly serious.

"I haven't said I'm going yet and besides...my boyfriend might be a bit upset about that last part."

McKinley pushes two plates of veal under the hot lamps and grabs the next ticket. "He'll be okay...we'll let him watch too. Maybe he's into that and you just don't know it yet. We have hidden depths, us lads...Isn't that right, Danny?"

Kate slides in beside me. She smells of crisp, clean white cotton and the dying notes of white musk. Her teenage breasts are fighting that constant battle with her uniform's tight blouse and not for the first time that night - every night - my eyes stray to the straining buttons and the enticing glimpse of skin and white lace between. "What have you got hidden then, Danny?" she half whispers near my ear. I almost cut the end of my finger off with the knife I'm using to julienne the carrots.

"Didn't you take the health and safety course at college, woman?" I recover my composure. "Never be flirtatious around a man holding a knife." McKinley's bell breaks the moment that I'm sure only I'm having. Kate turns on a sensible heel and heads for the door, gathering up the warm plates as she passes.

"Dirty little cow," McKinley massages his crotch in the same way he checks fruit for ripeness. "Hurry up and sort her out for fuck's sake, big man. I can't take much more of this."

He's not alone.

A few weeks later, Ellis asks me something as we get on the bus to college, something which shuts me up for the entire journey.

"Can you ask Deb what Monica thinks about me?"

There's so much wrong with this question that I don't know where to start. After the synapses in my brain stop fizzing and normal service is resumed, I start to sort through each disturbing part in order.

First, "Can I ask Deb?" Where has his head been for the last four weeks? Ellis inhabits the room next to mine - there's actual physical proof - and shares common areas within our crumbling student cess pit. We are friends, best friends, and drinking buddies. We live together. We sometimes work together. We get high together. We go to clubs and gigs together. We do pretty much everything together - with the obvious exception. And yet, he appears to have absolutely no fucking idea that I haven't even seen Deb in the street since she gagged on my cock and sprayed the bathroom with alcopuke. In what world am I in a position to call her up and ask here anything?

Second, "Can you ask Deb what Monica..?" Okay, even if the embarrassing sexual encounter and utter bastardness of my behaviour ever since I shovelled her limp and foul-smelling form into a cab a month ago had been forgotten and forgiven, why would I want to talk about Monica with Deb? And while we're at it - *Monica*? What happened to MC Steak Hammer? It was Ellis who rolled back one night after a session with some old school friends to reveal that little, ahem, moniker. Now he seems to have forgotten the nickname and is now referring, almost lovingly, to the MC by her first name. *I* am the only person he calls by their first name. It's all "Filthy Rob this..." or "Rob the Nob that..." or "Old McJock stole my Penthouse". Now we have *Monica*.

And third, in its entirety: "Can you ask Deb what Monica thinks about me?" This is the question put by someone who really cares enough about what the outcome may be but is so insecure as to want the enquiry to be put by proxy. This is what hits me and what clears up all the wooziness induced by the first and second part of my analysis. Ellis hasn't got a clue what's been going on with me and Deb because - and I now only realise this for the first time - he's been shagging the MC every other night and I've hardly seen hide nor hair of him at home for a good three weeks. They obviously haven't come up for breath long enough to discuss my unchivalrous misdemeanour or Debbie's shortcomings in the *Deep Throat* department. They've been too busy with each other. Too busy forming some embryonic bond – hence the reference to Monica! He's discovered she's a person! Jesus, this is serious. So serious in fact, that he actually wants to know and really cares what she thinks about him. You only want that information when you have already formed an opinion on the other person, most likely favourable, and want to either get the confirmation that you're not wasting your time or risking your emotions, or that it's a one-way road and you should cut your losses with your heart still intact. Fuck. He's falling for her. It's then, as Ellis gives up waving his hand in front of my face, that I realise why I've been so struck dumb by this. I'm jealous.

The silence continues for most of the day. We barely exchange words in any of the classes and I sit alone in thought during the breaks trying to get my head round this. Ellis and I, with the Scotsman and Filthy Rob, are supposed to be the Lads. The women who come and go are supposed to do just that. There's no room for any of them to stay permanently. Plus, there's a whole big ocean of fish to fry out there and while our angling average is relatively low at the moment, our trawling status as single blokes (McKinley excluded, he's just unfaithful to a degree) at least gives us the option to dip our rods when there's a chance of a bite. Once one of us lands the big one, the ship will start to list.

Or at least that's the party line.

As I said before, I'm shocked to find out that I'm jealous. Of course I'd rather be shagging every second night than not and with someone I connect with, even on just a purely physical level. Ellis, against the odds, could be the first of us (again, forget the Scotsman – and Mutton Jane doesn't count in Rob's case) to find himself attached.

"You're quiet today," Ellis asks me in the pub at lunchtime. "You've not said a thing since I asked you about talking to Debbie. What is really that bad with her?" Actually, I've had worse - which is a sad indictment of my love life since I split with Anna.

"It's not about Debbie," I admit. "She's just another face."

"Is it Monica then? Do you have something against her?"

Apart from stealing my best friend from me, literally muscling her way into our lives and giving you everything I'm hugely shocked to find out that I want for myself? "No, man. I think it's cool...It's just...What is it?"

"That's what I'm asking you, geezer?"

"No, I mean, what is it between you two? Is it serious?"

Ellis blows out his cheeks and gets a rabbit-in-the-headlights look on his face. "I dunno, man. Things are happening and I don't have a fucking clue what they are or what they mean. It's all new. I mean, you know, I'm always up for it, mad for it...But I have to say, I don't know how to deal with what's going on...you know...inside."

I resist a Vernon-related quip. "She's gotten to you, right?"

Again he blows out his cheeks and gets a thousand-yard stare. "Pretty much." I realise in that moment that the self-preservation of the group means nothing when a friend is in need. I decide there and then that I have to call Deb - for Ellis. Just after I've watched the England game at the pub tonight.

It's a typically raucous affair despite the fact that it's one of those pointless friendlies, this time against Uruguay. But that's never the point. This is England after all and in these parts, the national team in action always leads to the boys throwing their full support behind it by drinking heavily and getting severely out of order.

Ellis is so hammered that he has developed a false identity, complete with intricate back story, and is regaling a group of stunned casual drinkers with his exploits on the QEII before the match is even 20 minutes old. McKinley, a man who hates football with a passion, seems intent on spending the full 90 minutes accusing Bob the Bastard of being a cheating Sassenach and watering down the beer; his eyes glazed and wandering lazily to any passing cleavage behind his misted up glasses as he does so. Rob and I sit in front of the screen and take delivery of countless pints passed over the many heads by the benevolent hand of Kirsty the barmaid. Not many regulars get this type of service. It came about purely by accident. The accident being the time Rob tried to get back from the bar during one match carrying five pints, two of which slipped from his hand and landed on an old man's head, gashing it nastily. It was agreed in the aftermath that, in future, the drinks would be brought to us and we could settle up at the end of the night.

It's only at half-time that I remember that I promised to call Deb. Kirsty has been very efficient and I'm already numerous sheets to an ever-blowing wind. I get up after deciding its probably best to bite the bullet now while my mouth still works only to realise that Rob is wearing an outfit made up entirely of items of my clothing.

"Oi, you bastard, you've been raiding my fucking wardrobe again."

"What?" Rob tries the innocent look but becomes sheepish when I sit back down to confront him at close quarters, fingering the collar of his - my - shirt. "Yeah...funny story, actually." It turns out to be one of the least humorous things I've heard all day, and I've already been told this morning that my gran has had another stroke. Turns out that Rob spent the night before and most of the day crouched behind the bins at the back of Jane's apartment block waiting to catch her in the act. Despite the lack of evidence that she is cheating on him - his current paranoid delusion - Rob is convinced his usurper came and went in the brief moments he spent asleep on some ripe bin bags by a corner of the yard favoured as a pissoir by the local strays. Knowing we were set for the game, he came round while I was at work and helped himself to some fresh clothes as, in his own vernacular, he "minged like a tramp's foreskin". By the time I've: a) told him to get a life and move on, b) told him he's putting his stinking clobber back on once we're back at the house and c) told him he's a twat - the match is back on and my moment to call Deb has passed. Kirsty spots the empty jars in front of us and plants a fresh pair of Stella's on the table without a word.

After enduring a terrible 0-0 draw which only really profited pubs up and down the country, I brace myself and make good on the promise I made to Ellis by calling Debbie.

"It's Danny."

"Danny? Danny who?"

"Danny! You know...Danny."

"Danny? Oh...*Danny*." The emphasis she puts on my name is less that of happy realisation and more the resigned disgust which normally comes from stepping in something. "What do you want?"

Not another blow job, if that's what you're thinking...although the eight pints I've just consumed briefly convince me that this would not be such a bad idea. Reason, incredulously, wins out. "I thought we could talk," I slur.

"Are you drunk?"

"No." The force and jovial dismissive nature of my assertion immediately has me pegged as a liar as well as a bastard and a drunk. I realise this isn't going well and remember I'm doing this for Ellis. "Okay, I've had a couple of drinks but it's okay...it's okay...because I don't want to talk about the embarrassing sexual encounter and the puking, that's all in the past...I had a tug after you left and it was all forgotten..." Smooth, Daniel. The receiver nearly freezes to my hand such is the icy silence crackling down the line. "I want to talk about Ellis and Steak Hammer."

"Who?"

"What?"

"You said steak hammer."

"Yes...yes I did." I flash a panicked look to the bar where McKinley is trying to tune a pair of highly offended breasts into his frequency. Inspiration strikes. "I'm calling from work. McKinley was...preparing a steak...with his shoe...and I was trying to tell him a hammer would be better." So much for inspired minds. That's just fucking rubbish. "Look, does Monica really like Ellis or is she just messing him about?"

"Hang on," the exasperated voice on the other end finally replies. I hear Deb shout into the distance. "Mon, it's that Danny wanker on the phone. He wants to know if you really fancy his mate." I'm not even slightly offended by how she refers to me. It's wholly justified and about three-times a week accurate. I hear a muffled, low voice rumbling in response before Deb's squeaky tones stab me in the ear. "Yeah, she likes him and no, she not messing him around. Happy now?"

Not entirely, no. Actually I'm more confused. What does this mean? Obviously it suggests that instead of taking him out and getting him really drunk...again...to get over the bad news, I'm going to have to face the prospect of these two disparate and seemingly ill-matched lovers seeing a lot more of each other. It means that if this is genuine, Ellis is going to have a girlfriend. He's going to be in a relationship. Dear lord. "What does she like about him?"

Deb sighs heavily. It sounds like a mouse having its last breath squashed out of it. "Mon? Why do you like Ellis?" The rumble rolls again. "She says he has a nice penis."

"Put her on the phone, Debbie." I rummage in my pocket and take out another 50p and increase my call credit. There's a slight disagreement and some cajoling on the other end of the line before Steak Hammer's dulcet tones pick up the gauntlet.

"It's not too long, not too wide but nicely straight with a slight upwards curve at the top which really rubs my..."

"Hold on," I interject before twenty quid's worth of Stella makes an unannounced return. "I just want to know if it's all about the sex. If you're just shagging him, fine. But he should know that."

"Why does he want to know?"

"He just asked me to find out if you really like him."

"Why doesn't he ask me himself?"

"Hang on." I cup the receiver with my hand and shout across the pub. "Ellis! It's for you." He peels himself off the wall and lollops over with ungainly strides which make him look like a new born foal trying to make it across a minefield. I hand him the phone. "You're welcome." Job, as they say, is a good 'un.

she's electric

Some people pursue fame; others acquire it as a consequence. Most people, at some point in their lives, entertain a dream where they're universally loved and admired but real life and its demands more often than not soon extinguish those fantasies.

There was a time when only the chosen few achieved fame, either proactively or not. Nowadays, you just need to have a self-respect deficit and a reality show audition to your name to be spread-eagled over a glossy two-page spread with your boobs hanging out or your crotch exposed. Kids now tell their career advisors that they want to be famous when asked what job they want in the future. They don't even specify in which arena they want to lust after acclaim. It doesn't matter. Fame's value has plummeted, its lustre dimmed by the cheapness of its availability. More than ever, it's seen as an occupation rather than the by-product of lauded achievement. Few actually understand what they're wishing for and even fewer are prepared for the shock of getting their heart's desire.

I wanted to be Jim Morrison when I left school (although I never told my careers teacher that). Not THE Jim Morrison, you understand, because according to most of his biographers he was a self-absorbed, alcoholic wanker behind the genius front man persona. What I wanted to be was that kind of generational icon; the mixture of artist and god whose words defined the era and who inspired the youth of the day to dream and create. I had this vision mainly because I was heavily into Morrison's band at the time and was enthusiastically experimenting with hallucinogenics in an attempt to swing open my own Doors of perception. Once I'd come down from that particular trip, I was faced with my own realisation that his level of fame would have been unobtainable and far too destructive for me anyway. If I wanted to be well-known or recognised, I would have to settle for low key recognition.

This was a good thing to realise. It saved me. Considering my lack of self-control it was entirely possible that a bloated Jim circa *LA Woman* would have been my fate had it not.

I still had a desire to inspire and reach out to the world with my words. Instead I ended up as a journalist. Cynicism aside, through this career path, I would get to a level where I could finally speak to a wider audience - although I started off telling a tiny spattering of people about local car accidents and the boundaries of size being pushed by dedicated horticulturalists and their unfeasibly huge vegetables at country fetes. As time went on, I got to the point where I had access to larger, more global readerships - although, in most cases, they were getting censored versions of my message. Eventually, I was lucky enough to find outlets where the editorial line was based on the nurturing of creativity not the advancement of circulation figures.

Now, although I don't have a reputation which could be considered anything close to celebrity (and wouldn't want one), my chosen job does put me in regular contact with famous people. While this can be exciting and revealing, I'm becoming increasingly convinced that fame is a destructive and evil power, and that the concept of fame was one of the more heinous escapees from Pandora's Box.

Rob started out just wanting to act. There were many reasons why he wanted to become an actor but, at the very start at least, becoming famous wasn't one of them as far as any of us knew. I suspect he wanted a mask to hide behind, for whatever reasons, and that he was more comfortable in other people's skins than his own. The less analytical assumption is that he was just extremely good at it and that it was actually his calling in life. Despite everything that has happened since stepping onto his destined path, I still have tremendous respect for Rob for pursuing his dream - even though it has destroyed his soul, broken his heart and turned him into a person sporadically capable of being a Class A dickhead.

After having to entertain the coven of fat slags who followed him over in search of some memorabilia (or a love child, perhaps), the Ponce reclines in his seat, swirling a fan's gift of brandy ostentatiously in its bell glass, and fixes each of us with a satisfied smile. It's good to see him. He looks...like shit, to be honest - his once exhaustively trained body now seeing the first strains of toxic bloat - but he seems at ease with us, which shouldn't be taken for granted despite our long friendship. It's unusual to see him like this these days. His past insecurities have not been assuaged by adoration. In fact, fame has fed his demons, not tamed them and new psychoses have been spawned by fornicating fears. So to see him relatively relaxed and balanced is a rare joy. This could, and probably will, change as the evening progresses. As well as middle-aged women trying to rip his clothes off, attacks of neurosis and paranoia come as standard with any night out with Rob these days. As does heavy drinking, narcotic abuse and lasciviousness. After lagging behind when these were our collective goals, the Ponce has since been making up for lost time in a big way. But for now, he seems happier than I've seen him in many a year.

"So superstar, how have you been?" I ask, leaning forward and aggressively grabbing his knee in a show of man-love. "It seems I can get more information out of your agent these days than I can from you, and even he's monosyllabic at the best of times."

"Try *Woman's Own*. There's always something about him in there," grins Ellis.

"You read *Woman's Own*?" McKinley never misses a trick. "You big girl. At least it's less damaging to your eyesight than *Hustler*."

"My mum has a subscription," Ellis sneers. "Which reminds me...This is really embarrassing," he mumbles to Rob. "My mum's actually a fan of the show. She asked me to get you to sign something before you disappear into the realm of daytime TV again."

"You should have said, wee man." The Scotsman has that evil glint in his eye. "I've got a pair of cacks I stole from her drawer that I used to wank into. He could have scrawled his name on those."

"I've got to have my barriers, Ellis," Rob winks and raises his glass. "You can never be too careful. They may say they're Danny Jones, but who knows who they really are? It could be that mad tart from Glamorgan who believes every word I utter on the show is spoken directly through the television to her." The sign of true soap opera fame - Rob has his own stalker. "Plus you know what I'm like...I'm terrible at keeping in touch." How things change. An admission of fault from the man who barely ever came clean about leaving a turd in the toilet, let alone owned up to any personal shortcomings. Maybe we won't have to spend the best part of the night massaging his ego after all.

"So have you shagged the nutjob then?" McKinley asks, getting conspiratorial.

"Of course," smiles Rob. "Shortly before I slapped the restraining order on her." McKinley and Rob chink glasses and cackle in a rare show of public camaraderie. The Scotsman is as hardy a supporter of the Ponce's career as the rest of us but, as with many things which show his hidden depths, he rarely expresses any fondness for Rob in social situations. It's understood secretly that Rob is loved by all but to admit that would just be wrong. Successful acting career or not, he's still Filthy Rob after all these years; the poor relation, the butt of all jokes. "Fame has its downsides," he adds, his face slipping unguarded into a weary frown before he catches himself and forces it into a fake but illuminating grin. "But not many."

"Yeah, sniffing coke off the arses of naked soap groupies must be hell," says the Scotsman.

"Cocaine is God's way of saying you make too much money," Rob winks back.

"No, Rob. Having a hand-made chrome and calfskin dog sofa designed by Louis Vuitton is God's way of saying you have too much money," counters Ellis.

"Who's got one of them?"

Ellis points an accusing finger at Rob who shrinks, mortified, in his seat. "I told you. My mum's a fan."

"Okay, so I may have gone a little overboard in my first flush of fame but you can't tell me you wouldn't have done the same," Rob eventually concedes. "Getting even a little bit of fame makes people do stupid things if they're not prepared for it."

"So is it as hard as all these wining A-listers will have us believe?" Ellis asks.

"How would he know?" asks McKinley returning to his default setting of piss-taker. "He's D-list at best. D minus, maybe. See me... Must try harder."

"What exactly do they achieve by moaning about their fame?" asks Rob, rhetorically. "I'll tell you... More fame. 'Oh, leave me alone, I just want to be normal. I don't want my picture in the paper.' Bollocks. If you don't want to be seen or photographed, it's a piece of piss to go unnoticed. If fame made it impossible to avoid publicity then *Us Weekly* would be as thick as *War and Peace* every week. Everyone would be in it. Do you see Clint Eastwood in there? Do you fuck. He's one of the most famous people on the planet and yet he never gets papped scratching his balls outside a Seven-Eleven. You get seen when you want to get seen. They love the fame. We all do."

"What's so good about everyone knowing what brand of toilet paper you use?" I ask.

"Because Joe Public's so interested about you that shit like that matters to him. You matter to him. You mean something to him."

"So Joe's on the bog, right, having a dump and he reaches over to rip off a sheet of the paper you use - because he now buys it because you mean that much to him - and as he's cleaning his arse he's thinking, 'this is what Rob's ringpiece must feel like when he's wiping his backside.' That makes you feel good? That makes you feel adored."

"It's a step towards immortality, geezer."

"Living on in the post-defecation satisfaction of strangers?" I question, incredulously. "You're fucking mental, man."

"That warm afterglow Joe feels? That's as much to do with me as it is the Andrex puppy."

"Sick puppy more like," mumbles the Scotsman.

I cock a thumb at the giggling Ponce and address Ellis. "Do you still want to be famous? This is what fame does you to."

"What's this?" Rob asks.

"Brian de Palma here still wants to make the next *Long Good Friday* but can't seem to get his arse out of his parole officer's chair."

Rob drains his brandy and leans into the table. "You're making films again? I'd be into that if you need a star."

"Only if you're prepared to play the Big Bad Wolf alongside a bunch of five year olds," I chuckle.

Ellis remains unfazed. "These bastards are still banging on about me getting out of the city and making a movie. Which is fine, I appreciate the encouragement, but I don't see Danny here coming up with a script or Jockstrap putting up the finances."

"I've got some spare cash," Rob says, becoming enthused. "What's the story?"

Ellis sighs. "There isn't one. Like I said, Danny hasn't come up with the script."

"When was I supposed to?"

"We were Lennon and McCartney, remember? 50–50...We were supposed to share the workload and creative input. You write it and I direct it."

"If I remember correctly, I kept up my side of the bargain and you did fuck all. My words stayed on the page. I can't remember you shooting a frame. And besides, that was over ten years ago, man. I haven't heard anything from you about that since the last time we tried to make something together."

Ellis frowns. "But you weren't supposed to stop."

"So the fact that you haven't gotten off your arse to make a film which could have made your dream come true is my fault for not coming up with a script that I was unaware that I had to write in the first place?" Part of me is actually as pissed off as I sound. A small part but it's pissed off all the same. It comes from a well of frustration I thought I'd capped years ago. "You don't feel that you have any responsibility in this?"

"What happened to that screenplay you boys were working on anyway," asks Rob. "I thought it was great."

"You don't know about that? Where have you been for the last 12 years?"

"Where haven't I been?" Rob smirks. "Seriously, you never told me about this."

Ellis slumps back in his armchair and sighs. "You tell him."

I take a deep breath and start telling the story of how the last joint project Ellis and I worked on back in early 1998 caught the attention of a production company in London but when it came to making a formal presentation, nerves and alcohol got the better of my erstwhile partner. "It was like Spud's interview in *Trainspotting*: my pleasure in other people's leisure. He was all over the place." I laugh but at the time it caused a ruction so severe that it led to a breakdown in communication which lasted well over a year. Even now, I feel the slow, dull rise of regret and resentment which comes from this memory. It was the only time in all the years we've been friends that I couldn't stand to be around Ellis. Shortly after the production company wrote back to us saying they'd changed their mind, I moved to Dublin. While my decision to leave was based on many factors, not just this one, the utter disaster surrounding the script and the subsequent messy rift between Ellis and I certainly contributed to it.

"That explains a lot," says McKinley shaking his head. He knows about the past rift but until now hadn't known the details. "Wee man... Seriously. You've got to sort it out."

"That was ages ago," Ellis protests.

"Exactly," counters the Scotsman. "And you've done fuck all since."

"Why do you always have to turn these get-togethers into an intervention? I'm happy, okay? Of course I could be happier but I'm sure Danny would prefer to write for *Rolling Stone* than the *Irish Times* and I'm sure Rob would much rather work in films than on some ropey soap. We all settle. Even you...Especially you."

McKinley screws his face up in mock confusion. "Why especially me?"

"You know."

"Then why am I fucking asking?" A silence settles over the table as the Scotsman and Ellis fail in an attempt to communicate telepathically. Rob and I, clueless and only mildly curious, wait for the mind meld to either succeed or come to an abortive end with one head bursting *Scanners*-like all over the peanuts and empty glasses. Thankfully the Korova's staff have finally cottoned on to the fact that Rob is actually semi-famous and as such, actual trips to the bar suddenly become unnecessary. A pretty Asian waitress sways over and takes our next order which I presume, along with reserving tables, is something they don't normally do. The tension eases as Rob hands her a credit card and tells her to keep the drinks coming until we say otherwise. "Jesus," gapes the Scotsman, seizing the opportunity to lighten the mood. "I never thought I'd see the day."

"How minted are you these days?" Ellis asks in equal amazement. "Minted enough to pay back the ton I lent you in 1997?"

"I'm on Channel Five," Rob replies. "It's hardly HBO." Rob's move into daytime soap operas surprised everyone, not because he jumped at the chance to work in a genre that we all thought beneath him but because his situation was such that he had very little choice if he wanted to keep working. An accomplished Shakespearean actor who'd blown audiences and critics away with his early stage performances, earning lavish praise which normally involved putting the adjective 'young' in front of names like Olivier and Gielgud, Rob had struck out for the big time after his formative years treading the boards by setting his eyes on cinema. A handful of small independent successes soon led to studio projects clogging up his agent's letterbox and the big time seemed his for the taking. But after the initial flood of offers (and a solitary role in a big money gangster flick) the offers inexplicably dried up. Rob suddenly couldn't even get a radio commercial let alone an audition for stage or screen. He was on the verge of considering pay-per-view Internet porn when *Billionaire's Playground* found its way to his representation. Despite the fact that it made the ill-fated BBC soap *Eldorado* look like *Hamlet*, Rob - faced with being a has-been at the age of 28 - leapt at the chance of donning a grey wig and trowelled-on layers of slap to play a character twice his age in possibly the worst series to ever be commissioned by Britain's bargain basement broadcaster. As it turned out, while good taste is timeless, bad taste has had an equally impressive career and has proved to be even more lucrative. The result being that pandering to the lowest common denominator led to the highest ever ratings for a show on Channel 5. Six years later and Rob is now a stalwart of a show that many thought would have brought the four horsemen galloping across the earth in half that time.

Rob has never fully revealed what happened to suddenly turn his ascendency into a nosedive. The impression we've been given is that he doesn't fully know himself. It's true that sudden stardom took his fragile psyche by surprise even though it was something he thought he wanted more than anything and it's possible that the excesses that followed may have muddied the waters of his memory - but I for one don't buy it. I think he knows exactly what transpired to reverse his Midas touch and turn everything to shit. He just won't admit it - to us or himself. I stop myself from once again turning the spotlight on this dark period in his career in the hope of illuminating a black hole in my friend's life and rally the troops for the evening's next engagement. "Who's up for a curry then?" General grunts of hungry approval abound.

Ellis checks his watch. "We better get a shift on," he says, twisting his wrist to display his timepiece. "We're going to have to cab it if we want to make the reservation."

five

Begging You

April 1995

It's an accepted taboo within the male community that you don't comment on another man's equipment when standing at a urinal. Not even in jest. Even making a joke about your neighbour's tackle (in addition to opening yourself up to physical violence or at least a wet leg) exposes you as the filthy penis observer you are. Looking at another man's todger is unacceptable behaviour - full stop. However. While I must stress that I don't spend any amount of time fantasizing about a bloke making a comment on my cock, I sometimes wish that some wag would casually peer over and, with pleasant (and red-blooded heterosexual) surprise, ask me what I've been feeding that thing. Only then could I deliver the killer pay-off: "blondes."

While this is in no way an original response (it's attributed to Schwarzenegger in *Total Recall* but it must have come from someone way cooler, like Keith Richards maybe), it would be, in the most part, true. The roadside casualties of my haphazard, careening course through love and relationships have, more often than not, been fair-haired. Anna was blonde. Julia, Natalie and Debbie were too. I'm sure this predilection for Barbie types has led to me overlooking a number of stunning brunettes. If I spy a group of attractive women, regardless of how gorgeous the dark-haired among them may be, the blondes will always grab my attention first - and then hold it. I'll then make those split-second, in-built male judgements which help determine which one of those I most want to have sex with. In 99 out of 100 cases, the brunettes never get past that first colour-coded selection.

All of which explains why, on my way home from college on a sunny late April afternoon, I'm suddenly straying from my regular course to follow the one and only glowing head of shiny yellow hair in the sea of mousey barnets and assorted headwear. Moments ago I was in my usual post-lecture, dream-like state (part monologue-induced coma, part drowsiness from a couple of lunchtime pints), now I'm swerving with determined alertness from the direct route back to the house through a maze of backstreets in pursuit if this beacon of potential beauty. Now of course blonde hair alone is no guarantee that the woman who wears that golden glory is going to have the face of an angel and the body of a *Baywatch* babe. But such is my fascination with this stereotype that I'm willing to forego lustful fantasies over the rest of the fairer sex on offer today just to find out. As the crowd thins out, I get to see more than just the enticing head of hair. Her body looks slim under a tailored three-quarter length coat, her legs long and elegant as she manoeuvres her way through the puddles and litter. The clumpy white shoes don't quite compute with the elegance on top but hey! Who wears shoes in bed? And if she's into that, I'm sure we can find some stilettos or hooker boots from somewhere.

I suddenly start to feel slightly exposed and pervy as we turn another corner and become the only two people walking down this quiet street. It gets worse when I realise in horror that it's a dead end. I still don't know what she looks like. While the package from behind looks tasty, she could still turn round and fix me with a questioning, slightly concerned stare from a face which would make Mother Theresa look like Claudia Schiffer. If she's fit, I could just come clean and ask her out on her doorstep, which would be what I would probably do anyway if she turns out to be a looker, creepy as it may seem after tailing her for fifteen minutes. If she's a dog, I'm left with the options of either looking lost or ringing a random doorbell and offering the bemused occupant a non-existent copy of *The Watchtower*. Blondie turns up a pathway and fumbles nervously in her handbag for either a door key or a can of mace. Time to choose: romantic pursuer, directionless moron or empty-handed Jehovah's Witness? Suddenly, fortune smiles on me. I see the brass plaque on the wall by her door and read the name of J.T Slater, Dental Surgeon. The white shoes are no longer a mystery.

"Excuse me," I pipe up in relief. "This may be a stupid question but is this Dr. Slater's dental surgery?"

Blondie turns round and melts my heart. Big blue eyes, button nose, lips you just want to bite. Score. "Yes it is. Do you have an appointment?"

"No, I'm hoping to make one." For tomorrow night maybe, around eight? A couple of drinks, maybe something to eat, and then back to mine for some cavity filling? "This toothache is driving me crazy."

She gives me a sympathetic smile which softens her English rose features to such an extent that I audibly sigh. "Come in and let's get you sorted out then."

I walk up the path behind her as she opens the door. Her hair smells of coconut with a hint of antiseptic; the rest of her has the unmistakeable aroma of sexy bitch. "This place is hard to find," I finally say after subtly and silently breathing her in. "I thought I was totally lost."

"So what's wrong with your teeth?" Ellis is heaping a gargantuan serving of spaghetti Bolognese onto his plate with one hand and sipping intermittently from the can of Carlsberg he's holding in the other.

"Nothing. Plus I'm shit-scared of dentists."

"She's that fit?"

I want to tell him that it wouldn't matter if Sarah was a quadruple amputee with warts and an eye-patch. It's a couple of months since I last got my leg over and that was with Natalie the unwitting porn star so I'm not sure if that even counts. I'm just thankful Sarah has a pulse, although I'm desperate enough for that not be a prerequisite. But I'm in no rush to verbalise my current situation. It's depressing enough being reminded of my enforced celibacy in the confines of my own head, let alone putting it out there in the world for discussion. There's also the fact that Ellis is getting plenty and I'm not yet comfortable enough with that fact to permit him to give me advice. Bearing all this in mind, I decide to keep my feelings towards my current failings with the opposite sex to myself.

"She's blonde and she's a nurse. The rest is just a bonus." (I forgot to mention that I have a thing for uniforms as well. This is another reason why I'm particularly happy that I decided to give in to my stalker tendencies earlier in the day.)

"Result," Ellis burps and slaps another spade of food on a plate and pushes it towards me before squeezing out a high-pitched fart with a smile. Another question as to how he has suddenly become a much-desired sex machine is added to my growing sense of incredulity.

I keep the dentist's appointment despite the crippling dread. In the hours before I leave to have sharp implements shoved into my mouth by a rough-handed sadist, I fight a long and hard internal battle. One part of me wants to call the whole thing off. Another part of me wants to go through with it, knowing a bunk-up may be the reward, but wants to take me to the pub first to get shit-faced. Another rides in on a white stallion and beats the other two down, standing over their bloodied corpses to declare in an Errol Flynn voice that "faint heart ne'er won fair maid or helped get thy end away." So I let the Marquis de Slater have his evil way with my molars in the hope that the excruciating pain he's taking great pleasure in administering won't resurface as some kind of psychosomatic reaction whenever I see his assistant, the lovely Sarah.

As it turns out, I do have a problem with my teeth after all and I have to make another appointment to go back for some minor work in a week's time. While I'm waiting for the receptionist to deal with an old man with the worst halitosis ever, I wonder if I should wait until the next appointment to ask Sarah out or do it now. She comes out of the surgery and puts my records on the receptionist's desk. She looks up and mouths "you were very brave" at me. I'm about to beckon her over and ask if she wants to get a drink after work when she turns and sashays out in a swish of blonde ponytail and white smock.

After loitering longer than I need to in the reception area, I finally get the chance to get a look at the staff diary. After risking a neck injury by craning over the receptionist's desk, I find out that Sarah's birthday is slap bang in the middle of my two dental appointments. I decide that, instead of waiting for my next visit to ask her out, I'll drop off a single red rose and a card at the surgery on her big day. It's corny as hell and more of a coward's compromise than a grand romantic gesture.

I go to the surgery at midday knowing Sarah will be off having a celebratory lunch with friends (the result of more stalking) and leave the rose and card with the sour-faced matron on reception duty. Believing that it would be unethical of Sarah to use my medical file to find out my phone number, should she want to, I include it in the brief message within the card. She calls that night shortly before I have to leave for a shift at the hotel.

"Thank you for the rose and the card," she says with a hint of embarrassment in her voice. "That was very nice of you."

"Look, would you like to go for a drink tomorrow night? If you're free." The line appears to go dead. I'm about to ask if she's still there when Sarah answers.

"Okay," she finally says, in almost a whisper. "Do you know the Stanley Arms?"

The Stanley. A nice, respectable, if a little codger-friendly, establishment just round the corner. Quiet, yet not too boring. More importantly, not a pub which is frequented of an evening by the people I would want to avoid while trying to get a near perfect stranger into the sack i.e. any of the boys. Ideal for an initial, nervous get-together with the promise of more. "The Stanley would be perfect." We agree to meet at seven-thirty.

Sarah calls five minutes before I'm due to leave to meet her at the pub. I'm standing there, all shiny and clean, although smelling like a cross between a tomato picker and a Russian cab driver thanks to the dodgy aftershave I found lurking in the back of the bathroom cabinet. I'm primed. I'm ready to show this vision of beauty why she should take the curiosity she has over her stalker to a new level of understanding. I'm not, however, ready for what she has to say.

"You know, actually, I don't think this is such a good idea." The tell-tale sounds of muffled jukebox music, quiz machines and the stifled giggles of her girlfriends suggest that she's not making this heart-breaking decision from a place of quiet reflection. "You seem like a nice bloke but I'm not ready to start seeing anyone right now."

Fucking bitch, why did you wait until now, at the end of a full two hours of shameless pampering and preparation, of psyching myself up in any mirror I pass, of pacing the floor with 'Cigarettes and Alcohol' booming out to give me strength? "Oh..." I tamely reply. "Okay. Maybe I'll see you around." The phone is already dead but I can still hear the laughing at the other end of the line. So much for the New Lad culture. Aren't I supposed to be the one with better things to do? Isn't it my heart that's supposed to be made of stone? Shouldn't I be the one now clinking pint glasses and pissing myself over the image of some perfumed tart falling to pieces in some dingy living room as the light at the end of another tunnel gets snuffed out on a whim?

I feel like someone has just booted me in the gonads. The spreading nausea of rejection empties me of the hope and anticipation I'd had just seconds earlier. I feel the bitterness and self-destructiveness gathering on the fringes of the void, waiting to fill the vacuum with hateful thoughts and the need to get violently drunk. I loudly call Sarah a whore and kick our deflated football across the room, knocking over a full ashtray and a thrift-shop lava lamp in the process. Mr. Sifter, disturbed from quietly urinating under the sofa no doubt, shoots across the room and up the stairs in a flash of ginger and stench. Then I do what any self-respecting lad would do in this situation and reach for the drugs and liquor.

I can barely hear the banging at the door over the rate of decibels at which Primal Scream's 'Rocks' is playing but hear it I still can. I'm just not going to acknowledge it. My narcotic-induced self-confidence and pumped-up ego is telling me to let whoever it is out there go fuck themselves and that this music is being turned down for no man. I'm strutting around the kitchen in an agitated manner when a dark shape falls unceremoniously into the backyard from over the fence. Grabbing the nearest thing to hand, I burst out of the back door with all the will in the world, ready to give the intruder the biggest beating of his life - only to find Rob sitting on his arse in the weeds, weeping quietly to himself.

"Jesus, Rob. What the fuck are you playing at? I thought you were a burglar."

"You haven't got anything worth stealing," he snivels from behind his lank hair.

"Yeah but no-one else knows that. I could have hurt you."

Rob looks up. "What were you going to do, wash me to death?"

It's only then do I realise I was about to take on Raffles the gentleman thief with a bottle of Fairy Liquid. "Are you okay?"

"It's broken," he says, his damp face glowing in the orange hue of the nearby street lamp.

"What is? Your leg...your ankle?"

"My heart, geezer. My heart."

I would have much preferred a snapped limb. Limbs can be set. Limbs have their own dedicated professionals at hospitals, people trained to make them whole again. Bones are easy. Hearts...man. Hearts can stay broken for years. There's nothing any team of surgeons can do in the case of a broken heart. All of which makes Rob's decision to turn to me even more pathetic. Out of all the people unable to offer practical help in getting over a broken heart, I'm the least qualified. I'm also in the worst frame of mind to give him any objective advice.

"I saw her with him...they were getting out of a cab together..." The woman in this story is of course Mutton Jane, the middle-aged psycho clusterfuck that Rob has been sniffing around for the past few months. While he talks about her incessantly and have seen the two of them together on occasion, we have only ever met her once. And that was enough. Rob brought Jane and an equally deranged friend of hers round to ours one night on the way to a club. Both women looked like they'd been mainlining ketamine before driving at high speed into Cyndi Lauper's wardrobe, barely escaping with their lives and dignity intact. Jane hung off Rob's shoulder like a blonde-bobbed, neon-sheathed cadaver and as he proudly introduced her she managed to raise her eyelids in acknowledgment while the other harpy slouched around slagging off the décor. Anyway, it seems that this demeanour was something of a regular state for Jane rather than a pre-club example of over-doing it. Now, by the sounds of it, she's sucked enough of Rob's life-force from him to survive and has now found a new source of youthful flesh to sate her needs. "Some bloke...fucking smooth townie type...gelled hair cunt..."

I pass Rob a can. I think briefly about offering him a line but then remember that he doesn't do shit like that. He has other destructive habits. Jane, mostly. I also fight down the urge to rant about all women being heartless sluts. Rob needs a friend, not a bitter victim of rejection. One at a time...

"Maybe he was just a friend," I weakly suggest.

"He had his hand up her skirt as they were waiting to get into her apartment."

"Maybe she keeps her keys in there." I'm not helping.

"He was fingering her minge, Danny! Fucks sake, give me some credit."

Okay, fair play. Rob is a lot of things but he isn't an idiot. But while we're handing out credit, some must be due to the Phantom Fingerer. Getting her warmed up on the doorstep as not to waste anytime once inside? Clever boy. Anyone wanting to sort that nasty old slapper out would be wise not to linger too long on the starter and cut straight to the main course before calling for the cheque. If he was really on the ball, he'd have asked the cabbie to leave the engine running outside. I can't imagine anyone wanting to have more than a ten-minute relationship with that woman. It's then that I remember the broken hearted friend sitting on the sofa.

"You're better off without her, man," I sneer. "Women just want to mess with your head and have control. They've played us into this role where we have to be sensitive blokes to get them and then they stamp on our hearts as soon as we're hooked. Fuck 'em." I don't really believe this but this coke is over-riding my decision to censor my bitterness. Plus, as he threatens to turn to jelly beside me, I start thinking that it might actually be good for Rob to hear something like this. He looks on the verge of wallowing. Maybe I can fire him up and snap him out of it before it sets in.

"But I loved her." Rob looks up at me with his red, puffy eyes.

Really? I mean, I can't judge whether the two of them were actually soul mates as we only saw them together on the fringes of larger parties and the time we actually met Jane she was almost catatonic. I've sat through some of Rob's poetic and cringe-worthy expressions of his feelings for this woman but I usually put them down to either the amount of alcohol consumed beforehand or the naturally occurring dramatic effect he injects into most aspects of his existence. I never once believed that all that mooning around and flowery language could be an authentic expression of love. I have to admit that, even now, I still have my doubts. The current evidence would be quite persuasive would it not be for the fact that Rob has form. His infatuations - obsessions, even - have been known to take on the cloak of love, only for that disguise to be shed and discarded (normally after a lengthy period of tearful mourning where he makes endless mix tapes) once a new possibility of lasting affection has caught his eye.

We're not so unlike in some ways, Rob and I - which is painful to admit. We're poles apart on the things which I rate highly in a human being; cleanliness and pride in appearance among them, but when it comes to women we are both basically looking for The One. (The similarities actually stop right there, come to think of it). I offset my seemingly doomed quest for a lasting relationship with the quick-fix comfort of meaningless sex (when it happens), whereas Rob tends to latch onto anyone willing to allow his odorous form to climb on top of them a couple of times - before hanging on for grim death. Rob doesn't know when to quit, whereas I normally don't get a say in the matter. Right now, I'm thinking this is less about love and more about the fact that Jane finally chewed her leg out of the bear trap of Rob's making.

"Seriously, Rob. Were you really hoping to spend the rest of your life with this woman? She was almost twenty years older than you and - I have to say it, mate - a bit of a fucking head case."

"She was my Nala...," he says with a straight face. "I was her Simba."

Dear Christ. It all comes back to me now. During one of the many times Rob went into the details of his and Jane's sex life - much against my wishes, I must add - he told me that they used to prowl around on all fours, growling and roaring at each other, before he mounted her in what I can only assume looked like some bizarre cross between a *National Geographic* documentary and a pornographic Help the Aged commercial. He explained that they had had the best sex ever after seeing *The Lion King* together and that the film had inspired the role play that eventually became the only way either of them could reach orgasm. Something Elton John probably didn't have in mind when he wrote 'The Circle of Life'.

Rob slowly gets up from the sofa. "Is it okay if I use the stereo in your room?"

"Go nuts, fella," I say, slapping his shoulder in a manly show of support and sympathy. "The spare tapes are in the drawer as always."

Knowing that he'll spend the next few hours deliberating over whether Love's 'Andmoreagain' should follow on from The Beatles' 'Something,' I leave Rob to his misery and head to the pub. I take my wounded pride to the Castle, safe in the knowledge that Sarah will be swilling Bacardi Breezers in some tacky theme pub in the city centre with her sniggering mates. I locate Ellis and McKinley playing pool in the back room and before I even get within ten feet of the doorway, they're pointing at the bar. I fight my way through what appears to be a visiting darts team and order three pints. Once armed with refreshment, I swagger into the games room, digging deep to find the narcotic bravado which I was brimming with earlier.

"Crap shag, was she?" says Ellis, his eye line staying firmly fixed on his shot.

"I wouldn't know, mate," I say, handing the Scotsman his beer and putting the other two on the window sill. "I would've probably dropped off before I got that far. Talk about fucking dim."

"Big man, you're not supposed to hold a debate with her, you know that, right?" McKinley takes a half-smoked joint out of the ashtray and drags it back to life by the open window. "You have the rest of your life to talk. You should be getting your end wet."

"You don't talk to your missus...or shag her, come to think about it," Ellis slaps the eight-ball down with an arrogant flourish and strides over to his pint.

"It's a bit fucking hard when she's on the other side of the world, wee man," says McKinley in his most condescending tone. "Besides, come back when you've been with your girlfriend for longer than it takes you to cum in your pants and then we'll talk about adult relationships, okay?"

"Girlfriend? I don't have a girlfriend."

"Face facts, man. Steak Hammer's your bird now. It is what it is." McKinley winks at me as Ellis goes pale. I sit down and take the joint which the Scotsman offers. "So what happened with the naughty nurse, Danny Boy?"

"I just lost interest very quickly. Anyway, she's history so let's forget about it. Oh, and by the way, Rob's back at our place crying his eyes out over Jane." Sorry, geezer, but when you're in a boat with no oars in a shark-infested sea, you always throw the weaker guy in to swim for help.

"Seriously? What happened this time?" Ellis asks.

"He was checking up on her again and spotted the Phantom Fingerer with his hands in her pants. It sent the poor boy over the edge."

McKinley comes up for air from his pint with a grin. "Excellent."

"You sad bastard." McKinley leads the way into the living room, pointing an accusing finger at Rob who's sat on the sofa again, surrounded by empty beer cans with *Brief Encounter* playing on the video. The Scotsman slumps down beside him, grabs his knee and changes his tune. "Poor wee lamb. You're better off without her. Rough as a badger's tadger and mad with it, that one." Ellis issues a torrent of expletives from the open door of a now empty fridge, the gist being that he is mildly miffed that Rob has helped himself to his stock of beers. I head upstairs to find the right soundtrack to the rest of the evening as Ellis storms back into the living room to demand funds for more alcohol from our shell-shocked house guest. Up in my room, the search for an anthem begins. Right, what do we have? The three of us who have just got back from the pub are well lagered up and high with it, so something upbeat is required to keep us flying. We'll get Rob into a few joints and we'll all soon forget about our troubles if the music's right. It's an important job and one which normally takes a lot of consideration but tonight the music picks itself. *Definitely Maybe* and 'Rock'n'Roll Star' in particular are perfect for getting things underway. Now, I just need to tee this tape up...Hang on. Oh my, what do we have here?

I come back downstairs with almost unrestrained glee. Finding out that Ellis has just nipped out to the corner shop is excruciating. I can't do what I'm about to do without him here. It will never be as funny the second time round so I have to wait until he comes back with a carrier bag of cans in each hand. Once everyone has a tin, I make my claim for the biggest bastard on the planet. I go to the stereo, put the tape in and press play. "Darling Jane..," Rob's most heartfelt voice drones out of the speakers and into every ear in the room. "Every time I look into your eyes, I feel so much...*emotion*." The breathless, desperate emphasis on the word causes the first stifled guffaw from Ellis. The look of shock in Rob's eyes is quickly replaced by a short, sharp, hateful glare aimed in my direction before resigned defeat eventually settles on his face as he accepts his fate. "I want to hold you again...to be yours again...Jane...I love you." Just before the full realization of what they've just heard turns McKinley and Ellis into quivering wrecks, the payoff arrives. Elton John's 'Can You Feel the Love Tonight?' kicks in on a rough edit and the room dissolves. "Bastard." Rob is smiling now. He knows he's been had. He knows he just has to take it and take it well so he joins in with genuine amusement. My initial plan was just to pull off a masterstroke of playful ridicule but in addition to that, I've accomplished something else. In that moment, both Rob and I see that this whole pursuit of happiness can be taken way too seriously at times. Sarah and Jane were never going to be The One. You take your knocks, you swallow the humiliation...and you get out there again. I make a mental note to cancel my next dentist's appointment. Fuck it. I'll get false teeth if I have to. I'm moving on.

The Passage to India on Cutter Street hasn't changed in almost fifteen years and for once its stagnation is a welcome surprise. The décor, which was never contemporary even when it was lovingly pasted to the walls some forty years ago, has retained that out-of-time quality that only faux velvet flocking can achieve. The staff are still courteous to a man; a level of efficiency and politeness which harks back to a time of pride in service that none of us are old enough to have experienced the first time round. Most appealingly, the prices are still authentically 1996. And even back then, it was dirt cheap to eat here. This was due mainly to the continuous price war which raged between the dozens of curry houses which gave the mile long stretch of road its unoriginal nickname - Calcutta Street.

A waiter who could be the same bloke who used to seat us back in the day welcomes us as if he is an old friend. He asks us how we've been - raising the likelihood that he is actually the same bloke who used to seat us back in the day - and banters about the weather as he skilfully manoeuvres us into a booth. He hands out menus like a blackjack dealer while making risqué remarks about our plans for the rest of the evening in a *Carry On Up the Khyber* kinda way (nudge nudge, wink, wink, say no more), and immediately puts our beer requests on a tab he secretly hopes will pay for him to go back to Mumbai for a fortnight in September. The chances are increasing that this is the bloke who used to serve us. He appears to know us by reputation. In fact, if he is basing his enthusiasm on his previous experiences of our custom, he's probably planning to invest our lager bill in a retirement condo back in Mother India.

As with all experienced curry eaters, the menus remain mostly redundant. We all have our own specialities and stick to them religiously. Ellis always has a chicken korma while the Scotsman more often than not goes for a meat vindaloo. I always prefer my flesh to be defined by species so I remain faithful to the tried-and-tested lamb dansak. Rob completes the predictable ordering by settling on his trademark chicken madras after going through the equally unsurprising charade of indecision. We only consult the menus when choosing side dishes but then it's normally just a selection from the usual suspects; Bombay potatoes, naans of various varieties, that sort of thing. We order four pints of Kingfisher and tell our beer wallah to keep them coming. The chore of choosing our meals out of the way, we relax and allow ourselves to be absorbed into the plush upholstery of the booth as the banter begins again.

"Can you remember when we almost moved into the flat above this place?" I ask Ellis, smirking at the memory.

"When was that?" asks Rob.

"It was during one of the many times you went AWOL," Ellis remarks. "You were off playing Widow Twankey or something."

"It was 1996," I clarify. "We had to leave Calvin Road by the end of the European Championships and I found a bunch of flats to look at, the gaff above this place being one of them."

"I still think it would have been a top place to live," Ellis reminisces. "We would have just had to shout down our order and then have them bring it up to us. It would have been like the British Empire had never collapsed."

"Aye, wouldn't that have been great?" deadpans McKinley. "Maybe you could have had a few slaves as well up there so you could have beaten them when you got bored with playing polo and spreading herpes."

"So says the man with a household full of staff," I counter. "How is life in the Raj, old bean?"

McKinley smiles devilishly. "Fucking excellent, big man. I haven't had to do a stroke of housework in over ten years. I've not made my own breakfast in about eight. I'd be lost without my driver too." The three of us laugh. The Scotsman doesn't. "No, seriously. I'd be fucking lost. I have no idea how to get from A to B in Jakarta and I've lived there for nearly fourteen years. I get up, my driver takes me to work. I leave work, he drives me to the pub. He waits outside, I stagger out about five hours later and then he drives me home. It's a fucking miracle that my legs still work."

"Was it is that you actually do?" asks Rob. It's a pertinent question as both Ellis and I have admitted to each other in the recent past that we still have no idea what exactly McKinley does for a living. We know it has something to do with the finances of either a non-governmental organization or international aid agency in Indonesia but if our lives depended on giving a detailed job description we'd be buggered. McKinley himself is never any help and again he says less than the bare minimum, adding weight to Ellis's assertion that he's either a drug smuggler or an arms dealer. I still harbour fears that he runs a pornography empire.

"It's a secret," the Scotsman winks. "I could tell you but then I'd have to kill you."

"That would be interesting," I say to Rob, as a silver tray laden with frosty glasses of Kingfisher arrive from nowhere. "Your scriptwriters would have to come up with a creative storyline for once to explain your mysterious disappearance."

"They're creative," Rob protests, a little too defensively. "What about that story arc where I discovered that the hand which I'd lost in that plane crash had been saved and was being used by my illegitimate son to frame me in revenge for how I treated his mother?"

"What?" McKinley shakes his head incredulously. Apparently he doesn't get the chance to experience the insanity of *Billionaires Playground* in Jakarta. "What?"

"Okay, my character - Roger Forester - is in a plane crash," Rob explains. "He's rushing to Monaco to stop his daughter's diamond thief husband from signing over the papers to the family business to a blackmailer when the jet crashes on take-off. He survives but loses a hand. The hand mysteriously goes missing only to be transplanted onto the bastard love-child who cut off his own just so he could have mine sewn on. Then he does all these murders and robberies - one-handed, I must add - leaving my prints at all the crime scenes. All because I let his mother, a cocktail waitress I'd shagged years ago, die in poverty."

"Doesn't everyone know that you lost your hand though?" Ellis asks, joining the bizarre dots. "Surely that's the best alibi ever."

"Except Roger Forester can't show any weakness," winks Rob. "He's involved in a massive international power struggle and any sign of fallibility - like a missing hand - would be exploited by his enemies and rivals, so he had an exact replica of his missing hand made by the world's best prosthetic surgeon. It's as if nothing ever happened."

"So Roger would prefer to go down for multiple murders and thefts rather than be shown as having a disability? That's not a very healthy message," I add.

"But he could still bring the surgeon in to bail him out as a witness if things got too tasty though," chimes in Ellis, who seems to be getting carried away with the plot.

"Ah," Rob smiles. "But Roger had the surgeon killed and his practice burned to the ground so there's no evidence of the hand's creation. That's the beauty of the storyline. It's a classic *Catch 22* situation and one of the reasons the show's up for a Chattie."

"A what-ee?"

"A Chat Magazine Soap Opera Award. We're nominated in seven categories."

"Fuck me," the Scotsman finally says after a pause of disbelief. "And all this time I thought you were a proper stage actor pretending to be a fucking crap soap star."

"It's not crap...I mean, I'm not crap," Rob sounds a little hurt but he's used to this by now so doesn't take it completely to heart. "Besides it pays well, it gives me good exposure and, you know, it's not like I've never done West End stuff and films. Those times are just round the corner again. I'm just paying my dues."

"I thought you were supposed to pay your dues *before* you got your big break," Ellis joins in. "Not pay them, get a big break, fuck it up and then have to pay them again."

"Be fair, Ellis," I say, surprising everyone including myself by defending Rob's career choices. "That film he did with Guy Ritchie wasn't awful."

"No but his Irish accent was." Ellis counters.

I have to concede the point. "Well, yeah...That's true."

"But the film didn't bomb plus I got some really good reviews," Rob adds. "And, you know, I was in a Guy Ritchie movie which didn't suck cock so that must mean something, right? That doesn't happen every day."

"Again, true," I admit. "So if the film wasn't shit, how come you didn't get any more offers after that and ended up playing a billionaire twice your age on some ropey Channel 5 lunchtime soap?"

"Because he sounded less convincingly Irish than Sean Connery in *The Untouchables*," Ellis declares. "...And thatsh the shicago way!" he adds in a passable impression of Connery's terrible attempt at being oirish.

"Are you mocking the Connery?" asks Rob, now genuinely hurt. "The man is one of Britain's greatest actors."

"No he's not," says Ellis. "He's the best Bond but he's not a great actor. And saying that is like saying that Boba Fett is the best thing about *Star Wars*."

"He is," argues Rob.

"No. He's the coolest. There's a difference," Ellis responds. "What does he do other than look cool?"

"Err..."

"He has about three lines. You can't say he has much emotional depth or acting range, right? He just looks cool and acts cool. Just like Connery." Rob sits there shocked, as if McKinley has just told him that his mum was the best shag he'd ever had and had produced the pictures to prove it.

"If you think about it, Rob, Ellis is comparing you to Sean Connery which, in your eyes at least, is a big compliment," I add, trying to ease the trauma.

"Look, you were great in that Guy Ritchie film when you didn't have any lines," Ellis continues. "You were massively watchable, geezer, I was dead proud. But when you opened your mouth...Jesus. It was a relief when Vinnie Jones stuck that screwdriver in your head."

"Maybe you should try a career in mime," I suggest as I see McKinley getting edgy over his untouched beer out of the corner of my eye. "Anyway, enough character assassination. A toast, gentlemen."

McKinley grabs his beer and raises it high above the hotplates and garish table decorations. "To dodgy regional accents and evil twins!"

"Evil illegitimate sons," corrects Rob with a smile. We all repeat the amended toast and quaff deeply from our glasses.

Our waiter creeps over somewhat apologetically. We wait with baited breath for some bad news regarding our curries but instead receive a bashful request. "So sorry sirs but we have a massive favour to ask of you." He is almost bent double as if expecting a strap across the back or something. It's slightly embarrassing. "We have been talking, the staff and I, and we realise that the gentleman here is Roger Forester from *Billionaires Playground*. We are huge fans, sir, huge fans. Could we please trouble you for a photograph?"

Ellis almost spits his beer across the table – again – and McKinley roars with laughter. I sit with an expression of amused wonder on my face as Rob nods accommodatingly at his number one fan – in this restaurant at least. "No problem, my friend," smiles Roger Forester in that rich and slimy bastard way of his. "Where do you want me?"

"Actually sirs, we would all like to get into the booth with Mr. Forester sir." With that, the whole kitchen and bar staff of the Passage to India surround our booth, agitating to take our places. Ellis, McKinley and I swap glances and then slide out, allowing seven diminutive Indians to crowd round the table. Rob slides back against the wall and leans into the table as the staff struggle to all get their arms round him. A small chef hands me a digital camera with a polite "please" before climbing onto the table and displaying himself like a main course. I manage to get everyone in frame – Rob in the centre wearing an expression which is more Roger Moore than Forester – and click off a couple of cheesy group shots. The entire staff then slide out, passing around the camera between them while cooing appreciatively at my photographic skills before shuffling off with beaming faces. "Thank you very much sirs," says our waiter. "This will be put in a place of high honour on our wall behind the bar. And of course your meal tonight will be completely complimentary, drinks included." He bows and scuttles away.

"Not such a crappy soap star after all," beams Rob, leaning back and winking at a couple of housewives who are craning their heads round their own booth to get a glimpse of the resident star. "I have to admit, I love the fucking fame."

"It's hardly a handprint in the concrete, big man," grins McKinley. "You'll be up there on the wall with the guy who reads the local sports on the telly and that tart who went on to do that travel show on ITV where she always gets bitten by monkeys." He slaps Rob on the back. "Nice one, Olivier," he adds with genuine affection. "You've got your face in the Passage to India. Shame it's only the restaurant and not the movie but fair play all the same."

The Scotsman's right. Considering what Rob was like when all this began, when we were all bright of eye, bushy of tail and cocky as fuck, it is a remarkable achievement. I mean, he's also right that Rob's been in show business for fifteen years now and his biggest claim to fame so far is having a Philips jammed into his cranium by an ex-footballer in a mildly entertaining gangster romp directed by the ex-Mr. Madonna. And now his mug shot is destined to take pride of place over the dusty optics behind the bar in the Passage to India. I'm sure even Rob expected to have achieved more than that by now. But fair play as McKinley said - given that he used to sleep in a public toilet on occasion and only wore clothes he could steal from his friends, you could say that he's made it, to a certain degree. It's just that when he left us in 1996 to tread the boards, we really thought that we were going to have the next Kenneth Branagh on our hands. Of course, we never admitted it to each other and it was a struggle to even admit it to ourselves, but Rob had talent, immense talent, and it seemed that against all the odds he had given himself a real shot at harnessing that talent and unleashing it on the world. While starring in a long-running and popular-with-housewives daily soap is hardly what you could call failing miserably, one has to wonder how the man who managed to learn four main Shakespearean roles concurrently in less than a month became one-dimensional series villain Roger Forester.

Sitting here as my three best friends take the piss out of each other as if no time has passed between us, I really start to wonder. We've been friends for so long that we remain under the illusion that we know each other but in every one of our lives there are gaps; periods - stretching to years in some cases - where we have no real knowledge about what was going on. My hands are only marginally ill-equipped with enough fingers to count how many times I've met up with McKinley in the last 13 years. Even though Ellis is just an hour's budget airline flight away, I only see him perhaps twice as often, on birthdays and at Christmas, and Rob - well, as he's the only one with an agent and never answers his own phone, I'd be lucky to grab dinner with him once every two years. Our friendship, as solid and beautiful as it is, is based purely on a concentrated three year period where we all lived in each other's pockets - in Rob's case, almost literally.

Even in that intense spell, Rob was missing for huge, era-defining chunks of it. He made it through the first day of Glastonbury 1995 - before an acid-inspired revelation took him away from us for the first time - but he completely missed the collective insanity of our first Amsterdam odyssey, the unbridled patriotic machismo of Euro 96 and the zenith of Britpop, the Oasis weekender at Knebworth. These three events, more than any other we experienced together, cemented the bond between Ellis, the Scotsman and I. Rob was off treading the boards, learning his craft and developing into the actor we all hoped he would be while we were working on becoming borderline alcoholics with drug habits and sexually transmitted diseases. Before he left, he shared in building our collective hazy memories of beer-fuelled bad behaviour, skirt chasing and substance abuse while never having the same taste and vigour for it. He was there as the nation's music swelled into a strong movement around us and dragged us along on a wave of euphoria into a period of wonderfully thrilling British rock while never really buying into the scene and the promise it offered. Rob dabbled while we indulged. He dragged a toe through the waters while we dived in head first.

Rob's lost years remain a mystery. While I can fill in the gaps through sketchy knowledge of Ellis and McKinley's existences and their sporadic missives and updates, the actor remains an enigma. We all have our end-products which we bring to the table in terms of where our lives are now but we don't know for sure how Rob got here.

Finally - after all these years, curiosity gets the better of me. "Thinking about the time we almost moved in above this place," I begin, "it makes me wonder what was going on in your life, Rob. You were missing for quite some time." McKinley and Ellis break off from laughing at a joke about the actor's star status in the restaurant - another Passage-related double entendre - and suddenly become focused. "Spill the beans, man. Where were you while we were getting high?" Rob shifts uncomfortably a first. This isn't how it's meant to be. Normally we spend our preciously few and far-between moments together harmlessly ridiculing each other. There's reminiscing, of course, but it normally only goes as far and as deep as who shagged whom and what drugs you were on. This is something else.

"Come on, Olivier," McKinley says, backing me up. "Give us some truth."

"What do you want to know?" Rob finally says after searching three faces for pitfalls and potential traps. "I've told you what I was up to - acting."

"Yeah, but you never said anything about the life," I reply. "You told us about the thrill and the buzz you got from being on stage but you never told us what was going on in your head when you took off with...what was that Shakespearean company called?"

"Shaven Avon." Rob says. He waits for further prompting. He gets none. I watch him slowly relax into his chair and he adopts that accessible yet false expression I've seen a hundred times.

"And don't give us the chat show routine," I say, putting a stop to the bullshit before it begins. "We're your mates, not fucking Jonathon Ross. Tell us straight up."

Our curries arrive in a flurry of white sleeves, silver dishes and polite bowing. We're left with enough sustenance to see us through the coming revelations. McKinley, Ellis and I dig in while Rob plays thoughtfully with his madras before starting at the beginning.

Sorted for E's & Wizz

June 1995

I'm beginning to wonder if I'm focussing too much on one aspect of this whole Lad thing while neglecting others. I've been rabidly chasing skirt for the best part of six months now (mostly fruitlessly and when I have caught said item of women's clothing it's quite often been from the bargain bin) and I still feel as disconnected from myself as when Anna broke up with me last November. I've consulted the oracle every month as soon as it drops through my door and it keeps telling me the same old thing; that it should all be about "girls, goals and go on my son!" The 'girls' part of the *Loaded* magazine mantra is quite obviously not happening to any level of satisfaction for me at the moment. (The 'goals' take care of themselves every Saturday, unless you're an Ipswich Town supporter like Ellis.) There's plenty of 'Go on my son!' but the encouragement is empty; it's a football chant, a rallying cry, not a quiet word of advice which might help. I've tried shagging old dogs for the pure pleasure of it. I've been on hugely depressing and sometimes scary blind dates. I've used and have *been* used and I've even made a porn film (- which reminds me, I've asked McKinley to show me the tape three times in the last fortnight and he's fobbed me off every time). Ever since Sarah the Dental Nurse blew me off two months ago, the nearest I've come to actually having any sexual physical contact with a real life female was last week at the hotel when Jailbait Alex swished past me on her way to serving dessert. Such is my current drought that this brief brush of her pert arse against my crotch will no doubt keep me in masturbation fantasies for a fortnight. The thing is, it's not like I couldn't get it if I really wanted it. Previous experience shows that you can almost always get a shag if your standards are low enough. Truth be told, it's not the women which are enforcing my current sex embargo. It's me. I can't be bothered. I haven't lost interest in sex, I'm just really fed up with looking for more and coming up with even less.

I'm not alone in this situation either. The foul smelling collection of unwashed clothes and emaciated sweaty flesh sometimes referred to as Rob has been in residence on our sofa ever since that fateful night he witnessed his ex, Mutton Jane, getting fingered by some townie tosser on her very own doorstep. He seems incapable of dealing with the loss of this woman despite the fact that they were barely anything more than fuck buddies. He claims to have loved her but we've heard that before from Rob, sometimes about women he's known for less than a week and on one occasion after speaking to a total stranger in the pub for five minutes. He's suffered on numerous occasions after having his clutches (often physically) loosened from some object of his obsession but this is the hardest he's ever fallen. It's as though all the break-ups and meaningless experiences have added up to this. Jane is his final straw and the fact that she's such a grotty one just compounds the misery.

Before slipping into his current waking coma of self-loathing and non-bathing, he did give me one insightful statement: "All the women I go for are damaged goods...It's like, that's all I deserve." Without realising it, Rob has hit the nail on the head. For whatever twisted reason it is which prevents him from being the person he could be, deep down I think he doesn't believe he is worth enough to deserve to find true love with a sane person. Until he does, he's destined to fall for mental old slappers like Jane.

As well as the obvious effect having a damaged tramp living on your sofa can have on one's living arrangements, the situation is prompting other unpleasant consequences. One rancid entity has usurped another and the previous incumbent is more than a little pissed off. Mr. Sifter hates Rob at the best of times but now he's claimed the sofa as his own, the cat has taken his animosity to new heights. He's worked it out that he can't out-stink Rob or maim him with the one good tooth he has so he's gone back to shitting under my bed, a habit I thought we'd got over after our peace was made. Apparently Mr. Sifter blames me for his sofa crisis, which is a tad unfair, and he believes that the best way to get Rob evicted is to target those with the power to do so, namely me. The ginger tom's reasoning appears to be that diminishing my resolve through a soiling campaign will ultimately be more successful than repeatedly reversing onto Rob with a soggy arse. However, for the time being at least, he's out of luck. Despite the biological warfare being waged under my bed, I have been unable to bring myself to throw Rob out. I'm not the only one of course. Ellis is equally weak but he has somehow managed to escape Mr. Sifter's shitting campaign. Mine is the only room which keeps getting carpet bombed. The cat obviously sees me as the human to deal with in these situations.

Despite the accumulating nastiness - both feline and human - Rob stays. He looks too pathetic to evict; whimpering in emotional torment in the living room most of every day - his attendance record at college is on life support - and spending his nights either borrowing money to buy cheap, yet strong alcohol before returning to the sofa or going to hang around behind the bins at the back of Jane's apartment block. I know he doesn't want her back, he just doesn't know what to do without her. He wants something to connect with but - just the same as me - I think he's tired of trying and failing to reach people. Deep down he just can't be arsed with all the rejection. Maybe that's why I can't throw him out. I feel and understand his pain. Pouring yourself completely into someone can be hugely damaging, especially when they pull the plug and you feel yourself being sucked down the drain.

That's why I'm thinking that we've been concentrating on the wrong part of what's important, what it actually means to be Lads. If this culture is all to do with remembering what it is to be boys while living as men, then we've forgotten the most basic ingredient: the gang. The gang is the embodiment of male togetherness at all ages and while we've been a group of friends for a while now, we've only used that as a launch pad for the pursuit of sex. We've been a pack, not a gang. The pack hunts together but usually, in our case at least, the kill is made individually and the carcass enjoyed in private and defended ferociously. What we need is a new pursuit which brings us together and makes us stronger, giving us a connection to depend upon. Women come and go but mates remain. Now the women have come and gone, all we have left is each other. We've been pursuing the Lad thing but have neglected 'the lads'. What we need is something to rally behind, something other than the endless quest to get laid.

Now college is over for the summer and I've no significant (or even insignificant) other to consider, I've been dedicating a lot of time - and hash - to figuring out what our next step should be and I've identified exactly what we as a gang should be embracing. Behind the "girls, goals and go on my son!" is a soundtrack which, until now, has just been the background music to the nights spent boozing and birding. It's been an undercurrent to the scene but things are about to change, I can feel it and others can too. The mood is changing. The magazines are talking about a new phenomenon. They're calling it Britpop. The musical wave which has been gathering strength for the past two years is charging towards the land and is preparing to sweep everything and everyone before it. The US grunge invasion has been in full retreat since Cobain died last year, and the home-grown insurgency is now ready to become a full-blown revolution. It's time to take the island back and this is exactly what we should be a part of.

"So, you're not going to shag birds anymore and just listen to music?" McKinley incredulously asks as service comes to an end for another evening. "Sounds a bit fucking Radio Four, big man."

"Look, I'm just sick of always having the pressure of getting a girl into bed as the ultimate target for everything we do," I explain. "I just want to have a laugh with the lads. I've checked out the Glastonbury line-up for this year and it's full of all the great bands we love...Oasis, the Stone Roses, the Charlatans...We can get utterly shit-faced and get out of order to some really loud music."

"Just for a change." McKinley watches Kate stomp in and dump a load of dirty plates on the child-slave on washing duty before giving her a lecherous wink and a waggle of the tongue. She tuts at him and blushes on her way out of the kitchen. "If I find a saucy little tart like her on the campsite, can I still get her tits out?"

"It's not off the menu, geezer..." I tell him. "It's just not going to be the main course."

Of course, just because Rob and I are currently swearing off women (actually, Rob hasn't exactly confirmed this, he's barely said anything coherent in over two weeks) it doesn't mean that this male bonding exercise fits in with everyone's situation.

"How long will we be away?" Ellis asks as he takes advantage of one of the rare moments when Rob swaps the sofa for the toilet to tidy the living room and allow actual oxygen into the place. Mr. Sifter races in, bounds onto the gloriously free space and does three rapid circles before settling down in the dip created by Rob's permanent arse.

"The festival lasts for three days, and we can probably tack one day on at each end for travel," I reply through a haze of air freshener. "Five days?"

Ellis pulls air in over his teeth in the time-honoured way of tradesmen faced with an inadequate quotation of time or money. "That could be a bit difficult, man. Things with Monica are a little delicate right now. Me taking off with the boys for five days might not go down too well."

What's the worst she can do? Fuck you in the arse with a big black rubber dildo? Oh, been there, done that...bought the Anusol. "So what's the problem?"

"The C-word," Ellis confides. "She's been mentioning it a lot recently. It makes me nervous." Ellis can't actually bring himself to call it 'commitment' hence the reference to the C-word. When he first started using this code a month back, everyone thought he had a problem with the vulgar name for the female genitalia. McKinley told him not to be such a sensitive C-word and get over it. Only then did he admit his fear of commitment. Commitment to Ellis is all wedding invites, booked churches and honeymoons in Mauritius. Considering he's going out with a recent divorcee, I'm pretty sure the MC is looking for something a little less extreme and permanent. I've told him so on a number of occasions when this has come up but he still can't see the difference between embracing the R-word (another impediment revolving around Relationship, rather than Rimming or Rectal probing) and walking down the aisle.

"Come on, Ellis. Five days. You have the weekend with her, we take off to Glasto, and then you're back to pick her up from work on Monday afternoon. Bunch of flowers, back to her place, Bob's yer auntie's live-in lover."

He stops sweeping a speculative broom under Rob's current seat of residence and sits up on his knees. He pauses in thought as the sound of the toilet flushing alerts us to the imminent return of our unsavoury house guest. "You're right. If she wants the C-word...at some point...then she's going to have to respect me. I'm there with bells on, geezer. Book me a ticket." He stoops to scythe a final arc under the sofa as Rob slouches back in. This last sweep unearths a hidden health hazard. "Jesus, Rob..." A pair of previously white designer briefs are flung out into the room on the end of the broom. The camouflage pattern on the rear and gusset were certainly not put there by either Dolce or Gabbana. "That's it. Get back in the bathroom and have a shower. Then get yourself on the bus and go home. I'll even give you the fucking fare!"

Rob blinks in the face of this tirade of abuse. It shocks him into speaking coherently for the first time in three days. "I can't go home. I'm not ready." Ellis picks up the soiled underwear on the end of his broom and storms out, heading towards the back door and the garden. "Danny, geezer, you know the score, right? I can't heal there. My mum and dad are rowing and it's not helpful."

"Rob, mate, you have to sort it out. Get yourself cleaned up and off home for a couple of days to give us a break, okay?" Rob looks defeated. "Look, we're planning a trip to Glastonbury, how about we chip in and shout you a ticket? Just the lads..."

Rob thinks for a moment. "Can I come back in a few days?" He goes to sit down again but Mr. Sifter hisses and then lets out a worryingly bubbly fart, making his feelings on the matter very clear.

"Yeah, but there'll be no more sleeping on the sofa," I say, hoping my compromise will also appease the cat. "You'll have to go home every night." Rob nods sullenly. Suddenly, through the open window, the sound of a muffled *woof* can be heard. Rob and I look at each other and head for the back door. Ellis is standing over Rob's underwear which is currently burning with a strange green flame. He looks up from the burning pants and waves a can of lighter fluid at Rob in a threatening manner.

"Anything else you've infested is going the same way. Got it?"

I hope the sofa isn't next on his list. The place is rented with the furniture included.

After being wrestled into making a contribution to Rob's ticket on the condition that everyone has to take his own tent (with Filthy Rob consigned to a bio-hazard containment igloo), the Scotsman signs on for "Four Go Mad at Glastonbury" this summer. He dusts off his credit card and gets on the phone as I sit in one of his battered leather armchairs and smoke a joint. Glastonbury 1995 - fucking magic. The plan is already flowering in my mind along with the mellow high. My dad has already reluctantly agreed to lend me one of his most expendable work vans so the transport is sorted. We'll have to get an order in on time with one of our various contacts to ensure we have as much gear as possible for the journey down there and to see us through the whole five days. I'm sure there won't be a lack of drugs on site but it's better to be safe than sober. I see us leaving the city on the Thursday morning, making it to Somerset by late afternoon, setting up camp before sundown and then heading off on a preliminary sortie around the grounds. Both the Scotsman and I have a hunger for hallucinogenics and previous experience of festival dealers tells me that if you buy early, you're less likely to be sold a dud. Even if someone sells you plain blotting paper on the Thursday night, you have the whole of Friday to locate some proper acid by the time the main band headlines that night.

And what a Friday! The return of Oasis. If ever there was any evidence needed that the music of our generation was moving into its ascendancy at lightning speed, then that evidence would be Oasis as headliners on the Pyramid Stage on the Friday night of the 25th Anniversary Glastonbury Festival. A year ago, they played an afternoon slot on the NME Stage. Now, their star has risen so fast and high that they're rated as one of the three top bands at the festival. *Definitely Maybe* has been one of the albums of the past year and Oasis are ready to eclipse that in the coming months with their second album. The chances are high that their Glasto slot will be used to showcase the coming anthems of 1995 and beyond. And we will be down the front tripping our bollocks off to them.

Still not enough evidence of the resurgent greatness of British music? How about the Second Coming of the Stone Roses then? After sleeping off the LSD in the morning, we'll be back up for some antics around the other stages by mid-afternoon. Maybe some heavy drinking and pot smoking for These Animal Men, or maybe a crafty E and a workout in the dance tent. All of which will just be a warm-up for the Saturday evening of adoration. Combined with some well-meant abuse from McKinley (a lot of "big poof", "queer bastard" and "sad fucker" despite the fact that he had already agreed to come), the appearance of the Stone Roses was the main reason for Ellis deciding to leave Monica behind for five days of larging it with the Lads. After initially agreeing, however, he wavered for an evening after spending a good two hours 'debating' with his bird over the coming trip. My secret weapon was always going to be the Roses, knowing Ellis to be a major fan. It worked. The wavering stopped and he committed to becoming a witness to the resurrection. As a result, come the Saturday night, we will be among the most evangelical of the congregation as the Stone Roses make their triumphant ascension.

Things never go as smoothly as planned, of course - especially when we're the ones doing the planning. During the two months between the Scotsman securing the tickets and the day of departure, Rob goes mental, then missing and Ellis and MC Steak Hammer split up. Twice.

Rob was on the road to recovery until Mutton Jane the nightmare hag decided to pay him an unexpected visit sometime after he was allowed back into the parental home. The coming Glastonbury trip had given him something to look forward to and focus his mind on. The idea that there was more to life than the eternal search for The One had eased his crippling neurosis and convinced him that time would in fact heal, just as all the clichéd advice claimed it would. Time, however, had also given the heinous Jane time to realise that she was unlikely to ever find a more hopelessly devoted moron to keep her aging old bag of bones warm at night. After the Phantom Fingerer had had his five minutes of playing hide the sausage with her withered old vadge, Jane came looking for Rob's last shred of self-esteem. Armed with a cuddly Narla from the local Disney store and a bottle of gin, the sanity vampire somehow managed to convince Rob that she had made a huge mistake and that he was going to be her Simba forever.

Meanwhile, the C-word was proving to be a real T-bone of contention in the Steak Hammer household. Ellis would set out for Monica's convinced that a romantic night was on the cards, only to storm back home three hours later to drag me down the pub to complain about the "mental shackles" she was forcing him to wear. (On one occasion, there were *actual* shackles for him to wear but that's a different story and one which, given the variety of their sex life, I don't feel I am prepared to go into.) This floating out/storming home scenario went on for three weeks until there was no more floating out and only staying home/drinking heavily. That was the first time they broke up. A month later, they were back together after a round of peace talks - only for a return to hostilities and a second rift a week later.

If all this wasn't enough to throw the coming legendary excursion into doubt, John Squire managed to dislocate his shoulder in a mountain bike accident and as a result of the guitarist's injuries, the Stone Roses were forced to pull out. Even the announcement that Pulp had stepped in to save the day failed to prevent another rather large cloud joining the growing storm over our Glasto expedition.

A week to go before the four of us are supposed to leave for the Glastonbury festival and Rob has not been seen since Jane left him for the new, young, sexy (and female!) secretary at work a fortnight ago. Elsewhere, Ellis and the MC are tentatively back together, seeing how things go, as they say, putting his involvement in the upcoming festivities in jeopardy again. I, meanwhile, have stopped giving a fuck about the pair of them. McKinley is still game for Glasto and I'm going even if I have to walk there on my own.

While all this relationship aggravation has been going on, I've been enjoying the lack of pressure in my own non-sex life. Drinking binges have been even more fun than usual (for me at least - Ellis, when he has been motivated enough to attend, has been morose at best), Warehouse nights have been even more about the music as the Glasto excitement intensifies, and there's been an increase in the togetherness of the lads - minus Rob, of course, who is missing, presumed unwashed. Ellis has found comfort and strength in the company of the Scotsman and myself during his recent trials while McKinley, experiencing one of the longer periods of enforced separation from his missus, has been a regular visitor at the house and a willing host at his own. He's even toned down the perving of late but I think this is less to do with our renewed commitment to the gang than the increased private yearning he has for his long-distance lover. I'm no way advocating a permanently celibate life for myself but right now, I feel that I finally have my priorities straight and I feel happier for it. Mates first, music second, drug abuse third (or maybe that's joint second, pun unintended). Women don't even feature in the top five at the moment. You've still got to make room for football and drinking after all.

After Ellis finally recommits to the trip, Rob eventually resurfaces a day before we're due to leave, acting as though nothing untoward has happened and looking the smartest I've ever seen him.

"Alright Danny? Ready for the off, are we?"

"Where the fuck have you been?" I ask, barring his way on the threshold out of incredulous anger. "We were about ready to sell your ticket. No-one has heard from you in nearly three weeks. Your old man has been round twice looking for you. He even put out a request for information about you over the PA in Pulse the other night." The recollection of the DJ making one of those announcements you get in department stores when a kid has been lost brings a smile to my face. Rob reads this a sign of thawing relations. He reads it wrong and tries to come in. I stand firm. "Hang on, you're not coming in until you tell me what's been going on."

Rob look sheepish. "I met someone."

This time the change in my expression does represent a true lightening of the mood. For the past month, I was concerned that my wayward friend had finally done himself in over some waste-of-space minger he met at a local meat market. This news that he has actually been spending time with someone other than Mutton Jane and looks the more happy and balanced for it fills me with relief, and no little amount of hope. "You're a dark horse," I grin. "When did this happen?"

"I'll fill you in over a cup of tea?" Rob presents this as a question because, despite my suddenly more relaxed demeanour, I'm still standing in his way, giving mixed signals over whether he's welcome or not. I finally clarify the situation.

"I'll get some cash and you can tell me over a pint."

The Castle's beer garden is expansive but for some reason seating space is at a premium on this Wednesday lunchtime. Maybe it's the June sun which is warm and bright, and the overwhelming feeling that summer has settled in for the duration. Kids play on the plastic climbing frame in one corner as assorted parents and friends enjoy their pub lunches and halves of ale nearby. The locals who normally inhabit the dark corners of the bar for most of the year are crowded round a long wooden table, wearing the same expressions they would have on a cold November evening. Rob and I have a small table for four to ourselves in the far corner. Once we're settled and have toasted Rob's return, he starts filling in the blanks.

"Well, you know about what happened with that fucking Jane bitch, right? She decided she wanted to be a lesbian this time and dumped me for this bimbo receptionist at her office. And yes, I did try and get a threesome set up before she jacked me in and she wasn't up for it. Neither of them were, actually. Anyway, then I met this bloke…"

"Bloke?" The surprise in my voice gives away the conclusion I've jumped to.

"This isn't a sex thing. You were right. I have been concentrating on the wrong things and getting my priorities all arse about face. I wasn't going to let that horrible wench ruin me so I after a couple of days of getting myself straight, I was on my way round to yours when I bumped into this bloke Aiden Craske, an old friend of my brother. Anyway, he was in the city with a travelling theatre group from back home and we just hung out for a couple of weeks. It was just nice to hear familiar accents…It kinda reminded me of a time before here, you know?"

A time before here. The reason *I'm* here is because the time before *this* is something I want to forget. I realise that this is not the case for Rob. I know he didn't have a choice about moving here. His parents' restaurant went bankrupt and he ended up here as part of the family deal when they moved job lot to the city to start again. Many of Rob's ends were left loose and the enforced relocation severed many bonds, creating new resentments in a home already riven by accusations and blame. Knowing some of the background really helps in understanding why Rob is such a basket case. "So are we finished with worrying about you and the lovely Jane?"

"I think so."

"Good. So Simba will be joining us on our rock'n'roll'n'drugs binge after all?"

"Fuck off."

"Glad to hear it."

After co-pilot McKinley gets too stoned too quickly and misses our motorway exit, leaving us to circumnavigate the North Circular at a snail's pace in blazing summer sun, we eventually escape London's tractor beam ring road and make good time flying through the southwest countryside. After negotiating checkpoints of stressed-out stewards and creeping past vans full of short-tempered and over-heated constables in the leafy lanes leading to the site, we slowly pull onto an already congested field of cars as the afternoon sun begins to wane over Worthy Farm. From our eventual resting place in the car park, the 1995 Glastonbury Festival looks more like the gasoline compound in *Mad Max II*, minus the flame throwers and crossbows. Far from being a welcoming sight for all those who have travelled from near and far to embrace the brotherhood of man in a celebration of love and music, the entrance would look only more ominous if it had a sign hanging on it which read 'Abandon hope all ye who enter here.' From left to right of the gate, as far as the eye can see, is a high, grey steel barrier. Apparently, this year's security has been heightened to prevent an expected illegal invasion of non-paying travellers gate (or should it be fence?) -crashing the festival.

"They should have just hung bars of soap all around the place," McKinley quips as we filter through even more checkpoints. Once wristbanded and through the final turnstile we finally take in our first view of the festival site from within. Rolling fields bend away in every direction, full of stalls, vans, tents and people of all colour, creed and persuasion. Circus freaks appear from nowhere breathing fire or looming down on us from vertiginous stilts as we haul our gear, open-mouthed, towards the main field through the wandering masses. We have already decided to pitch camp on the hill overlooking the main Pyramid stage as to make the most of every sight and sound from the throbbing heart of the site and thankfully, due to the enormity of the festival, the thousands of people who are already here have been swallowed up by the various camping fields around the inner circle, leaving the hillside of our choice barely touched. We lug the camping gear about two-thirds of the way up the hill and set up our small village of four tents in a wagon circle, securing the perimeter with a handy rope left behind in the van by one of my dad's labourers. We're travelling light and only have with us what we can afford to lose should we get robbed so we're sorted and back down the hill in no time.

Sitting on a picnic bench in an eating area surrounded by open circus tents, we take stock. "Pretty surreal, huh?" I offer, as a group of semi-naked, green painted water nymphs walk past eating cartons of Chinese food.

"Maybe we don't need any acid after all," adds Ellis, who's bent over a half-rolled joint.

"Don't be silly, wee man. We always need some acid."

"Need some acid?" a voice chips in. "Got some nice California Sunrises. Just five quid a tab." The owner of the voice makes himself comfortable on the corner of the bench and looks hopefully from one face to the next. The ethnic threads and dreadlocks label him as a crusty but his demeanour suggests he could possibly be a trustworthy sort. Casually-dressed, wide-boy dealers are often on the scam while hippies tend to be the real deal - most of the time. McKinley eyes him with suspicion. He's not a fan of hippies.

"Five quid's a bit steep. We'll take four for three quid a pop."

"Four quid."

"Three-fifty."

The hippie hesitates. "Deal." He spits on his hand and offers it to the Scotsman.

"Nah, you're alright." McKinley's stony glare withers the hand. "Let's see the gear then." The hippie furtively takes out a small, zip-lock bag from a pouch on his belt and lays it on the table for inspection. The tabs are pre-cut and have perforated edges, a good sign that they're not just bits of cut-up fag packets. Each has a golden sun embedded in it. McKinley looks from the tabs to the hippie and back again before handing over fifteen quid. "Keep the change."

"Nice doing business with you, geezers. Have a good 'un." With that, the hippie hops off the bench and melts into the crowd.

"That was easy," says Rob.

"Aye," says the Scotsman. "A bit too easy. Keep your eyes open for anyone else selling tabs. We should get some back-ups in just in case."

No-one gets to find out whether the California Sunrises (or the back-up microdots we bought on the way back up the hill after a few beers) are the real thing until Friday morning. I wake up first and crawl out into blinding sunlight. Our little village has been engulfed by a city which has sprung up overnight, turning our enclave into just another suburb of a sprawling tent metropolis. I stand and blink at the settlement which stretches down the hill before us and back up to the summit behind us; a forest of flags flutters lazily in the warm breeze, while fellow early risers surface and stretch and yawn in encampments the length and breadth of the field. A long-haired bloke tying his hair back under a Pink Floyd flag nearby raises his hand in greeting. I wave back. Glastonbury 1995. Let's have it.

By the time I've crapped in the relatively-typhoid free toilets at the bottom of the hill and made my way back with four recyclable cups of extremely strong Trade Fair coffee, the others have crawled from their pits. The Scotsman is toking on a large reefer while Ellis brushes his teeth, gobbing foam and mineral water down the side of Rob's tent as he rinses. Rob doesn't notice. He's too busy directing his bare six-pack and pecs in the direction of a nearby camp of disinterested girls.

"Oi, Adonis. None of that," I say, striding over the rope perimeter and handing out cups. "This is a Lads event. No sex. Drugs, booze and rock'n'roll only, remember?"

"Speaking of which," McKinley wheezes before passing me the joint in exchange for a coffee. "When are we going to try this acid?"

"I reckon we should neck one now," says Ellis, securing his shades and breathing in the aroma of Arabica beans. "If it's crap, we'll drop the microdot. If that's crap too, we'll have time to get some more before the 'Sis come on."

"If they're good, though, then we'll be coming down before they're on stage," I muse.

"Then we'll drop the others."

"I reckon two of us should do the dots, the other two do the Sunrises. Then we'll know for sure," the Scotsman proposes. Ellis and I nod in agreement while Rob continues to preen, unaware of the discussion taking place. "Or one of us could have a dot," says McKinley, pointing at Rob, "and we have the others?" This is even more to our liking. Microdots are notoriously unpredictable. It's always best to try them on a lab rat first.

"Open wide, Robert." Ellis hits the target first time as Rob turns round in surprise and gets a microdot in the mouth.

"What was that?"

"We're dropping the tabs and then going for a wander," I say, taking receipt of a Sunrise.

"You gave me acid?" Rob looks freaked. "I've never done LSD before."

McKinley, Ellis and myself exchange concerned glances. "You said you had," says Ellis.

"Yeah, well I haven't," Rob confesses.

"Well, you have now," says McKinley and swallows his own tab.

"This should be interesting," I say, ducking into my tent for shirt and sunglasses.

As it turns out, both the California Sunrises and the microdots work just fine, depending on your perspective, of course. I'm enjoying a few early rolling waves of psychedelic colour when Rob grabs my arm as I'm waiting in line for some bottles of water.

"What's fucking going on, Danny? Where are the others? Why is it just you and me?"

I look over at Ellis and McKinley who are sat on the ground nearby, giggling over a pair of dwarves dressed as a bride and groom. "They're right over there, man. It's cool. It's all good."

"You're going to leave me, aren't you? You've planned to meet up with them later once you've ditched me."

Uh oh. If acid greases the wheels of the subconscious and opens up doors into the unknown corners of the mind, the mind in question should be as settled as possible before allowing such powerful stuff to work its magic. Unfortunately, we didn't have time for a decade's worth of expensive therapy before giving Rob his first trip. As a result, a whole army of insecurities and issues are on the verge of being unleashed in a lysergic nightmare that could consume us all. I'm not equipped to deal with this. We need an expert. I whistle over at Ellis and McKinley and summon the Scotsman as Rob's increasingly terrified gaze flickers from face to face. "Houston, we have a problem." I nod over at Rob and McKinley spots the danger signs.

"Fucking hell."

Rob starts to pant and his eyes bulge. McKinley, in the early stages of his own trip, takes a deep breath and leads Rob out of the queue on rubbery legs and sits him on the grass. Rob starts blathering and pointing at me, which isn't helping with the balance of my own sanity, but he begins to visibly chill as the Scotsman starts to talk him down. Ellis wanders over from a daydream.

"What's going on?" he asks.

"Rob's having a bad one."

"Nice."

McKinley lays a reassuring hand on Rob's arm before coming back over. "He's off his fucking tits, man. He thinks you hate him and want to dump him here. I'm going to have to baby-sit him or fuck knows what's going to happen."

"But what about the bands this afternoon?"

McKinley sways slightly and takes a couple of deep breaths as his own acid tide washes over him. "I'll take him around," he eventually replies with a thick tongue. "Let's meet at the tents at six. Things should be better by then." He hopes. With that, the Scotsman takes control of the extremely delicate Rob situation and leads the stricken acid casualty calmly into the crowds. Talk about the blind leading the blind...

"So, what should we do?" asks Ellis, wide of eye and bushy of tail.

I shake off the recent weirdness to find that I'm actually really quite fucking high. "Let's have some, matey."

It would be fair to say that in terms of having some, we take everything Glastonbury has to offer and then go back for seconds. By the time we stumble out of the steaming masses to reconvene at the tent, Ellis and I have seen purple and pink waves of cosmic light stream from the Ash drum kit, watched Rick Witter of Shed Seven glow, sparkle and levitate like Jesus at the ascension, and physically throbbed in spiritual synergy with the boys from Dodgy. The blazing sun of the day turns to a hazy dusk as we sit in our tent circle floating uneasily on the first sloshing waves of the comedown. Our babbling has calmed to a combination of almost normal conversation and reassuring deep breaths by the time McKinley and Rob weave their way home. Rob looks he's been through a mangle but appears placid and centred while McKinley just looks knackered. Somehow, at some point during its own psychedelic odyssey, the Scotsman's altered mind showed some forethought and provided him with enough clarity to buy some amphetamines. Instead of crashing and burning, we're now going to be either speeding away from the scene of a potential accident or accelerating straight into another brick wall, depending on your outlook. Right now, the future is gathering below us. No-one can see further than Oasis headlining the main stage tonight. So we snort our lines, neck more tabs and take a slow chemical stroll through the creeping darkness towards the warm spotlights and crash barriers.

The California Sunrise is much more to Rob's liking. When Liam Gallagher rolls onto stage and waves his tambourine in his general direction, Rob's face lights up beatifically. His eyes expand to drink in the scene and all its swirling, pulsing euphoria. The rest of us are feeling the intensity of the microdot trip which nearly sent Rob over the edge and when the band settles into a rolling jam, the music sends wave after wave of tremors through my body. The wisdom of getting even more fucked up and positioning ourselves in the middle of the mosh pit directly centre stage is immediately called into question as the intro to 'Acquiesce' cranks out. The shivers and nervous anticipation almost blow my head off. But that's nothing. Seconds pass, the guitars go into overdrive and then the whole place kicks off. Its bedlam! Without even making the conscious decision to do so, I'm jumping up and down, forced from the earth and back again by the motion of the bodies around me. I frantically search for the others and see Ellis frozen in a suspended moment of utter surprise, his bug-eyed skull caught in freeze-framed shock by a camera-flash strobe. The Scotsman grabs my shoulder and I manage to turn. His expression is a mixture of manic excitement and deep-rooted fear and he's laughing like a lunatic in my face. Somewhere to his right, Rob is having a religious experience; his arms stretched to the heavens, his palms splayed, his eyes tightly shut, his mouth straining open in a drowned-out rapturous scream.

Everything stops making sense until Liam makes a dedication to the Stone Roses: "This one's for our mates who can't be here coz one of 'em can't ride a bike...but never mind...'Supersonic' for the lads." As one, the four us come together to form a sweaty, foaming nucleus as the drums signal more madness to follow. 'Supersonic' for the Lads. Not the Roses - the Lads. This is for us. For all of us. This is why we're here. This is why we're together. Some unexplainable energy lifts us out of our lives at the moment Noel's guitar sends its swaggering chords out into the Somerset air and keeps us removed from all fear and doubt for over an hour until Liam's farewell: "Have a good one...goodbye...see yer later!" Then they're gone but the emotion remains. We're left to wander the site that never sleeps for eternity, or so it seems, smiling and cackling at the sights and sounds of people enjoying hedonistic freedom. Eventually, as a cold sun creeps over the surrounding hills, spreading weak light over the misty fields, we trudge back with unwanted food and an even less desired latent sickness. It's Saturday and today we'll do it all again.

I wake up around midday feeling like I spent the previous night eating caustic lime while a circus strongman hammered a tent spike through my left eye. I'd puke but there's nothing inside me and I'm scared that if I did, my head would split in two. I retch at the rancid heat of the tent, clutch my pounding skull and drag my carcass to the opening to gasp for air and/or die. As my eyes cross and waver in and out of focus, I can make out the Scotsman's decomposing corpse oozing out of the opposite igloo, arse first. Squinting left and right, I locate the others. A half-naked Rob (top half, thank God) is pouring a bottle of mineral water over his head while a grinning Ellis thrusts a cup of coffee in my face.

"Afternoon."

I free my furry tongue from the roof of my cotton mouth. "You're chirpy," I rasp.

"I'm off my face again. I highly recommend it."

I slither into the world and take the coffee. Life, if you can describe it as such, is all around. I try and find any evidence of my own. No luck as yet. "What are you on?"

"Just weed. Guess who I saw at the coffee stand? Fucking Robbie Williams."

"Bollocks. You're high."

"Bleached Barnet, fat arse, tracksuit...Fucking Robbie Williams, man!"

"Did you call him a cunt?" The Scotsman pipes up, proving reports of his death to be greatly exaggerated.

"No, actually," replies Ellis slowly, considering this. "That was a missed opportunity." He stands from his crouching position and kicks McKinley in the leg. "Come on, get it together." The Scotsman farts his displeasure. "Someone said Robbie was on stage with Oasis last night. How fucked up is that?"

"You know we probably weren't the only ones tripping, right?" I say after forcing down a mouthful of bitter, tar-black coffee. "What no milk?"

"It's like a refugee camp down there, man. We're already running out of stuff. And don't bother taking a shit today...or for the rest of the weekend for that matter. It's foul down there. Full of bangers and mash. I saw a bunch of crusties turn one Porta-loo over with some poor fucker inside. He climbed out covered in the crap of a thousand people looking like the *Creature from the Black Lagoon*. Seriously dodgy goings-on in this place, geezers."

I retch again at the thought and the toxic coffee mixes with some unexpected bile. "What's new, Rob?" I ask.

Rob rubs his hair with a t-shirt and turns his face to the sun, reliving last night's revelations behind his closed eyes. "I was off the planet last night. There was a lot of weird stuff going on but, I have to say, everything today seems in order. More than it has any right to be actually. Feels like some things clicked into place, like I was moved into a totally new space."

That's deep. I didn't expect that. "What about you, Jockstrap?"

"Kill me now," McKinley moans as another, slightly more liquid fart escapes.

"I'd get yourself some Pampers, geezer," I suggest. "We've got another big day ahead of us."

After the all-out war of Friday and a night spent in the trenches, we wisely choose to pick our battles on the Saturday. The main objective is surviving Pulp in the headline slot so the majority of the day is spent lazing in the sun on the sidelines as the day's line-up passes before our bloodshot eyes. McKinley is still suffering and sleeps through most of the afternoon on the verges of the ebbing and flowing crowds, missing Jeff Buckley and most of the Boo Radleys set on the main stage before we drag him to the acoustic stage. Rob, meanwhile, wanders off to check out the dance tent on his own leaving Ellis and I sitting cross-legged (and the Scotsman once again prone) in front of Billy Bragg. My house mate's previously euphoric high has settled into a deeper level of stoned and he looks pensive as he pulls on a joint.

"When you were with Anna," he says out of the haze, "how long was it before you realised you were a proper couple?"

I think for a moment as I adapt to the switch from day-dreaming and talking shite about the bands to deep conversation. "It never felt like we were a couple while we were getting to know each other," I finally reply, accepting the reefer. "There was so much other stuff going on. I was working and she was studying. Each day we just discovered new things about each other. Time just passed in each other's company. We were just being together." I realise two things very quickly; that Ellis has packed this joint with very strong grass and that, in my compromised state of reminiscence, I've failed to answer Ellis' question - both of which contribute to why he seems slightly thrown for a moment before asking it again.

"So when did you realise?"

"I suppose it was when Anna started talking about going to university," I slowly reply, trying to relive moments from our last months together in my current stoned fog. "It had been ticking along on an even keel until then. Suddenly the dynamic was changing and I had to look outside the bubble. I started thinking about what was supposed to happen next and realised that I'd had this girlfriend for nearly three years. Three years! It was quite a shock. I mean, we weren't teenagers anymore by then. Three years in an adult relationship and you're almost hitched." I see Ellis retreat into himself a little further, probably out of fear. I didn't think that last statement through, given his unease at the moment with Steak Hammer's increasing demands for him to embrace the C-word. "But even though it had been three years, we still didn't consider it to be serious." I quickly add, throwing him a mental rope to hang onto while lying through my teeth. I don't add that in my loved-up state before the break-up, I'd considered asking Anna to marry me.

Thank fuck she dumped me before I went that far over the line. "It was fine as it was, just being together...or so I thought."

"I've never had a...thing...last for more than two days let alone two months," Ellis admits, claiming back the joint. "Is she right to want the C-word from me? Am I in the R-word?"

"Mate, the fact that you've been with her for two months shows a real level of the C-word, by your standards. Actions speak louder than words, fella. Just keep on keeping it on. That's if you want to." Ellis nods slowly in a non-committal way. His eyes glaze over and he goes back to processing his thoughts and emotions. He shouldn't have to say anything to her. He's showing everyone what he wants by still being with her. Hopefully he'll now realise this. The harder job will be convincing Monica. She needs to realise that it's a big fucking deal that he hasn't made a run for the hills yet.

Speaking of which...

"I know stuff gets nicked at festivals but this is taking the piss." I'm standing open-mouthed (which helps when you're speaking in outraged shock) with the Scotsman and Ellis by our tent circle...which is now a tent triangle. Rob's igloo is missing. Ellis strides over the currently (and obviously formerly) useless rope barrier to survey the apparent crime scene.

"Hang on..." He bends down between his and McKinley's tents and comes back up holding a crumpled note which has been stuck to the side with chewing gum. He reads the note and then kicks what he thinks is an empty beer can into the surrounding tents. It's not empty. Luckily the now soaking wet neighbouring tepee is. He then hands the note to me in disgust.

"Don't tell me...the mad bastard's topped himself," says the Scotsman.

"Worse than that," Ellis sneers. "He's moved to Wales." I read the explanation for the absence of Rob and his tent out loud:

Boys,

Gone to stay with my brother Brian in Snowdonia to sort my head out. That acid really got me thinking. I need some distance from the city and our routines so I can figure out what I want. I'll be back for the start of term. Happy shagging.

Rob.

And then there were three.

By the time Pulp arrive on stage, any latent disappointment over the no-show by the Stone Roses has dissipated from a capacity crowd eager to see what Jarvis Cocker & Co. are really made of. Even the hard-nosed Roses fans are bowled over as Pulp grab Glastonbury by the scruff of the neck and set about blowing everyone away, myself included. When they play 'Sorted for E's & Wizz', the victory is in the bag. "Oh is this the way they say the future's meant to feel?" asks Jarvis Cocker. "Or just 20,000 people standing in a field." It's more like 100,000, Jarv, but we'll let you off. "And I don't quite understand just what this feeling is...But that's okay cos we're all sorted out for E's and wizz." Nothing wins over a crowd faster than a song about drugs when everyone is off their tits. It doesn't matter if it's a cynical statement of futility because no-one knows and no-one cares. It's okay coz we're all sorted out for E's and wizz...and acid...and dope...and lager. Following that up with the life-affirming 'Disco 2000', the atmosphere changes from pleasantly surprised to joyfully hedonistic. Ellis, McKinley and I have shed our preconceptions along with the afternoon's comedown sickness and are now lurching like epileptic puppets at the end of Cocker's spindly fingers, as he bends his newly converted followers to his will and leads them into council house bedrooms and kitchen sink affairs. With the festival in the palms of their hands, Pulp unclench to deliver a confident and perversely-charged performance which turns songs into anthems and an also-ran band into Britpop legends. By the time they hit us with the double-whammy of 'Babies' and 'Common People', many of the sweating, gurning masses have forgotten about the *Second Coming*. Pulp are a *Different Class*.

Only as the set comes to a close and the creepy neurosis of 'I Spy' rolls over our heads do I spare a thought for Rob. You missed a truly magical moment here tonight, geezer. You'll never know what you gave up. You may have headed for the hills but we made it to higher ground.

The three of us spent a good hour slagging Rob off in the wake of his departure. We accused him of being a lightweight, a fucking let-down and a coward. Now, as we walk away from the dying strains of Pulp's ultimate triumph amid a sea of happy faces, I begin to see that we may have got only two out of three right. Rob can't take the pace, not just of something like Glastonbury but the times he's living in. He strives to be part of it, part of the movement, part of the gang but there are too many contradictions between the life he lives and the life he wants. That's why he regularly crumbles. That's why he can be so delicate. That's why he can't be relied upon. But a coward? No. We got that one wrong. I won't say this to Ellis. I won't even say this to McKinley. But I think Rob shows more bravery than any of us. No-one shows how they really are as often as Rob. We see this as weakness and all part of the image we have of him as the poor relation or the village idiot. But is being yourself, despite what that might mean, a sign of weakness? Is leaving a situation in the hope that you can return stronger and more focused an act of cowardice? I don't think so. Rob is a fucking weird geezer, there's no doubt about that, and he's everything we say about him and more at times. But he's our mate. And he certainly isn't a coward.

seven

Rob's Story

Of course I lied about doing acid. I'm not stupid, despite what many people think. First of all, I lied to fit in. Then I lied to avoid the harassment which I knew would follow as soon as I admitted I'd never tried LSD. Then I lied to cover up the lie.

If anyone of the lads knew what my state of mind was like back then, they would have understood but no-one really knew because I never really said. No-one really said anything. We all talked a lot but we never really *said* anything. There were times when someone opened up a bit and let a bit of soul shine through but usually the guards stayed up. It was not the time to talk about feelings - that brief time had quickly passed and had been shat on by the return of macho belligerence - it was a time to indulge and to be seen indulging. Everyone had to be bulletproof. So I was bulletproof. At least I tried to be.

I was naïve to think that I didn't need to say anything to my friends. I thought my behaviour was a clear enough indication that I was very close to being off my fucking rocker without having to take mind-altering drugs to get there. I didn't need acid - my life was a trip. It was a constant bad one.

Ever since the façade of family security and stability shattered and we were forced to leave our lives in the hills for the hell of city living, part of me started to die. It was okay to have dreams when you could wander through the valleys and forests, planning how you would make them come true. Even having such an isolated and lonely childhood was made bearable by having those dreams - visions of making something of yourself by doing the one thing you loved to do even when you had no idea at the time what that thing was. That didn't matter when you had time and space to imagine the possibilities. I didn't care that I had no inclination what my calling was. All I knew was that I had something inside me worth expressing and that when the time came to broadcast my talent, it would be appreciated and I would be loved. It's what I wanted, deep down. I suppose that's what we all want. To be acknowledged and adored.

Coming to the city, of course, didn't automatically send me tumbling down the rabbit hole. I was thrilled by it at first. The wilds of Wales were fine for the dreams but the reality would need a much more vibrant setting in which to materialise. If I wanted to find out what it was that was brewing inside I would need the opportunities the city offered. Now I know this makes me sound like fucking Mowgli but I wasn't exactly raised by wolves. I wasn't born in the green and grey wilderness, unless that's what you consider the suburbs around Bristol to be. I'd done the teenage drinking and the experiments with sex in the piss-fragrant underpasses and stairwells of the city and knew what urban living could be like. It was just that I felt more suited to isolation when I was forced into it by the badly-thought out choices of my parents. When my contemporaries were smoking hash and becoming teenage mothers in inner-city high schools I was attending small town schools and reading biographies of Peter Sellers and Tony Hancock on blustery rocky outcrops. (I always loved the dramatic symbolism and felt my chosen tortured persona could develop best in these rugged surroundings.)

I embraced the move across the country at first. I hated the fact that we still couldn't escape the family failings - the lack of business sense which destroyed my father's business, the disappointment and resentment that killed my mother's love for him - but for pursuing my own dream, it seemed a good decision. Fate may have destroyed my parents' marriage and their livelihood, in turn alienating their oldest son and heaping a greater weight of expectation on their youngest (me), but it had handed me the opportunity to take the next step. A step which would allow me to escape the bitterness now festering in a home a quarter of the size of that we'd been forced to leave. My parents were beyond saving so I instead decided I'd save myself.

Not knowing what my calling was resulted in many fights at home as my father's own self-loathing became so great that he thought it necessary to burden me with the excess. "Don't end up a loser like me," he would beat his chest while saying. "Become something, for Christ's sake. Just get off your arse." Such constructive criticism eventually forced my hand. I took the place on the local college's media course out of sheer desperation, to get out from under his stamping feet and away from his incessant demands to find my way in life. Maybe media would be my calling, I thought. If it wasn't, at least it may lead to it in some roundabout way. I mean, no-one joins a media course to really end up in the media, do they? It's like any course in the humanities area - it provides two years or so of random direction while keeping your off the streets long enough to decide a career in insurance would be more satisfying and lucrative. I didn't know what I wanted from it but I sure as hell didn't want to be an insurance salesman, but I also didn't want to be a journalist or some lackey researcher for Esther Rantzen either. I chose media over the business course on offer because I thought the people would be more stimulating. And they were. There were definitely a lot of stimulants.

This is where things started to unravel. It wasn't the people - I am, after all, currently sat at a table in an Indian restaurant with the three closest people I have to family; friends from that very time and course - and, despite its short-lived nature, it wasn't the media training which wrecked me. It was the era. I had been plucked from obscurity by fate's twisted hand and rather than being placed in an environment where a suffering artist could discuss Balzac over espressos and cigarettes, I was relocated into a garish, testosterone-driven hyper-reality where the merits of tits and football were regularly argued over pints. I wanted Sartre and got *Loaded*. Literally.

The shock of those first few weeks in the autumn of 1994 was such that I almost lost myself there and then. Here was an embryonic culture and movement driven by recklessness and abandon heading away from me at breakneck speed. I was in danger of being left behind. We were all new. We had all been dumped here alone. But groups were forming and I was in danger of being the one left on the fringes, shell-shocked by the growing animalistic energy around me. I was torn - I needed to find myself for so many reasons, to escape my roots, to discover my future...but here was a phenomenon that wouldn't wait for me to find out what I wanted. If I didn't want to be cut loose from this burgeoning cult, for what it was worth, I had to grab the coat tails of it as they whipped past. And besides, maybe my future would materialise in the maelstrom.

Soon I found that I didn't need to worry about my family, my prospects and my dreams. This reality was all-consuming and intoxicating. I was searching for myself and I found a version of it that was liked and acknowledged among the marauding misfits of the fledgling Lad culture. So I embraced that version. I became Filthy Rob. This was mainly because it was even harder to survive in the eye of my father's increasingly speedy breakdown when I appeared to have even less direction than before. So I slept on sofas - usually at Ellis and Danny's place - and when friends were unavailable, I slept rough. Public lavatories, derelict buildings, even the college grounds in warmer weather (although I still didn't make it to lectures on time even when I was sleeping on the step of the media block). But Filthy Rob didn't care. Filthy Rob took the ridicule and enjoyed being the butt of jokes because Filthy Rob was a person people were talking about. He was a personality - which was ironic because at that time, the one I'd arrived with had been completely obliterated.

Filthy Rob was my first role and initially I embraced him. I drank with the best, I drugged with the rest (mostly only weed as chemicals scared me in those days) and I could out-Lad many of the peripheral hangers-on with my outrageous behaviour. Filthy Rob didn't care - he had no reason too. No-one expected anything but the worst from him. Being Filthy Rob was great - but only because it drowned out the increasingly painful voice of self-doubt and insecurity echoing from the prisoner within.

Things really changed when the focus moved from the drinking and substance abuse to the fascination, nay obsession, with getting laid. I have always argued - with myself, mainly - that the Scotsman was responsible for adding this dimension to our lives. When McKinley showed up, Danny was still dealing with the fallout from his relationship ending and although he gamely chatted up birds and got the odd snog, I could see that he was still damaged by that. His own excesses were covering up the screams of his own demons. Ellis was a novice at everything. He couldn't drink, he took way too many drugs before knowing his limitations, and I suspect that he was probably still a virgin by the time we all started college. He was a blank page and Lad culture was writing its rules and manifesto all over him. As for me, I'd had girlfriends back in Bristol but that was at a time when sex was something to get out of the way, something to say you'd done rather than a thrilling pursuit. That changed with McKinley's arrival.

I never quite got the Scotsman's deal. He was attached to a long-term partner who worked overseas who we never saw (until much later). They'd meet up when McKinley had university holidays but most of the time I think the relationship was conducted over the phone. The rest of the time he seemed to be as free as any one of us. He was the most sexually charged out of all of us and pursued wanks and blowjobs like a shark hunting prey. Yet I never heard and definitely never saw anything to suggest he had sex with anyone. He did, however, encourage everyone else to do this - specifically Danny to begin with. They were always chasing after waitresses at the hotel or getting into situations with random slappers. Ellis started to get roped into this scene when Danny and the Scotsman had some apparent low-level falling out over some shag which went wrong. I remember seeing some poorly filmed skin flick of Danny fucking some drunken tart from the Warehouse and after that, the Scotsman's active involvement in Dan's sex life dropped off. He seemed to take on a consultation role after that and this was when Ellis got involved in a number of ill-conceived blind dates, one of which actually made a man of him.

Weirdly enough, I was the most successful with women at this time - but of course this was entirely relative.

To keep up with the seemingly constant drinking, I had to take a job at Amir's Kebab Emporium just to earn enough to fund my developing alcoholism. It barely amounted to enough cash per week to buy a round on pound-a-pint Thursdays and it did even less for my self-esteem. Working the graveyard shift at a take-away on the corner of clubland was asking for trouble - and I regularly got it. Drunken abuse, food thrown in my face, actual physical violence - and this was just from my friends. It was a nightmare; a recurring, lamb and chip fat-soaked nightmare.

However paltry the monetary gains were, they did allow me to keep up my social engagements. After one particular shift where I actually finished work in time to enjoy a night out, I decided I needed to let off steam so I accompanied Amir to Speakeasy's with my kebab money burning a pathetically small hole in my pocket. And that's when I met Jane.

Jane and I were the classic example of a co-dependent, destructive relationship. She was old and crazy, I was young and desperate. She wanted to regress and I wanted to mature. She wanted sex, I wanted love. We both wanted sex, actually, but while getting regular filthy portions of it, I fell in love with her - just out of the sheer need of feeling love, of feeling anything which had the illusion of being real. Jane was not the sort of person who anyone should fall in love with. She was selfish, she was abusive and she was addicted to everything going. I gave her one of the things which kept her going but I never got what I ultimately wanted and needed from her in return. By misreading her insatiable need for intercourse for emotional attachment, I fell into the oldest trap - mistaking sex for love. But even a vegetarian can convince himself a bloody steak is a tofu burger if he's hungry enough, right?

Of course, this was doomed from the start but a) I didn't see it in my blinkered state and b) I wouldn't have cared either way. I was getting fucked left, right and centre at a time that my contemporaries were beating themselves to a pulp in Vaseline-fisted loneliness. Filthy Rob was suddenly the Alpha Male. When Jane had had enough, however, the fall from that particular pedestal was so severe that it knocked a heavy dose of reality into me - and it was not pretty.

At first, it was the heartbreak. I honestly felt that it had been love with Jane. I'd manufactured an emotion from the fag ends of our bizarre union and, not knowing any different, had labelled it love. So when this evaporated, I was in bits. This was the first of the very rare moments that I felt that one of my friends showed true empathy. Danny was the closest to understanding how I was feeling and the way he seemed to adapt his opinion and approach to me from that moment on suggested to me that being dumped by Jane could actually bring about a positive change. Danny and I became closer after that. I'd been right about him being damaged by losing Anna and I suspected that, deep down, he could see the growing futility in our existences at that time. He treated me with a bit more respect and understanding after that and really came through for me on a number of occasions. McKinley and Ellis never really knew how hard I actually took Jane's betrayal and just saw it as something I'd brought on myself for getting involved with a middle-aged mental patient. But Danny saw something of himself in me and my situation - although I'm sure he would never admit it.

I lurched along after that, pining for attention and warmth from any female I could get my hands on. They were all band-aids. They were never a remedy or cure. The disease I was suffering from hadn't even been caught from Jane. She herself had been a symptom. I was craving the thing I was missing from the moment I arrived in the city and which I had lost as soon as I had bought into the empty dream of Lad utopia. I needed the one person I could trust and rely on: I needed myself. But I had absolutely no fucking idea who I was or where to find that person. Luckily, I met someone who seemed to have a map.

As I mentioned before, my brother had always been a twat. He was known in Bristol as being one of the biggest and that's saying something. That should tell you how big a knob he really was. But somehow, despite being a total cock and an aggressive, bullying arsehole to boot, he had some sorted people as friends. While he was drawn more to the rugged, manly pursuits afforded him by our relocation to the Welsh countryside, the majority of his new friends in the valley appreciated the more artistic side of life. Where they found common ground, God only knows, but I'm glad there were enough shared interests between my brother and Aiden Craske for Aiden to have stuck around long enough to form a bond with his friend's younger brother.

I was wallowing in my post-Jane phase when Aiden Craske suddenly appeared in my life again, presumably shoved my way but that cack-handed claw of fate which had brought me to the city in the first place. After being made homeless by Danny and Ellis - despite being evicted in such a helpless state, I'll always be grateful for the three week couch residency they provided - I'd steeled myself enough to head home with a bag full of apologies and no less amount of bullshit. Convincing my dad that I was starting a new, I at least managed to secure a new base from which to wander aimlessly love-lost in the city. While doing so one day, I bumped into Aiden.

Those two weeks in his company were just what I needed. He was a breath of unsullied-by-Lad fresh air. Talking about the Welsh countryside made me ache for wide open spaces and beautiful isolation, listening to his take on the world as it currently appeared was inspiring and watching him work with his group of young actors at the Haymarket was like a flashbulb going off in my head. I watched every rehearsal. I went to every performance - matinee and evening. I watched humble kids transform into raging, larger-than-life characters at a flick of a spotlight. I saw multiple personalities and multiple opportunities emerge at every swish of curtain up. These people were not slaves to the current culture but wraiths taking on whatever forms they needed to pass seamlessly through it. I'd found what I'd been looking for.

Before I made my mind up to follow this new life, I had a lot of things to put right and settle in my old one. I went to Calvin Road that day to basically say my goodbyes but Danny inadvertently convinced me to postpone my new life for more of the same. It was my own weakness of course. I still wasn't totally free from the intoxicating rush of lager madness and the promise of hedonism. I was going to have to start from scratch again by building myself a new personality but I wasn't ready to leave Filthy Rob behind. He'd taken quite a while to develop and had quite a cult following. With Filthy Rob, I was guaranteed exposure and attention. Whoever came next would have to work even harder. But I was willing to make this leap in time and so I made a decision to have one last fling before packing my bags. So I agreed to go to Glastonbury. Plus, you know, the lads were paying for my ticket. It would have been rude to let them down.

As I said at the start, there were a number of reasons why I lied about taking acid. When that microdot started to work its black magic on me, I was painfully aware of the most frightening one. I was suddenly fully aware of who and what I had become. I felt as if my skin had been flayed from my bones and that all the painful scenes from my life were being broadcast on the shiny, wet surfaces of my exposed flesh. I felt as though I was a walking, oozing cinema screen, showing a life-long study of humiliation and hate on repeat for all to see. Of course, these scenes were only playing on rotation in my extremely compromised mind and that the chemicals were adding the whole 'skinned alive' aspect but even listening to McKinley explaining that in soothing tones didn't make it any easier to grasp. Every decision I'd made since arriving from Wales, every moment where I forgot myself on purpose, every descent into oblivion was flashing before my eyes. It was like the deathbed revelation of the damned, like being shown all the reasons why I was about to be dragged to Hell. The heavy doors which kept the truth safely locked away in the part of my brain reserved for denial had been crow-barred open and all that ugly reality had barged its way out into my consciousness. If I ever needed a reason to escape this incarnation, here were about a billion of them.

Just as Danny stepped up when I needed someone after Jane dumped me, the Scotsman did me proud with his chaperone job at Glastonbury. A seasoned tripper, he knew exactly what to say, exactly where to take me and exactly what to do when the demons looked to be winning. There were times when I was on the verge of the deepest fear and he talked me back from the edge. I was ready to plumb the depths of the sea of despair but he was there to keep my head above the murky waters. In the months which followed, I was never spared from his sometimes brutally frank piss-taking but I did enjoy moments of pure honesty and support from him. Again, something changed in my relationship with

McKinley that day. We found a way to understand each other a little better.

You would have thought I would have baulked at another trip after that nightmare but in the rolling waves of the dying high I realised that this was as bad as it could get. I'd seen all I had to see about the worst of myself and my situation. Another acid journey could even take me through the other side into recovery and revelation.

Coupled with the intensity of my emotions generated by the Oasis show, the second trip blew my mind in a completely different way. At times the microdot made me want to kill myself just to escape, but the Californian Sunrise showed me beauty and hope in what was going on around me. I'd been shown how I'd failed and now I was being shown how to put things right. I wasn't cut out for Lad culture. I was always looking beyond it - and that was never the point. Lad was about the here and now, doing what you wanted in the moment and fucking the consequences. I'd always been one for looking to the future but this ideal had chained me to the present. Watching Oasis - five blokes from nowhere with nothing but raw talent - convinced me that the time was right to break free and go in search of what could come next. Oasis had believed. They had fought through the hard times, of being shackled to a way of life and now they were leading a generation. Every song spoke to me: I could be *Supersonic*, I could *Live Forever*, I was going to look ahead and not back in anger. In those moments when I was removed from fear and given strength by the thousands around me and the five blokes on stage, I made my decision to leave. The next day, as the lads recovered in various parts of Worthy Farm, I did just that. I left.

I promised the boys in my leaving note that I'd be back for the start of the next term but that was never an honest target. The media course was over for me and I knew it. I'd blown every assessment, had my quota of referrals and warnings, and had been hunting around, begging for extra borrowed time. I knew it didn't matter if I was there to enrol or not in September. I'd be out eventually. So I didn't even consider that in the months I spent back in Snowdonia. I cleared my mind of all the things that didn't matter anymore while hanging from cliff faces. I threw out my collection of denials and spring cleaned my self-esteem while canoeing on white water. I was not back to stay, I wasn't even bummed out when I found out Aiden was on tour, I was there to get things sorted for the next phase. It was clear in my mind that acting was the way to go so after putting up with my brother's shit for about two months, I packed my stuff again and hitchhiked across the country. It took me three days.

As expected I was kicked off the course just before Christmas. I'd been biding my time since getting back and had identified possible routes towards my now obvious destiny. My ever-generous father gave me a helping hand by kicking me out of the house as soon as my career in further education had been terminated and I soon found myself relying on the heavily-disguised charity of Peruvian Tony.

I knew everyone thought that I was in the worst state of my life at this point; no college, no home, no hope, no direction...living with a homosexual dwarf who was obviously in love with me. Everyone, even those friends who thought they knew me, believed I'd hit rock bottom. And yes, it did look bad - to all those on the outside. But for me, it was the moment I'd been waiting for. Think about it - I was free of the hopes and dreams of my father, out of an education system which was railroading me into a career I never wanted, and removed from the eye of the Lad hurricane by moving away from the madness. To all but Danny, Ellis and the Scotsman, I was persona non grata. I didn't exist anymore to many of those who'd known me as Filthy Rob. I'd been abandoned to my sore-arsed fate at the hands of a serial bender. But I was now free to build on the revelations that had come to me at Glastonbury and then in Snowdonia.

Of course, it's never that easy. I may have had very few ties but I also didn't have a job which meant I had no cash. Tony implied that the rent would be forgotten if I were to cross the sexuality boundary but I would have preferred to go back to Amir's Kebab Emporium on ten pence an hour rather than sell my ring piece for a room in the Peruvian's kingdom of depraved insanity. I needed that address to get the government hand-outs I was after but I also needed a base away from the throbbing bird and beer culture across the city in Calvin Road. I couldn't get distracted. The limelights and greasepaint were calling and I was eager to answer their call. While waiting for my opportunity to weasel my way into the Haymarket Theatre, I took more of Tony's dubious patronage by working cash-in-hand at his salon as a general dogsbody. Eventually, the dwarf's madness and those two harpies he had working there persuaded me that I needed a more pro-active approach. I'd been frequenting the Haymarket bar on and off for a few weeks, mingling with audience and actors alike, getting my face known, when the opportunity to tend bar arose. I grabbed it with one hand and stuck the fingers of the other up in Tony's direction. I now had access to every performance, every dress rehearsal and - more importantly - every dandy director and camp casting agent who fluttered by. As fate would have it, however, the casting couch was never dusted down in my honour because my guardian angel - Aiden Craske - swooped in once more to save me from sacrificial sodomy.

Even though I was spending most of my days at the theatre at this time, I hadn't abandoned my old ways completely. I was just keeping my appearances to the minimum. I was still there at the Orchard for pound-a-pint Thursdays and made the effort to get at least two Warehouse visits in a month but I was weaning myself off this routine in preparation for what I expected to be my final flit. The others didn't know this, of course. I often disappeared for days, even more so in recent times. It didn't cause any concern or raise any suspicion - which is why I was factored in as the fifth member of the Hartington Hotel's jolly jaunt to Amsterdam.

I would have put in a fine, final performance had I gone. The idea of transporting our well-rehearsed mayhem to the continent, to the City of Sin, did appeal in a way. As I said before, the scene was seductive. There's something incredibly uplifting about being out of control. To be let loose in a foreign land where even fewer rules apply (in your own head, at least), was a huge temptation. I was ready to let Filthy Rob die in a haze of weed, continental beer and red light abandon. His epitaph would have been a list of bars, coffee shops and brothels from which he was banned on his last day on earth. But I feared I would have been lost again had I gone; convinced that this way of life was not only exciting but sustainable. So instead, I ignored the phone and cut my Thursdays and Saturdays out completely. I dropped off the radar in the hope that I'd be left alone.

This is when my Guardian Angel chose to reappear. I'd missed Aiden's return to Wales by about a week but my brother had informed him of my desire to tread the boards in my absence. He passed on my number at Tony's but thankfully Aiden thought it better to approach me in person and so he made his way across the country from Bangor to make his offer eye-to-eye. Luckily, the misshapen claw of fate had waved a bony digit in the direction of the Haymarket before he got anywhere near the Kingdom of Mad Tone. Aiden's company Shaven Avon was at the end of its current run and in a flurry of nervous energy and excitement, he had immediately started to conceptualize the group's next tour. Those actors who were available had already gathered and were running through initial rehearsals as we spoke. He presented the plan to me over a coffee at the Haymarket and I agreed to join before he could even mention what roles he had in mind for me. This was my chance. The dream which had eluded me for so long was now a fully formed opportunity and one which was within my grasp - along with adoration and acknowledgement, a wealth of personalities like off–the–rack suits to choose from, and a life never having to be any kind of Rob – Filthy or otherwise. I immediately handed my notice in at the bar before scrawling a note to Tony on the back of a flier Aiden had with him advertising the proposed tour and writing an explanation letter to the boys. We swung by Tony's flat to pick up my things, dropped the flier and the letter on the kitchen table and then set a course for stardom.

Stardom in its most basic form is still stardom all the same to someone who has never even had a sniff of the real thing before. Being well–known as a deflowerer of maladjusted virgins is not really the kind of fame that should be promoted. Seeing your name up in lights, however small their wattage, is far more acceptable – which is why Shaven Avon's Random Acts of Thespianism tour was like getting the lead in a Scorsese movie for me. I knew that I could do silly voices and that I could mimic anyone perfectly after only seconds in their company but I was blown away to discover I could learn word perfect, parallel Shakespearean roles. Everyone else was equally amazed and I quickly gained a standing of respect within the group despite being the new boy. Soon it went further than that, and therein laid the problems to come.

The first tour was great and the loving response from the audience, the plaudits from my peers and the willingness of Britain's theatre groupies made it one of the best times of my life. Shaven Avon also benefitted and Aiden was asked to extend the tour, adding an extra four months to the run. I was sure that I was never going back to the city again and that this was now my life – and I was fucking insanely happy about that. I needed to be on stage. I craved the roles and asked for more. I wanted Aiden to push me, to force and bend me into shapes and people outside of what was becoming my comfort zone. I was just too good. It was too simple. I fucked dozens of young wannabes during that tour, not because of an insatiable need to conquer but because every lay was easier than the last. I was looking for a challenge. I stopped drinking beer because it took too long to drink and made me punchy and slurred so I swapped to whiskey which made me edgy and angry. I hated the way weed slowed me down so I stopped getting stoned and started getting high. The coke was just a little pick me up at first but soon I was sweating nervously if I didn't have a gram in my pocket. My ego was way out of whack by the time Danny managed to get in touch with me to invite me to a reunion party at McKinley's, an event to celebrate his first return home in a year and to mark the 1997 general election which Labour looked in good shape to win.

We were almost at the end of the third extra month of the run when I told Aiden I was going back to the city for the weekend. He wasn't happy. Such was my level of control by then, I'd dispensed with all understudies. If I wasn't there, the Random Acts became a lot less random. Fuck it, I told him. We had a good run. I was thinking of moving on anyway (I hadn't been doing anything of the sort until that powder-inspired moment of spontaneity). Fuck you, he told me. Fuck you too, I replied and walked off the tour, leaving my Guardian Angel mortally wounded like a dumb pigeon caught in the air rifle crosshairs of a ruthless child.

Of course, I didn't understand what a total cunt I'd been until a few years later when our paths would cross again. Aiden had given me my break and had helped construct the dream. I had repaid him by shitting on him from a great height. I hadn't even stabbed him in the back. I'd stood in front of him and gouged out his heart with a dessert spoon while he watched. I was eventually to find out to my detriment that my star wasn't the only one to have risen in the years which had passed since my betrayal.

I look around the Passage to India and see my friends sitting here at this table, all wondering why my career nose-dived after appearing in that Guy Ritchie film and I can't tell them the truth, despite revealing a lot more of myself than I thought I would this weekend. I'd much rather let them believe the curse of Filthy Rob returned and brought his sack full of bad luck with him. I'll even let them believe that my admittedly terrible Irish accent put paid to my embryonic movie career. Anything's better than telling them that Aiden Craske had become one of the most powerful producers in the West End over the previous decade and that after hearing that my career had hit a relative high, he made damn sure that it never went any higher...

Before Vinnie Jones executed on screen what Aiden had effectively done off it, I'd been carried along by ambitious agents who chose to see pounds and dollars instead of the addictions to cocaine, hookers and single malt which were addling this once hungry young tyro. I had screwed my way through wannabes and has-beens, also-rans and non-starters, nobodies and personalities. Not once had I found anyone who wanted to know Rob - which was a fucking stroke of luck because by the time Roger Forester came to save me, I again had absolutely no idea who Rob was.

eight

History

Christmas 1995

When Rob disappeared on the Saturday at Glastonbury in search of whatever he thought he may find in the rugged mountains of Snowdonia, we all expected him to be back for the start of the next college year as he'd promised - despite his notorious record for being full of shit. However difficult and frustrating he may have found the first year, he was still in a position to start the next term which was a minor miracle considering the amount of referrals and warnings he'd had. It had been made clear to him - to all of us, in fact - that the second year of the course would be much more exciting, much more practical and much more fulfilling. Everyone was going to be given a clean slate and the chance to really get to grips with the full gamut of media possibilities. Rob, as ever, decided the best way to get a clean slate was to piss all over it. In fact, such was his disregard for the chance of redemption he'd been offered, the rest of us were putting the finishing touches to our end of term projects and hanging Christmas decorations by the time a fully-bearded, unwashed, cross-country hitch-hiker known as Filthy Rob deigned to darken the towels at Calvin Road once again...

Rob's meeting with Course Leader Susan lasts for over an hour which is surprising when you think it takes less than a few seconds to say "welcome back" or "you're off the course." Expecting a quick decision either way, Ellis and I agree to wait for him outside the office. Ten minutes pass and Ellis sticks his ear to the door. Rob is in the middle of a soliloquy about his life: "And even then, as a ten-year-old, I wasn't sure..."

Ellis sighs. "He's on one about his upbringing again. We'll be here all fucking day."

"Is it the true version or the bullshit version?" I ask. There is more of a difference than just reality and lies. Rob rarely stretches the true version out to more than quarter of an hour, even if his life depends on the listener being convinced. The bullshit can go on for hours. Ellis presses his ear against the door again.

"Losing my uncle in the assault on Goose Green hit me hard...Only his Victoria Cross and his Falklands service medal helped me through that time...I knew I had to join the Paras after that."

"Fancy a pint?" Ellis asks.

The Trowel is full of rowdy office workers when we get there. A bunch of insurance firm lackeys are bellowing out Slade's 'Merry Christmas Everyone' by the bar while a tipsy group of shop girls giggle over their staff party turkey under cheap plastic snowmen and nativity scenes from Chinese sweatshops. Christmas. Bah humbug. Seeing couples sloppily grope each other under the fake mistletoe just makes me even more up for a shag. Luckily, this is the one time of year when even the sad and desperate can get laid thanks to that most romantic combination: yuletide alcohol and Christmas cheer. However, there is another factor which may inhibit my ability to prey on drunken slappers looking for a festive leg-over. My self-imposed sex embargo, decreed in a fit of insanity before the Glastonbury festival almost six months ago, has since been fully endorsed by the United Nations of Women. It appears that the General Assembly of Female-kind met at some point while we were larging it in a field and agreed that not having sex with Danny Jones was a good idea and passed a resolution to that effect while I was in absentia. Now I can only overturn my own motion if the Council of Birds agrees to it. Or gets drunk enough to forget the whole stupid thing - which is what I'm hoping for. I've long since abandoned the idea that being a Lad is more about embracing the music than getting my end away. I think it's only right that the opposite sex does the same.

Ellis and I are squeezed between two fat, sweaty accountants at the bar, trying to order, when something starts poking me in the small of the back. I struggle to turn and with my neck contorted I spy the top of someone's head about a foot below me. It's Peruvian Tony.

"Where is he? Where is Rob the Bastard?"

I twist myself round, leaving Ellis to get the beers in, and address the midget staring up at me with defiant eyes. "And a Merry Christmas to you too, Tone."

"Bastard Rob owes me money. Where is he?" Peruvian Tony does two things regularly. One is cut hair, which is his profession, and the other is demand money whether he's entitled to it or not, which is his hobby. Most of the time he believes he deserves it, either for some favour or act of benevolence. At other times, he's just trying his luck. In this case, considering Rob is apparently involved, Tony probably has a case. "He no pay me fifty quids I gave him last week. He complete and utter bastard. I no find him nowhere."

"You live with him. Can't you wait until he gets home tonight?" When Rob got back from Snowdonia to find that his dad had thrown him out of the house again, he moved into Tony's spare room and started working as a slave at the salon. No one thought it was a good idea. We still don't. It's a widely accepted belief that Tony is quite clearly insane.

"You tell Bastard Rob, he out on his fucking arse if he no pay me back." The South American dwarf turns to leave. "Oh, this present from Debs." He spits on my shoe and gives me the finger before storming out like an unfairly sacked member of Santa's workforce. I stare at the watery gob on my trainers and make a mental note never to get my hair cut at Tony's again, especially if that mad bitch Debbie is intent on holding the scissors.

Half an hour later, Rob ambles into the considerably quieter pub wearing a face like a slapped arse. The lunchtime crowd has dispersed and Ellis and I beckon him over to our table under an illuminated Father Christmas who looks like he's on E. Rob orders a pint of bitter and takes a seat.

"So?"

"Slag kicked me off."

"Even after the Falklands story?" ask Ellis. "That one usually slays them."

"What are you going to do?" I enquire.

"Work at Tony's, I s'pose." Rob dejectedly takes a sip of his drink and stares at the weak head as it evaporates on the surface.

"That reminds me. That mad fucking midget was in here earlier. He says you owe him fifty quid."

"Do I bollocks? He hasn't paid me in a month. That was wages in lieu." Rob quickly seizes his anger and blows out his cheeks. "This is not the new start I had in mind when I came back. No home, no money, no course. Just a shitty job sweeping up hair for a mental homosexual dwarf."

"What you need is a good night out, geezer." I smile. "Let's put that fifty quid of Tony's to good use."

There is so much right about this evening and yet a lot of it is alien and out of place. On the one hand, I feel at ease because the sounds and smells of the Warehouse are as comforting as ever while the recognisable silhouettes of Ellis and Rob, which become illuminated by the flashing strobes from time to time, remind me I'm in the company of friends. But then I remember that this is a Wednesday night, not a Saturday. It's not even a Thursday, the only acceptable alternative to the usual. I am also very aware that everyone - and I mean everyone - from our course is down here tonight. Including the lecturers. This was someone's ill-conceived idea of the perfect end to of an evening of bonding over warmed-through seasonal pub food. This is BTEC Media's Christmas Party.

The crowd I arrived with (in a less arrogant and confident manner than usual, I must add) is a strange, unsettling mix. There are those - mainly the girls for whom the 'Like A Virgin' look never got old - who usually frequent such townie dens of inequity as Chrome Dreams and the equally heinous Speakeasy's; there are some of the peripheral lads who sometimes roll up and latch on to our Saturday night extravaganzas and then there are the poor souls who rarely, if ever, venture out of their bedrooms. In addition to this, there at the bar, in all their tweed-jacketed, inappropriately open-shirted maturity, are the academics that time and fashion forgot; the people charged with our education and development.

I'm torn between lording it over them all in a place where I consider myself to be royalty and blending into the shadows that creep into the corners and which would afford me the cover I need to slip out unnoticed. The majority of my course mates stand around in a huddled group as if they are bound by some pact of collective protection watching Film Theory Clive and Marketing Liz, both adults who should know better, unwittingly create a scene from *Dirty Dancing* in the midst of a heaving mosh pit. The large amount of alcohol I consumed to get me through the pre-club meal is proving to be glaringly insufficient. I join Ellis and Rob at the far end of the bar away from the shocked throng of cellar dwellers who are having their brains pulverised by 'Girl from Mars' by Ash.

"This is really fucking surreal. I'm not sure if I can handle this." I motion to a bar maid who I fail to recognise, an unusual event which adds to my growing discomfort.

"Can you handle getting your leg over?" Ellis asks over his shoulder as he shields the fact that he's skinning up a small reefer from prying eyes.

"That's a stupid question if ever I heard one," I reply. "But I have even less chance of getting laid in this place tonight than I usually do. Unless you're suggesting I prey on Claire Holmes." Poor Claire. Those Deirdre Barlow glasses she always wears make her eyes look like they're about to pop out of her head at the best of times. Tonight, she looks like a bush baby on acid. It's fair to say she doesn't get out much and when she does, she always has her Walkman on pumping the calming mantras of Take That into her unsettled mind. She currently looks petrified by the aural assault raining down on her from the speakers above.

"She looks like she needs some tequila," Rob grins, and orders a couple of shots. He gathers them up, winks and heads over to where Claire is trembling.

"All I'm saying," Ellis continues, "is that I would keep an eye on how much Sadie Brown is drinking." He gives a knowing nod. "A little bird told me in the pub earlier that she has the hots for you."

Sadie Brown. I've never really thought about Sadie Brown. I mean, she's not unattractive. I suppose you could describe her as pretty but she has that kind of undeveloped look that some young girls have. You can see that she has potential but her features just don't look comfortable in each other's company at the moment. She could grow into a real stunner or her face could never really get on with itself and she could just end up being okay. Plus I've never been able to look past her friends, the Speakeasy's Coven. She always hides in the background behind Fran and Ruth, which isn't hard because they both play in the women's rugby team and both are big enough to beat the living crap out of me. Luckily I get on with both of them, they're quite a laugh, but when the banter gets going Sadie never says anything. She just smiles softly behind her shaggy 80's curls.

Ellis passes me the joint and I discreetly pull in a lungful. "Aye aye," he nudges me in the ribs, forcing a plume of pungent smoke out over the bar. "Looks like it's game on, fella." I cough and wipe the tears from my eyes in time to see Sadie and the Coven set up a line of shots on the bar. I catch Sadie's eye just before she necks her vodka. She smiles enticingly at me. My groin stirs, completely without permission. Game on, indeed. Seems like discussions over lifting the sex embargo are well underway.

As the night progresses, the feeling of apprehension I arrived with is buried under a flood of Red Stripe, an increasing miasma of ganja smoke and the effects of some nasty but effective speed that Ellis purloined from an old school friend in the toilets. As my fears sink, my ardour rises. It seems that everyone's inhibitions have been cast aside, for good or ill. Half a bottle of tequila has sent the previously meek Claire Holmes into a frenzy and she is thrashing around to 'Parklife' while preventing a scared-looking Rob, who looks intimidated by more than just the dirty pigeons, from escaping the clutches of the monster he has created. The lecturers hang off each other to form a sweaty, 12-legged groove machine which moves like an unsteady scrum through the masses of flailing kids, while the Coven - and Sadie in particular - look to have become fully paid up members of the Britpop revolution (as well as major shareholders in Smirnoff). As Blur metamorphoses into 'Reverend Black

Grape', common sense is trampled in the rush to get to the dance floor and before I know it I'm grinding myself against a happily surprised Sadie Brown. The messed-up funk has the whole crowd cutting a fierce rug so my initial burst of attention towards Sadie doesn't look as unsubtle as it might do in less hedonistic situations. The feel-good factor is high and any awkwardness which may have arisen from the two of us making a transition from fellow students to something more intimate in such an uncoordinated and inebriated way is lost in the surrounding insanity.

The intensity subsides when Black Grape makes way for Cast's 'Fine Time' and the change in tempo allows Sadie and I to actually dance together. It's then that both of us realise what's happening. We're actually on the verge of getting off with each other. Any relationship we had before this moment is about to be ruined forever in favour of something involving the swapping of bodily fluids. In the spirit of this new understanding, I swap the dry humping for slower, rhythmic pelvic pressing. I pull her into me with the one arm I now have hooked around her waist. The other arm is completely out of control, by the way, as if all the speed has ended up in that one limb. But as it's not interfering with the intimacy which is happening below the belt, neither of us seem to be bothered that one half of me looks like I'm frantically hailing a cab. Sadie has both her arms loosely around my neck as she sways and pushes against me. My arm moves up her damp back and pulls her onto me and I feel her small tits flatten against my chest through her flimsy shirt. I feel the softness spread and from the centre of that fleshiness, her hard nipples dig into me like football studs. I suddenly make that split-second decision to do all I can to get her into my bed tonight. The next thing either of us know I have my tongue in her mouth and at that moment I feel this usually shy young woman mentally throw caution to the wind and fall into me.

We spend the next half an hour on the side of the dance floor locked in a heady, pounding embrace, our mouths crazily sliding all over each other's faces. It can't look pretty but I'm currently in no mood to give a shit. My mind, despite having to multitask with the varying effects that the alcohol, weed and amphetamines is having on it, is quite clear on one topic: I want to fuck this girl. And soon. I'm just about to suggest we follow my wayward arm's advice and get a taxi back to the house when the coked-up swaggering intro to 'Supersonic' thuds through the club. From nowhere Ellis and Rob appear, scream "GIN & TONIC!!" in my ear and drag me away into the heaving masses. I'm so convinced that I'm on a done deal, I don't protest. I just put my faith in the Gallaghers and let myself go. I'm positive I've done enough to ensure she'll still be there or thereabouts when I'm done feeling supersonic.

As the song ends, I extricate myself from the dying strains of the final guitar refrain and the clammy clutches of my mates and lurch out of the human Somme to the place where I left my shag. She's not there. After a quick scan of the dimly lit areas, I locate her by the bar. She seems to be gleefully giving details of our tryst to her fellow Coven sisters. I get the urge to stride over and bask in this situation but something stops me. This something is five foot six, with long brown hair swept back into a swishing ponytail, and wearing a tight t-shirt with the motto 'Big Boots No Knickers' on the front. It isn't just the intensely full, pouting lips or the deep brown almond-shaped eyes, or even the rock hard breasts that stop me going over to Sadie but the whole presence of this girl. She stands less than a metre away from me but I feel like I've already physically walked into her. I can feel her impact on my body. She looks directly into my face and smiles a wonky grin.

"Danny, right?"

And you must be the angel sent to save me from this lifetime of loneliness and meaningless sex. "That's me."

"I'm Kelly." The moronic look and slowly gaping mouth tells her more information is needed. "Stuart's mate? We met at the Bluetones gig a couple of months ago." Stuart, that little wanker. I'm going to have to get to know him a little better and stop taking the piss out of that ridiculous hat he wears whenever I see him.

"Oh yeah. How is he? I haven't seen him in a while." And if you are indeed a mate of Stu-pid, and hang out with him, I'll be sure to rectify that as soon as humanly possible.

"He's here actually. I'll let him know you're about. Laters." And with another one of those heart-melting, lop-sided smiles, she disappears into the crowd. As I frantically search the sea of bobbing heads in vain, trying to catch sight of that enticing ponytail, Sadie appears in front of me. She plants a soft kiss on my lips and looks up at me with sparkling, hopeful eyes. It suddenly becomes obvious that she isn't the dirty slut I was hoping for and that she is actually one of those nice girls who want love and companionship to develop from situations like this. Sorry love. You're about eight months too late.

"Hi. Did you miss me?"

I try to shake Miss Big Boots No Knickers from my mind and concentrate on what appears to be my diminishing chances of getting some no-strings-attached sex.

"I did, babe. I thought someone may have made you a better offer."

"Well, I haven't heard what you've got to say yet, so I wouldn't know."

All, it seems, is not lost. Maybe wedding bells are not ringing in this bird's head and the sound she hears is actually the banging of my headboard. "How about we get out of here and go back to mine. Ellis won't be home for hours and we'll have the place to ourselves."

The spark of hope in her eyes turns to trepidation. "I came with the girls. I just think I should go when they go." She starts to see me for the heartless sex pest I am but gives it one last try. "I'm not saying I don't want to. It's just a little fast for me."

Nice girls. Civilization would be damned without them. They keep us all on the straight and narrow. They offer us hope and the promise of salvation. Ultimately, this is what I've been searching for: someone who wants to build on the obvious attraction and heat to create something beautiful together. But this is quest I've since abandoned, or at least postponed. And besides, Sadie Brown is not the person I want to build that with. Sadie Brown is not a forever and ever. Sadie Brown is a right here, right now. In all honesty, she isn't even that anymore. If she'd been easy, then I would have enjoyed her - a lot - and then maybe spent a week or two regretting it over the festive period before suffering a month or so of awkwardness back at college. But she was never a pursued target. She just wandered into my crosshairs. She's nothing more to me now than a come-and-gone.

"That's okay," I smile, and kind of nod my head towards the bar. "It's my round. I better get them in before the lads lynch me." I don't stay long enough to actually see the physical effects of my thinly-veiled rejection but, as I plot my course away from her, I can feel the crushing of Sadie Brown's spirit in the vacuum behind me.

I order three beers and discover that I seem to have misplaced my conscience. Sadie Brown and I were never meant to be. There was nothing in the previous year-and-a-bit of knowing each other that ever suggested that something like this would ever happen. In total, our flirtation and near consummation of lust lasted a mere thirty minutes tops. If we were ships passing in the night, then we would be speedboats or jet skis, chopping up the waves between us before accelerating away from the dissipating surf we created. I convince myself that neither of us have lost anything from this brief encounter and, to keep the nautical metaphor going, it's already water under the bridge.

"So are you getting into Sadie's pants or not?" Rob's slurred voice reaches my ear just milliseconds after his arm has bent round me to grab his pint. Ellis's lanky form slides up on my other side and takes possession of the other glass.

"It's not going to happen," I say. Instead of revealing the fact that she wasn't up for the cup, I take the Laddish option. "She started to ming, so I decided to move on." I'm learning. Fast.

"B.O?" Ellis chuckled. "You let a shag go for stinky pits?"

"Man, I'm telling you, if she smells that bad up there, imagine what she's like down there."

"Mr. Sifter's salmon dinner," Rob replies sagely. Ellis and I nod in silent agreement. Now I feel a bit of a shit. Bailing out of a snog situation because there is no hope of a shag is fair enough but then fabricating a story about the girl's personal hygiene to excuse yourself is a bit low. And I know that one of these two, most probably both, will cite vaginal odour as the reason why Danny dumped Sadie the night of the BTEC Media Christmas Party. It will be a rumour that will dog the poor girl for the rest of the course, if not the rest of her life. She'll probably end up with a nickname like Kipper or something.

Out of the gloom, a hat which would make Jamiroquai look like the most understated person at Royal Ascot appears with an annoying little tosser positioned directly underneath it. Stuart monkey-walks up to us, snapping his fingers in Rob's face.

"Nice one, our kid. Knowworramean?"

"Why are you pretending to be a Geordie?" says Rob. Rob hates Stuart. Ellis hates Stuart. I don't hate Stuart. I just can't stand him. There is a difference, albeit a slim one. It boils down to how much time it takes for us to really get spiteful towards him. For Rob and Ellis, it's immediate whereas I can take about ten minutes of his inane bullshit before I want to drop his gagged and bound carcass in the river. While the other two slip into their hatred modes in preparation for the usual bout of merciless ridicule, I look past Stuart in the hope that Kelly is in tow. I spot her on the fringes of the crowd in front of us. She stands a few feet away and smiles at me. She knows. She knows we all think he's a pointless little twat. That's why she won't come over. She's giving me an escape route. I brush past Stuart and leave him to his fate.

"You know I work for the advertising standards authority," I whisper in her ear. "I'm going to have to check if that slogan on your t-shirt is true." She looks up at me with the filthiest look a woman has ever given me, hooks a finger in my belt and pulls me towards the exit.

The blokes' toilets are always the better bet if you're looking to shag a bird in a club. The women's bogs always have a fucking great queue out of the door even on quiet nights and there's always a big group of tarts readjusting their hair and whacking more slap on in front of the mirrors. You'll never find a free cubicle and the girls will always make a big fuss either over the fact that there's a bloke in their precious piss parlour or that one of the sisterhood is being a randy whore. Having it off in the gents rarely comes with that same set of problems. Lads dash in, piss out their pints and head straight out to the bar to restock. The only drawbacks are that their bogs reek to high heaven and blokes are more likely to throw up all over the sit-downs.

Luckily, on this occasion, no-one has been caught out by a pre-Warehouse curry or succumbed as yet to the watered down lager.

Kelly drags me into the toilets without a care. She uses the big boots of said slogan to kick open an empty cubicle door and slams it shut behind us. As she's fumbling at my zip, I'm following up my chat-up line by hoisting up her short skirt to check on the authenticity of the statement. Contrary to her t-shirt's claim, the Doc Martens she's wearing come with flimsy, lace panties.

"Oh, you are in big trouble," I growl.

244

"Just fuck me," she pants and after I've literally ripped her underwear off, she leaps up and wraps her legs round my waist. She roughly guides me inside her and we're off at a rate of knots. She's so light that I can hold her up easily and can use my strength elsewhere. She hangs onto my neck and bites my ear so fucking hard that I'm sure she's drawn blood. She's repeating my name over and over again in short, breathless little squeaks and if it wasn't for the amphetamine coursing through me, this would be enough to make me blow my stack on its own. The cubicle rattles like an earthquake is rumbling under the club as we fuck like these are our last moments on earth.

The whole nature of what just happened convinces me that as soon as we're back in the club, Kelly will disappear into the crowd and I'll never see her again. She'll be this amazing memory that will only get better and more embellished with time. Or we may see each other on occasion but *this* will never happen again. We will smile knowingly, silently remembering that moment when we rocked that small patch of world under the last cubicle but one. But instead of a 'wham bam thank you Dan', Kelly takes my hand and leads me past the seething faces of the Speakeasy Coven and the trading of insults between Stuart and the lads to the chill-out area at the far end of the main room. There she sits me down in an armchair, slides onto my lap and starts kissing me tenderly. Behind the 'what the fuck?' level of utter surprise, I'm totally blown away. Who the hell is this girl? Who's paying her? If this is someone's idea of a Christmas present, then I'm not going to be wanting another one for about the next decade.

The level of disbelief continues when I wake up the next day and find Kelly asleep next to me in my bed. The spent johnnies on the floor are all the evidence I need to answer the first questions which fill my mind on waking. It's true! I DID spend all night shagging this delicious young woman. I then wonder why we bothered to go through a box of Durex back at the house when I can't remember using one in the frantic toilet fuck of the night before. It's then that the brain-creasing pain kicks in and I realise this is as far as that thought process can go in my current state. We'll pick that apart at a later date, one when the chainsaw massacre in my head is over and done with. I carefully lay my head back on the pillow and listen to the sound of my brain sloshing from one side of my skull to the other. This, and presumably my pathetic groaning, causes Kelly to stir. I brace myself for the usual awkward excuses and the rapid exit but instead she opens her eyes, smiles, sighs a satisfied "mmmm" and snuggles under my arm. This is getting ridiculous. When is reality going to kick in?

"What time is it?" she purrs.

I squint at the clock on my wall. "It's either nine-thirty or quarter to six."

"Did you never learn how to tell the time?"

"That's not the problem. My eyesight is a little messed-up at the moment."

Kelly props herself up on an elbow and lazily kisses both my eyes. "Is that better?"

"Nope. Now I'm blind."

She leans over me and grabs my watch from the table beside the bed. I feel her body heat warm my very soul and her soft hair brush the side of my face. If I am being taken for a ride here, it's worth every minute. "Okay, it's almost twenty to ten. I have to meet my mum in the city in about 30 minutes to go Christmas shopping."

Okay, that's plausible. She's letting me down gently. If she'd said she had to give her Granny a bed bath, then that would be more in keeping with my previous experiences at this stage. But this could be true. "You don't need to get me anything, you know."

"Don't worry," she smiles. "I'll be back tonight to give you your present." She kisses me on the lips and rolls over me onto the floor, giving me my first real look at her full naked body. Just wrap a red ribbon round that and I'll be very happy indeed. She dresses quickly but then seems lost. "I had knickers on last night, right?"

"Err...yeah. That was my fault. I owe you a pair. I got a bit carried away."

"What colour do you like? Red, white...black?"

"Err..."

"Silky, lacy or cotton?"

"Err..."

"I'll come up with something." Kelly winks and leans over me and kisses me goodbye. "I'll come over at about seven-ish. Maybe we can go for a drink. Talk a bit, even."

"I can talk." I can barely put these short words together at the moment but I see a lot of paracetemol in my future so the evening might not be a total disaster. She kisses me again quickly and leaves.

After an hour spent trying to put together the events of the previous evening, fending off the increasingly ripe Mr. Sifter's attempts at joining me in bed and occasionally wincing in chemically-induced anguish, I finally get up and slope downstairs. Ellis and Rob are engaged in what appears to be a titanic struggle for FIFA International Soccer supremacy on the Sega, while Stuart of all people sleeps soundly, wrapped in what appears to be a curtain, on the sofa. The sound of clinking spoons and mugs, along with the strains of a boiling kettle, catch my attention. As no-one seems to be acknowledging my existence in the living room; I pass wraith-like into the kitchen. I find McKinley on tea duty.

"You're a bad bastard," he says, with only half a smile on his face.

"Good morning to you too." I stand next to him and look out onto the grey day. "Are you making coffee as well or just tea?"

"I'm not sure I'm allowed to make you anything, big man." The Scotsman indicates that he's under some kind of order from the silent twins in the other room. "You are, as they say, persona non grata."

"What did I do?"

"Not what. Who." Ellis comes in after presumably annihilating his woeful opponent yet again.

"I wasn't aware of any list. Who was I meant to be doing? Sadie Brown?"

"That's another thing," Ellis adds. "You'd better watch yourself. The ladies rugby team aren't too impressed with you, old son."

"Okay, but what's the first thing? What's the problem with Kelly?"

Rob comes in and shuts the kitchen door. "She was Stu-pid's bird. Well, at least he fancied her first. And you went and shagged her. That's out of order." All three of them pick up a cup of tea and look accusingly at me.

"Hang on, you hate him."

"That's not the point, geezer."

"Was he knobbing her?"

"No."

"Has he ever knobbed her?"

"Probably not."

"Then what's the problem?"

Silence. McKinley takes this cessation in hostilities to cave in and start making me a coffee. As their argument and basis for being pissed off seems to be in tatters, neither Ellis nor Rob enforce the ban on hot beverages. "The thing is, he really fancies her and has done for years," Rob of all people finally says. "Even when she was out of reach, he still felt like he had a chance. Now you're banging her, his dream is over."

"Were you up all night bonding or something?" Rob ignores the question. "Look, it's not like she was a virgin until last night, man. Believe me, she knows where everything goes."

"But you're his friend," Ellis pipes up.

"No I'm not. I just dislike him less than you two."

"Same thing."

Pause of incredulity. "What?" I look to the Scotsman for an injection of his usual wisdom. "Say something sensible please."

McKinley passes me the most welcome coffee in the history of the human race. "Seems to me she was fair game. If the wee bastard hadn't made a move, then it's his own fault. But," he hesitates, taking a sip of his tea, "you should talk to him. And you, you smelly cunt, you should tell Danny what you were up to last night before judging anyone about who they're shagging."

"Rob got laid?"

Long embarrassed pause. "I deflowered the Take That freak," he mutters.

Longer pause of utter disbelief with additional stifled hysterics. "I just have one question...," Ellis finally says after getting a tenuous grip on his self-control. "Could it be magic?"

"Fuck off," Rob mumbles, or something similar. It's hard to tell exactly as the kitchen descends into hilarious chaos at this point. Despite all our fragile states, McKinley for once excluded, the tension is lifted thanks to the fits of laughter rattling the windows. Our outbursts wake up Stuart who wanders into the kitchen looking dazed and confused. The boys swallow their giggles, grab their teas and leave me alone with him.

At this point I should provide a little background on Stuart. When we all started college together, Stuart was the weediest of the weedy; an almost pre-pubescent boy-child seemingly cast out by an uncharitable kindergarten and thrust into further education from somewhere out there in the cruel, cruel world. He lacked social skills...any skills, actually...and as a result suffered at the hands of those types who prey on such easy victims. Lecturers, mostly. Nobody stood up for him - until one day, I did. My intervention that fateful day saved him from a kicking but it would never be enough to truly save him from a lifetime of beatings he seemed destined to be heading for. Yet that one charitable act made such an impression on him that I became - as far as only Stuart was concerned - his friend.

Then, just when it looked like he would either be found dead or kicked off the course (perhaps both, but obviously not in this order - the system isn't that brutal), Stuart got a job with the local BBC. Nobody knows how but suddenly he went from being bully fodder at college to being a gopher for a mildly successful morning talk show host, which basically equates to the same thing but with better pay. His ego expanded exponentially and he became the epitome of the media tossers we were all hoping to avoid in later life. He grew a goatee, he dressed in an alternative way and when Britpop hit, he got himself an Oasis haircut and suddenly started talking in a terrible fake Mancunian accent. He flashed his cash and bragged about the circles he was moving in. Those who pitied him before hated him now.

Stuart's circle of 'mates' in the city was varied but he mainly hung out with a group of old school friends, all of which treated in him in a slightly (only slightly, I may add) more humane way than we ever did. Kelly had been his first girlfriend when they were eight and they had stayed friends all the way through high school. Stuart's love apparently had never died - which is why I now find myself sitting across the kitchen table from him, about to smash his already broken heart into smithereens.

"So, Stu. It's been a while."

"Do you love her? I love her."

"Err...Look, Kelly's great. And I think I could get really into her..."

"She coming out of a hugely messy break-up, you know." He fixes me with this faux-intense beady little piggy stare he uses when he's pissed off. It's far from intimidating. "Her ex really screwed her up. She doesn't deserve something like that happening again."

"Stuart, listen. I think she's amazing but we only really met last night. We'll see how it goes." I'm treading as softly as I can but he's running out of road.

"If you hurt her, I'll fuck you up."

"Okay, easy tiger. You've got a job, you haven't developed superhuman powers. I can still swat you like a fly."

"I'm just saying..."

"Make yourself a tea." I actually mean get your shit together and leave in the next half an hour. "And don't let the others see you crying, for fucks sake. They're like a pack of hyenas when they sense weakness." I push a box of tissues his way and leave him to compose himself in private. Poor bastard. Love, eh? And this is what I'm searching for? This is what I want for myself? Be careful what you ask for...

The next two weeks with Kelly are fantastic. The intensity of the sex increases with every night and my creaky old bed takes a real hammering (as does Ellis's patience - we never sleep at hers). On top of that, we actually manage to develop an embryonic relationship away from the bedroom. We meet for drinks, we talk about stuff, we go dancing, we spend some of that mythical 'quality time' together. For someone who has resolved not to get involved with anyone and play the field, I'm surprised to discover that I'm actually quite smitten. Maybe it's because I wasn't hunting for it. Maybe not looking for something serious was the best way of finding it. Could this mean that Kelly is The One?

As Christmas Day nears, it actually feels like we have become, dare I say it, boyfriend and girlfriend. We agree that we'll do the family thing over the festive period and then meet up again once all the tinselled fuss is over to see the New Year in together. I'm careful not to tell her that I'll miss her, even though I'm not looking forward to trading long, naked lie-ins for a few days in rural/parental hell. A fortnight is no way long enough for even the most needy person to develop abandonment issues. Plus Kelly is cool as fuck and street with it. She's hardly the type who'll find it endearing that her man is pining over his gravy while his father carves an unnecessarily large Bernard Mathews turkey. Instead, on our last meeting before going our separate ways, I pull her roughly to me at the bus stop and kiss her passionately. Breaking off as the number 32 pulls up, I wink at her and lightly slap her arse. "Behave yourself," I grin. She gives me a naughty schoolgirl look of feigned innocence and hops on the bus. She blows me a kiss through the window as the bus pulls away.

Christmas Day comes and goes without any major incidents. My perfect brother and his perfect family deign to grace the event with their perfect presence. I spend the day drinking the beer I had to bring with me as my mother will only buy wine for the festive period as she tends to get her Christian festivals mixed up ("It's the blood of Jesus"). I share a couple of cans with my Granddad in front of *Goldfinger* as the kids do their best to give my old man a coronary in the back garden and the Golden Child sips Sainsbury's best Merlot in the kitchen while my mum, partially-paralysed Gran and sister-in-law slave over the dirty dishes. My brother is such a dick. The spirit of festive goodwill continues to find the door to sexual equality bolted firmly shut in my parents' household, especially when Keith is in residence.

Facing three more days of family bliss before returning to the city for New Year, I take off into town on Boxing Day to try and catch the football - any football - on the television down at the Crown. I'm drinking my way through Arsenal's 3-0 victory over Queens Park Rangers when Kevin Bensley, an old school friend and fellow student at City College, rolls in with a couple of lads I know on a nodding basis. Kevin spots me from the bar, waves and makes the time-honoured mime which suggests a refill. I give him the thumbs-up and a couple of minutes later, he's sitting beside me and we're toasting each other's health with fresh pints. After the usual catching up small-talk, Kevin becomes conspiratorial. What he has to say ruins my year and casts a heavy shadow over the one about to begin.

"Man, sorry to hear about you and Kelly Davis. She's well fit. You must be gutted." After making it very clear that I have no idea what he's talking about and after he's said 'shit' about forty times, I eventually get the details from his perspective.

It seems that Kevin and his boys spent Christmas Eve in the city pubs before heading back to the sticks to honour their own family commitments. While they were in a rather crowded pub in Kelly's neighbourhood, Kevin spotted her at the bar. Knowing her through a mutual friend, he attempted to get through the throng to wish her a Merry Christmas. However, before he made it, her ex-boyfriend appeared on the scene and made it very clear to all those who had eyes that the ex- part of that title was no longer applicable. Kevin, after a few more 'shits', then made it very clear to me that it didn't look like a one-off and that Kelly and this Gary tosser appeared to be very much back together.

"I don't get it, geezer. From what I hear, he used to knock her about," Kevin says by way of yet another apology. "He's a bit of fucking nutter, that Gary. Off his rocker..."

I'm on the last train back to the city that night after making my excuses to my parents. I can't process this with my mother banging on about TV repeats in one ear and my brother's snide comments about careers in the other. My train limps into the station at kicking-out time and I have to traipse across the city through belligerent Christmas pissheads and drunken slappers dressed as fairies. The house is empty when I eventually get there and I give bitter thanks for that. Even Mr. Sifter is off having whatever fun incontinent, heavily-balled tom cats get up to during the festive season. Ellis isn't due back until New Year's Eve, when we were all supposed to head down to the Warehouse together to ring in 1996 in style and, to be honest, I'm glad he's not here. I need to brood in silence and solitude. I need a clear head to go through all the questions which have been turning over in my mind since that fateful meeting in the Crown. Can I trust Kevin? Can I trust what he saw? He was hammered, by his own admission, but he was genuinely mortified when I told him I had no idea that Kelly and I had split up. Would she really go back to that wanker after he beat her up? What can he offer her that I can't, other than a black eye or a fractured rib? After sitting in the dark for an hour nursing an untouched can of lager, I decide that I'm not the one who can answer these queries. The shops are open tomorrow and Kelly will be back at work.

I fight down the nausea from the moment I wake up at eight but it still takes me until ten-thirty before I'm ready to leave the house. I call McKinley just before I'm about to head out and we arrange to meet at the Orchard for a liquid lunch. I figure whatever needs to be said between me and Kelly will be done and dusted by midday. I can then focus on getting seriously shit-faced, either out of sheer relief or the need to drown some serious sorrows. It feels like it takes an age to get to the florists; my feet drag along the damp pavement, spraying the remnants of slush onto the bottom of my jeans. I make a reconnaissance pass of the shop behind a group of idling tourists. From safely behind the winter jackets and woolly hats of the out-of-towners, I see Kelly tying bundles of twigs in the back of the shop. Cheryl, her boss, is nowhere in sight. I quickly double back and go straight into the shop while my courage still holds. The doorbell alerts Kelly to my presence and the fact that her face drops when she sees me tells me all I need to know. I'm here four days earlier than I should be and there's no sign of delight. The lack of enthusiastic greeting on my part makes it very clear I'm not here because I couldn't stay away. We both know why I'm here and how this is going to go. She comes slowly out of the storeroom and stands behind the counter. There's no wonky smile today. Her beautiful, dark, almond-shaped eyes can't stay on my face for longer than a second at a time.

"I'm sorry, Danny," she finally says. "There's just too much history there."

"I heard. And yet you're still going back to him."

"I always felt so much safer with you." Her eyes dampen.

"It isn't enough though, is it?" She shakes her head slowly. The doorbell goes behind me and an elderly couple come in. They seem to understand the scene before them and wander off towards the pot plants at the far end of the shop. Kelly wipes her eyes as I put a small wrapped gift on the counter, something I wanted her to have on the stroke of midnight on the last day of 1995. "Bye Kelly. Look after yourself." I walk out and don't look back.

As Rob is wrapping up his life story over dirty plates and dregs of beer, my phone begins buzzing in my pocket. I check the number to see if it's somebody worth talking to or someone who can be called back after the actor finishes his lengthy soliloquy. It's my other life calling. Immediately the internal conflict starts again. I'm already feeling very comfortable with being this version of me; one of the lads. Now I'll have to revert to my other self, the one I'm struggling with on a day-to-day basis. McKinley sees my reaction to the caller ID and unsubtly disconnects from the conversation around the table in the hope of eavesdropping on mine. I slide out of the booth to take the call outside, denying him the chance.

"How's it going? Is everyone there?" Usually the question is 'is everyone okay?' but because Rob's involved, the enquiry has to be amended to take account of the actor's atrocious reliability issues.

"Yeah, everyone made it. Even Rob...Although, as you would expect, he was late."

"Did Ellis give him a hard time?"

I chuckle to myself as it dawns on me for the umpteenth time tonight how little things have changed since we were unruly lads in this very same city. "Ellis is more stressed out than ever, which is unsurprising considering, so yes, Rob got a real mouthful. He took it well though."

"Stardom hasn't turned him into a complete egocentric prick then?"

"Not complete, no. He's still about 25 percent self-doubting basket case. Nothing will ever destroy that completely, not even daytime television."

The tone on the other end of the phone softens. "Someone wants to have a word with you." There's a muffled exchange between the two most familiar voices in my life and the receiver is noisily passed from one to the other. A soft accent, a combination of my own and the Irish inflections which have been infiltrating since birth, floats down the line.

"Daddy, why aren't you here?"

"Hey sweetheart, how was school?

"I miss you. When are you coming home?"

"I only left this morning, Leah. It's like every day when I go to work. I'll just be gone a bit longer, that's all. I'll be home in a couple of days."

"Aunt Manda said you were being naughty. You have to behave yourself, Daddy."

Cow. Indoctrinating my child in the Church of Bitter Bitches. "I'll be good, Leah, I promise. Can you put Mummy back on the phone?" The phone sounds like it's dropped on a table and the two familiar voices have a short but stern exchange before the more grown up one returns. "So, I take it Amanda called."

"She just wanted to know when you'd be in town." Why? So we can meet and catch up over tea and scones or shop for accessories together at Harvey Nichols? "Just drop by if you have time. It won't kill you to say hi. She is Leah's godmother." Yes, and she's also been my grimacing, miserable nemesis for as long as I've known my daughter's mother. I grunt a non-committal response. The voice on the phone smiles. "You won't be naughty, will you Danny? You're only allowed to be naughty with me. I'll wear that outfit you like if you want to be naughty when you get back..."

Play the game. Don't give yourself away. She doesn't need to know or hear the doubts in your voice. "If you want me to stay faithful it's not a good idea to turn me on when I'm hundreds of miles away, especially considering the company I'm in."

"Well, do what your daughter tells you and behave yourself," the voice grins before taking on the tone reserved just for me. "I love you, Danny."

How long I waited to hear Karen say those words, way back in the mists of time, in that other age. When she said them for the first time, everything fell into place, everything felt right. My choices and decisions were justified, my sacrifices more than worthwhile. These days, these words weigh on my shoulders like a hod full of bricks - and I hate myself for feeling this way. These expressions of love buckle my back; they push down on me, adding pressure and responsibility when once they set me free. Three little words. Partner. Child. Family. I should consider these the treasures of my life, not sources of unhappiness. But lately, the doubts and questions have been rising. Am I happier now than I was before? The fact there is no clear answer right now terrifies me. "I love you too," I reply lamely, hoping that lack of commitment that causes my gut to cramp doesn't transmit through my voice. "I'll see you in a couple of days. Kiss Leah for me."

Ellis comes outside for a cigarette, or at least a smoke. He pulls a small single skinner out of his Marlboro packet and furtively sparks it up as fun seekers totter past on unfeasibly high heels in the direction of the city's cattle markets. He doesn't notice the quick change of expression as I bury my guilt and dig up a cheery façade.

"Do you get drug tested at work?" I ask him as he struggles to hold in a deep lungful.

"No," he wheezes. "The yanks do it but thankfully we haven't taken that on yet."

"Do you ever feel slightly hypocritical that you spend your days trying to get people out of a life of crime while at the same time making it harder for people, like your dealers, to break the cycle?"

Ellis chokes on the weed and coughs out a hail of phlegm onto the pavement. "Fucking hell, Dan. What's with the Paxman treatment? I just wanted a quiet smoke."

"I'm just wondering, man. I just wanted to know if anything had changed to make you cut down on your intake." I take the joint from him as he catches his breath and regains a semblance of composure. "I mean, I don't smoke half as much gear as I used to. Even less than half, actually. And I've been pretty much clean of Class As since Leah was born."

Ellis leans back against the wall and takes a deep breath. "Did having a kid bring this on?" I'm not sure if he means my line of intense questioning or the end of my prolific drug career.

"To a certain extent," I wheeze, answering both possible enquiries with the same answer. The ganja is quick to exert its influence over me, a lot faster than I expected and it's unsettling how alien this feels. Back in the day, it would take a mountain of green to get me high, such was the level of our consumption. I could imbibe all manner of chemicals and still manage to operate better than most straight people in social situations. These days I can barely form a sentence if I've even had a whiff of dope. Right now I'm loath to admit it but it's been that long since I had a proper smoke that I'm in danger of having a whitey right here outside the Passage to India and spewing up my lamb dansak all over the street. My former self would be having a very stoned laughing fit if he could see me now. I take some welcome gulps of air and find my neutral space. I steady my capsizing mind and breathe through the growing unease. "You can't be off your tits when there's a toddler running around, man. They're into everything. And having drugs in the place...No chance. There was an incident not long back where some little kid necked his mum's E." I click my fingers for dramatic effect even though the tragic story needs none. "Dead, just like that."

"Heavy." Ellis looks shocked and more than a little wasted too. I'm wondering if his formerly prodigious intake has been as seriously reduced by his own set of changing circumstances.

"Besides, I very rarely have any time to get shitfaced these days," I add, more than a little sadly. "I need to get stuff done on time or I don't get paid, and if I don't get paid, my kid doesn't get new shoes. I know it sounds like something out of a fucking Dickens novel but it's true. I can't be all drugged up these days because people rely on me. It's not just me I'm taking care of anymore." The weight of this realisation and others force a deep sigh of resignation from my cloudy lungs. "Plus my body doesn't seem to react in the same way anymore...It's like it's had enough. It would rather raise the white flag than do the white line." I pass the joint back to Ellis who seems surprised and a little disappointed to see that there's still a lot of it left to burn. "Fuck, man. When did we become these people...these adults? I can't remember giving my permission for any of this to happen."

Ellis takes a short toke on the spliff and grimaces. "Life is what happens when you're busy making other plans, geezer."

"Or while you're off your face for five straight years."

"We did cane it quite a lot, didn't we?"

"Too right," I reply. "That's why I don't regret that I don't large it like that anymore." My lie convinces no-one. "We did more than our fair share."

"Good times," Ellis says, looking as though he's missing a departed friend. "Good times." I get the sense that he's steeling himself for something as he sighs deeply and takes on a more serious countenance. "Are you still pissed off about the screenplay fiasco? It seems like there was still something a little raw back there in the pub earlier."

His directness blindsides me. "It was a long time ago, man," I say somewhat uncomfortably, once again avoiding the actual truth. "We were different people then."

"That's not what I asked." He draws deeply on the joint and his face flushes. He hands me the burning bush and exhales, eyes bulging. I take the reefer and consider the situation we now find ourselves in while puffing gingerly on the weed. Ellis recovers from his head rush and watches me intently, adding to the sense that this is a crossroads moment. We're away from the numbers and in a frame of mind where this could finally be resolved. I shake the mildly forming sense of paranoia out of my head and decide to take this opportunity that my friend has so bravely offered me.

"I'm not pissed off about what happened anymore," I say in all honesty. "I would have liked to have made a film with you, or even just had one of my script ideas optioned by someone but everything happens for a reason, right?" I take a long pull on the joint, feeling at ease again with its now familiar effects. "What does piss me off is that you blew a great chance for you to make a change."

"What do you mean?"

"Are you happy Ellis?" I pass him the reefer and give him my own intent stare. "Is being a parole officer enough for you? Will it ever be enough for you?"

"It's a job," he mumbles.

"That not what *I* asked."

Ellis takes a moment and his hard features soften. "What do you think?"

"I think you are more pissed off with what happened with the script than I ever was. I think you still blame yourself for denying yourself that chance you always dreamed of having and for some reason that's why you still sabotage the chances you get. I'm pissed off that meeting wasn't enough to change things for you there and then, that you didn't take that disaster and turn it into a learning experience and get straight back out there." I'm flowing with the thoughts now as the dope-greased wheels of my psyche spin fluidly. "I also think that you're still trying to beat your brother. I still don't know what you think you have to do to win this...I don't think there's any winners when you're trying to be someone other than yourself...but you're your own man these days, whatever you choose to do. You don't need to gauge your own success against Sean. I would like to think you have a higher opinion of yourself than that. I'm only pissed off that you haven't realised that yet." Ellis looks shocked. The burst of THC subsides and I suddenly find myself in a vacuum of clarity. "Sorry, man...You did ask."

He blows out his cheeks and takes a moment. "You asked if I was happy," he says thoughtfully. "I am happy, for the most part. My life has changed so much for the better in the last year. Okay, so I'm a parole officer instead of a director. That does eat me up sometimes but not as often as it used to. I have a life now, or at least I'm building one which I can be happy and satisfied with. So what if my job isn't my dream. Maybe it doesn't have to be. I don't fuck my job up like I do these stupid wedding videos I keep agreeing to do, so that must mean something, right?"

I look at Ellis, digesting his words and realise for the first time that I've been less of a friend than I should have been over the past few years. These are words I've never heard before - and only because I was so wrapped up in who I thought Ellis should be to even ask. Instead of accepting him for whom and what he has become, I've been judging him on my own perception of who I think he should be. I've been ignoring the fact that he has found his own way in life, a way so different from the one I expected from him, and have resented the fact that - in my eyes - he has been letting a huge talent go to waste in pursuit of a dead-end job. How patronising can one person be? I forgot to ask if what I wanted for him is what he wanted for himself. I forgot to ask if he was doing something he loved even if it wasn't the thing he loved most. "It means a lot," I finally say. "It means that you're committed to do the best you can do. It means that it's important to you." I hesitate for a moment. "Are you actually a good parole officer?"

Ellis smiles. "Yeah, man. I'm the bollocks."

I grin back. "Well, there you go then." In that moment something changes between us. A cloud which has hanging over us for years suddenly disperses and things become a bit clearer. I feel I know and understand my friend a little better now. He relaxes and I get the feeling a weight has also been lifted from his shoulders. He scrapes the burning tip of the joint along the wall of the restaurant and puts the extinguished half back in his cigarette packet. "So..."

"So..." Ellis echoes. A silence settles between us. Ellis looks puzzled. "What?"

"How are you feeling about the wedding?"

"Man, you promised you wouldn't mention the W word tonight. We made a deal."

"I thought it was the M word which was out of bounds."

"M word?"

"Marriage."

"Fuck, man...you're doing this on purpose."

"Don't be such a little kid," I smirk, enjoying the fact that I'm making him slightly uncomfortable like in the old days. "It's happening. Get used to it. Not talking about is not going to change the fact."

"Yeah but it's alright for you, isn't it? You've always been the more sorted one when it comes to women. It's a piece of piss for you, relationships and stuff."

I realise at that moment that my friends have as many black holes in the story of my life as I have in the stories of theirs. They all look at me as the one who got what he wanted, the man who found what he was searching for. They think it was easy. It wasn't. "Contrary to popular opinion, man, I was as lost as everyone else back then. Let's face it - we were all carrying more fucking baggage than Posh Spice on a shopping trip. I was no exception especially at the end when you all thought I'd made it." Ellis stops looking like a rabbit caught in the headlights, mentally puts his own issues aside and gives me his full attention. "You all think I left the city and went straight into domestic bliss. It was nothing like that. I didn't have a clue what I was doing, man. I went from a time of being completely off my face with you lot every day...chasing birds, getting out of order... to a completely alien situation where everything was different. Nothing brings home the fact that things are never going to be the same than a complete collapse of perception. That's what happened when I left. Everything I knew fell away." Ellis takes out his cigarettes and offers me one even though he knows I don't smoke anymore. Despite not having lit up a straight since packing them in on the day Leah was born, I take one. I need to get things out in the open and right now it feels like a cigarette will make that an easier exercise.

"Did you ever think about coming home?" Ellis asks, providing a flame.

"To what?" I wheeze, holding in the first sweet lungful of smoke. The nicotine joins with the other poisons coursing round my system to give me a short but intense head rush. "Not only had my world changed but *the* world had changed. The party was finished - everywhere. There was nothing cosy to go back to. The life we had was over."

"But everyone was in the same boat," Ellis muses. "I was dealing with it here, Rob was facing up to new realities on the road, McKinley was having culture shock on the other side of the world..."

"Okay so it was happening to everyone; the crowds were changing, the music was turning into something else, the optimism was slowly ebbing away...But those were all gradual warning signs that you sadly accept over time if you stay in a familiar setting. If you're safely in your comfort zone, it's much easier to deal with the changing tide. But try going from living the carefree life of the Lad to living with a woman you barely know in a city miles from home with no mates and a new job at a time when everything which defined you as the person you thought you were is being stripped away...It's like being dunked in a barrel of ice water and coming up to find you've been given someone else's life."

"But you still had Karen," Ellis says, sounding nervous again. "That must have meant something."

"Of course. It would have been a thousand times worse without her but being with her in those early days was one of the biggest parts of the headfuck. Okay, you could say at least I had a bird but at that can be as much of a pain as a comfort. I had to change my ways completely and almost immediately to make it work. I didn't realise what that would mean and how that would change my life. It was fucking hard, man. You're starting at the very beginning again when you move in together. You're learning about her, getting to know parts of her she hasn't shown you yet. I was trying to handle this while not knowing who the fuck I was."

"I bet all the shagging helped though, right?"

"Mate, you think it would be on tap but it all depends on whether you're getting everything else right in your life. If you're fucking up, you're not fucking her. I couldn't piss about anymore because so much was riding on us making a go of it. We were in it together which meant my whole attitude had to change. Suddenly everything mattered. Just weeks before, nothing really mattered. I was scared. I didn't feel bullet proof anymore. Things could hurt me. Things could affect my life. But I suppose that's when things started to fall into place slowly. When you start feeling more vulnerable, your outlook changes." Ellis drags hard on his Marlboro and gets a faraway look of fear in his eyes. In my effort to be more open about my own experiences, I realise that I've completely disregarded the needs of my target audience. Ellis is skittish about relationships at the best of times. With his impending marriage on the horizon, a badly placed word could send him scarpering over it. I switch to a course of reassurance, in turn choosing to not follow through and face my own demons. Ellis is another who won't benefit from hearing about my insecurities. "Look, my life only started to work out when I made the conscious effort to give it a helping hand. You remember? Karen and I almost never made it because I was being such a dick. Only when it looked like my chance was dead and buried did I finally man up and grab my one chance while it was still there."

"Is that what I'm doing?" Ellis asks, almost pleadingly.

"Ellis, you made that choice years ago," I smile. "This just the icing on the wedding cake."

"Funny." His face relaxes and a slight smirk plays at the corners of his mouth.

"Should we finish the joint before going back in?"

"We'll have that on the way to the club," he winks and grabs my shoulder, shaking it briefly in a show of acceptance and thanks.

The club. Of course. This reunion, this stag night wouldn't be the celebration it was planned to be without a visit to the Warehouse.

Few places define our friendship as solidly as the Warehouse. Few places hold as many memories or provoke the same feelings. It was not only the most superior club for miles around during the best (and worst) days of Britpop but it was also a home from home. If anyone of us had shown up on our own, there would have been dozens of people we could have joined up with and had a top night with. It was our crowd. We were known. We were the faces.

It wasn't only the comforting knowledge that we could swan about like royalty in there and banter with all manner of regulars as if we owned the place which made the Warehouse an essential location during our halcyon period. The Warehouse was also a wall-to-wall Lad's playground. You could score anything you wanted in there, from cheap drugs to cheap thrills. The girls were the best in the city; fit, funny and up for it. The gear was (mostly) pure and affordable, punted out by (relatively) honest, stand-up geezers who knew not to fuck you over because you'd buy from them every week.

And the music - man, the music was everything we could have ever asked for and more. It wasn't just the tunes of the day but the ancestors of all what was currently great. Generations of excellent vibes would play non-stop for hours, segueing into each other with love and knowledge, following the eclectic branches of the British musical family tree.

You always knew what you were getting with a night down the Warehouse and rarely were we ever disappointed. I suppose this is one of the reasons why I'm in two minds about going back.

You know what they say: the more things change, the more they stay the same. I never really got what that was supposed to mean. Things that change to a greater degree, by the nature of change, become something completely different. If they stayed the same, they'd *he* the same, right? So I always thought that 'they' were talking out of their arses when they said it.

That is until we finally complete our meandering journey from the Indian and walk straight back into the 1990s. The Warehouse may have had a few new coats of paint since we were last lurching around the old place, and a few fake walls of dangerously low height to drunks have been added but otherwise it looks much the same. The dubious, brown tiled floor is showing its age after nearly 20 years of being pounded by clubbers and gig goers and the stage is looking battered and splintered but these things only add to the warmth of reminiscence emanating from the dingy hall. There, by the speaker tower to the left of the stage, is the gash in the wall left from McKinley's ill-conceived stage dive during an early Shed Seven gig (the obvious bend in the nearby light rig providing evidence of its own role in the ensuing carnage); the fraying chip board corner on the right still bearing the scars of Ellis' attempt to join Paul Weller on stage, a dark map-like stain on the same old stage curtains where I mopped up a mosh-pit nosebleed. It's all still there - the evidence of our former life within these battered walls.

Our current condition is also reminiscent of the state we would be in when we rolled through these doors back in the day. McKinley and I have been drinking pretty much from the mid-morning onwards and Ellis has been racing to catch up ever since he left work. While not a topic of conversation he likes to pursue, it's pretty much accepted that Rob is following in the meandering footsteps of such great thespian drunks as Oliver Reed, Peter O'Toole and Richard Harris and so probably had half a bottle of scotch on the two-hour drive up here. Factor in that we've been smoking ganja intermittently for most of the evening and Rob has probably had a sneaky line or two in his Bentley, we're pretty wasted on arrival. All the more reason to push the envelope, or in this case the small folded paper wrap Ellis has in pocket. After Ellis caves under the weight of the Scotsman's argument for getting the cocaine out, one by one we slope off to the toilets. Maybe it's evidence of a misspent youth but these toilets hold as many memories for me as the dance floor, which is why I choose the last cubicle but one to hoover my line.

This used to come easy to me. There never used to be questions and dilemmas but the nervous thrill ahead of taking any drug these days comes with a certain trepidation which is why I hesitate for a moment, looking down at the roughly chopped crystals on the cigarette-burned lid of the cistern. These are the moments I've been missing; when I can smoke a quiet joint away from the pressures of work or snort a furtive line miles from my family. Anticipating these moments builds an excitement in me which is missing from my everyday existence and I look forward to being that Danny Jones again, just for a moment. Lately, I've been wondering if being that Danny Jones again on a permanent basis is what my life is missing; the freedom, the constant chance of escape, the myriad options available. But now I'm here at the crossroads again and for a second I hear my daughter's voice: "you have to behave yourself Daddy." I briefly consider brushing the powder into the toilet bowl and honouring my child's request. The conflict shoots back and forth for a second more. "Daddy's done a lot worse, sweetheart, and besides...the only person he's hurting is himself. You're safe, mummy's safe and Daddy can handle it." As the sharp acidity blasts up my nostril and a squirming elation begins in the pit of my stomach, I laugh to myself at the absurdity of it all. My experiences in this place, in these toilets, in this cubicle, seem like they're stories from another person's life. It's hard to believe, given how much has changed, that the Danny Jones now feeling a swelling narcotic rush is the same one who once considered the Warehouse his second home. Even though we seem intent on trying to recreate that same magic tonight, none of us are the same people who lorded it over all in this place. To be here now, so off my tits, more mentally compromised than I've been since...well probably the last time I was here some years ago, is surreal. Maybe the more things change, they really do stay the same. Maybe they weren't talking out of their rectums.

Back out in the club, I watch my best friends begin to morph into familiar animals. McKinley has a mad glint in his eye and a slightly aggressive expression on his face - a sure sign that the coke will soon start bringing out the most acerbic side of his nature. Ellis looks uncomfortable in his own skin; edgy and wired with a straining chin which wouldn't look out of place on Easter Island. Only Rob looks at ease. Gak suits the Actor. He's always been an ego junkie, whether it's love, adoration, booze or cocaine that caresses and fluffs it. He embraces the artificial power it gives him. It gifts him with another mask to wear.

Positioned by the loyal old bar, pulled towards its sticky embrace once more, the voices of old friends boom from the ageing speakers all around us; Liam, Damon, Jarvis, Justine... Closing my eyes, it's Saturday night again. I'm rocking a skinny-fit Fred Perry tennis shirt - white with red and blue piping, my jeans are boot cut, my trainers scuffed and retro - my battle-scarred Adidas Sambas. My hair curls in front of my ears and behind, spiking precociously on top, a grown out Beatles cut flirting with Faces-era Rod Stewart. Ellis is beside me, his Keith Moon target t-shirt drenched in sweat and beer, his pale 501s filthy at the knees after skidding in a puddle of Red Stripe, his crew-cut glistening with unabsorbed pearls of perspiration. Shamelessly perving on my other side, the Scotsman peers myopically at passing breasts, turned out immaculately in a plaid Ben Sherman, button-downed collar done up tight, dark Levis and desert boots. His suedehead cut and Heinrich Himmler glasses give him a slightly right-wing vibe but it's okay - the brutal look is in, it's very British without the previously associated nastiness; the aura of fascism suspended for the Britpop generation. Somewhere on the fringes, the rag-tag figure of Rob loiters suspiciously, his attempts at leering less subtle than McKinley's. Dressed in an old denim jacket of mine, a tan corduroy Western shirt discarded by the Scotsman and presumably his own jeans and Caterpillar boots, he nods drunkenly along to the music while ogling women, his floppy Brett Anderson hair hanging lank over his jagged features.

In my mind's eye, a raucous crowd of designer-clad Lads and Ladettes cut a fierce rug in front of us, lost in the anthems of the day; Lacoste and Ralph Lauren do battle to 'Roll With It' and 'Country

House', while Puma and the Three Stripes go toe-to-toe over 'Common People' and 'Connection', and blokes in checks and birds in vintage sportswear dance, flirt, booze and cop off under a constant aural onslaught of sublime British rock.

McKinley nudges me, sticks a plastic pint in my hand and I'm suddenly back in the 21st Century. The music remains the same as in my memory, the crowd before me as young and well-dressed, only subtle changes suggest that fifteen years have actually passed in a blink of my mind's eye. The style is slightly different, the attitude more so. There are fewer beer louts, less obvious sexual activity, and instead of knowing they look good in their clothes and going for it, everyone seems painfully aware of the damage they could do to their clobber should things gets totally out of control. There seem to be fewer risks being taken, less abandon.

And then there's us. Four thirty-somethings (well, three and mid-40s McKinley) showing early signs of wear and tear and a definite age difference to those who occupy the kingdom we vacated and the throne we abdicated. I suddenly get the feeling we're standing out, like four potential undercover coppers checking out what The Kids of today may be getting up to. Old Bill trying to look in touch but failing. My minimalist, post-punk styling - all slim black suit and Beatle boots - suddenly feels like I'm trying too hard. Even the Pretty Green t-shirt under my Paul Smith tailoring - which is a genuine nod to the part of me which still keeps the dream alive - could be misconstrued as a cynical attempt at ingratiation. Ellis looks like the officer who got the wrong decade when doing his research. He looks almost identical to the Ellis in my memory with only a smart black roll-neck replacing the mod t-shirt. He stands there in that old, stinking, heavy Parka of his, scanning the crowd as if he's readying for a snatch raid. The Scotsman, on the other hand, would be the one we call Guv - a study of middle-aged restraint in ironed slacks, sensible loafers, dress shirt and leather bomber. If anyone would be leading the operation, it would be Detective Inspector McKinley. Rob would be the loose cannon who dresses like he's on a stake-out even when he's off duty. For someone enjoying gainful and not un-lucrative employment in a daytime soap, he dresses like a cross between a tramp and Morpheus from *The Matrix* - long, leather trench coat stretching to his dirty Blundstones while hiding a shapeless Aron sweater and grubby jeans in-between. He is Withnail to everyone else's I. Together we look a far cry from the uniformed gang which used to stand out for different stylistic reasons back in the day.

"Glad to hear that they still know what the top tunes are," says Ellis, taking a rapid swig of his beer and tapping an agitated bowling shoe along to 'Live Forever'. Rather than assuming some messianic, centre-stage pose while off my tits on Class As like I would have done in the past, I nod along, both in agreement to Ellis' statement and to the Oasis anthem of belief. I feel strong on the powder but it also stokes latent insecurities of my place in this current Warehouse dynamic. While Ellis looks primed to try and emulate his glory days as the human windmill on this very dance floor, I'm not ready to take those steps into that new reality just yet. Somewhere inside, I fear the feelings and decisions a commitment like that might generate.

"Looking at the state of the place, the record collection probably suffered from the same lack of funds that the minor repairs did," scoffs McKinley. "They probably couldn't afford anything new."

"Come on, excellent music will always get played, whatever era you're in," I say. "Why are we still listening to the Stones, the Kinks...the Beatles?"

"People still listen to Beethoven," adds Rob. "I listen to Beethoven."

"Fucking what?" McKinley exclaims in mirth, his belligerent side beginning to assert control. "Beethoven? You, who used to beat off to

The Prodigy while spying on the girls school tennis lessons through your old man's binoculars? When did you get cultured?"

"I'll have you know that I've always had an appreciation of Ludwig Van," Rob retorts. "He's just not very good to wank to."

The Special Branch quartet crack up en masse. "If you're so into the finer things of life these days, why do you still dress like you've robbed a wino?" asks Ellis as the hilarity subsides. "You look like Arnie in *Terminator*. You probably went up to some geezer in the street this morning and said 'I need your clothes and your motorcycle.'" Ellis' robotic Austrian accent raises more smiles and heralds the return of some long over-due piss taking. "Come on, man! You're a fucking TV star - buy some decent threads for once. I'm sure you can afford it now."

"So says the man in the fucking minging mod blanket," McKinley quips.

"Is that the same Parka you always used to knock about in?" asks Rob, showing no signs of fragility.

Ellis nods with pride. "The very same, geezer. Fifteen years and still going strong. Parkas are like German Shepherds, man. Treat them right and they'll give you years of loyalty and protection."

"Aye, smells like an old Alsatian as well. Did your mum's dog have it for a bed or something? Jesus..." The Scotsman takes a whiff of Ellis' coat and wrinkles his nose. "Tasty."

"This, matey, is a quality bit of clobber," Ellis retorts. "Proper Quadrophenia style. Besides, I work in the parole office. I'm not a daytime soap star - so what's your excuse for looking like a dosser?"

"This, I'll have you know, is what London hipsters call Boho Chic," Rob camps, striking an exaggerated catwalk pose.

"Homo chic, more like," McKinley mumbles near my ear.

"Anyway," Rob continues unaware, "I never bought into the fashion like you boys did. I always thought it was a bit pathetic that everyone would sing along to 'Supersonic', claiming they wanted to be themselves, when they were all dressed and acting exactly the same. Irony was not enjoying its most popular spell back in those days."

"So you actually had a reason for looking like you'd woken up in a Sally Army jumble sale," I playfully snipe. "I always thought it was just because you were a lazy, stingy bastard with no style."

"Look, I'm doing okay these days," Rob continues, "but I'm not Tom Cruise. I can afford a nice suit if I want but that's not me. It never has been." He flaps open my suit jacket for dramatic effect. Rob's response leads to the Scotsman and Ellis eyeing me up and down for the first time since we all came together a few hours ago. It's as though they now see me as I am now, not as Britpop Danny. I can see them comparing their memories of a Lad decked out in sportswear to the reality of the man standing before them. "So are you attending a funeral while you're here or what?" asks the Scotsman, deadpanning as cuttingly as any time in the past. "Or have you regressed to your teenage Goth years?"

"I like his style, man. Don't knock it," says Ellis, gurning appreciatively. "Suited and booted. It's very Strokes, very Interpol. They're not really my taste musically but at least they look cool."

"I never thought that you'd buy into the Yank scene, Danny," sniffs Rob. "I thought you were dyed-in-the-wool Britpop, like, forever and ever, amen."

"Yeah, Danny was such a massive Oasis fan that he always ordered the soup at the college canteen 'cause he got a 'Roll With It'," smirks Ellis.

"Ha ha, very fucking funny," I sneer, although he's not too far off the mark. I was - am, always will be - Oasis 'till I die. But things changed. Faster than any of us really expected or were prepared for. "I've never abandoned my allegiances," I say, perhaps protesting a tad too firmly. "But you have to move on. Besides, what was the alternative? Oasis were bloated on coke and fame, Pulp were drowning in self-loathing and paranoia, Blur were adrift in a massive identity crisis...Everyone was dealing with the consequences of the excess and as a result, the music suffered. That's why fucking Robbie Williams became so huge. All the decent bands went into rehab and pop stars took over. Do you think 'Angels' would have been so huge if the Gallaghers hadn't pissed it all up the wall or Damon hadn't lost the plot?"

"'Angels' is a tune, man," Rob says with no hint of sarcasm.

McKinley aims a mimed face slap in the Ponce's direction. "Shut the fuck up, gaylord, and get the beers in." Rob frowns and turns to the bar, hailing the staff for service with a royal wave.

"My point is, we had it so good that we weren't ready to accept that it was over," I continue. "Britpop was dead the moment Knebworth ended. Nothing was ever going to top that. When a movement gets that big you know it's on the verge of eating itself, just look at Spike Island and Madchester. The bands just can't sustain it after something that huge happens, it all becomes a massive binge and sooner rather than later the place is full of casualties." I really feel the coke now. I'm starting to bulge in my skin; hot rushes accelerate up and down my body, and my mouth is running out of control. For a moment I think I'm going to lose it, that I may have overdone it and that I'm going to need help. But it soon passes and I start feeling holy again when Pulp's 'Party Hard' begins grinding out of the weary PA system.

I was having a whale of a time until your Uncle Psychosis arrived...

Why do we have to half-kill ourselves just to prove we're alive?

"This is what I mean," I grin, nodding towards the speakers and thanking the benevolent gods of emphasis. "No album sums up the end of the good times like *This is Hardcore*. It's the sound of Britpop going cold turkey. Once we'd all come down and faced up to the reality that it was all over, anyone with any taste started looking for the next thrill...and for me, bands like The Strokes were it."

Rob hands out the next round of beers as Ellis and McKinley consider my observations with glazed expressions, grinding teeth and jutting jaws. "What about you, wee man? We know the Ponce here got into Boyzone but where did you end up?"

"I went back to the past," Ellis says, his twitchy legs already taking on a life of their own, suggesting it won't be long before he's out on the floor. "Me and Danny kind of went in different directions at that time." In more ways than one...

The musical routes Ellis and I followed in the wake of Britpop's demise reflected the changes which were taking place in our lives and relationship at the same time. The road we'd been travelling on together for the previous four years split at a junction in 1998 and we sped away from each other after that on very different journeys. Our words to each other have never really touched on this but our divergence has been clear for years in our musical tastes. While we retain our common bond over the music which soundtracked our years together, the preferences we have favoured since emphasize the time spent apart and the different people we have become.

After ending the silly feud over the screenplay debacle, we kept the camaraderie alive by maintaining one of our oldest traditions – the exchange of music. It all began in the mists of time with mix tapes at college as a way of displaying our colours, of presenting each other with touchstones for our fledgling friendship. We then moved onto more eclectic and rare collections during Britpop as we hunted down influential material from the distant past, climbing through the family trees of our rock forefathers. Finally, after we went our separate ways, it mutated into a competition; CD-burned experiments in one-upmanship. The deeper we dug for new music the other may not have heard of, the more our musical tastes expanded and sped away in different directions. It has always given me a weird sense of satisfaction that I can send albums full of far-flung indie and obscure post-punk revivalism and still get old skool mod and Motown classics in return, although - more often than not - Ellis comes up with stuff I've never heard of and subsequently like. It gives me another reason to feel smug and superior - selfish emotions I like to revel in from time to time. It confirms my position (in my own mind, that is) as the person who moved on, the one who evolved. I stop short of verbalising this. Making a statement of your progress tends to negate it. It also makes you look a bit of tit.

McKinley keeps quiet for once and lets go the opportunity to make his own statement. He realises that he's out of his depth a little. He's been out of the cultural loop for some time now even though Ellis and I have been fighting over him for years; inundating him with copies of the albums we've been pelting each other with in our musical war of attrition in the hope of securing his loyalty. Feeding his dwindling interest in music with pirate CDs and bootlegs from Thai markets, the Scotsman has been bypassed by at least two important musical movements since he flew out of our lives in the dying heat of the summer of 96. I know him well enough to know that he still has the spark and that the albums we loved to death fifteen years ago still keep him connected but I also know that we are in danger of losing him behind in the past. While trumping Ellis always gives me great pleasure (- knowing that his love of nostalgia keeps him digging for undiscovered gems reassures me that even if he is going deeper into the archives, he's at least keeping up the search), revealing McKinley's stagnation would give me none. I watch him waiting for a change of topic and decide to save him - and myself. Further analysis of my continued willingness to buy into youth cultures and styles despite my age may instigate the debate which sometimes rages in my own head: is it sadder to live in the past, or be the old fart gate-crasher at the party of the present? I've yet to find a satisfactory answer and I'm always left wondering what the alternative is. Going in search of the answer right now is not the best course of action. I sense my godlike aura slipping. Danny Paranoia is approaching the gates.

"Okay, try and spot the young 'you' in this place tonight," I offer brightly, sweeping the previous discussion under the rug. I start the distracting game with an easy one. "That bloke over there who can barely stand up has to be the new Ellis." A tall, awkward-looking lad is clutching a spilling pint to his breast like a crying child, rocking it back and forth as if comforting it as the music creates drunken movies behind his tightly closed eyes. He blows out his cheeks intermittently, a sure sign that he's coming to the end of the pleasant part of his evening. I've watched my friend sway and struggle much in the same way on countless occasions.

Ellis laughs in that slightly annoyed way of his when he respects the comedy but resents being the butt of it. He scans the crowd for revenge. "Alright," he eventually says, "the geezer in the corner begging that tart to go home with him, that's the 2010 vintage Danny Jones. Look at him, he's probably using the same lines too."

"I've got an alarm clock," deadpans the Scotsman. I silently concede this point because, sadly, this is true. I actually used that once - when a conquest refused to spend the night because she had work in the morning.

"Come on, it could be the start of something beautiful," grins Ellis.

"Fuck off, I never said that," I protest, a little too aggressively. I know I've been guilty of outright lies to get women to go to bed with me but I'm pretty sure that I never resorted to cheesy crap like that. That was always Rob's approach. "You're thinking of the Bard there," I add, pointing at Rob while avoiding further post mortem investigations into my past pulling technique. "Remember that time he was wandering round with those chat-up lines he cut out of the *Mirror*? You were actually reading them out to birds' faces!"

"I bake my own bread." McKinley's memory is sharp. "That was a classic."

"Did you see the sunset last night? Wow." Ellis has his own favourite. "Did any of them ever work?"

"Of course not!" laughs Rob. "But that wasn't the point, was it? Remember the score cards? They weren't supposed to get any of us laid, were they? They were just for the laugh, just us being Lads."

McKinley and I exchange slightly guilty looks. "They got me a blow job," says the Scotsman sheepishly.

"That girl I gave full marks to tugged me off behind the pub," I also admit. "She was well nice."

It's Ellis and Rob's turn to trade expressions, this time of surprise. Rob's face soon slips into a comic-bitter scowl. "Bastards," he mutters as if no time has passed between then and now.

"Come on, we've stopped playing," pipes up Ellis. "Where's the new and barely improved Rob then?"

Four pairs of eyes scan the crowd for a lurching, badly-dressed letch in need of a good wash. McKinley wins. "By the stage, right of the speaker. There's the sad fucker." The resemblance to 90s Filthy Rob is unsettling. The youngster in question stands out in a sea of self-consciously dressed clubbers due not only to his shabby attire but also for his obvious lack of self-awareness. Just as Rob always appeared to be at ease with the fact that he was Pig Pen in our own *Peanuts* gang, so this bloke looks totally unconcerned that he looks as though he may have only recently woken up in a wheelie bin. The amount of alcohol he looks to have consumed is also helping. The world around him, with all its pressures and expectations, seems a universe away as he flails

279

drunkenly around, his unfashionable long hair drenched with sweat and booze whipping the back of his plaid lumberjack shirt like a cat-o-nine-tails.

"Good for him," says Rob, raising a glass in the kid's general direction. "He doesn't give a fuck. And why should he? I never did."

"Yeah, right," says the Scotsman. "You were such a carefree individualist."

"I was," Rob retorts. "I still am."

"Bollocks, you gave a fuck. Of course you did," McKinley responds, the beer and drugs adding menace to his conviction. "That's why you were fucking mental...that's why you're still fucking mental. My missus got you spot on the day she met you. You were always hiding from something - and you still are. That's not the behaviour of someone who doesn't give a fuck, that's what you do when you do give a fuck what people think...and when you don't know how to handle it. You didn't have a clue who you were then and I bet you have even less idea now."

"To be fair, man, weren't we all like that?" I step in before the Scotsman gets too nasty. "I didn't know who I was back then." I'm not all that sure now, to be honest. "It was just easier for some of us to cover it up than others. We all had ways of hiding what was going on but different reasons for doing it. Rob went into acting and we hid behind the Lad thing. Who can say how much of any of that was actually real?"

McKinley stares at me and sways a little as Ellis drifts off into thought. Rob taps his plastic pint glass onto mine and raises it towards me. "Exactly, Dan. We all had masks. Fucking spot on."

The Scotsman blinks and tries to get me into vision. The weight of the developing conversation appears to be too heavy for him as he puffs out his cheeks. "Big man, I need to get some air. I'm well off my tits." With that, McKinley staggers his way through the crowd towards the exit to the beer garden. It seems I'm not the only one riding the peaks and troughs.

"I think we may have just blown his mind," I grin.

"And he thinks I'm in denial," adds Rob. Ellis remains silent and in thought. At that moment the stirring, rhythmic beats of a much-loved anthem thud from the trusty sound system. Again, but this time with my eyes open, I have a vision of the past: I look at the snap-shot expressions of joy on the faces of Ellis and Rob and the same old unspoken agreement passes between us. 'Supersonic'. Any worries I had about looking like a sad old fart among a sea of bright young things fly out of the window as Noel Gallagher's guitar hooks pierce my skin and drag me into the gathering storm. We've been here many times before; lost in Liam's sneer, drifting in narcotic bliss, moving involuntarily in time with the primal swagger. We're here in the present but also here in the past. We're in the sweaty chaos of a warm Glastonbury night while swaying by the Orchard's jukebox on a regular Thursday. We're sat nodding along, stoned out of our gourds in student bedrooms but at the same time celebrating victory in ecstatic rapture among the Knebworth masses. It's not about time and it's not about a place. It's about every time and every place. We're transported to every part of our lives in which this song has been the soundtrack and for those four-and-a-half minutes we're everywhere at once and nowhere at the same time.

The spell is finally broken as Oasis make way for Babyshambles and the kids storm the dance floor, reclaiming it from the old guard. Ellis it seems has other ideas although it's hard to know what's going through his mind as his automatic, even spasmodic, dance moves continue as if the change of song has passed him by. He's lost in music. He's caught in a trap. Rob and I smirk at each before the Actor nods towards the beer garden and we leave the Parole Officer to dance merrily alone in his private world. After we deposit the lukewarm remnants of our last drinks on the bar, Rob buys a pair of fresh, cold lagers and we head outside into an evening struggling to fight off the coming chill of deep night. As we take a couple of seats by the canal (intelligently cordoned off from the water's edge), I spot McKinley having some sort of internal battle with himself in the distant corner. I kick Rob's shin lightly and nod towards where the Scotsman is pacing.

"Should we call him over?" asks Rob.

"I think he needs a bit of space," I smile. "If I know McKinley, he had more than just the one line in the bogs earlier on. He's probably got a lot more going on in his head right now than the rest of us."

"How are you doing?"

I take a deep, welcome breath of unsullied air. "I was on the verge back there for a while," I admit. "I was actually quite badly pissed and then the charlie brought on a bit of a heavy rush but it's evened out now. I'm just nicely buzzy now. You?"

"Supersonic, mate," Rob grins back. "It's strange to be here again. A lot of memories. Not all good, either." Rob's smile dims. I see the face of my friend from years back, the one who used to confide in me, the one who allowed the mask to slip from time to time in the knowledge that we shared something the others didn't have. Or at least we thought so at the time.

"That's what spun me out earlier," I say, feeling at ease with what appears to be the Rob behind the curtain. "So much has happened since I was that person and then to find myself doing exactly the same thing in exactly the same place... Man, talk about two worlds colliding."

"Well, you're not doing *exactly* what you used to do here." Rob's face settles as he finds himself in a safe place with me. "You did a lot of fanny chasing here. We all did...with varying degrees of success. I don't see you doing that now."

"That's true," I say, nodding slowly and casting an eye over to where the Scotsman is now gulping in lungfuls of oxygen between reciting calming mantras. "Even so, it's good to be back," I sigh, feeling a new rush of chemically charged enthusiasm surge through me. "I've missed this."

"Really?" Rob's questioning tone clips my heels as I'm about to take a slightly woozy wander down memory lane.

"You haven't?" A sudden crackle of interference disrupts the wavelength we've been sharing. For a brief moment, barely a couple of seconds long, we share a silence as two strangers would. It's an uncomfortable and unnerving one for reasons I don't quite understand. "I know you're on the telly now and are probably better off financially than the rest of us put together but you really wouldn't want to go back to the freedom and hedonism of those golden days if someone gave you the chance?"

"They weren't all golden," Rob says, a wistfulness creeping into his baritone voice. "You may have had a better time of it than I did, or even Ellis, but you can't say that bad shit never happened to you."

Again our line of communication suffers a disruption. This time it's like a crossed line cutting in from the past. The sounds are unclear but the echoes have a unsettling effect on me. As if reacting to some subconscious prompting, the incoherent vibrations set off an unsettling wave of nervous nausea. Something from my memory is trying to get through… "Okay, it wasn't all rosy," I say, trying to raise the tone of my voice to contradict my statement, "but what I wouldn't give for the space and time just to live like that…like this…again. It was the best time of my life. Shagging around, getting off my face, larging it all over the shop…What a great time to be young. Right? What could top that?"

"What about when your kid was born? Or any moment when you looked at Karen and Leah and felt complete?" Rob stares into my face with eyes I haven't seen for over a decade. I see the face of my friend from years back, the one who used to confide in me, the one who allowed the mask to slip from time to time in the knowledge that we shared something the others didn't have. Or at least we thought so at the time. I see a man who would kill for what I have. "Getting pissed up with your mates is a laugh, Danny, but surely what you have sitting at home is more precious than a life stumbling around in shitholes like this with friends who should know better." The sloshing sickness of recollection returns as the memories I've been suppressing finally hijack the airwaves to deliver their crystal clear message. There was laughter; raucous and genuine enough to risk losing bladder control at times. And there were bright lights and luminous people; shining moments of intimacy and magic under the glow of a youthful sun. But there was also darkness and loneliness; moments of loss and despair away from the crowd with no-one to hold and no-one to talk to. The caves you crawl into for shelter on a long journey of self-discovery are not always lit by the welcoming fires of fellow travellers. Many are stony and cold. A few even play host to the odd wild animal.

I look around at the youthful victims of the Crisis Generation as they stumble and screech around with obliviously happy and short-circuited minds. They'll survive these days the only way they know how; partying through the dark of a recession with the distant lights and sounds of wars they have no real knowledge of sparking on their compromised peripheries. They'll feel that nothing can touch them, that nothing can affect them - until it becomes their struggle and their fight. Because, eventually, we all inherit the world. And it pays to be prepared. It pays to have more than just a reliable dealer and a local pub where everyone knows your name. When the harsh glare of reality turns on you, the barflies and the pushers won't be there to comfort and help you. They'll scuttle into the corners. The real people in your lives will stand by you, wanting to love and be loved by you as the real world shakes into focus. These are the important ones. Why would I want to return to the lonely dark of safe denial when I can stand together with the ones that matter in the beautiful but frightening light? To shy away from that, to crave a return to a life of sleep, a comfortably numb existence devoid of deep interaction, would be a coward's choice. Besides, a wise old Scotsman once told me that we don't have to fully take sides but to accept life's balance: we're all light and dark, big man. We're all light and dark.

"Maybe you're right," I finally say as the veil of denial slips away completely. "Maybe it's not the life I miss but the way we were. We were all elements which made up a whole, and I thought that whole was the most fantastic thing ever. Real friends. You're lucky in life if you can have that, even for a few years. If you can keep hold of them, even when your lives change, then they're the real deal and you're truly blessed."

"Yeah, you're right there" Rob says, drifting into his own introspection. "Real friends. True friends."

I see I'm losing Rob to the dark side and haul him back. "Hey, you know you're loved, right? We've always bullshitted around, and took the piss but we've always been all for one and one for all. That's never changed and never will, okay? Like we always said, women come and go but mates remain."

"The women have come and gone alright..." Rob's voice sails off on a passing breeze and his craggy features sag, making him look a lot like Roger Forester without the aid of make-up. Before he completely disappears inside himself, Rob gains a foothold and forces a smile, as plastic as the glass he now raises to me. "But look at you now, eh? The woman of your dreams, a beautiful little daughter... That's an amazing feat, man, to come out the other side and have a nucleus like that at the centre of your life. It was what we wanted, remember? To find The One. Never lose sight of that, man. You found The One." The One. This is what we shared, the quest to find the one true love of our lives. Rob was as committed to the search as I was but he was never as well equipped to deal with the fact that it was an odyssey filled with rejection and disappointment. Every woman who came his way was The One, from mad middle-aged cougars to hormonally-charged baby fanatics racing against biological time. He always ended up with women who wanted to use him for some reason, be it to help them retain their youth or to provide the seed to birth their obsession. When he couldn't provide what they wanted, they would cast him aside along with his overpowering desire to be loved. My quest was painful in a different way. I knew I would have to experience the lows in an effort to discover the highs. But while this should have given me an edge of optimism to know my chances were increasing with every failure, each discarded bed partner added a little blackness to my soul. It made me question my worth as a human being whereas Rob had no self-worth, he just questioned the unfairness of the world. I eventually found my salvation. Rob continues to search for his in the wrong places. "I know I've blown my chance," he sighs. "Maybe I was stupid enough to blow more than just one. Who knows if I'll ever get another."

"Come on. Look at the women you've been going after. Soap opera groupies and mad old badgers like Mutton Jane and Faye the Sperm Stealer?"

"Who?"

"That lunatic with the intense stare and baby obsession McKinley set me up with once. You and her were at it during the election party in '97."

"Was I?"

"Yeah, man. We watched you."

"And you'd been there before me?"

"No chance, man. She was a fucking nutcase."

"Sounds par for the course...," Rob's voice tails off. "Most of my conquests have been certifiable. You'll never find The One in the loony bin."

I grab his knee. "Rob, can you honestly say to me...all bullshit aside, I know we're high and drunk but try and be honest... Have you ever felt true love before?"

"I don't know."

"Then you haven't," I say. "Which means you haven't blown anything. It's all yet to come, man. Just don't fuck it up when it does because you'll know it when you feel it - and that will be your chance to grab it."

Rob shakes his head slowly. "My life is a sham, Danny. I spend my days living the fabricated life of a 60 year-old billionaire for the titillation of housewives, regurgitating lines that some third-rate hack churns out every week in return for cash enough to fund his meth habit. When I'm not Roger Forester, I'm the actor who plays him, a failed Shakespearean prodigy with no grasp of the real world. My life is a superficial swimming pool filled with sharks and I'm the king of the shallow end. The only time I ever feel real, when I ever feel close to being me - Rob - is when I'm with you boys. It doesn't have to be here, it can be anywhere. You guys are my family and my home. When I'm with the lads...it's the only time I don't feel completely lost."

"Other people can make you feel that way too...if you give them a chance." Two barely teenage girls trip and slide past us towards the darkest corner of the beer garden, their fluorescent garb slipping off bony shoulders and sliding off childlike hips, exposing H&M thongs as they struggle to negotiate tables and chairs. The more unstable one barely makes it to her intended plant pot before she drags up a gut load of watery vomit.

"There's a deficit of genuine people in the world, Danny," Rob says, watching the sadly familiar sight of the allure of excess winning its fight over common sense. "There are too many actors in life, too many masks...No-one's brave enough to show you who they really are. There's too much to lose...I should know."

"Haven't you figured this all out yet?" I ask, somewhat incredulously. "Yes, there are risks to exposing yourself...your true self...and as you know, you have to take a lot of hits. But the rewards are much greater when you meet someone willing to do the same." The non-puking Lolita tending to her overly-refreshed friend looks over and flutters her mascara heavy lashes in Rob's direction. A well-practiced pout follows along with a straightening of the back which pushes her B-cups out and up. Just when it looked like Rob had negotiated his way to the boundaries of the wilderness, the Devil reminds him of the many accessible yet empty pleasures he would be leaving behind.

"Maybe it's just too much hard work being real," he says hypnotically, locking into the stare coming from the nearby Fuck Me eyes. "Perhaps it's easier if we keep it fake. No-one gets hurt."

My tenuous grip on Rob's collar as he dangles over the precipice of the Grand Canyon of Self Loathing and Destruction is starting to slip. I need to get his mind off this - fast - before he plummets to the rocks below. "Hey, what say we find somewhere a little more salubrious to go tomorrow night...if we survive tonight that is," I say brightly. "Nothing heavy, just a few drinks in a bar where the women are on the legal side of puberty. Maybe you just need a change of scene, you know? Forget the easy lays and groupies, you need to identify what you want from a partner. How would you describe your ideal woman?"

"Sane?" A genuine smirk flickers across his face as he breaks eye contact with Lolita and returns it to me. My grip tightens.

"That's a tall order in these parts but we'll see what we can do." We tap our plastic glasses together and toast more positive futures.

"Which one of you queers has the powder?" A more stable and slightly more affable McKinley suddenly swoops in from nowhere and invades the moment. "Sort it out. I'm starting to feel the effects of twelve hours of drinking." I look at Rob and a huge smile involuntarily breaks out across my face. He winks and smiles back. I laugh, almost out of relief at a successful rescue. We're back.

It soon dawns on us that the delicate paper envelope of coke we are so relying on is currently in the sweaty, possibly moist pocket of a certain whirling dervish. "Jesus, it'll be a fucking mothball by now. Where is the wee man?" As one we leave the seriousness of the beer garden behind and return to the frenzied abandon of the dance floor. Ellis is soon located doing something that resembles the Twist by one of the speakers, his eyes bulging, his chin rigid and his pallor pale. Detective Inspector McKinley frisks him and locates the wrap. It's a lot thinner than it was half an hour ago. "Fucking hell, man," the Scotsman chides. "And you call me a greedy bastard. He's had half the gear!" Before Elis can be interrogated further, the electronic glam of Kasabian's 'Shoot the Runner' stomps out over the PA and passes an electric current through our overly-refreshed friend. Ellis careens into the moshing masses like a marionette on methedrone. McKinley shouts well-meant abuse at him but the vibe has him in its clutches and the words are lost. "I'll have the wee bastard when he's done," he mumbles in my ear and points to the bar. I'm eager to find out what's happening with the Scotsman so I suppress the urge to follow Rob into Ellis' wake and choose to accompany McKinley in his search for more alcohol instead. He orders another pair of pints and leans back to observe the ensuing chaos that the Ponce and Wee Man are creating among a crowd of intimidated teenies.

"I thought we'd lost you back there," I say, taking receipt of my drink. "Everything okay?"

"Big man, I'm fucking off the planet. I need some more of that Gianluca or I'm gonna get seriously messy before the night's out."

"I know what you mean, it's anchoring me down," I agree. "But you looked like you were struggling to get it together in the beer garden."

"It's just been a while since I've done so much. You get your hands cut off if you get caught doing shit like this in Jakarta. They'll chop your balls off given half the chance." He glugs down half his pint in one go and belches his dissatisfaction. "Christ, the beer's shite in here. We should get off and have some champers and a bit of toe action at the strip club soon. This place is starting to twist my melon." He turns to the barman. "Big man, your beer's shite. I want my money back."

The barman leans over even though I'm sure he heard what the Scotsman said. Everyone else in a ten-metre radius did, even above the thudding music. He actually has something he wants to say discreetly. "Listen lads, a word of advice. Things are a bit different in here these days. We have a private security firm doing the bouncing and they have a bit of a reputation so maybe it's time you moved on. Your mates on the dance floor are catching the eye a bit and these blokes don't think twice about kicking the shit out of people and throwing them in the river."

McKinley spies a couple of bomber-jacketed Neanderthals edging their way round the edge of the crowd in an effort to get into position to abduct Ellis and Rob. "Aye, aye," he says, tapping my arm and alerting me to the unfolding drama. In a shot I push myself away from the bar and start wading through the bodies to get to the Toxic Twins before the bouncers mount their assault. Like a lifeguard yanking two toddlers from the surf just before a shark attacks, I collar Ellis and Rob and drag them back towards the bar as the bouncers make a frustrated pass of the front of stage area, their quarry getting further away from their jaws by the second. McKinley applauds as we approach and then downs the rest of his rancid beer. "Right," he grimaces. "Time for some quality muff."

nine

You Do Something to Me

March 1996

The Scotsman and Ellis are the dream team at the hotel tonight. It's Mormon Week in the city and the hotel is full of respectably suited-and-booted young men with name tags and lecherous, leathery old farts who ogle the waitresses behind their wives' backs and hide their sinful, priapic thoughts under freshly laundered napkins. Dennis was extremely keen to get the three of us in but I told him I had plans. Even if I hadn't, I would have made some. Mormon Week freaks me out. All these blokes with serene expressions, swarming around the footie stadium in their charcoal grey Next three-pieces looking like some highly-focused insurance salesman cult. The First Bradford & Bingley Restorationists or something. They fill the streets around McKinley's house from dawn to dusk during their seven day mission, threatening to ring door bells or thrust inoffensive-looking but heavily coded literature through your letter box. I'd much rather fight my way home through hordes of drunken Man United fans trying to find their way to the train station than navigate the pin-striped tribes of fundamentalists. Even the prostitutes relocate during Mormon Week, which is ironic considering it could be a bumper week for some of them if they stuck around long and late enough after the gatherings are over.

It's even worse at the hotel. The slightly shabby but strangely alluring grandeur of the old place gets a sudden blast of pseudo-religious whitewash when the Mormons are in town. I'm sure the Hartington becomes, along with the Great Wall of China, only the second man made structure visible from space. Not because their patronage gives it some supernatural growth hormone but because the radiance from the general atmosphere of rapturous joy and sacred cow smiles surely lights up the hotel like a supernova. I find it distasteful and false, and if I had a say, I'd tell them to set up camp somewhere else and spread their "love" on another hotel's bed sheets. But Gerry the Boss loves the Mormons. Apart from the fact that they keep his listing ship afloat every year, he gets "uplifted from their positive nature" quote-unquote. Rumour has it; he and Angela also enjoy the uplifting bouts of sexual abandon which go on between hotel rooms in the reserved wings. But that's all conjecture. No one has ever seen the photos Barry the Barman claims to have. They are, after all, his insurance and retirement package rolled into one. As he often takes great pride in saying, in hushed tones of course, he would be a fool to let them out of his sight.

So, I'm glad to be off out of all the weird, Twin Peaks surrealist fakery and cheaply attired hypocrisy tonight. I have a date. To be more accurate, I have a secret date.

Why secret, you may ask? At a time when any news of a potential shag situation is celebrated within the group with manly cheers and raised glasses of alcohol, you would think I would be mad for the kudos. Ordinarily, this would be the case. However, there are certain ways of doing things at the moment; ways which influence many aspects of life, including how you choose your potential sexual partners. There are certain clothes you need to wear; a certain attitude you need to have, and certain bands you need to be listening to. In most cases, the renewed belief and confidence in being British is influencing all these aspects of life. Don't get me wrong, I'm all in favour of this and am a fully paid up supporter. I have the right number of Ben Sherman's hanging next to the tasteful cross-section of Fred Perry polos in my wardrobe; I am fiercely patriotic when need be but without crossing the fine line into fascism and nationalism, and the next Oasis release is circled in red marker pen on my Loaded calendar. I for one am loving this resurgence but the code of the day makes certain trysts a little hard to stomach in certain circles. One particular circle which would find the tryst in question worthy of a month of piss-taking is thankfully doing the six to eleven shift, serving members of the Church of Latter Day Saints with knock-off salmon McKinley got for twenty quid and a crate of Holsten down the market while off his head on magic mushrooms. This, and the fact that I had a genuine excuse, leaves me free to pursue my object of forbidden lust.

Of course I don't have an actual date. That would suggest that my current run of extreme bad luck and lack of any discernible charm or sexual confidence had been conquered. I will, in fact, be sharing the young lady in question with about 800 other people, not all of them men. This isn't one of the Scotsman's accidentally attended "social group" meetings - there won't be any wife-swapping or flesh pot key exchanges...unfortunately - it's a Belly concert.

Watching bands which have a high popularity rating with the opposite sex has its own set of obvious advantages. Bloke bands - Pop Will Eat Itself or Ned's Atomic Dustbin notwithstanding - usually have at least one fanciable male in their line-up. This will attract teenage girls like a bunch of damp-gusseted moths to a leather-clad flame. Girl bands, on the other hand, bring out those who see the lead female as a role model. In both cases, those young ladies at the front are too busy fantasising or idolising to realise that it's not just the crush behind which is forcing this bloke's penis into their thigh.

Cheap thrills aside, the concert hall can offer the gig pervert many a consenting illicit rendezvous if luck and bravado are on his side. One such situation kept my right hand busy throughout the whole of one cold and lonely winter. It was an erotic experience straight out of McKinley's imagination, just without the spanking and vegetables. Back in the last throes of Baggy sometime in 1991, I shuffled myself along in my C&A flares to see The La's and got more than a night of jangly Mersey pop for my troubles. After one of my sporadic forays into the crowd for a bit of jumping around, I had retired to the steps at the back of the standing area to catch my breath. Most of the crowd was crushed into the first ten feet in front of the stage so those around me were hardly fighting for space. All of which meant that I was slightly surprised when a girl I'd previously seen on the fringes started dancing immediately in front of me. I was just about to get slightly annoyed, given the amount of vacant floor on either side, when she reversed into me and started rubbing her arse on my knee. Taken aback at first, I then shifted position and bent my knee, giving a more solid, pointed quality...y'know, just to see what would happen. This more tangibly hard surface inspired the young lady to rub harder and she began gyrating her backside on my kneecap. No-one around me seemed to be taking a blind bit of notice in the gloom of our corner and after coming to the slightly obvious conclusion that this was not some act of clumsiness on her part, I rested my hand on my knee and stuck my thumb out to give her something to work on. It was definitely to her liking and after riding my thickest digit for a minute or two, I went for broke and slipped my hand up her skirt. It then became very clear that this had been turning her on for quite a while. It wasn't long before she had her hand on my crotch, massaging my cock through my jeans as I went to work in her pants. Then, just as quickly as this situation arose, it was over. She pulled herself off my finger and bounded into the crowd. She never looked round once during the whole thing. That memory made that particular girlfriend-less period much more bearable.

The other advantage of going to see a more bird-friendly band is that if you fail to feel up or cop off with any of the audience, a sexy female singer or guitarist offers a welcome compromise. Feeling as shit about myself as I do right now, pursuing and conquering a nubile Belly fan is unlikely so tonight my adoration and undivided attention will be directed towards the band's leader, Tanya Donnelly.

I've attended a number of concerts in my time where lusting over the female singer relegated the actual musical experience into a distant second place. On more than one occasion, in fact, the deluded wank fantasy totally bypassed the musical taste barriers, leading to some very ill-advised concert attendances; I remember a patchouli-scented pursuit of Julianne Regan of Goth gypsies All About Eve during my early teens, followed by the throbbing need to see Wendy James roll about in lace while Transvision Vamp violated my ears and credibility. But there have been worthwhile pursuits; getting down the front for the Primitives (twice) for a close encounter with Tracy Tracy was particularly thrilling, while an evening pressed against a crash-barrier just feet away from the blonde-bobbed cuteness of Darling Bud Andrea Lewis left me with the horn for days.

Now of course, it should be Justine Frischmann of Elastica (in my case, however, being the picky bastard I am, it's actually Donna Matthews) or Echobelly's Sonya Madan (whose penchant for dressing as a schoolgirl is admirable) and, believe me, hot British indie chicks such as these rock my world - BUT...tonight I am going to have to be a filthy traitor and consort with the transatlantic enemy.

Why are we currently getting so incredibly excited and animated over a handful of good, new British bands? Because since we hung our bell-bottoms up and gave the flower pot hats to our dads to do the gardening in, it's all been about America, plaid shirts, greasy hair and 'I hate myself and I want to die.' It's like the One Love generation never existed. Ever since Madchester sloped off in a drug-induced stupor, we've been playing our Happy Mondays records smooth in the hope that the sleeping giant which is British musical creativity hears the alarm clock of a million voices crying to be saved. Now, it seems, that giant has not only stirred but has woken up, stretched and after finding some grungy Stateside bastard has drunk all the beers while it was asleep, has put on its Chelsea boots and is giving the Yank a swift kick in the bollocks. It's been so long since we've had anything of our own to celebrate that we're over-compensating by larging it like never before. And as a result of being led out of the darkness by these new bands, we're loath to show any kind of allegiance and support for anyone else. The Brits are back and they deserve the undying and sole support of the country's faithful, or so certain manifestos would have us believe.

Of course, not everyone has bought into this musical nationalism. Hence the sell-out show tonight. The more enlightened souls are here tonight solely for the music, regardless of which side of the Atlantic it comes from. Me? I'm hoping not to get spotted by anyone who'll question my Britpop credentials, which labels me both a sheep of the current pop culture and a shallow man willing to cross into enemy territory just to ogle a girl with a guitar.

In all honesty, of course, I'm not totally against the music either. This isn't another Wendy James moment. Ms Donnelly provides a very aesthetic focus but her tunes are pretty good too and Belly are doing well over here despite the media-hyped hostilities. They have an edgy US underground take on the current Brit sound which appeals to the rockier side of my nature. So when the lights go down and the crowd start to whistle and scream in anticipation, I move out of the shadows and stand not that far away from where I fingered the mystery La's girl four years ago.

The band seem overwhelmed by the acceptance of the crowd and respond by tearing through the majority of their 1993 album, *Star*. A particularly raucous *Feed the Tree* has me down the front, forgetting my flock-mentality for three minutes of exquisite college rock. The segue into new material gives me the opportunity to exit the mosh-pit and make it to the bar where I pay two-quid for a drink I could have passed freshly from my own bladder for nothing. I'm standing by the sound desk with a plastic glass of pony urine in my hand when I feel someone stand beside me and fix me with a sideways stare. I endure the feeling of eyes on my face for a few awkward seconds, hoping that it's not the British indie Gestapo, before I slowly turn to the left to face my inquisitor.

"Fancy seeing you here."

Karen. There is a God. "Hey, stranger. I thought I'd lost you forever." My relief is genuine, not because my secret American dalliance remains protected but because I honestly thought I would never see this girl again.

"Well, I said I'd be around somewhere," she smiles into my ear. "And this is somewhere."

I check the vicinity for any signs of Karen's bodyguard. "Are you here on your own?"

"No, I came with a couple of friends but they're, you know, *a couple* so they're off doing whatever couples do when they see bands together." He will be protectively holding onto her from behind, tapping a polite foot but not really listening to the music while fantasising over another pint. She will be immersed in the band and trying to dance while attempting to break free of the possessive bear-hug her bloke has her trapped in.

"No couple's night for you, then?" It's not the most subtle way of finding out of there is an attachment in her life but then again if I was as direct as Karen can be, we would just spend our conversations firing truths and clipped, intrusive enquiries at each other.

"No, I'm not seeing anyone, Danny. Why don't you just ask?"

Ask what? Ask if she's seeing someone? Ask why she ran out on me that night in Probe? Ask if she wants to ditch Belly and go somewhere less crowded where getting naked wouldn't be such a big deal? My head is full of questions, not all of them for Karen. "I tried to track you down after that night in Probe," I admit. "I wanted to see you again." Okay, what was that? That's the kind of admission you make in the dark of the bedroom once you've found out, through a bout of rigorous sex, that the feelings of attraction are mutual. Only the naïve use the truth at this early stage, I should know this. But this girl has a power that makes me want to be honest from the start. It's very unsettling.

She avoids dealing with my statement but her reply suggests that what she just heard wasn't exactly bad news. "So, do you want to walk me home? I have to be up early for work in the morning and I'm not such a huge fan of the band."

If I wasn't wearing everything I arrived in I would be running for my coat right now. Actually, I would probably just leave the fucking thing behind. I can always buy a new one. "Okay. I think I've heard enough too." I awkwardly start towards the exit, not knowing if I should lead, follow or walk out beside her. I stop her by the t-shirt stand. "You do have a key to get in to your place, right? You're not going to run off again."

She dangles a set of keys in front of me. "If I do, it won't be for that reason." She leads the way and that wonderful arse beckons me to follow once more. A mixture of feelings swamp me. Apart from the obvious ones which are stirring between my front pockets, I'm sick with excitement and nerves. What's going on here and why do I seem powerless to stop it?

The university auditorium is a fair walk from the city centre so I'm pleased that it's unseasonably mild for early March. As we cross the car park and onto the main road which rings the campus, I realise I have no idea where Karen lives but I'm hoping it's far enough away to give me plenty of time with her. Wanting to get a firm address which I'll burn into my memory and one which will give our current aimless wandering some direction, I break the silence. "So where are we heading?"

"I want to show you something," Karen says and takes my hand, leading me into the inky blackness of Centennial Park. My previous experiences of going into deserted parks with girls in the middle of the night have all been good (with one exception). Despite not being able to see a thing in the thick band of oak which circles the rolling fields I know from daylight visits, I feel confident that this one will keep my almost 100 percent record intact. The trees soon give way to the huge, sprawling parkland which rolls away from the city limits and into the surrounding countryside. Stepping out of the darkness into the moonlight feels like passing over the threshold into another dimension. We're only a few hundred metres from a busy road but it's silent here apart from the swishing of our feet through the long grass.

"Wow. This is very cool," I whisper, not wanting to break the spell.

"This isn't what I wanted to show you," Karen says. She lets go of my hand and starts running. "Come on," she calls back. Remembering my one bad experience, when an indiscretion I thought was a secret came back to bite me in the arse - and steal my clothes, I quickly give chase. I follow her down the hill and into a glade I've never seen before despite my many visits here as a child. There, in the centre of what looks to be a naturally formed coliseum, is a once ornate, crumbling bandstand. The moon illuminates the hexagonal structure like a spotlight, making it glow almost magically. But it also shows up its state of disrepair; its flaking iron balustrades, its holey roof, the random missing floorboards. Karen walks up the broken steps and stands in the middle of the bandstand, looking up. She turns with a smile brighter than the moon and waves me over. I climb in and stand beside her. She then sits down, pulling me to the floor.

"Lie down and look up," she whispers, reclining on the musty floor. I react as if in some kind of dream, almost floating into a lying position beside her. Looking up at the stars through the battered and gaping rafters, the world stops. Neither of us speak for what seems like eons.

We lie there watching the heavens wheel overhead as this piece of rock we're on turns through space. Clichéd as it is, nothing puts the irrelevance of daily life into perspective like the great unknown. It is also raises questions about existence. But not tonight. I spend too many of my waking hours wondering why I'm here, what I'm supposed to be doing and why love remains elusive. I'm not going to waste this cosmic pause on such egocentric crap.

After a while, I return to earth and tune in to Karen's breathing and the humming presence of her body next to mine. My heart rate and breathing which had been calmed by the solar system suddenly quicken again as I remember myself and remember this girl. This situation, so removed from any which I've experienced with anyone over the last few years, feels unreal and too perfect to be happening to me. It's a world away from nights down the pub with the lads, a universe away from the drunken pursuit of slags in some nasty club. It feels like something which would happen to someone in a romantic novel or a chick flick movie. It feels like a moment two lovers would share. Except a ten-minute snog is as far as 'this' - whatever 'this' is - has ever gone. Part of me feels that this is the perfect opportunity to take things further, or at least pick up where we left off but the majority of me doesn't want anything to spoil this moment. I don't really understand why but the thing I thought I wanted most from Karen isn't important right now.

"I was surprised to see you at the gig tonight," she says dreamily. "I didn't think Belly would be your thing."

"What do you think my 'thing' is then?" I ask, turning my head to face her.

"Well, you have the hair, the clothes...I've seen you in action remember," she pushes herself up on an elbow and looks at me. "You're a Lad."

Usually I would be celebrating this fact. It's the aim of every single one of the tribe to be accepted as such. If you follow the easy steps, read and believe the material you're given, then - if you do it right - you should get the recognition. But from Karen's mouth, it doesn't sound the same. Suddenly, for some reason, I feel less inclined to wear my badge with pride. "I'm just me," I reply, trying to hide the slight tones of hurt in my voice.

"Sometimes, probably. Like that night in Pulse, like tonight...like now," she says. "Why were you on your own? Where were your mates?"

I wouldn't be lying if I said that they were at work. But it is more complicated than that. If I'm being honest I would say that I was there alone and in secret tonight because I wanted to be. I wanted to be me, Danny Jones, not one of the lads, just for a night, just for a change. It felt weird - I still had the Britpop hang-ups - but it felt good. She sees this. She sees a difference. Does she *understand* me? "It gets a bit much sometimes, doing everything together, and doing the same things. I needed a night off."

"So who are you now, right now?"

I sit up and cross my legs in front of her and offer her my hand. "Daniel Jones. I don't believe we've met."

She smiles and kneels in front of me. "Karen Anderson. Nice to meet you." She takes my hand and shakes it softly. "You know, I think we have met before." She leans forward and kisses me lightly on the lips. "Yep, I'm pretty sure you're the same guy."

As well as experiencing that same electrical charge I got in the aptly name Pulse, I feel something of a weight leave me as I shuffle forward and meet her oncoming lips in a second, more passionate kiss. It feels like I have nothing to prove and no-one else to be.

The kissing becomes more intense but, just as before, Karen makes it very clear how far she's willing to go. It's all very passionate but my left hand gets the message that her jeans are staying on after being relocated to her clad arse from her front buttons for the third time. My right is allowed to frantically explore her chest but only on condition it stays above the cloth. Her hands, however, are in my shirt and all over my bare chest but it seems the 'not below the belt' pact is a mutually applicable one, despite my continued efforts to direct her further south. Suddenly, in a disappointing flash-back to our previous encounter, Karen pulls back and composes herself.

"What time is it?" she asks.

"Do you have somewhere else you need to be because this is really nice," I say, somewhat incredulously.

"I've got to get home and the night buses are really crap from around here."

"Wait, you don't live around here?"

"No. And nice try, Danny. I'm not giving you my number or address yet."

"Why is that again?"

"Time, Daniel."

I look at my watch in the beam of moonlight streaming through the gaping hole overhead. "It's almost eleven."

"Shit. The last 38 goes from the Boundary in ten minutes. Fancy a quick jog?" She gets up and rearranges her clothes and hair, which is weird given we're now going to have to sprint to a gate about half a mile away.

"I was hoping for a quick something else but if we have to."

Eight minutes later I'm gasping like an asthmatic as a calm and collected Karen flags down the Number 38. She kisses me quickly and whispers in my ear before jumping on the bus: "Keep looking for me." I'm torn between demanding some kind of explanation and having a cardiac arrest but it's too late to choose. Again, she's gone.

On the unfeasibly long walk home (no bus for me - all my cash must be scattered over the floor of the bandstand) I try and process the events of this evening. This was something entirely different from the night in Pulse. This could not be explained away as some drunken, opportunistic grope. After our first meeting, I was left with the feeling that Karen had crossed me off a long list of unrequited crushes, that I had been a loose end which, by twist of fate, had dangled itself in front of her again. But tonight was something else. Just the fact that we met and kissed for a second time changes this situation between us. My belief that Pulse was a one-off has been proved false. My conviction that Karen had taken all she needed from me in those brief heady moments in the dark has been wonderfully shaken. And not only is there a second act in this story but what a second act! This was intense in a way that the heart-bursting tryst in the club never was. This was less physical. This was spiritual. This was magical. Fucking hell... *What is this?*

The fizzing thoughts racing through my head and the not unpleasant churning in my guts keep me occupied as I make my way home. An hour after Karen got on the Number 38, I'm still drifting in a state of heady confusion. I float over the threshold and crash land in reality.

"Kelly?"

Ellis comes out of the kitchen with a cup of tea wearing a concerned face and nods towards the hallway. He hands Kelly the tea which she takes with shaky hands before leading me out in the hallway, closing the living room door behind us.

"She turned up at the hotel in a right state, geezer. She said she needed to see you. I didn't know what else to do with her. She's a mess."

"Has she told you what's going on?"

Ellis shakes his head slowly. "But the bruise on the side of her face says a lot." He taps my arm sympathetically. "Oh, and Mr. Sifter shat under your bed again. I opened a window but you'll have to fish it out. It's pretty toxic." He raises his eyebrows. "Not your night is it, fella?" He then heads upstairs, leaving me with a blast from the past, an explosion for the future and a landmine under my bed. I take a breath and go back into the living room. Kelly looks up at me, smiling weakly and I see that her left eye is beginning to close above a swelling red crescent. I try to bury the sickness and anger I feel but she sees it growing in me and stands up. She tentatively puts her arms round my waist and pulls herself close to me, as much to reassure me as to get comfort for herself. As she starts to sob, nothing can stop me from wrapping myself around her, a much too late attempt at protection. What happened between us and all the things I went through to forget about her are irrelevant now. She needs to feel safe and I'll do whatever it takes. My body remembers what it feels like to touch her and old emotions and smouldering desires flare up again in the depths. But this is not about us. Even if that had been the reason for Kelly being here, I would still be dousing those flames. That part of us is over. But this is just beginning.

"Tell me what happened, Kelly." The shock of seeing her face like that is compounded by the utter fragility I see in her, the absence of confidence which has literally been beaten out of her. As she sits back down and shrinks before me, I search for that presence which always bowled me over. There's no trace of it. I kneel in front of her and take her hands in mine. "It's okay. Tell me."

"We had an argument...Gary just went mad and lashed out. I didn't know where else to go. I can't go home, he'll go looking for me there."

Fucking Gary. Lunatic or not, if I ever see this wanker... "What was the argument about?"

Kelly looks up from her wringing hands. "You." The surprise on my face suggests further information is required. "I'm pregnant."

You know when people say that they saw the colour drain out of someone's face? Well, there's also a feeling which goes along with that which makes the exterior effect of hearing such news aptly pale into insignificance. It's the feeling of your flesh turning to cold, rubbery putty and the sensation of all the warm blood from your face turning into icy acid. It trickles over your sunken cheek bones like a contaminated mountain stream flowing over jagged rocks before washing into the pit of your stomach in a whirlpool of churning bile. That's where I'm at about now. "Pregnant? Are you sure?"

"I'm sure I'm pregnant...I'm just not sure who the father is."

Okay, one thing at a time. This baby thing is not going anywhere for the time being so let's stick with the first situation. I need to focus on this because the room is starting to spin and I feel like I could puke. "And Gary hit you because you told him I might be the dad?" She nods sadly and starts to cry softly again. I get up and sit beside her on the sofa, taking her in my arms. "First thing you have to do is tell your parents and the police that he hit you."

"I can't!" she sobs. "My dad will kill him."

Yeah, well, sounds like old Gazza has it coming. "They have to know, Kelly. If you tell the police, which you have to do by the way, then they'll find out anyway." I'M NOT READY TO HAVE A KID! I STILL AM A KID! "We'll talk about what to do about the other thing when this is sorted." AAARRRGGHHH! CURSE THE PENIS! "I promise it'll be okay." WHERE'S MY PASSPORT! RUN! GET OUT OF HERE! "You should stay here tonight but call your mum first, okay. Let her know where you are. You can tell your folks about Gary in the morning. Then I'm going to call the police."

For someone who may or may not have knocked up a girl after a frantic, pharmaceutically-charged shag in the toilets of a night club, I can be remarkably responsible when I choose to be. However, if I had been responsible when I *should* have been, one part of this hideous mess may have been avoided.

Kelly cries for another five minutes before composing herself and calling her mum. After hiding the ganja plant in the bathroom and talking Kelly out of having a shower before the coppers arrive - something to do with destroying evidence, I saw it on *Quincy* once - I call the Old Bill. I cradle her through another ten minutes of sobbing before they arrive. Kelly gives a statement to a sympathetic female officer while her brutish male colleague grills me as if I'm the one who slapped her about.

"So you're not Gary."

"No."

"Who are you?"

"Danny Jones."

"Have you ever hit her, Danny Jones?"

"No."

"What's your relationship with Miss Davis?"

Fuck buddy? Father of her child? Resident superhero? "Just friends."

"You look familiar..."

No I don't. "I get that a lot."

The female officer tells Kelly that she has to come to the police station in the morning with her parents then she and Maniac Cop leave, presumably to go and pick up Gary the Wanker. I look at the clock and it's almost two in the morning. While Kelly takes her shower, I mine-sweep for Mr. Sifter's deposit and waste a can of air freshener on my carpet. The furry bastard watches me through the window from the flat roof outside while he limbers up for his nightly operatic performance. I flick him the Vs and aggressively pull the curtains shut as Kelly creeps into the room. I put her to bed before grabbing my sleeping bag and heading for the sofa downstairs.

"You can sleep here if you want." Kelly pulls the duvet back. She looks fantastically vulnerable in my old faded Charlatans t-shirt and her flowery boy-shorts. For a millisecond, I forget that she is with child and sporting a black-eye. Then I regain my senses.

"Tell you what, how about a compromise," I whisper. "I'll sleep on the floor. Just in case you need me." I go to kiss her but stop myself in time. I take her hand instead and squeeze it. I notice that she's wearing the Claddagh ring I bought her as a Christmas present last year; the one I gave to her as we were splitting up. I don't mention it. I don't want to know why she still has it and why she feels the need to wear it. What's past is past. "Everything will be okay," I whisper. Whether my lie was convincing enough or not, I can't tell. Kelly is asleep before the words are out of my mouth.

Even if I was laying on the most comfortable bed in the cleanest, quietest, most freshly aired room, I would still not be able to sleep. Turmoil is like a duck-down feather floating on a millpond in comparison to what's going on in my head right now. Earlier this evening, my main concern was whether I should allow myself to fall in love with the luminously strange and elusive Karen Anderson. Now my thoughts are consumed with visions of crap-filled nappies, dead-end jobs and domestic hell. Okay, it could be worse but not much worse. At least Kelly is fit. Or, at least, she is at the moment. What would childbirth and the pressures of becoming a young mum do to her? Maybe she'd turn into an ugly, bitter fishwife and make my council estate purgatory even more of a living nightmare. No more energetic sex sessions and experimentations with inserted objects, I can tell you. Just a life of shitting, puking and nagging. And as I count the seconds to the sweet release of death, getting fat and depressed over how my ambitions had crumbled, I would dream of the time when Karen Anderson showed me the stars.

she's electric

The arrival of the Camel Club on the city's nightlife circuit is another indication of the upwardly mobile status the council has been pursuing in the last few years - if you consider a lap dancing bar to be the kind of establishment you need to put your fiefdom on the map. Having a lap dancing bar in your city says much about the way society is going in terms of its progress: general moral standards are on the slide, local pervs have a lot more disposable income and certain women are in the position where stripping for cash seems like a good idea. None of these suggest that your locality is heading towards the pinnacle of civilization.

This is not to say that I am frowning down on the Camel Club from a gilded pedestal of outrage. Far from it actually. I'm willingly standing outside in the queue to get in with a hugely excited Scotsman, a slightly tentative and flagging Ellis and a heavily disguised Rob in tow. I'm just glad this place didn't exist when we were living here. There'd be no prizes for guessing where the majority of our hotel wages would have ended up.

It was hoped that our walk from the Warehouse to the Camel Club would have helped with the increasingly dubious state we're all in. However, after berating Ellis for most of the journey for holding the coke to ransom, McKinley had promptly taken control of the stash and chopped out a few thick lines on the bonnet of a parked car. With a new course of medication working its magic, we'd made good time up a hill which is notorious for its energy-sapping length and the number of post-club casualties it has claimed in the past. While our newly imbibed superpowers meant that we were at our destination a lot quicker than we normally would have been, it also meant that the four of us arrived looking more than a little glazed and confused.

"This is a really bad idea," mumbles the Actor from behind the Arab scarf he has wrapped round his face, his eyes no doubt darting around for paparazzi behind Ellis' sunglasses. "All I need is for some maggot from *Heat* magazine to spot a coked-up Roger Forester waiting to get a tug from some provincial stripper and I'll be back doing voiceovers for Carpet City commercials before you can say Bobby Davro."

"No-one would even notice you if you weren't dressed like fucking Yasser Arafat," I complain. "We'll never get in if they think you're going to blow the place up."

"There's no such thing as bad publicity, big man," chuckles McKinley, his anticipation and ardour rising as we near the door. "Look at Charlie Sheen. That fucker could be found with a headless hooker in the boot of his car and he'd still get work."

"What time is it?" asks Ellis.

"Time to get some tart's legs wrapped round your neck," laughs the Scotsman. "What's the problem, wee man? Are you going to turn into a pumpkin or something?"

Arafat props up Ellis' sunglasses and squints at his Rolex under the light of a flashing neon camel. "It's one-thirty."

"Man." Ellis sounds like he's reaching the end of his endurance. "I'll stay for one more round and then I'm heading home. I'm wasted."

"Someone needs another pick-me-up," whispers McKinley in my ear. "Alright, you gay bastard. Just the one and then we'll call you a cab." The Scotsman winks at me and taps the side of his nose. We shuffle towards the velvet rope across the entrance to the club and try and look as straight and respectable as humanly possible, although it seems a futile gesture considering the type of venue we're about to enter. The head bouncer looks down the line, his eyes under a furrowed brow resting on Yasser Arafat's furtive attempts at looking discreet.

"How many, gents?"

"Four of us," I say in my most chipper and personable voice.

The head bouncer counts down the line with a pork sausage finger. He finally points the meaty digit at Rob. "What's his problem?"

"How long have you got?" mumbles McKinley.

"He's a celebrity," I say quickly as a flash of annoyance appears on the bouncer's face. "He's scared he's going to get noticed."

"Who is he then?" So far the bouncer is not impressed.

"Have you ever seen *Billionaire's Playground*?"

"Never heard of it." It looks like we've shit out playing the fame card. Rob sadly takes off the scarf and props the sunglasses up on his head. The bouncer suddenly becomes more animated. "Fuck me, it's the bloke from that Guy Ritchie film...the one where Vinnie Jones sticks that chisel in his head!"

"It was a screwdriver actually," Rob replies, his compromised state allowing his bastardized Bristol-Welsh accent to infiltrate his usually affected Estuary English.

"I thought you were Irish?" The bouncer asks, making Rob's day. "Four is it lads? No problem." He says something incomprehensible into his headpiece and gets a burst of static back in reply. "There's a VIP table with a complimentary bottle set aside for you gents. Shawna will show you to your seats. Have a good night." The bouncer unclips the velvet rope and shows us inside, slapping Rob on the back as we pass.

"Nice one, Yasser," grins the Scotsman as a young West Indian hostess comes to meet us and leads us to our discreet booth where four champagne flutes and a chilled bottle of Cristal is waiting for us. The change in Rob's demeanour gets an immediate and astounding boost. He looked to have been retreating from us back at the Warehouse but getting recognised for one of his better film roles rather than his Channel Five day job seems to have taken him to a new level. It's great to see. It was looking like the happy part of the evening was already over for Rob and so no one uses the moment to turn praise into ridicule.

Rob actually seems the most at ease in this current situation, an indication that his life has had its fair share of VIP moments. He expertly cracks the champagne open with aplomb and pours four frosty glasses without spilling a drop. He passes them round and makes a toast.

"To the four of us, for keeping the bond strong." He raises his hand, indicating that there's more to come. "And especially to Ellis. The reason we're all here tonight."

"Hear hear!" We all glug the Cristal down in one and three of us gasp our satisfaction in unison while Ellis catches a retch in his throat. He certainly doesn't look long for this world. McKinley refills the glasses as Rob catches the attention of Shawna the hostess.

"Shawna my sweet, please keep the bottles coming and we would like a bit of company in a little while so if you can sort that out, I'd be most grateful." Rob hands over his credit card and winks. Shawna smiles back and sashays off towards the bar with three pairs of eyes watching the rhythm of her walk. Only Ellis fails to notice the hypnotic music generated by her hips. He's too busy scanning the club from our vantage point on the raised staging area to the side of the main runway.

"Wee man, you look like you're expecting to get busted," McKinley says, handing Ellis a fresh glass. "It's all cool. We could do a bunch of rails up here and no-one would give a fuck. The Ponce is splashing the cash so we're VIP. Chill."

"It's like *Carlito's Way*, man," I add, using a tried-and-tested device in an attempt to take Ellis' mind off whatever is troubling him. "You're Carlito Brigante, motherfucker to the max!"

"I think I'm having a bad one," Ellis mutters, pulling the tight collar of his jumper away from his neck as beads of icy perspiration roll down his temples. Apart from everything he's imbibed in the last few hours, the sweltering heat in the club can't be helping his delicate state. I'm sweating up too - probably as much from the toxins in my bloodstream as from the unnecessarily efficient heating in this place. As I slip off my jacket, the envelope which Bazza gave me back in the Hartington falls out of the inside pocket and lands on the floor.

"Got some naked photos of your missus in there, have you?" smirks McKinley. "Get 'em out for the boys then." The conversation in the bar earlier suddenly comes to mind and guessing what might be inside the envelope, I choose to keep its contents a surprise. This will teach the bastard a lesson. I chuck the envelope onto the table without a word. "I've often wondered what she looks like in the buff..." The Scotsman tears the envelope open like an excited child opening presents on Christmas morning, albeit one consumed by inappropriate fantasies. "I bet she's got a lovely set of..." He holds one of the photos up to the light. "Jesus Christ!" He shoots a horrified look across the table at me before his burning eyes are drawn back to the picture. "Fucking hell, man...that's nasty..."

Rob picks up the envelope and takes another of the photos out. He has to rotate the picture a number of times before its subject matter becomes clear. "You sick bastard," he says and hands the photo across the table to Ellis.

"Where did you get these from?" asks the mortified Scotsman. "They're brutal!"

"Is that..?" stutters Ellis. "What are they doing with that hosepipe?"

"These," I beam, satisfied to have disgusted all and sundry, "are the notorious Mormon Week photos. Bazza passed them on when I was at the hotel earlier. He said he didn't need them anymore."

McKinley can't tear his eyes off the image in his hands despite it causing his face to crease in sickened shock. "There must be about six blokes there...I never knew Angela had it in her."

"Well, she's definitely got it in her in this one," I grin, passing another sordid snap across the table. The Scotsman baulks, a rare sight. "And yes, that is a goat."

Ellis suddenly turns a ghostly white, slides out of the booth and looks nervously around. "I need the shitter. Anyone know where the bogs are?" He doesn't wait for an answer before stumbling off. His increasingly pale skin shimmers under the pulsating light as he totters between chrome railings over disco-lit floor tiles. He's approached by a dancer who strokes his arm enticingly but she quickly steps out of character when Ellis gags. She points worryingly at the entrance to the toilets and keeps her distance. Ellis makes a beeline for the gents, one hand struggling to keep down the vomit which is threatening to turn projectile. We watch with amusement.

"It's not a stag night until the groom-to-be goes home in an ambulance," smiles Rob.

"Stag night? Fucking Bambi night, more like. Check him out." We watch Ellis stumble his way towards the toilet like a newly born foal.

"He's definitely having a bad one," I say, stating the obvious.

"I thought he was going queer on us," says the Scotsman. "He never was at his most comfortable with the birds."

"And yet he's the one getting hitched."

"Aye. What a shocker." With Ellis out of earshot, it's safe for us to finally address the real reason why we're here, back in the City of Dreams (or Nightmares) Past. One of the conditions Ellis had laid down when we said that we would be throwing him a stag party to celebrate his impending nuptials was that we wouldn't mention that the event had anything to do with his coming marriage. It gave him the fear, he said. After all the shit he'd been through with Monica in their early years together, when he couldn't bring himself to say the words 'relationship' and 'commitment' - reasons for more than one damaging break-up in their collective history - he still couldn't really face up to the reality that he was getting married.

"Whoever thought he'd end up proposing?" muses McKinley, gathering up the offending photographic material and putting it back in the envelope before furtively chopping a thin line out on the table top. "And to a woman as well!"

"Yeah, he always seemed to love the booze and drugs more than anything else," adds Rob. "He was mad for getting pissed and stoned, that one."

"But remember, apart from McKinley, he was the first one to get a proper girlfriend when he started seeing Steak Hammer," I say. "Believe me, that was the real shocker."

"You're telling me," says McKinley, rubbing a nostril. "When I first met him I thought he was so far in the closet he was in fucking Narnia." We enjoy another laugh at Ellis' expense and toast our currently absent friend. The Scotsman chops out another couple of rails and offers round the rolled-up note.

"Did Ellis ever have anyone else...like, ever?" he asks, refilling our glasses again.

"He had a thing for Jailbait Alex at the hotel...and I think she was keen on him but nothing ever happened between them," I reveal.

"Puking on her couldn't have helped," adds the Scotsman. "Anyway, he was probably too scared to sort her out. He only became a man after Steak Hammer took him in hand...or should I say, up the arse." Again, Ellis provides us with a moment of hilarity in absentia. "I would have shagged Alex though," McKinley muses, "but then I would have shagged any of those waitresses given half the chance."

"Yeah but instead of that you got me to do it," I smile.

"To be fair, big man, I only got you to shag Julia Jugs...and that mad bint from the Warehouse," McKinley laughs. "And that one wasn't just for me. You did it for the boys."

I actually did that one for me. I was desperate at the time. Actually, I was desperate most of the time. "That reminds me, I want that video." I trust McKinley with my life. I don't, however, trust him with a homemade porn film in which I'm starring with some drunken slapper I pulled in a nightclub. The notorious Rachel tape hasn't been seen since the Scotsman left for Jakarta over thirteen years ago and knowing that porn films have that uncanny knack of going missing only to turn up where you least expect them, I'm still more than a little nervous about the whereabouts of my one and only credited performance in an adult feature.

"Danny Boy, don't worry. I've still got it. Like I said, it's under lock and key."

"He's probably going to show it at Cannes," grins Rob. "Or screen it at your wedding,"

"Exactly, which is why there's no ring on my finger," I say. "I'm not getting hitched until that film is either in my possession or burnt in front of me."

"I'm truly hurt, big man..."

"Why aren't you married, Dan?" asks Rob, waving over at the bar for more champagne. "You two have a kid. I thought you'd want to do the right thing."

"I do, but not while the bastard Scotsman still has that porn tape." McKinley cheers. "You're holding back the march of holy matrimony, fella."

"Seriously..." Rob takes receipt of the next bottle and signs the bill.

"I prefer to have at least three kids with a woman before I'll even consider marrying her." Rob playfully aims the champagne bottle at me as if he's holding me at gunpoint. I give up. "We just don't see the point in it," I admit. "It's nice for everybody else involved and believe me, my mother is as keen as anyone to see her grandchild have upstanding parentage, but for us, it's just a piece of paper."

"I bet Olivier here is too busy knobbing all those young soap groupies to settle down," McKinley says, punching Rob on the shoulder. "I'm guessing you're not the marrying kind."

Rob winks at McKinley. "You know the score, big man," he says, doing a note-perfect impression of the Scotsman. "Too many tarts, not enough time to shag 'em all."

"Cheeky bastard."

A great performance again by Rob. The tears of a clown. As he breaks open the champagne in another obvious display of largesse, I scan his face for those cracks in the persona which appear when a nerve is touched. And there they are: the dimming light in his eyes, a more pronounced hollowing of the cheeks, the almost intangible tightness of the smile. I've been there when the façade has slipped enough times to recognise these subtle changes in expression which everyone else fails to see. I've been there when Rob has opened up, when Rob has cried, when Rob has been left broken-hearted. I took notice at those times. I watched and listened when the others ripped the piss out of him for being "a big poof" or a "sad bastard". I know that deep down he aches for the chance to meet someone who could be his wife; a woman who loves him for who he is and not what she can get from him, a woman who can respect him. I also know, even after all these years, what Brenda said on the morning after the Labour landslide still rings true - Rob feels that he doesn't deserve the best so he hunts down the nutters and the whores. They at least make him feel that he's right; they reaffirm his self-loathing and enable him in his self-destruction. It's tragic really. Really tragic. But perhaps our conversation back at the Warehouse will give him hope. I sincerely hope so.

"Anyway," Rob continues in his own voice after the barricades have gone back up, "I'm in a completely different situation from you two. You've both had your fun but now you're a couple of breadwinners."

"Fuck off!" My expletive is tinged with both humour and incredulity.

"Cheers, Ponce...just kill me now." The Scotsman levels a stony glare at Rob.

"What I mean is...You two lived it large back in the day," Rob explains. "I tried but it made no sense to me. You both had bigger plans. You both knew that the party would end which is why I think you went for it in such a big way. I didn't have a clue what I wanted or what was going to happen. I was too wrapped up in the angst. Now I'm finally in a position to enjoy myself, like you did back then. I'm just a late developer."

"Aye, in that case, you've got a bit of catching up to do. Get your drugs out. We've finished this one off - and don't lie about not having any. I saw you wiping your nose back in the Warehouse bogs."

"Speaking of bogs," I say, "is anyone worried about Ellis? He hasn't come back yet."

"If Olivier gets his charles out, I'll go and check on him." Rob slides a thick wrap across the table towards the Scotsman. "Jesus, when were you going to tell us that you had fucking Pablo Escobar's personal in your pocket? Dodgy bastard." McKinley doesn't wait for an explanation. He's up and swaggering his way through the hostesses and dancers towards the toilets before Rob can tell him it was the reserve stash, in case the Scotsman himself got greedy with the gear Ellis was supposed to get. Perversely, it was Ellis we should have been watching.

"It's weird seeing him again," Rob says smiling as McKinley cops a feel from a stripper on his way to get even higher. "He hasn't changed a bit and yet something's different. It must be age and responsibility, I suppose."

"He's a complex one," I grin, watching the chided Scotsman almost gambol to the toilets. He got me through a lot shit in the past. There's more to him than meets the eye."

"Yeah, I've seen that side too," admits Rob. "But he's still the biggest pervert and piss-taker I know."

"Don't misunderstand me," I reply. "He's a great listener and has more wisdom than most people would give him credit for but he's still a dodgy fucker. He's older but I'm not sure he's any more responsible." My mind suddenly going back to the conversation that almost took place back at the hotel earlier today. Despite all the revelations we've had so far, McKinley has cunningly avoided talking about the situation which occurred when he came back home to sell the house. We've bullshitted around about the past, revealed a few details that had not been public knowledge and heard about the secret life of Filthy Rob but the Scotsman has yet to spill the beans. He's not going to get away with it again.

"He still doesn't open up much, does he?" Rob muses, sipping thoughtfully on his Cristal. "You were right about what you said in the Indian. We don't really know a lot about what's be going on with each other since we all went our separate ways. I guess we'll never really know about the Scotsman's other life. He's too canny."

"Is he fuck. I have a feeling there's a lot more to come from him tonight. When you get him going, you'll be surprised how deep he can go. He just needs the right kind of encouragement. What do you say we move onto the harder stuff, if your plastic can stretch that far?"

When McKinley returns from the toilets without Ellis, looking more agitated than he did when he left, a fresh tray of gin and tonics adorn the table. The Scotsman wastes no time in taking on more intoxicants.

"Is he still alive in there?"

"He's got more yak than Tibet," McKinley grins, reporting back on the current state of Ellis. "He's turning himself inside out in there. Don't worry, I cut him out a line on the cistern for when he's finished puking. That'll sort him out."

"So," pipes up Rob. "What's the deal with you and Mrs. McKinley these days? Finished having sprogs yet? I have to tell you, I was surprised at the speed that you got her knocked up. I'm guessing it wasn't planned. " Rob's right. The Scotsman didn't wait long before adding a child to his new list of responsibilities when he first arrived in Jakarta, albeit without actually making the conscious decision to do so. Within five years, he and Brenda had accidentally spawned three little McKinley's and tied the knot - both in matrimony and the Scotsman's balls. It had been a whirlwind of change that had left the freshly vasectomised McKinley reeling. Proud as he was of his brood, tinges of regret often peppered his less guarded moments leaving me to wonder if his masterplan had reached fruition too quickly, leaving him with no time for reflection or adaptation. Rob's enquiry prompts a nervous look to cross McKinley's face - it could have been a brief manifestation of that same regret or just a cocaine tremor - either way, the Scotsman looks unsettled. His defences look to be wavering so I take it as a sign to push on in a bid to the Scotsman to bare some of his soul for once.

"Man, we've seen some drastic changes, eh boys?" I say, trying to keep the atmosphere jovial. "Kids, marriage, careers... We would have shat our pants if any of that had come our way back in the 90s, right? None of us were ready for all that back then."

"You had a scare, big man, remember? That tart you shagged in the bogs at the Warehouse." Kelly, of course. How my life would have been different had her kid turned out to be mine.

"Man, I was not up for fathering anyone's child back then, especially Kelly's."

"She was tasty, though. Fucking lovely arse if I remember," the Scotsman drools.

"But you seem to be made for the job," Rob adds heartily, slapping McKinley's knee. "It didn't take the love machine long to get on with the baby-making. He was off overseas and the next thing I hear he's got a wife and she's dropping kids left, right and centre. Right man? It didn't take you long to get the full monty. Fair play. If family and responsibility is your thing then why hang about, right?"

McKinley shifts uneasily in his chair, his face struggling to hide another moment of turmoil. "Yeah but we're still the same lads at heart though," I say. "Tonight proves that. It doesn't matter what changes, we still get the urge to make the same mistakes and act up as we used to once in a while. I suppose it reminds us of the old times. It's just that as you get older, it makes less sense to do those things. You have more to lose."

Ellis wanders back from the toilets looking happier than at any time in the past two hours while McKinley continues his own internal battle. "What are we talking about?" Ellis says, taking his seat and knocking back a G&T.

"We were just saying you have more to lose when you get older."

"I just lost about ten pints and a whole Indian meal, so yeah...I suppose you're right." Ellis waves over to the bar and smiles. "Sometimes losing something can make you feel a whole lot fucking better!" He snorts up a milky stream of escaping snot and then wipes his nose.

"I fucked Manimal." The Scotsman drops a bombshell on us out of the blue. Time stands still for a moment. Expressions remain frozen on faces. The air feels like it's been sucked out of the room. Only McKinley moves, his face turning to each of us in turn, begging for someone to say something. Finally I oblige.

"Say that again."

"I fucked Manimal." McKinley almost pukes the words out this time, like his body is doing everything it can to hold them down but something more powerful inside is forcing them out - like his conscience or his soul maybe. At first a look of stifled amusement passes between Rob and myself until we make the connection between the story of the past and the reality of now. Ellis looks suspiciously unsurprised. So that's what it was all about. McKinley had broken the code.

"When you came back to sell the house?"

"Aye."

"That makes you two practically related," Rob eventually says in a ham-fisted attempt at easing the developing tension.

"How did you work that out?" I ask, perplexed at both Rob's statement and his inability to successfully inject diplomacy into this potentially awkward, painful conversation.

"Well, Manimal is Leah's godmother, right? And you're Leah's father..."

"Yeah, and..?"

"He fucked Manimal." Rob crosses his arms and nods with satisfaction at an argument he presumes to have been well presented and executed. "That makes you almost family." The incredulity spreads around the group and Ellis, McKinley and I sit there in dumbfounded silence for a moment as Rob relaxes comfortably in his twisted logic.

"That says so much more about you and your messed up family than it does about my situation, gaylord," McKinley finally says. "And that in itself is comfort enough, so thanks for being a bigger fuck up than me."

"So now do you know what I was referring to when I said you of all people have settled for your lot in life?" Ellis is now more lucid that at any other time during the whole evening.

"I'm guessing from your lack of surprise that you knew" I say with a slight accent of accusation in my voice.

Ellis looks humble. "Not leaving the city may mean I miss out on more exotic opportunities but hanging around allows me to keep our story alive here," he says. "It may be all in the past for you blokes but for me it's still everyday life. It's not a chapter in the past for me. It's page after page. So yeah, I was here when McKinley came back to sell his house and I was here...although not *right* there...when he shagged Amanda." McKinley seems happy to let Ellis take the lead for now. His wired features twitch and his darting eyes flicker from face to face but he remains silent. "Just as we meet up when we can, Danny, so me and Jockstrap took the opportunity when he was last here. It just so happened that he also used that opportunity to slip Manimal a length."

"It would have been nice for someone to have given me the heads up when it happened...seeings as me and Amanda are related." Rob raises his glass at me as I shoot him a withering glance.

McKinley returns to the fray. "There's not much to say unless you want me to go into the sloppy details," McKinley shrugs. He sits back apparently opening himself up for questioning with a resigned look on his face. "I'll give you the gory details if you want."

I for one do not want to hear about what Amanda is like in the sack. She haunts me enough as it is, lurking in the background of my family and our common history. The last thing I want to add to that ghostly feeling of always having her around is the imagined sights and sounds of McKinley hammering away between her ample thighs. What I do want to know, however, is how it happened and what effect it has had on my friend's life. I'd also like to know why both he and Ellis kept it a secret from me when such conquests were once reasons for celebration. "Leave out the shagging and just tell me why neither of you told me."

"Big man, would you have admitted it?"

"I've had my fair share of slappers, man, and I've always confessed... or at least had one of you bastards blow the whistle on me. Either way, the truth always came out."

"But this was different," adds Ellis. "This wasn't a random fuck. It meant something, right McKinley? That's what you told me. This is what I meant about him settling for the life he has more than any of us. Admit it, Manimal gave you an escape route and you were ready to bail. Instead, you went back to Brenda, swallowed your guilt and stuck by her and the kids despite being unhappy." After all the temptation McKinley passed up during our glory years, he succumbed at an even weaker moment; a moment when his life looked to have stalled. When there was a future, he had more to lose. When that future became the day-in, day-out, he caved in. When the fight looked to have been won, he was blind-sided. He took his eyes off the prize.

"Jesus. Really?" I can't believe my ears. I've been under the impression, ever since the day I met him, that McKinley was following a plan which would culminate I him living happily ever after with Brenda and any future children. Now I hear that he was so unhappy with his life and the completion of his plan that he was willing to throw it all away for Manimal.

"Bizarre as it may seem, the Ponce was actually pretty close before," the Scotsman says. "Manimal is so close to your family that I wasn't sure how it would go down if I told you I'd sorted her out."

"Mate, you know me and Amanda have never been close," I reply. "I don't give a shit that you screwed her. I don't even care that much that you didn't tell me, although you should have. I'm more spun out by how it actually happened and why. Especially after you spent the whole of the nineties denying yourself."

McKinley slides the wrap over the table towards me. "Get your mind on this, big man. I'm going to explain what happened and why I think it happened, so have a line, get another drink down you and get comfortable." Shawna deposits another tray of gins in front of us as McKinley prepares to unburden himself.

ten

Charmless Man

May 1996

Rob's gone. Again.

Just like the last time, we're among the last to find out. Peruvian Tony turns up on the doorstep demanding cash – again.

"He say you have my money. I want my money."

"Tony, I don't know what you're talking about?" As usual. Peruvian Tony rarely makes sense.

"Rob. He gone. He no pay rent. He say here you will pay rent." The midget waves a letter at my navel. I snatch it from his tiny mitt and scan through Rob's spider-scrawl handwriting to find the evidence. Somewhere between a scribble and what appears to be a doodle of Rob as a muscular superhero flying away from the city, I find what Tony's referring to.

"Bastard."

"See? You pay month's rent. Rob say so here. See?"

"I'm not paying you anything. No one here agreed to cover what he owes you."

"But Bastard Rob owe me seventy quids."

"Go and sort it out with his old man."

Tony blanches. "Old man even bigger bastard." The midget thinks for a moment. "You call old man. You get money from bastard old man."

"Sod that. I'm not getting involved. This is your problem, Tony." Some vital information is missing here. In all the confusion of being shaken down by an insane dwarf at eight in the morning I've forgotten to ask. "Where's he gone anyway?"

"He run off to join circus," Tony spits. "Here." The midget hands me an envelope with half a coffee cup ring on one corner and another sketch of a buff Rob holding something which looks like a large vibrator. On closer inspection, I see it's supposed to be an Oscar. Mr. Sifter stealthily approaches from across the street, obviously in search of a second breakfast, and lightens my mood by quietly spraying the back of Tony's leg on his way into the house. The dwarf doesn't notice. "You call bastard old man. You get my money."

"Fuck off, Tony. It's not going to happen." I can still hear him complaining bitterly through the letterbox after I've slammed the door in his face. I stand in the hallway and open the envelope to find another semi-literate letter scrawled on the back of a cheap, photocopied flier.

Boys,

This place has done my head in again so I'm off. That bloke Aiden from back home turned up the other day and asked if I wanted to join up with his theatre group for a tour. Too right I do. So I'm going to be an actor and shag loads of top tarts. No more of the dregs for me. Should be done in about six months but could be away for longer if it works out. May never come back, not for good anyway. Will be in touch.

Rob.

P.S. - Don't give Tony any fucking money.

Well, I didn't see that one coming. I thought Rob had taken the job at the Haymarket bar just to get access to the totty that rolled up there for performances. Little did any of us realise that the sneaky git had been setting himself up for a career treading the boards. Fair play. It's about time he did something with that huge talent of his rather than tossing off around the city like the rest of the spongers. Hi–diddle–dee–dee, an actor's life for me. I turn the letter over to read the flier:

More Bard Than You Can Shake a Speare at

The Selective Works of William Shakespeare

acts of random thespianism by

THE SHAVEN AVON COMPANY

you buy your ticket – you take your chance

performances could include any of the following*

✄

A Midsummer's Night Dream

Hamlet

Much Ado About Nothing

Macbeth

A Comedy Of Errors

✄

*or possibly not

Huh?

I don't see any of the others until that evening at the hotel. Ellis has spent the day dreaming about sex and drugs over cheese and ham at Tesco's (if only the housewives knew what corruptible thoughts the polite young man on deli duty had cast over their stilton) while the Scotsman has been cramming for the exam he'll be attempting to take soon after we get back from our latest trip. I show McKinley the flier as soon as I come into the kitchen.

"Shaven Avon? What is it, some kind of underage sex show or something?"

"It's Shakespeare, geezer. He's off being a luvvie."

"I knew it. He's a fucking bandit. All those sad birds he's been after looked like blokes. It makes perfect sense." He grins as Jailbait Alex comes in to start work. He hands her the flier. "There you go darlin'. Something for you."

She takes the flier and reads it. "Shakespeare? I saw the film at school. It was shit." Bless her. Not the brightest bulb in the chandelier. The Scotsman presses on.

"You could join them though, right? Bet yours is a right little shaven haven."

After finally understanding what he's implying, Alex blushes but tries to hide her embarrassment and maintain her facade of sexual experience. "Pervert. You'll never know." She quickly exits before she had to endure any more of the Scotsman's harassment.

"Like candy floss round a paper cut," he chuckles. "Peachy."

"Can we focus here?" I try and snap him out of his pubescent minge fantasy. "We're a man down. Again."

McKinley shakes the image of Alex's downy undercarriage from his twisted mind and smiles intently at me. "Big man, don't worry. He was never going to come anyway. Now we know for sure that there'll be plenty of space in the car. He would have just minced around the place, ordering small sherries and talking like Alec Guinness all the time. We're better off without him."

After service, as usual on Saturday evenings before the weekly misbehaviour at the Warehouse begins, we find Ellis enjoying a pint and a bit of banter with Barry in the bar. Before saying anything, I hand him the letter. He reads it in silence and then turns it over to read the flier.

"That explains why Peruvian Tony came into work today, ranting about Rob's dad."

"You didn't give him any cash, did you?" I ask.

"Did I fuck. I had security throw him out."

McKinley and I nod approvingly. Dennis the Manager strides in, full of his own self-importance as he is whenever the owners are too drunk to show up and leave him in charge. He leers at the three of us, nodding at each of us in turn. Looks of mild amusement pass between us, unnoticed by our hovering boss.

"What are you degenerates up to this evening, eh?"

"Having a pint," McKinley deadpans, pointing to his glass.

"Or ten more like," Dennis chuckles, knowingly. "Don't overdo it. Save some space for the coming extravaganza."

"I'm sure we'll be fine, Dennis," McKinley says. "We're not leaving until Thursday."

"I'll be in perfect condition. I'll be unstoppable." With that affirmation, he strides off again to berate Jailbait Alex for some minor cutlery indiscretion or other.

"Are you sure about this?" I ask the Scotsman, the architect of the 'coming extravaganza'.

"Trust me, big man," he raises his glass and a devilish smile spreads across his face. "This is going to be immense."

Recent events have led me to question why Dr. Frankenstein made such a fuss when assembling his monster. All that farting about with body parts and lightning, he should have just paid attention to the simplest of instructions: just add alcohol. While Frankenstein was actually attempting to play God and create the miracle of life rather than setting out from the start to build a rampaging horror, we, however, had other ideas. To be honest, at the start, we had *no* idea. But when things started to get out of control, rather than yelling at Igor to lob off its head, we fed our monster more.

Which is why McKinley, Ellis and myself are sitting in an Amsterdam strip bar debating the wisdom of running out on our designated driver, who is currently trying to gobble a banana out of a bird's snatch live on stage. We have no-one to blame but ourselves, and yes, a whole fucking squadron of mutant chickens have come to roost. Six months ago, Dennis was a quiet, slightly strange hermit in his late 30s, living in a basement flat in the east wing of the Hartington. He barely saw daylight, except through the windows of the establishment he'd given his entire working life to and the tinted versions of his one and only love, his jet black Saab 900. He was the hospitality industry's version of a pit pony. When he did venture out of the hotel grounds to blink in the sunlight, he usually spent his rare moments of free time aimlessly cruising the streets of the city listening to dross like the Lighthouse Family - or driving the short distance to his mother's house. It would have been fair to say that his was a sad and simple existence...until we came along. Now, half a year almost to the day since we decided to show him what he was missing out on, we are watching him being serviced by a fifteen stone Oprah Winfrey look-a-like while over a hundred international voyeurs cheer him on.

"What have we done?" I say, laughing in the mirthless, joyless way of the deranged.

"It's like a car crash," says Ellis, in shock. "It's terrible but I can't look away."

"Fucking hell, he's giving it to her from behind now." McKinley, the man responsible for this weekend away, is torn between disgust and his natural response to live sex shows, i.e. getting severely into it. Ellis and I turn away from the stage and motion for two more beers. McKinley downs what's left on his and adds a third to the order. "Put it on the performer's tab," he says, cocking a thumb towards the stage. The bar man nods. This was one of the reasons why creating our own Boris Karloff seemed like such a good idea at the time. We soon discovered that when under the influence of minimal amounts of alcohol and marijuana, Dennis soon forgot who had paid for what. As a result, he paid for everything.

"Part of me wants to go back to a simpler time..." I muse to Ellis, who nods before we both burst into fits of laughter. "This is mad. Who would have thought it?"

"The bastard has form, remember?" McKinley spins round on his bar stool and once again braves the show. "Remember? My place...After that first night with him down the Warehouse? Well fucking dodgy."

That was where this all started. It was my birthday. Just over a year since both McKinley and I started at the hotel. We decided it was going to be a big one. We'd celebrate my twenty-third and combine it with a belated one-year Hartington anniversary bash. The excitement was high and it was the talk of the kitchen for at least a fortnight before the big event. Everyone from the backroom staff had been asked to join in so it seemed only fair to invite Dennis, given that he had spent a good portion of the two-week planning phase mournfully eavesdropping. As usual, he would be working that day but such was his enthusiasm to attend (stoked by the intensity of McKinley's encouragement), he managed to get off a couple of hours early.

On the big day, we started out crawling round the city's bars as early as opening time of that morning, and had decided against taking it easy. In the run-up to lunchtime, the most popular tipple had been pints of snakebite made from a combination of Special Brew and Scrumpy Jack. Lethal stuff. After a pub meal that none of us could later remember eating, the drinks took on a more responsible nature but the quantity continued unabated. So by the time Dennis turned up at the pre-arranged 'staging area' (McKinley's kitchen) for the night's revelry, everyone was arseholed. He was quite shocked at what he saw on his arrival: lines of birthday coke were chopped out on a silver tray, the old cigar box full of pre-rolled joints was open to guests and a couple of bowls of magic mushrooms were available as pre-club snacks. McKinley had to take him to one side and give him some ground rules, mainly 'what happens in this house, stays in this house, yerknoworramean?' Dennis understood and took possession of a large Bacardi and a joint. If any moment in the many that followed could be pinpointed as his first stumble on the slippery slope, that total immersion into the way we did things was probably it.

As with all slopes, when you're at the top, it's all downhill from there. And so it was. The Warehouse was rockin' that night and we were all flying. But Dennis made us all look tame. He was a madman. It was like someone had forgotten to lock the cage of a literate Tasmanian devil while stupidly leaving a mound of amphetamine in a bowl marked 'food' on the table by the door. At one stage, he was so off his face - literally chasing women through the club, screaming - that he didn't notice that the Scotsman had taken control of his wallet. By some miracle, we managed to make it to lights-up without any encounters with the security and headed back to McKinley's to start the slow, painful process of returning to earth. Dennis, meanwhile, had other ideas. Once back at the house, and with 'Fool's Gold' rolling through the ground floor at high volume, Dennis smoked a lot more hash, drank a lot more rum and eventually showed his true colours - and nearly everything else. Lost in the psychedelic pastures of his severely compromised mind and entranced by this unknown haunting music, he began to strip...and then feel himself up, unhinged and castaway in his own private peepshow performance. The initial hilarity on our part soon turned to concern...and then fear as our hotel manager, lost in an erotically-charged pharmaceutical high, threatened to bring little Dennis out to play. That's when we urged McKinley, who was crying tears of laughter by this point, to stage an intervention.

We thought in the days that followed that we would lose our jobs, that the total disregard and disrespect would be punished with redundancy. But when it was eventually time to go back to work, we were met by the new Dennis, a man with a completely different perspective on life: "That was the best night of my life," he drawled. "When are we doing it again?" Morrissey had been right. November had truly spawned a monster.

Finally, the show on the stage is over and we can open our eyes again without fear of our sub-conscious blinding us out of self-preservation. Dennis, overly-sated and sweating, joins us at the bar with the applause of his audience drowning out the next act's introduction. "Do you hear that?" he says, drunk both on alcohol and adoration, "I'm golden. Amsterdam loves me."

While I take my fair share of responsibility for the creation of Dennis the Menace, McKinley must assume the majority of culpability for the jolly we are currently on. I'm not entirely blameless though. It was my idea to plan another break. I really needed a weekend away to bury the remaining feelings attached to Kelly's pregnancy, preferably under a deluge of continental lager and burning bushels of strong weed. I just had to mention this to the Scotsman and events then took on a life of their own.

As I lay on the top bunk, trying to stop the room from spinning while the others snore and fart around and below me, it soon becomes clear that I haven't actually thought this through properly. I'm finding out that once I finally get over the whole baby thing, I still have to deal with the fact that I am alone and that my best chance of finding The One has evaporated in the meantime. I haven't seen Karen Anderson since the night Kelly and her fertilized egg crash-landed back in my life. Truth is, given all the shit that has gone down, the image of her has been blown away by the whirlwind. Far from freeing my mind from the stresses and losses of the past few weeks, the beer is making me morose and melancholic while the ganja is taking my brain down long, unwanted walks down memory lane. Even the scantily-clad treats on offer in the scarlet-tinged windows only remind me of what I'm missing rather than inspiring me to get it for a reasonable price. The potential sex, drugs and alcohol binge I hoped would finally lay all my recent ghosts to rest and pave the way to a brighter future is not helping in the way I thought it would. I talk myself out of this chemically-charged state of analysis and repeatedly assure myself that everything will be okay. Tomorrow is another day.

Thank God for the distractions provided by my travelling companions. McKinley sits across from me nursing a hangover and a fresh pint of beer. It's 10.30 in the morning and we've stumbled our way out of the sweaty, minging confines of our hostel room to get some air and stock up on breakfast in the weak heat of a nearby pub terrace. The most important meal of the day, according to the Scotsman, is steak and chips washed down with a flagon of ale, most of which is sitting untouched on the table before him. The struggle he is dealing with appears to be threefold. Firstly, the deep breaths and sweating suggest that he is engaged in a decision making process regarding vomit. This seems to be at odds with the second; the alien concept of not immediately drinking a beer which is put in front of him. The third, judging by the constant trouser re-arranging, is the need to lose the load he's been carrying around with him since he arrived in the city of sin.

Ellis, looking like a cross between Jimmy from *Quadrophenia* and a deathly pale Stevie Wonder, sits beside me huddled in his parka, his head lolling from side to side as if he's about to break into a rendition of 'Superstitious'. I take a break from taking bets on which of McKinley's basic needs will win the fight and watch my rubbery housemate with interest. I suspect that the real reason his melon is rolling around without restraint is because his neck can't deal with the pressure it's under. It could be his dangerously enlarged brain or the weight coming from the pair of massive shades he is wearing which is causing the imbalance but I finally settle on the chemical version as the reason for his strange demeanour this morning. Entering into the spirit of Amsterdam is only one reason why Ellis went at things full tilt last night. He and Steak Hammer had another of their bi-monthly fallings out before we set off and for once, Ellis didn't allow her to guilt him into making any concessions. From the bunker of my room upstairs, Mr. Sifter and I heard every word. No-one was going to stop Ellis enjoying himself with his friends, apparently, and he was going to go "super fucking large" this weekend and blow off steam after handing in his last piece of coursework at college. Monica seemed quite convinced that Ellis was "having a fucking laugh" if he thought he could just take off to Amsterdam at a moment's notice - especially with that bunch of animals he calls mates. (That's us, by the way, in case that was in any doubt). Monica, as things turned out, would "have to deal with and stop being a bitch." Ellis could "piss right off" and "not bother sniffing around" when he got back. The door slammed after that and Ellis has been wearing a brave face ever since.

Except for this morning. He's currently wearing a very sullen expression with additional green tinge. The fallout of that fight and Ellis' initial attempts to go "super fucking large" in a bid to forget it all are painfully evident in the woeful sight before me.

Sitting next to the Scotsman, Dennis looks a lot healthier than anyone in his situation has any right to. Soon after his Tony Award-winning performance at the Banana Bar last night, he started hitting the hard stuff in a big way. While we stuck with pints, Dennis indulged in a spot of spirit tourism - the act of randomly making your way through the optics behind the bar, sometimes combining liquors which had previously been unknown to each other. He also bought himself a small pipe at some point during the evening, rendering the lengthy and complicated process of rolling a joint while hammered redundant. As a result, when he wasn't imbibing Calvados and Blue Curacao, he had the pipe stuck to his lips like Popeye on Thai stick. Any normal human would either be still in bed at this point or on a slab with a tag on his toe. Not Dirty Den. He has taken receipt of a homemade cheeseburger and is wolfing it down greedily between gulps of effeminate Bucks Fizz.

Me? I'm just happily taking it all in. Happily, because despite the jabbing pain behind the Wayfarers and the acidic event happening in my lower intestines I'm gradually forgetting about the situation back home. It's day two of the Amsterdam extravaganza and I'm finally starting to focus on other things.

"You boys staying here for a bit?" McKinley asks from amongst the carnage of his internal battlefield.

I look over at Ty-Dennis-Saurus Rex devouring his brontosaurus burger and then at the Nodding Mod. "It certainly looks like it," I reply, thankful that no-one is ready to move on quite yet.

"Right. I'm going for a tug." As the Scotsman gets up and slaloms off in the direction of the nearest peepshow, I pay myself the winnings of the bet. The penis wins. But then again, the penis always wins.

"I have to throw up," says Ellis out of the blue. He pushes himself upright, sways unsteadily for a moment and then weaves his way through the tables towards the darkness of the pub.

"Don't call her!" I shout after him. Once my self-generated amusement subsides, I wait for a break in the gorging opposite me to check in with Dennis. "So, Den. What do you think?"

He chews his final mouthful thoughtfully, like a cow working out long division. Swallowing doesn't bring us to the answer any time soon and he blinks slowly at me for what seems like a couple of hours before eventually answering with a lazy grin. "It's fantastic. I want more." It's clear that he isn't talking about ground meat and deep fried potatoes.

"What are you up for today?"

"Everything." No hesitation this time. "I'm going to get my nipple pierced first. And then I want to party." His normally languid drawl is tinged with malevolence, sending a chill down my spine. He nods slowly at me, his bulbous, watery eyes narrow and his Nosferatu smile spreads like a slowly opening gash below his beaked nose. Truly disturbing. As I'm in the process of shaking the dread that has settled on me in this brief moment, Ellis reappears with some colour in his cheeks and a flowerpot of Hoegaarden in his hand. He sits down, props his sunglasses up on his head and sighs.

"Man, that's better." He takes a fast couple of lugs on his beer before letting out a roar of satisfaction. "Who's up for shagging some prozzies today then?"

"I'm going to have two at a time," slimes the rabid dog formerly known as Dennis Collins.

"Top bloke," grins Ellis. "Male or female?"

"I don't care. I want it all."

Ellis and I exchange surprised looks as Dennis cackles from across the table. A lighter-looking McKinley eventually ambles into view with a broad grin on his face, giving us the thumbs-up as he makes his way across the terrace.

"Better out than in," he smiles. Ellis nods in agreement, presumably in reference to his recent Technicolor yawn. "What did I miss?"

"Ellis chucked up and Dennis is a little hotel-motel."

"Excellent," the Scotsman laughs. He sits down and slaps Dennis hard on the back. "Get them in then, yer queer bastard!"

Three more pints and a relocation to a reggae-themed coffee shop later, I find myself floating somewhere above northern Europe with only Ellis for company. Apparently the masturbation break McKinley had enjoyed during breakfast was just the first of many. He and Dennis left for the red light district about an hour ago and neither has been since. In that time, Ellis and I have bought and consumed some of the strongest gear known to man. As my body remains seated under a mural of Bob Marley, my mind is off orbiting the earth while my soul looks down on myself from the corner of the smoky basement's sunburst ceiling. Am I dead? If I am, it's not that bad. A little confusing, but not scary at all.

"Dan? Did you hear what I said?" Ground control to major fucking space cadet. Reading you loud and clear, Ellis. I'm just floating in a most peculiar way.... Experiencing intercom problems right now due to the fact that the three components which make up my being are on different planes. My brain throws on its thrusters and heads back to my earthly form but my soul has no intention of taking up residence quite yet. It still seems intent on watching our conversation from its position above me. Things become a little more disconcerting. "I'm out of my fucking tree, man," body and brain replies. Soul nods in agreement from its corner.

"It's heavy stuff, huh?" Ellis looks very stoned but sounds like he's dealing okay, albeit at half speed. Remembering his initial inquiry, he tries again. "So did you hear what I said?"

"About what?"

"You were talking about Kelly and that it was time to move on, and I asked you if you had any other irons in the fire before she showed up again."

I was talking about Kelly? Was that before my three-way split or after? Maybe that was what sent mind, body and soul to their own separate corners of the universe. Whenever it was, one or more parts of me believe it's time to get over the whole baby drama. The body feels in agreement - no sickness or longing in the stomach or chest. The mind is the organ processing all this and is not adding any awkward questions to proceedings. The soul, my soul, slowly floats home - alone. No real heartbreak and no nagging doubts. Kelly and I are truly history. Planet Earth is blue and there's nothing I can do. But what happens now?

"Danny, man, for fucks sake," Ellis draws on the unnecessary and potentially life-ending spliff he's been rolling since I once more slipped into stand-by mode. "Do you have a woman lined up back home to help you get back on the horse or not?"

"There's shitloads of them out there and ready to go for the price of a slap-up grill." McKinley ambles in, alone. "You can probably find a horse out there too if you look long enough."

"Have you indulged, Mr. McKinley?" Ellis wheezes, barely containing a lungful of smoke.

"Just one off the wrist...The early afternoon trade looks a bit desperate."

"Where's the deviant?" I ask, my brain finally making sense of the simple arithmetic problem it was set on McKinley's return.

"I left Dennis the Menace negotiating with an Asian mother–daughter combo," the Scotsman says as he sits and takes the joint from Ellis. Both he and I zone out as McKinley searches our faces for more responses. "I see you've had a productive afternoon so far."

Actually I'd call making my peace with the Kelly situation a highly successful and worthwhile exercise. Now comes the hard part.

While the idea of paying for sex may combine many aspects of Laddish life - wantonly splashing the cash, treating women as objects, indulging in immoral pleasure - I have to admit I'm not comfortable with the concept. It's hard to say why given its obvious advantages. It's not like my upbringing ever included a lecture on the evils of picking up prostitutes. Imagining my mother struggling to explain the mechanics of the transaction does raise a smile and no small amount of regret though. Despite the lack of any embarrassing parental treatise on the topic, something in the way I was subconsciously educated and socially engineered has instilled a belief in the wrongness of paying for sex. This is a pain in the arse because right now, I have a hard-on for a cute Latina whose olive-skinned and lithe body is daring me to come to the door and do the deal.

McKinley's earlier assessment had been correct. The afternoon trade certainly had the air of desperation about it. For every young gem smiling demurely from a room in the shadowy back streets, there were a dozen fucked-through grannies plying their tired trade from garishly public windows on the main thoroughfare. Men with apparently no taste and no shame mixed with young families and retired couples in crowds negotiating the pretty but sadly corrupt streets of the red light district. Locals shopping for quiet evening meals walked by without a second glance as shaven-headed Brits asked retirement-aged madams if they took it up the shitter. Walking around in this utterly bizarre situation while stoned out of my mind, the whole spectacle soon took on a very surreal nature.

With an afternoon's worth of drugs and alcohol coursing through me after hours spent in the relative sanctuary of a nearby bar, I am now standing in the evening gloom, struggling with my conscience and the throbbing, nervous excitement growing in my jeans.

McKinley is in a room around the corner, justifying to himself that banging a young Thai girl within an inch of her life lacks the emotional connection needed to officially make it an act of cheating. Dennis, after necking a couple of pills he bought off some dodgy dealer on a nearby bridge, was last seen heading for a bar called the Cock Ring to "push the envelope". He and his freshly pierced nipple have not been seen since. Ellis, meanwhile, was practically dragged into a booth by a female Dolph Lundgren look-a-like about 40 minutes ago for a pounding which would make the death of Apollo Creed in *Rocky IV* look like a tickling fight.

I'm still standing in the alley across from my Latina, watching her pornographic Marcel Marceau act aimed at convincing me of the damp heat of her crotch while excitement and doubt battle for supremacy in my confused mind. As I ask myself again why it would be so wrong to pay for the privilege of hammering this sexy little minx, a group of shaggy, denim-clad Germans roll up to her door and start negotiations in broken English. The fattest and sweatiest of the group takes a second to make the decision I've been agonizing over for the last ten minutes and enters the room to wild Teutonic cheers. As my Latina closes the door behind Hans (or maybe Horst), she gives me one last look. It might say 'maybe next time' but it could easily be a plea for help. Either way, it's too late now. My mind has been made up for me. The curtain closes and I check my watch. I have half an hour before meeting the others so I head back towards the lights and sleaze in search of a reflective pint and peace and quiet enough to construct my lie.

The Latina experience brings back the feelings of confusion I'd struggled with previously but now they seem to want to do battle with my willingness to leave all that shit behind. This should be a celebratory weekend, not another of my notorious, self-inflicted guilt-fests. There are many reasons to be cheerful. I dodged a baby bullet and discovered that, when faced with an old flame in need, I didn't take advantage of the situation and screw her. I actually did the right thing and in doing so, I discovered that I am ready to move on. But to what? I've spent the last few weeks fretting over paternity tests and a future completely dominated by unplanned offspring to think about much else. Now I know that Kelly's baby is the spawn of that thug Gary, I should get my life back. Except, when I think about it, I'm not that sure that I want it. As I stand on this bridge, watching the pleasure seekers and curious tourists pass on the canal banks on either side of me, I can't help thinking that I'm at a personal crossroads. I can go back the way I came, muscle the Munich mullet heads out of the way and ride that sexy senorita until I blow my load and a million brain cells in a crescendo of relief. I can go back and answer that call of the wild, the howl of the pack, the cry for last orders. Or I can go forward and leave the red lights behind. I can explore the other side of the canal.

A decision like this really puts things into perspective. The whole Oasis versus Blur drama last August has nothing on this. There the choice was an easy one, like choosing Adidas over Puma. I'll always side with Oasis because they are way cooler and offer us a future. Blur may have won the battle but Oasis are certainly winning the war. Listen to *What's the Story (Morning Glory)?* and then put on Blur's *The Great Escape*. One is the sound of our generation strutting out of their bed-sit parties and claiming the streets, while the other is a sad attempt at keeping the masses happy and comfortable, a last desperate throw of the cockney dice. The time for pale ale and a knees-up is over. What we need now is a proper revolution. Maybe this is the perfect time to go for what we really want and not settle for any substitutes. It's 1996 and time to sort the men out from the Lads. Talking of which, McKinley and Ellis amble into view from adjoining alleyways. Ellis has a sheepish look on his face while the Scotsman, as usual, looks in need of a drink. They weave their way through the masses and onto the bridge.

"So, big man, did you get a portion of spicy salsa then?"

Man or boy? Back or forth? Oasis or Blur? "Nah, I didn't fancy it in the end." McKinley raises his eyebrows but doesn't say a word. He holds his surprised stare for a moment before his features soften. Ellis turns and looks down the canal in silence. "What about you two? Did you get value for money?"

"I've had better," the Scotsman admits with a sniff. "The lass blows fifty blokes a night and she still can't do a decent job." He coughs up a wad of phlegm and gobs it into the water below. "Just can't get the staff...could've got a better suck down the pub for nothing and spent the guilders on lager. Fucking tarts."

"What about you?" I ask Ellis, who is doing his best to appear invisible. "Looks like Ivana the Terrible was ready to give you a good run for your money."

"'S'alright." He never even looks up from his brooding.

"She didn't do a Big Vern on you, did she?" The Scotsman winks.

Ellis turns round from staring over the bridge. "You told him?"

"I...may have mentioned it...yes, I told him," I admit from behind a façade of disbelief at McKinley's indiscretion and creeping amusement. "Come on, man. No need to get up the arse about it."

McKinley cheers and we both descend into fits of laughter. Ellis is having a harder job seeing the funny side of things. "Mate, that was personal shit. That was between you and me."

"And you never told him about Diego Maradona?" This is a nickname given to a particularly ill-advised, and apparently not-so-secret, pick-up I'd made in Chrome Dreams one night. The name is kinda self-explanatory but Ellis fills in the gaps anyway.

"Danny, she was short, fat, hairy and had thighs like a fucking sumo wrestler. Of course I was going to tell him," Ellis protests. "But this is different, man."

"How is this different?"

Ellis looks at me and then at McKinley. About a hundred indifferent people cross the bridge before he answers. "Because I love her."

"Jesus..." The Scotsman actually looks physically stunned. I'm appropriately gob-smacked - and also strangely impressed.

"I never shagged the Russian tart," Ellis continues. "I stood there with the money in my hand and all I could think about was Monica."

"Monica?" asks McKinley out of the side of his mouth.

"Steak Hammer." I whisper in muted reply.

"I've never been in love before but I'm sure this is it...," Ellis adds, his words stumbling out. "And you can call me a big poof and take the piss as much as you want but it won't change anything. This is how it is...and it's fucking scary...but there it is." He takes out his Marlboros and lights one, drawing deeply on it. "Thinking what it would be like without her makes me feel sick," he says, looking up and fixing us, one after the other, with a look of deep conviction. "This fight...It made me realise, I have a choice to make. I think I've made it." This is not the kind of revelation either of us was expecting on this trip so a moment of awkward silence passes before either McKinley or I speak. The Scotsman pipes up first.

"Thank fuck for that. I was beginning to think you were a bender like Dennis the Pennis." I laugh out of relief and Ellis visibly relaxes. I kick him in the leg and give him a wink which means 'nice one' in the Male language. "Speaking of the deviant, where is the queer bastard?" McKinley searches the crowds for a sign of our errant bisexual driver for about five seconds. "Oh well, fuck him. He knows where the hotel is and if he doesn't, tough shit. I need a beer."

Significantly or not, we leave the red light district behind and wander off towards the city centre. After finding a relatively civilised pub in a lively square, McKinley takes our orders and joins the queue at the bar. Alone for the first time since his declaration of love, I take the opportunity to congratulate Ellis.

"I think it's great," I blurt out. "You and Monica. I think it's great."

"Well, who knows what's going to happen, eh?" Ellis shrugs it off. "She may do one as soon as I tell her. If I tell her. If she even lets me close enough to tell her."

I'm not having that. "Come on, man. You've found someone you love. That's huge. That's what it's all about. All you need is love, remember? No one is going to belittle that, and if they do, they just don't understand what it means. And Monica's been after this from you for months, of course she won't do one. She'll take you in those big old muscle-bound arms and hug the skinny crap out of you."

Ellis looks genuinely surprised. "Thanks, Dan."

"No worries, man. It'll be a white boy day, I guarantee it." I reach for his cigarettes and help myself to one. "I have to admit I'm a bit jealous," I tell him, lighting the Marlboro. "Not of the dildo buggery..." I add as he grins self-consciously. "Well...maybe a little about that too but mainly because you've made a connection. All the birds who have come and gone, not one has ever really gotten to me."

"Really? Not one?"

There was one. The One. But because of all the things that have happened recently, I stopped looking for her. I stopped searching. I didn't keep my end of the bargain. Maybe I broke the spell. Perhaps now she'll be gone for good, never to be found. McKinley comes back with three large tankards of Heineken and brings me back from my moment of selfish reflection. "Anyway, this is about you," I pipe up cheerfully, as the Scotsman places the heavy glasses down on the table. I take a tankard and struggle to raise it in Ellis's direction. "To Ellis and Steak Hammer. Long may she tenderize your meat!"

"And shag you up the arse with Big Vern!" adds McKinley loudly, drawing interested glances from those who can understand English on the surrounding tables. "By the way, does she really bash cocks like she's pounding sirloin?"

Again, despite the large amounts of alcohol consumed on the way back to the hostel, sleep does not come easy. I lay in the dark and consider Ellis's commitment. He's come such a long way in a short amount of time. The wayward über–Lad has found direction. More than that, he's found someone who has made him want to change his ways, change his life. Whether he's ready to accept it or not, he's found love. Isn't that what we all really want? Isn't that what *I* really want? Man or boy. Back or forth. Oasis or Blur.

The sun has once again got his hat on so the four of us decide on another *al fresco* breakfast on the sun terrace of the local pub. In contrast to yesterday, however, only one of us is looking and feeling like death. I'm pleased to say it's not me but unfortunately, it's our designated driver – the man charged with getting us to our 8pm ferry sailing from Calais. Why we decided to do the cross–channel route, I'll never know. It would have been easier to get across to the Hook of Holland from Harwich but Stirling Toss wanted to open the Saab up on the French motorways. Now we face another arduous journey south through Belgium to get to our continental hop–off point with Dennis looking like Keith Richards warmed up. He blundered into the hostel last night at about four in the morning, reeking of amyl nitrate and vegetable oil while chuckling demonically to himself. From the small amount of information we managed to glean from him before he retired to sleep in the bathroom, it became clear on which side of the fence he had finally decided to set up his stall. Just before launching into a painful two hours of retching, Dennis officially came out to us. Apparently nothing convinces a person of his sexuality like being tethered to the Cock Ring's bar like a steed outside a western saloon. A night of being led back and forth from the dark rooms out the back also helps. It appears you *can* lead a horse to water and make him drink, and a lot of other stuff too, especially if you feed him on poppers and lube him up enough. Thankfully, Dennis is too close to death this morning to regale us with more tales of wanton sodomy. Still sporting the tell-tale crescent of the toilet seat on his forehead and a smattering of pubes we hope he got from the rim, Dennis is putty in our hands. We pump him full of caffeine and force him to eat a full English in the hope that before we have to leave around three o'clock this afternoon, he'll be back to his old deranged self again.

"One of us can always drive us back if he doesn't make it," I offer.

"Don't talk about me like I'm not here," mumbles Dennis, weakly. "And no-one but me commands the cockpit."

"So you said last night," Ellis replies, raising smiles.

"I won't have any homophobia in the Saab," Dennis growls, wagging a flaccid finger. "Now I'm out, there'll be none of that. Is that clear?"

"I don't like the new Dennis," I joke. "He's a bitch."

"So, you big gay bastard, do you feel better now you've accepted what we all knew about you from day one?" McKinley slaps Dirty Den on the back and nearly knocks him face-first into his plate of egg and bacon. The Scotsman hauls him back upright with a strong grip on his shirt and steadies him.

"I love dick," Dennis says slowly, seemingly unaware of what just happened. "And I feel fantastic." At which point he convulses into a well-lubricated coughing fit which makes him leak from every facial orifice.

"And you look amazing too!" I add, moving my own breakfast away from the toxic spray. "Right, I'm going to take this opportunity to stock up on some more ganja for the way home. Anybody want anything?"

"How are we going to get it back?" asks Ellis through a mouthful of beans on toast.

"Leave it to me," I wink. "I have a cunning plan." I leave the Three Stooges behind and head for the familiar pungency of Smokies, the rather obviously named coffee shop just round the corner from the hostel on Rembrandtplein. (I concede that, when it comes to thinking up names from coffee shops, there are a couple of things that need to be considered. First, one must consider the type of people most likely to be naming the shop. While major smokers may, on the face of things, be just the type of artificially inspired creative types to come up with something mind-blowing for a name, chances are that when the smoke has cleared, none of the great titles can be remembered. Finding themselves still in need of a name, we come to the second most crucial and influential point. Coffee shops have very few uses beyond the obvious. So when the amnesia hits and the need for a name continues to be an issue, most proprietors will think about their establishment's main purpose and settle for the bleeding obvious - Smokies, Head in the Clouds and the like - before building up another six-skinner.) Despite the morning being barely old enough to qualify for its title, the place is heaving with solitary heavy-lidded punters drawing on their first THC of the day and groups of serious looking stoners huddled around hookahs in their conspiratorial corners as techno at ear-bleeding volume rains down on them. Smokies is not alone in this most confounding of Amsterdam phenomena. In my experience, most coffee shops incredulously favour the aural assault approach when it comes to setting the atmosphere. How can a place which has done so much to nurture stoner culture and give it a spiritual home get the music so wrong so often? Apart from the reggae bars, very few coffee shops seem to understand that dopeheads require mellow vibes, not thudding oppressiveness and electro death-from-above. (Maybe Ecstasy bars are a concept better suited for such music - but what fun would those places be? Groups of sweaty, shirtless lads pacing in corners, yearning for more room to experience universal love. No thanks.) One of the most popular conversations between smokers under fire from excruciatingly high bpms must surely be "what music would you play if *you* owned a coffee shop, man?" Personally, I would go for a solid base built on the more restrained aspects of the 1960s; some *Rubber Soul* and *Revolver*, maybe the Stones circa *Let it Bleed* or choice cuts from *Beggars Banquet*, perhaps some *Village Green Preservation Society* Kinks, a smidge of soulful Hendrix and a bit of Traffic. That kinda thing. I'd throw in the Stone Roses and some *Pills 'N' Thrills* Mondays when the buzz gets going and maybe some Marvin Gaye and those of his ilk when things seem a little too fraught. I have very definite ideas but the general consensus among those who like to mix bongs with their songs is that melody is paramount. Flowing with the music and not being drowned by it should be a given, just as straying into territory inhabited by any Floyd album after *Meddle* is widely acknowledged to be asking for trouble...

As I hunker down under the carpet-bombing Euro-thrash in the queue for drugs at the teller window, I strain to hear a young woman who looks like she should be at home studying for an art history exam explain the advantages and disadvantages of the myriad strains of weed and hashish she has under the counter.

"The Northern Lights is quite buzzy but has a mellow edge...The Crystal Haze is a little more intense with some nice visuals, but it's quite smooth...the White Widow is pretty strong, and gets you really fucked up...that's why we sell it in smaller quantities..." The three Welsh lads in front of me hold a very short discussion and plump for three bags of the Widow. An expression which says "I warned you" flickers across her face - I catch it, the Taffs don't - before she pushes three bags of ominous grey-green grass through the hatch. The resignation in her voice suggests this is a scenario which she has seen play out many times before: "Enjoy." The Taffs grab their new stash and greedily scuttle off towards an empty booth and have already started skinning up by the time it's my turn to order.

"Hi, how are you today?"

"I'm good, thanks," I reply, before wondering what it is about me which pegs me as an English speaker before I even open my mouth. "I'm after some solid. What can you recommend?" The Teller pushes a laminated and garishly designed menu through the hatch before running off the types of hashish in much the same way as she explained the weed. Given that they only have three choices, I take twelve grams of each; the Nepalese, the Moroccan and the Afghan. As she's locating the various containers of hash, I look over to see how the Welsh lads are getting on. A joint the size of the Olympic torch is being passed round in what appears to be a very localised example of London pea soup fog. Somewhere in the haze, one of the sheep worriers is having a coughing fit which is so guttural that it's audible over the incessant, ear-splitting blips and beeps. While I fear for his lungs and his long-term mental health, his now slit-eyed friends are finding the whole scene hilarious. That is until they both start hacking their guts up in unison. Happy days... I pay the Teller and stop myself asking her what makes her think I'm English as I catch my reflection in the mirrored wall. Who was I ever kidding? Anyway, I thank her and wander back out into the contrasting, heavenly bustle of Rembrandtplein, swapping the heinous racket of the bar for the somewhat more soothing clang of trams and bicycle bells. It's just as I'm getting my thoughts together before locating the others when I'm beckoned from across the square by a pair of hypnotically familiar buttocks. Various belief systems and previous knowledge cross swords.

No...It couldn't be. Not here. If it is who I think it is then who should *I* be? My decision of the previous night to start moving away from the hardcore Lad towards a person someone could love is still raw and in flux. I was hoping for more time to get to grips with this new version of myself before having to try him out in a real life situation with the girl of my dreams. Oh well, no time like the present...

"Karen?"

Seven tired faces sporting almost matching diva shades turn and look at me in slow confusion. The lack of reply or confirmation from any of the seated zombies has me doubting my initial conviction. For a moment I'm caught in a seven-strong jet black, eyeless stare. It's like I've just gate-crashed a Bodysnatchers anniversary reunion or something. I expect them to all scream a high-pitch, alien wail at me before tearing me to pieces for interrupting their margaritas and human enslavement plans. Thankfully, before this can happen, one of the pairs of fly glasses is lifted to reveal a sunken gaze which confirms a couple of important things. Firstly, it's human (just) and secondly - I'm even more thankful to see that I was right - it is Karen, although a version with a lot less luminosity as usual and with red, rather than the more familiar hazelnut, eyes. I knew it. I never forget an arse. "Danny? What are you doing here?" The other Bodysnatchers turn their deadly gaze from me and start whispering together over their breakfast cocktails. I hear my name mentioned among the low murmuring. I try to appear nonchalant.

"Well, you know, you said to keep looking for you," I grin, trying and failing to exude easy charm. "After exhausting all the usual places, I thought, you know, why not try something a bit further afield?" So this is the bloke you're going to be, eh? The sappy tosser with a line in sad humour? It needs work, Dan. Karen gets up from her seat and takes me by the arm, leading me away from the table of Bodysnatchers towards the bar. She guides me onto a stool and sits on the one beside me. The surprise of seeing her here dwindles quickly into a curiosity about what *she's* doing here, her current state and the less-than-happy vibes I'm getting from her in relation to my unexpected presence. I try and raise the temperature with some unnatural joviality: "Surprise!" Okay, this guy *has* to go.

"Danny, why are you here? How are you here?" These are the questions of a mind not quite in full working order. Karen pinches the bridge of her nose to emphasise the struggle. This frostiness convinces me that the pleased puppy persona should be abandoned right here and right now.

"You don't seem too chuffed to see me." I frown. "Heavy night?"

Karen squints at me and mentally churns a few gears. I can almost make out the sound of crunching behind her furrowed brow. "It's just...seeing you is a bit of a headfuck, that's all." Headfuck? Where did that come from? Hardly the level of considered, philosophical turn of phrase I'm used to from this girl. "I have a really bad hangover and dealing with the world in front of my eyes is really hard right now. Seeing you pop up out of nowhere has spun me out a bit. It's just a bit much right now." Okay, I'm not so naive as to think that Karen is an untouched, virginal hermit who sits in her room waiting for the right moment to resurface and change small parts of my life but I have to admit, I'm also a little spun out. I thought - I hoped - that she was above all this...boozing malarkey. I thought I'd found someone who could teach me the right balance of fun and moderation; the girl who could save me from the downward spiral of pound-a-pint nights and mornings waking up with stray dogs. I didn't expect to discover that there was a Hyde to her Jekyll.

"So what are *you* doing here?" I ask, again dodging the same question for a second time. If she was on the ball, she would have done the simple math by now: Lad + Amsterdam = sex, drugs and drinking. The sex part would be an error but then she's not to know that. The simple addition would have severely compromised my chances of convincing her that I was more than just the Lad she sees me as. Luckily, she seems to be having more trouble keeping the contents of her stomach down than coming to conclusions.

"It's Emma's hen weekend," Karen eventually says after a series of deep breaths. "We flew in yesterday and have been drinking ever since." I cast a glance back at the table of equally compromised Bodysnatchers and identify the bride-to-be by way of the L-plate stuck on her back and the splash of recent vomit on her shoes. The betrothed also appears to be drooling into her Bloody Mary. Some lucky geezer has got himself quite a catch. "There was a strip club...I think," Karen continues, slowly. "A lot of buff blokes with their cocks out..."

Hang on..."Do what?" I sound a lot more upset than I have any right to be. "You went to a dick show?"

"It's a hen party, Daniel. What do you think happens? A night at the opera?"

Fair play. However... "And you like that sort of thing? Geezers swinging their tackle about?"

"It was a laugh, Danny...Anyway, why are you getting all aggro about it?"

Good question - and I could give her a thorough answer but right now I need to be somewhere else. My world was already on its way to being turned upside down, now it's being shaken from side to side. "I'm not aggro," I reply, in a manner that negates my statement. "I am wasting my time though."

"Sorry?" Karen sounds tired and confused. That's still no excuse.

"All this 'search for me' bollocks...If I'd known that you're just like all the rest underneath the cryptic romance stuff I would have just looked for the nearest strip joint. I wouldn't have spent the past year twisting my melon over you, trying to work you out. I would have just looked for the nearest gang of drunken tarts, cheering on a bunch of swinging pricks. Thanks for messing with my head."

"What...?"

"I gotta go," I say curtly. "The boys are waiting for me. See you around."

"Danny..."

I swagger out of the café as best I can while hiding my anger and bruised male pride, sneering my way past the Bodysnatchers table as the future Mrs. Lucky Geezer barfs into her handbag. Classy bird. I storm off through the crowds in a fug of indignation. What the hell just happened? Twelve hours ago I stood on a bridge and made the decision to change my ways to become the man worthy of such a beautiful and sorted young woman. Now it looks like I needn't have bothered. I should have taken the path back into the red lights and fully embraced my inner caveman. Far from striving to be a new man, I should just go back to being the old one. It seems more in line with the real Karen Anderson, the one who drinks from morning till night and likes to have strange penises waved in her face.

I find Ellis and the Scotsman frozen in disgust as Dennis twists a thick golden ring through his recently pierced nipple, revelling in the blood and apparently delicious pain. My return is welcomed with overenthusiastic relief as it distracts Den from his masochistic jewellery obsession and gives the others a chance to tear their eyes away from the disturbingly enthralling sideshow.

"We thought we'd lost you," Ellis says, getting up from his chair a little too fast. "Want a beer? I need a beer. Anyone else for beer?" He doesn't wait for a reply but makes straight for the bar, happy that the spell has finally been broken.

"Did you get a quick shag in then, you filthy monkey?" McKinley's wicked glint has returned to his clouded-over gaze. "Some tasty speciality acts out there this time of day."

"I could do with a nice cock," drawls Dennis, putting his mutilated, raw nipple away.

"You've had quite enough of everything, you mad bastard," McKinley replies earnestly, causing deep cackles of malevolent mirth from the monster. "So come on, Danny Boy, did you find yourself a nice bird?"

"Almost," I say. "But she turned out to be just like all the rest."

Dennis is in his element at the wheel of the Saab. It's as though the car is an extension of his body, like he's incomplete without it. His mood, which hasn't dropped below ravenous all weekend, is suddenly soothed as he calmly negotiates our way out of Amsterdam and onto the motorway heading south to Belgium. He is a study in concentration and skill, man and machine in harmony. All those years with only a four-wheeled friend for company has given his driving an expert edge. Despite his chaotic and borderline psychotic reinvention over the past eighteen months, once in control of his pride and joy, there is nothing but the open road and a comforting synergy to occupy his thoughts. He doesn't twist his nipple ring once.

His passengers also contribute to the Zen-like quality of the early stages of the journey home. McKinley is out for the count beside me in the back of the car while Ellis daydreams silently as Holland speeds by his passenger seat window. Alcohol and drugs have sedated them in different ways; the Scotsman's energy has been sapped, leaving him in need of down time while Ellis has a cinematic inner-eye to keep him occupied. (Speaking of drugs, the malleable hash I bought is currently moulded around the inside of the Saab's rear lights - a little trick I learned somewhere on life's rich and varied highway). Me? As the minutes and miles roll by, I sit and try and work out what my next move in life will be.

I arrived in Amsterdam in need of release after the baby scare and all the shit Kelly stirred up. I just wanted to forget about it all and break free of the shrinking world which had threatened to imprison me during these last three months. When I finally managed to breathe again, I found my breathing to be shallow and panicked. Was a constant run of knocked-up, domestically abused ex-girlfriends to be my lot in life? Was an existence of dodging bullets and inappropriate women the wages of my sin? It all came to a head on the Road to Damascus (or Bridge to Damrak, if you like) last night. Free of the stresses of the past twelve weeks or so, I woke from that nightmare to find my mind confronted with a potentially life-changing set of choices - and I made the harder one, believing it would lead to salvation. But then, a chance meeting with my potential saviour threw it all into flux again. My saviour turned out not be the shepherdess I needed but another wolf in sheep's clothing. Now I'm faced with another choice: sticking with my decision and becoming the black sheep of the family or turning back to the flock.

All this aside, the overwhelming feeling I have as we creep along in a queue at a checkpoint on the Belgian-France border is one of bitter disappointment. I was convinced Karen Anderson was The One.

"Boys, I think we're going to have to deal with the cops here." Ellis sounds nervous as the occupants of a car two vehicles in front of us are grilled by gendarmes with Maglites and semi-automatic weapons.

"Tell them we've been to Brussels," says McKinley. "Look respectable and say we've been sight-seeing."

We look more like a team of Serbian hit-men than a bunch of culture vultures but no-one argues with the Scotsman's plan. There's no time to formulate an alternative either as a French copper dressed like something straight out of the Pink Panther comes up to the passenger door and signals for Ellis to wind down the window.

"Bon soir, monsieur."

"We've been to Brussels," blurts out Ellis. Smoothly done. The gendarme shines his torch into the car, spots the two unshaven assassin look-a-likes in the back and the mess of Rizla papers and spilt tobacco on the floor. His mate comes up to the driver's side, takes one look at Dennis and orders us to the hard shoulder.

"If we get spun," McKinley whispers in my ear, "drop Dennis in the shit. We'll get home somehow."

Five minutes later, the four of us are sitting in the small control room in the central reservation watching a couple of butch policewomen go through our bags on a table in front of us. Outside, as curious tourists creep past in their cars, two coppers are pulling Den's Saab to bits on the side of the motorway. Another stands by with what I'm hoping is the worst narcotics dog on the French force. The doors are in pieces but no-one has even gone round to the rear. All that, however, is about to change.

"What eez theez?" says one of the lady coppers, holding up a pathetic bag of what looks like turf clippings.

Dennis turns a shade paler than usual. They're lifting it from his bag. "Gras savage," he offers, combining some scattered remnants of his school French as way of an explanation. Two burly male officers standing by the door watching the traffic pass are alerted to the discovery. The next thing we know, we're being marched across the parallel highway to a police station which now looms out of the darkness on the other side of the border crossing.

"Have you ever heard of bringing coals to Newcastle, you daft bastard?" McKinley growls at Dennis. "Bringing home-grown on a trip to Amsterdam...for fuck's sake."

The police station, if you can call it that, is ominously empty and deathly quiet. It's really just a large, magnolia-painted room with a bench (on which we nervously balance), a large desk and chair in its centre and four small doors in the far wall behind. Much to our collective dismay, there are a number of wooden bats and truncheons hanging on the wall beside us. Two other officers appear and confer with our escorts. All colour has drained from every British face by the time one of the officers approaches us and mumbles something incomprehensible in French. Taking this as a request for the first interviewee, I decide to volunteer. I raise a hand and just before I stand up, McKinley offers his advice once again.

"Blame the deviant."

Two of the officers lead me to one of the four doors on the back wall. The door is unlocked and I'm shown in. As soon as I realise this is no interview room (no desk, no chair, nothing), a sense of foreboding bubbles in my throat like bile. "Streep," says one of the coppers, and makes a head-to-toe gesture with his truncheon. I'm starting to wonder if, after all this, I'll be less concerned about finding the right woman and more concerned about finding the right man.

There are few things which can send a shiver down the spine like a surgical glove snapping into place. The sound of latex constricting around a brawny, hairy wrist and the muffled screech of the rubber stretching over sausage-like fingers can make the slackest of sphincters shut up shop. Combine this with the vulnerability of standing naked in a locked room with two foreign police officers and the mercifully brief yet humiliating probing that follows and you can understand why, when I'm released from the cell, I can only shake my head at the lads in response to their worried, questioning expressions. There really are no words. Once I'm gingerly seated, the cops dispense with the niceties of asking for volunteers and start picking from the other three. Ellis is next.

"They're going to need a bigger torch," McKinley says. I can't help but smile. Gallows humour at its best.

Eventually, when we've all been searched (Dennis takes longer than anyone but denies accusations that he asked for a second opinion), the cops escort us back to the border post in the central reservation. Our luggage is returned along with, surprisingly, the *gras savage*. Apparently, on closer inspection, the pathetic home-grown didn't even technically rate as an illegal substance - a fact that adds insult to our superficial internal injuries. We're shown to the Saab which has been reassembled and allowed on our way. Dopey the Superdog and his handler have completely missed the ganja in the rear lights and when we're far enough away as not to attract attention, we erupt in cheers of relief and victory. What's a bit of rough anal fingering when you can smoke the memory away with some of Amsterdam's finest hash in the comfort of your own home? We make it to the ferry and once safely on board, we treat ourselves to a well-deserved drink and toast getting one over Le Frogs. After the first mouthfuls of freedom are savoured, McKinley taps his pint glass to call us to order.

"Boys, I have to say, this was a fucking epic weekend. Legendary, even by our own standards. Its mythic status will no doubt grow in bars all over the land in time but one thing should be said at this point: when it comes to the anal probe, what happens on the road, stays on the road. Know what I mean?" He looks each of us in the eye. Neither I nor Ellis have any problem with this rule. Dennis looks a little disappointed. "Alright, you can crow about it to your bandit mates but leave us all out of it, okay?"

"I'll say I was rodgered by the cops," Dennis states belligerently. "I'll be a god."

"Just keep us out of it, you mad gay bastard."

With that, our ferry sets sail. We're homeward bound.

eleven

McKinley's Story

I never really knew or cared for that matter if the boys understood what was going on with me. To be honest, I didn't fucking know myself half the time. I just knew that I'd come into this situation from a completely different angle from everyone else. Not just because I was older and I had a bird, but because they were finding their way every day whereas I'd found mine. I was just on the hard shoulder waiting for the breakdown lorry to pick me up. The fact that it took about three years to get going again was a bit of a surprise but I knew I would be on my way eventually. I suppose the others also knew deep down that this wasn't the be-all and end-all. But I knew exactly what I was working towards and where I'd be. I was on a holiday from real life. What a fucking vacation that was...

Just like every holiday, there are times when you don't want to go back and I'd be lying if I said there were never times when I thought about giving in totally to the life we were living. The chances to do so came by every single day; the birds we met made me want to ditch the bastard complicated long-distance arrangement I had with Brenda and spend my life shagging top tarts until my knob turned black and dropped off. Wild drunken nights fuelled by beer and drugs made me want to forget about the painfully mature career I had set myself on course for and tempted me to spend my life as a part-time chef and perpetual student working his way through never-ending humanities degrees while spending grants and piss poor wages on getting permanently shitfaced. The crack we had, the camaraderie and gang bond was such that I regularly had to fight the urge to abandon dreams of an international lifestyle in favour of the womb-like comfort of this small city, filled with familiar faces and local hang-outs. How easy it would be for life to carry on like that. How unchallenging it would be to live for casual sex, narcotic japes and routine madness. The reality of how utterly soul-destroying it would actually be to still be that McKinley when celebrating my fourth decade of life was never lost on me which is why I never gave in to those urges. Life had always shown me that just as bad times would always make way for good times, good times could quite often lead to great times.

Of course, shit is generously spread throughout a person's life. The passage between good and great would undoubtedly be littered with piles of crap. Life is a municipal park - green, expansive and peppered with freshly curled dog landmines with your name on them. I'd just stepped in a fresh steamer when all this began which is why I was glad that the lads came along when they did - and that they were more fucked up and damaged than even I was at the time.

Ask Danny, wee man or the Ponce who was the most sorted one out of the four of us and I'll bet a crumpled tenner on them saying that it was me. Ellis was a fucking leery virgin with an blind appetite for chaos, the Ponce was a sadistically brutalized basket case with no self-esteem, and Danny was a heart-broken lost soul searching for unattainable love. Of course I'd stand out as the most sane and sorted next to that bunch of sad fuckers. I was a university student doing an economics degree, as well as being a qualified chef and one half of a relationship with ten years on the clock. My credentials suggested I was a man with a plan whereas the other three were a bunch of boys stumbling about like Stevie Wonder on acid. And there was a certain amount of truth in that. I did have a plan but when I came to the city to execute the last part of it, I was in such a fragile state from completing the previous stage that I was totally unprepared for what was about to happen.

I'm not going to bore you with the details of my early days. Suffice to say, I had a shit childhood and basically brought myself up. As soon as I was old enough to get out of that situation and support myself, I did. I was never more focussed than in those days when my very survival depended on completing the early stages of self-education and improvement which I called Phase One. Contrary to what some people will tell you, there aren't people who can help you in a situation like mine. At least, there aren't enough of them to go round which means most of those deserving of support rarely get it. I was one of those who slipped through the cracks. Faced with very stark choices - and being witness to people close to me making the bad ones - I put everything into following the right path as well as I could. I slipped many times and was led astray more than once - inevitably, considering I was basically an orphan raising myself on the streets of Glasgow - but I always found my way back. Once on the (relatively) straight and narrow again, I made a pledge to always look ahead, never back to where I'd been and where I'd come from. I would never talk about my family. I would be my own family, and perhaps one day be the start of a new one with its own history.

Keeping this kind of focus is fucking hard work at the best of times but this was all happening at the same time that my hormones were raging and my cock was stiffening at the drop of a hat. I'd come up with a plan which required me to work my bollocks off to get enough money to fund each stage of self-improvement which would eventually result in a life so far removed from the one I was born into that it would be that of a completely different person. I would be that person. But I didn't count on the effect that women would have on my grand plan or how they would be instrumental in making this new person such a randy bastard.

I found out very early on - as Danny would some years later - that hotels are a hot bed for wild sex opportunities and filled with impressionable and corruptible young girls. I was 17 when I got my first live-in job and the goings-on in the hotel I moved into made Roman orgies look like Tupperware parties. When the staff weren't shagging each other, they were shagging with the guests. I was to find out as my career in the hospitality industry progressed that infidelity was as common as having eggs for breakfast. My boss had gone through all the waitresses at least once before I got there and was halfway through going through them again by the time I made trainee chef. His missus was no better. She was regularly caught sucking off all manner of bar staff and had a six-month fling with a salesman who used the hotel as a second home (and knocking shop). The smell of moist teenage girls and pheromone-charged male staff hung in the air constantly. It was only a matter of time before I would become intoxicated by this atmosphere. The straw which broke the camel's cherry finally came in the form of the rampant wife of my boss.

Someone once told me that they found it hard to believe that I was ever a virgin. They couldn't imagine a time when I was not getting my end wet in one orifice or another, such is my reputation for unbridled perving. But of course there was a time before sex and before the overwhelming pursuit of tits and muff made my life a constant struggle with self-control. Strangely, it was an experience which would have put the majority of young boys off sex forever which set me on this slippery and slightly fishy-smelling path of sexual abandon. Being one of the live-in staff had numerous advantages but there were also a number of cons to go with the pros. I had a roof over my head, three square meals and a regular wage which allowed me to enjoy those precious hours away from the hotel in any way I saw fit I (more of that later). Unfortunately, being almost permanently on-site meant I was seen as being constantly available and was first in line for early and late night duties, such as preparing the kitchen for the next day's breakfast service. One particularly late night, these duties suddenly included licking out the Boss Lady.

I'd had my hands in a few of pairs of knickers at this point but I'd never done oral and had never even come close to getting my end away so having the Boss Lady hoist her skirt up, sit herself on the stainless steel preparation table and present her minging old badger to me was quite a shock. When she commanded me to "eat it", I mistakenly started by using my teeth (a technique she was apparently not averse to and which was only refined after a plea from my first real girlfriend two years later). Once Boss Lady had been chewed on to her satisfaction, I was practically wrestled to the floor and roughly inserted inside her. With the reassuring words: "Don't worry, I've had a hysterectomy" she began riding me like a fucking mental rodeo clown, complete with cries of yee-haw and a few giddy-ups. Bucking like a middle-aged bronco, Boss Lady clamped down on me and drained me of my virgin oil before screaming like she'd been stabbed - which she had been, in a way. After gushing and panting all over my meat dagger for a few moments, she hopped off and walked out of the kitchen without a word, leaving me slightly bemused and not a little chuffed. I'd had sex, after all. It didn't matter that it had practically been rape. This wild and mildly unsavoury rutting with the Boss Lady continued on and off for a year, during which I learned a lot of new tricks which I began teaching to those waitresses who were not currently being serviced by the Boss Man.

This crash-course in sex not only set me on the road to obsession but also led me, for the first time since taking my first steps into employment, off my chosen path. I was no longer concentrating on the plan. I was constantly thinking about getting my leg over. The objective had suddenly become getting as much fanny as possible, not becoming the new man with the new life. My new vice was soon joined by others which would threaten to derail me.

Shagging waitresses and nymphomaniac hotel hags is like shooting fish in a barrel. They're all easy pickings once you have your aim and your technique down. There's no escape for them once you have them where you want them. But it gets a little fucking boring after a while and for a young bloke eager to taste as much of the world's crotch as humanly possible, it soon becomes a sort of vaginal cabin fever. I'd already started to gravitate towards pubs and clubs in my spare time in pursuit of bands and music, an interest and love I'd had since that time which belongs to another age and another person - the rare, happy moments of my childhood. I would sit with my head against the radio for hours listening to the hits of the day and then when things started to turn to shit, I'd lock myself away with my mum's record collection, drowning out the arguments with the Beach Boys and Rolling Stones. Seeing bands live had also been part of my early search for sanctuary. I'd sneak into bars in Glasgow to watch any band and any type of music. I even snuck into a Clash gig at the Glasgow Apollo on a freezing January night in 1980 after hiding all day in the dark corners of a loading bay. That turned out to be one of the defining moments of that particular life. Joe Strummer's lyrics spoke to me and gave me hope. Those songs formed the embryonic basis of the plan to get a life. It also inadvertently contributed to my straying further from the path.

It wasn't a huge leap to combine my love of music for my now insatiable desire for sex. Going to see bands put me in contact with strange and alluring women - new, potential conquests drawn to Siouxsie and the Banshees or gathered to watch XTC. Birds at gigs seemed even more up for it than imprisoned hotel staff. At first I couldn't work out why. That is until one shag bought me a beer and then got her drugs out.

Escaping the cocoon-like environment of the hotel, armed with a bulging arsenal of shag moves and growing sexual prowess, the world seemed a less hostile place. Life was still a struggle as far as I was concerned but one which was no longer just about keeping your nose clean but about beating the millions of other randy males to the numbers of available women. In evolutionary terms, it was survival of the fittest. This was a challenge I accepted with relish and while pursuing tarts like a man with only days to live, I began losing sight of the bigger picture I'd painted for myself during my previous period of trial. Sex was everything - that is until that fateful day when I was inducted into the world of alcohol and narcotics.

If I hadn't been so obsessed with my vices, I would have realised that a destructive pattern was emerging, one which I'd been witness to in my previous life. Addiction had torn my family apart and for most people coming from this type of upbringing, this would have been reason enough to have followed a sober, celibate life - or at least one of moderation. Not me. I knew what I was escaping from but I thought it was the results of that life I was desperate to avoid, not the elements which brought it to such a drastically premature conclusion. I wanted to be a better man than my father, I wanted to have more options than my mother and I wanted to avoid making the same mistakes as my brother. I didn't realise at the time that I was creating a whole new set of pitfalls for myself.

For almost two years I was in a situation that ten years later I would be scared shitless of repeating again. What should have been a transitional period in my new life, a step to greater things, suddenly became my existence. I'd settled for a shit job, a life full of casual sex, drink and drugs. It seemed good enough. I was having fun, and I was barely out of my teens at this point so why the fuck did it matter? My reasoning was that I'd been denying myself any time to grow up in the same way that most kids did so what did it matter if I did a little catching up? But when you're waking up and hitting a bong before breakfast, downing five pints at lunch before working the rest of the day under the influence of speed and cocaine, you're not catching up. You're on a treadmill, running hard every day and night but not getting anywhere.

Before too long I was unaware of any time passing; each day was the same, each night a repeat of the last. There were subtle changes. I'd do acid to mix things up, or wake up to a few lines rather than waiting until I started work. But the effect was the same. I was fucked and I was fucking up - big time.

Then one day I met Brenda.

The whole point of starting a career in the hospitality industry was never to be a fully qualified chef, although I somehow managed to reach that unplanned target during my time shagging my way through the female staff while on inhuman amounts of chemicals. It was always about the cash. The hotel business kept me off the streets and gave me a solid base to build on, and a qualification I could always fall back on should I need too, but the main focus for entering a trade which basically kills all chance of a social life (unless you're really determined) was to earn and hoard enough money for Phase Two. This was going to be the next step which got me out of the blue collar work force and onto the lower rungs of the higher education ladder. To get to Phase Three - a degree course which would eventually lead to a lucrative career and world travel - I first needed to get the qualifications needed to make it to university.

I'd done okay at comprehensive school, considering I had no home of my own and was relying on the charity of friends to see me through my exam years, but I needed a couple of higher level passes to be considered for university. I'd always had a mind for numbers so once the requisite amount of cash had been saved (an amount which surely would have been larger and reached so much faster had I not discovered wine, women and song), I applied for a foundation course at the local college.

I was sat in the college canteen on my first day when I saw her. I won't lie and say that it was love at first sight, mainly because I had no fucking idea what love was. My thing was sex and looking out for shaggable wenches. The hairdressers and beauty school students were pinging constantly on my radar with their big hair, big tits and tight uniforms. Brenda didn't tick any of those boxes but I noticed her all the same. I think she stood out because of the supremely confident, almost arrogant air she gave off - and the heinous tartan two-piece she was wearing which made her look like a maiden aunt rather than a student. While you could imagine the beauty tarts with stockings and suspenders under their tunics, Brenda screamed woolly tights and grandma knickers. She was so out of place. Here we were, in this Glasgow shithole, full of hopeful kids unwittingly being set up for lifetimes in McJobs and here was this painfully uptight, middle-class matron swanning around through the middle of it all expecting to be taught how to conquer the world.

As it turned out, this dowdy bird soon became a constant in my life, not because I soon found her hidden depths of passion, humility and humour and convinced her to love me forever but because she was to became the daily pain in my arse. Having Brenda in my class was like spending eight hours a day in the company of the lovechild of Hitler and the Riddler. When she wasn't trying to invade Poland - or at least run the class - she was elongating simple tasks by hours with her incessant questions. Everyone hated her and she didn't seem to care. For her, the rest of us (and this included the lecturers) were just blurs on the periphery of her tunnel vision to success, black shapes on the sidelines of her narrow focus. We were the road kill she had to drive over on her path to glory and greatness. I couldn't fucking stand her.

Although I had managed to get my act together enough to get out of the hotel business and into Phase Two as planned, the vices I had acquired still wanted to be indulged in. They say there is a time and place for experimentation and that time and place is college. I now had a new target to aim for but just as birds and partying had hindered the speed of my progress in Phase One, so the demons I thought I'd beaten down to get here would resurface to offer potential fuck-ups aplenty. Now living in the halls of residence, my life became a schedule of parties, late night drinking and running round the campus high as a fucking kite.

The halls were an endless source of ill-advised sexual liaisons, drinking and drugging and even though I'd sworn to myself to keep my focus this time, it wasn't long before I'd become the life, soul and pervert of every party.

One night, at an off-campus soiree thrown by some hugely hip second-year engineering wankers, I bumped into the most unlikely yet familiar face. Dancing with careless abandon, lost in her own world of tequila and Tears for Fears was Brenda, whirling like a trouser-suited dervish in the middle of an almost empty room. I'd come looking for a quiet spot where I could hoover a couple of lines and had stumbled into a scene from one of those 80s teen flicks where the dorky bird is invited to the cool party by accident and becomes the main source of ridicule. I'd arrived just before the college quarterback and his mates find her enjoying herself and then humiliate her by ripping her dress off or dumping pigs' blood on her head. With no football team in sight, I watched her from the doorway, grinning to myself as I calculated how many ways I could use this against her. It was then that her eyes snapped open, she stopped dancing and she stomped over to where I was standing.

"Are you just going to stand there, McKinley, or are you going to dance with me?" She knew my name. She must have left one ear open while absorbing all the information we were supposed to be compiling for future use and taken notice of the world around her - including me. The arrogance was still there but there was something softer about her as she stood there grinning at my discomfort. "You know how to dance, don't you?"

"Aye," I said, digging up my Govan accent in a vain attempt to add edge to my rapidly disappearing air of cool. "But I don't dance to shite like this."

"What do you dance to then?"

"Err…"

"Do you drink then?" she said, growing rapidly irritated. "Big tough guy like you must like a drink."

"Aye, I like a drink."

"Great," she smiled, her face lighting up and turning it into a completely different proposition. "Then you can buy me one. I'm bored of this place. Everyone's too fucking cool to have a good time."

The next thing I knew we were sitting in a loud pub round the corner from the party, necking whiskey. I'd barely said a word since Brenda had gotten in my face about dancing some 20 minutes previously. After she'd barged a corridor through the crowds to get to the bar, ordered six hits of Glennfiddich and then dragged me to a table, she'd opened up about why she was in Glasgow and what she intended to do with the rest of her life.

"What about you? You don't seem the type to be chasing a dream. What are you doing on the course?" She rattled of the questions in much the same way as she did in class.

With two fast shots of single malt in me I decided to take control. "You have a lot to say woman but do you ever listen?" I got in her face for the first time. "Every day, I hear your voice. I hear it when you're not even fucking there because that's all I ever hear when I'm in that place. You're in my head, asking questions and being a snooty cunt. How can you ever think that you're learning anything when you don't shut your fucking mouth long enough to process what's going on?"

Brenda looked stunned. She sat there in silence for what seemed like an age as I gradually started to feel terrible for shouting and swearing at her. I was just about to apologise when a smile spread across her face. "You think about me? I'm in your head?"

"Easy, darling..." I say, relaxing. "It's not like I start choking it when you come to mind."

Her smile spread broader. "Not yet, sunshine," she said. "But give it time."

I wasn't interested in giving it time and certainly didn't find my wank fantasies suddenly filled with the urge to drag down Brenda's woolly tights with my teeth - at least not for a few months.

In the weeks following the party, Brenda seemed to appear in my life more and more, and piss me off less and less. In class I actually started to challenge her when she attempted to close off arguments or explain something as a given. As well as dragging me back onto the path of academic pursuit, which I had stumbled off in a drunken daze not long after starting the course, she was covertly steering me onto the straight and narrow when it came to my shagging urges. While the arguments we had over economic theories and approaches fired my imagination and interest in the subject, the heat from those arguments started to get other things burning too. My loins, to be precise. Believe me when I say, and this is a conservative estimate, I spent 80 percent of my free time trying to work out what was making me want to have sex with Brenda and 20 percent working out how I was going pork her. Soon enough, the ratio was reversed.

On the surface, we couldn't have been more different. She was a middle-class only child brought up in the more affluent areas of Edinburgh while I came from a brood of scrapping, biting, nasty working class fuckers from the rough end of Govan. Before we met, my idea of a social evening meant pursuing the best ways of rendering walking and talking impossible. Hers involved staying up all night, gassing about Rimbaud and Proust. I'm not fucking stupid but I could never see any fun in sitting around, talking about French Formula One drivers until dawn. (Brenda actually liked this joke and I credit it as the one which got me my first blowjob off her.)

Chalk and cheese, opposites attract, all that bollocks...I don't know to this day why it worked out and why we were suddenly so good together that we decided to get together and stay together. But we did. (If I'm pushed to make a guess though, I reckon it's because she'd never been fucked right until I sorted her out. When a woman physically growls or makes any involuntary animal noises when you're having sex, you're pretty much golden after that.)

So, I had a girlfriend. My first real girlfriend. It was scary until I started to realise that while variety may be the spice of life, there's nothing like having your own herb garden. Before, I thought the thrill of sex came from having a lot of different partners. Once I found myself with Brenda, I realised that you could get up to far dirtier and kinkier stuff with a girlfriend than you could with a one-night stand. If I'd tried to do some of the stuff I persuaded Brenda to get into with a bird I'd just met, she would have cried bloody murder and I would have been on the front page of the *Daily Mail* faster than you could say "Scotland's Depravity." This helped to ease the fears I was having that saddling my cart to a single mare meant that I was missing out on all the best horseplay.

Even though things were great, it messed with my head on a regular basis. I'd started off wanting to improve myself and reach my targets just for me. I'd set off alone on this self-improvement and salvation trip with only me in mind, with my focus on the prize of getting out of the shithole I was in and away from the whirlpool of abuse which had dragged so many people I'd known into it. It was hard enough to amend that plan and that target when I discovered birds and shagging. It was a daily struggle not to give in to all the pussy in the world and fuck off my ideas of a great career in favour of a life on the job. (I didn't know it then but even having a solid, loving relationship was never going to be the solution to that struggle.) I'd managed to find a balance between the pursuit of sex and my plan, only for drink and drugs to come along and fuck it all up. Even finding a way to get shitfaced while pursuing my dream seemed easier at times than living my life for two which was what

- as the weeks turned into months - my relationship with Brenda became. But just when I thought I wasn't cut out for battling through life as one half of a partnership, the lone wolf got a dose of domestication. I wouldn't say he became a fucking lap dog but he got way too used to having his tummy tickled.

I'll give Brenda her dues. She knew I was a bad bastard and knew what I was capable of and yet most of my shortcomings never got in the way of our relationship. I never hid any of the drinking and drugging from her but as our situation changed and we became more involved, my excesses in those departments did tail off - especially after we started living together. We both liked a drink – that was never a problem – but she was less keen about the drugs so I chose my moments and kept the sporadic binges secret from her. She played it very well. I was still convinced I was a bad lad but all the time she was building up the importance of the other side of me - the one searching for a better life. We'd get out of order and have huge nights out on the lash but the increasingly sober moments were spent exploring the many opportunities which would be waiting for us out on in the world. In time, even getting off my tits became less of an urge as we spent more and more time together looking ahead. Brenda got me back to focusing on the plan and before long we were talking about a joint vision where our separate dreams would be combined into one objective. She convinced me that following my path - which, unbeknownst to me, was now our path - would be so much easier now it wasn't just me fighting for the future. It wasn't just me stamping down my demons. I wasn't just responsible for my own progress but partly responsible for hers too. As such, I was back to being totally committed to the path that I was stomping down; eyes on the prize with tunnel vision, barely sniffing a drink, craving a joint or rubbing my cock.

Which is why, when Brenda told me she'd been offered an internship in Jakarta and that she was going to take it, I felt cheated.

We'd both graduated with flying colours and I was already looking into possible university courses in Scotland when she suddenly changed her vision of pursuing a degree and decided an internship would be a more practical route. Always the idealist, Brenda wanted to be working at making things right in the world as soon as possible and the opportunity to do so at a respected non-governmental organization was one that she thought was too good to pass up. I would have agreed had it not been at the fucking end of the earth. I'd been thinking along the lines of a shared future for some time at this point and had been focused on arriving at the point of looking for work together some four years down the line. That she was taking that leap now struck me as a betrayal. I hadn't rewritten my plan to include her - I'd practically ripped up the original and signed on to this new partnership agreement. Now my partner was fucking off round the world.

I could have gone with her. I could have taken this as my opportunity to start another unplanned phase which, with a little bit of tweaking, could have fitted into my bigger picture. But this wasn't how I'd planned it. Even before this became our future, my future rested on getting the highest level of education I could get to give myself the best chances to get as far away as possible from my old life. Indonesia was pretty fucking far from Glasgow but only geographically. I would have still been under-developed in the developing world. I wasn't ready.

We fought as only two pig-headed, stubborn-as-fuck Scots can: endlessly, viciously and mostly under the influence of whiskey. On most occasions we were so caught up in the fighting that we didn't see that they we still wanted the same things but at different times. We still wanted to be together and we still wanted to reach that target of a shared life together. Eventually, after all the futile tears, we agreed to stay with each other but I would stay here. For this to work, however, Brenda had some conditions.

"I'm not stupid," she said as we prepared to go our separate ways together. "I know what you were like before we met and I'm under no illusions as to what you're like now. We're only probably going to see each other for about three months out of every year of your degree. There'll be opportunities for you with other women, no doubt. But if you really want this, if you want us, and if you really want the future you've been fucking scrapping and fighting for over all these years, you will not put your dick in another woman." Bitch. She couldn't have just tagged this to our relationship; she had to bring my whole life and eternal soul into it. "You know I'll find out if you do - and if you do, there won't even be a goodbye. This will end immediately." Her voice, measured and calm up until this point, started to waver. "Don't do this for me, that's not what I'm saying this for. Do this for us. We've come a long way and can go a lot further but that great future relies on you not screwing around." She smiled and kissed me. "You got that, sunshine?"

At that point, I was happy with the deal. It didn't seem any different from the way I had been living. Since we'd got together I hadn't even had a wank over another woman let alone touched one. I hadn't spewed up through drinking or smoked myself into oblivion for months. I was more centred and focused than ever. I didn't only have my career target to aim for but my personal one too. It might not always be easy but as Brenda jetted off for Asia, I was sure that I could do it. I wanted to do it. That was half the battle won.

Or so I thought.

I never realised how much of a stabilising influence Brenda had been until I moved down south to take up my place on the university course in the city. We'd bought the house together (or, more correctly, Brenda with the help of her filthy rich parents had bought it) as an investment and for somewhere for me to live while I studied. Just the fact that I had made it this far, from the gutters and shite of Govan to the verge of an economics degree, through my own determination and conviction (and in

376

spite of the external and internal pitfalls which had threatened my progress), convinced me that this was possible. It would be just another challenge, like the many others I had overcome to get where I was. But I didn't fully appreciate how much Brenda had steered me back onto the path until she was no longer there to guide me - and the only like-minded individuals I found myself relying on were blokes who appealed to the more wayward side of my character.

What followed after I hooked up with Danny, Ellis and Rob is well-documented. What is less well-known is what I was actually feeling at that time - in terms of emotions, I mean. My groping of random breasts and arses is a matter of record. As I said at the beginning, everyone thought I was the most sorted. But my turmoil was as complicated and crippling as any Danny Boy, wee man and the Ponce were dealing with.

I'd had a lot of practice of dealing with my love of alcohol and drugs. As I've made clear, I had managed to balance those urges with my more overwhelming desire to avoid their most damaging effects. Seeing my father and brother succumb to the darkest depths those substances can drag a person into had always been the only incentive I needed to keep those particular demons at bay. Through serious experimentation, I soon found that I could master them, knowing how far I could go without losing myself or my dream. Sex, on the other hand, had never seemed to be a problem - until I couldn't have it. Suddenly sex was the lorry with a drunk driver at the wheel which I never saw coming. I'd avoided becoming a victim of other people's addictions but sex would turn out to be my own. In reality, it always had been. I was far more hooked on it than the beer or the weed. I'd just never gone cold turkey. And the battle to stop myself from getting out there and scoring some hole was about to get a whole fucking lot harder.

Only when I was presented with the opportunities she warned me about did I realise that, by supporting my dream while shagging me senseless, Brenda was not only keeping me on the straight and narrow but she was also keeping me out of the whorehouses and strip clubs. She wasn't only steering me towards my goal but also steering me away from the cheap sluts and easy lays. To make matters worse, just when my sex demons were beginning to scratch at the door, Lad Culture hit and suddenly everything with a pulse was out to get shagged.

Until Lad reared its bulbous, throbbing head I'd managed to keep my dick to myself. So much so in fact that, until I met the boys and started to have a social life again, my early university days were spent beating myself to a pulp in front of anything which could vaguely pass as pornography. See? I was committed to Brenda's request. It would have been easy to throw myself into the mix as soon as Fuck a Fresher week began and shag my way through my four year degree if I hadn't been. But cursed as I was with this idea that falling off the sex wagon would ultimately lead to the complete obliteration of my plans and dreams, I chose to wank myself silly instead.

That is, until I found myself in familiar surroundings.

Taking the hotel job was necessary as student grants were never calculated with the recipient's intake of drugs and alcohol taken into consideration – which, taking into account that most of anyone's student grant ends up either down the union bar or in some fucking hippie dealer's Guatemalan hemp wallet, is more than a bit stupid. So I had to work and what could I do other than crunch numbers and come up with ideas how to save the world economy? Cook fry-ups for ungrateful bastard pensioners whose eggs are never quite right. The committed me who entered the Hartington for the first time was under the delusion that the fear of fucking everything up would be enough to keep my perving instincts at bay must have been in the running for the Nobel Prize for the world's most naïve cunt. It was like handing over the keys of the bar to an alcoholic. The Hartington was an all-you-can-eat buffet of young – and not so young – girls. It soon became very clear that I'd blindly stepped into a time machine while off my face and ended up very near the beginning of my story.

Now if Danny had been a bloke with a steady girlfriend, eyes fixed on a good job, and who liked a beer now and again, I could have survived the hotel and used the waitresses and cleaning staff as alternative fantasies to those in the sticky pages of the old copy of Reader's Wives which was keeping my right hand busy. But he turned out to be a fanny rat with a growing appetite for excess and a dearth in identity which made him rich pickings for the New Lad recruiters. And then when Ellis turned up - Jesus, I'd never met anyone so in need of a shag in my life. When these two, and then the equally desperate Ponce, became my people of note, I knew that I was cast out in the wilderness with a big jugged, damp-gusseted she-devil whispering in my ear day and night. If I didn't find some way of bending the rules, I was going to have be castrated just to make it to graduation.

This is when I added an amendment to Brenda's policy paper. I wouldn't shag around, as agreed, but while adhering to the letter of the law - do not put your dick in another woman - I managed to justify to myself that if women were to grab my cock, give it a stroke or rub it all over their tits, I wouldn't be breaking the agreement. Plus, I would not be totally giving in to the addiction which I feared would drag my off the straight and narrow and leave me bleeding anally in the nearest ditch. Hand jobs, tit wanks and other sundry sexual acts which didn't include penetration would be my methadone supplement. In this way, I wouldn't feel the need to get myself a sex heroin habit even though the streets were awash with shag skag. I didn't count on the fact that just as junkies get hooked on the drug that's supposed to save them, I would totally fall into the world of slap and tickle.

I never felt an ounce of guilt, to be honest. I was keeping faithful in the terms of our agreement and I never got emotionally involved. If there was a bird who I really liked, I'd just set Danny up with her and live off the buzz of the Proxy Fuck. I got great satisfaction, and not just the sexual kind, from watching his progress and conquests. Being involved in the planning was a laugh, hearing about the execution was titillating but ultimately, having a hand in Danny Boy's slow discovery of who he was and what he wanted gave me a real sense of achievement. I'd struggled my whole life to find the answers to some of life's questions and random personalities had helped me when I need them. Being there for Danny and helping him find his way made me feel like a proud father - one who sets his 'son' up with cheap tarts and then celebrates with drug and alcohol binges. Okay, so I wasn't going to win any Parent of the Year prizes but guiding Danny as much as I did, I like to think I contributed to making him the man he eventually became.

Dabbling in the love lives of the boys gave me a safe thrill. It was like jacking up scouring powder when there wasn't anything else around but it kept me from careening into another dark alley, that of finding someone else - a person who would divert me eternally from the goal. Someone who would make me crave the easy life. Someone who would make me happy to settle for a life of kitchen work, nights in the pub and free time on the gear. Someone like Manimal.

The four years in the city literally went by in a blur (which is not surprising, considering). Before I knew it, I was working in Jakarta and living with Brenda again. It took us a while to readjust - or rather, it took her a while to readjust. I don't think I ever did. It's flippant to say having not had to face the experience (although a few Thursday nights in the Orchard came close) but I started to understand how hard it must be for soldiers to come back from war. Surviving Britpop and Lad was like coming home from a two-fronted military campaign. The fighting was for identity, sanity and community. The bond formed between those beside you in the cultural trenches as you battled your demons, your insecurities and regiments of scantily-clad drunken slappers was as tight as that between troops living together in real foxholes as the bombs fell.

Even though I'd been airlifted out and de-mobbed, I still bore the scars and still held the camaraderie and brotherhood from those years close to my heart. It's hard, if not impossible, to move on from that.

I threw myself into my job. I'd made it out of another difficult phase and was so close to the dream that I could smell the success. But it felt empty. In the first year, I questioned if this was really what I wanted. When we went back for a visit on Election Day in 1997, it hit home harder than ever. While the nation's party was certainly over by then, even though the Labour landslide suggested the good times would continue to roll, there was still the echo of great days in the city. The lads were still in top form even though they had attempted to move on too. It was strangely comforting to see them still struggling to come to terms with what real life may have in store for them.

I was with them there. Life wasn't as complete as I imagined it would be. I had the woman, the career, the international lifestyle - I had everything I wanted to escape to. And yet, I'd lost something of myself. I'd left a part of me somewhere along the way. I tried to find it by getting back into drinking but my body couldn't handle it like it used to and the booze led me further away from where I thought this part of me might be. I gladly took those rare opportunities to meet up with Danny and Ellis in the following years to get fucked up and try and find that missing quality in drugs, but again it wasn't the same. I couldn't find the missing part in the safe places and situations of the past.

The arrival of my three sons in fast succession removed the ache for a while. Three beautiful boys, full of life and personality. Little bastards, every one of them, but how else were they going to be, considering the source of a good portion of their DNA? I suddenly started to wonder if the life I'd chosen for myself was what I really wanted because these little unplanned miracles had never featured in any part of my plan. Their arrival totally blew the plan out of the water - but they gave me something unimaginable. Maybe this was the plan all along?

We'd always thought that we would eventually move back to the city and live in the house as a family but it became increasingly clear that it was never going to be home. I for one didn't want to move back there. There were far too many shag beasts in the closet and potentially awkward reunions in the street for me to feel completely comfortable there. Besides, Danny was in Dublin and the Ponce was wherever the work took him. Spending my advancing years with Ellis the Parole Officer, moping over halves of ale and moaning about what could have been, would have sent me to an early grave, as much as I love the wee man. I was all for moving on so I agreed quickly to Brenda's idea to sell-up.

It was weird to be back in the city alone. It wasn't the first time but it had been many, many years. I'd started off here on my tod rattling about in the old place while navigating the first year of my degree and the multitude of strange, unnerving urges I was having away from Brenda's calming influence. Once our gang had formed at the start of my second year, I was hardly ever alone. Now, some thirteen years after we took the place by storm, I was wandering the streets anonymously, failing to recognise a single face. I did however recognise a pair of tits. Faces and names come and go but for the professional pervert, a nice set of jugs is forever. I'd just signed all the necessary paperwork with the estate agents who were putting the house on the market after speaking to Melons about the possibility of her and wino Jerry turning their long-term tenancy into home ownership and thought I deserved a drink. I wasn't exactly sure where I was until a dodgy looking backstreet brought me out onto the Haymarket. I was overcome with nostalgia almost immediately and so, after getting my head round the fact that Probe had been turned into a heinous multi-floored gastro pub, I decided that this was more than a fitting venue for toasting my final goodbye.

However, I didn't expect the clientele to still be the same as it was in 1994.

"McKinley?" A voice drifted to my ears from somewhere behind me but it could well have been the walls whispering to me. "I thought it was you."

I turned my head and my eyes immediately zoomed in a couple of old friends - leftie and righty. "Jesus Christ, Manimal." It must have been the combination of the venue and the sudden breast blast from the past but I suddenly regressed to my Lad self before I could stop myself. "Sorry. Amanda."

Then she did something I'd never seen her do before. She smiled. "I never really knew why you boys always called me that."

"Do you want to know now?"

"Not really." She did it again. She smiled. It was unnerving, mainly because when she did it her face changed completely. She became strangely attractive to the extent that I stopped staring at her puppies and concentrated on her eyes. "How are you?" she continued. "It's been a couple of years since I last saw you." Danny's kid's christening, in fact. As godfather, I had to go through the whole rigmarole of promising to keep Leah on good terms with the Lord - like I'm best qualified to do that - and share that responsibility with Manimal...I mean, Amanda. At the time it was a pain in the arse, especially as Amanda was being her usual bitch self (which seems to be her default setting whenever Danny's around), but at that moment I was actually quite glad we'd been through all that together. It gave me another topic of conversation to hang onto other than the one which began: remember when I fondled your tits in this place and tried to shag you? We chatted amiably for a few minutes on how Danny, Karen and Leah were getting on, whether I'd seen them lately, how often she'd been over to Dublin - when she said once a month, I could see Danny's screwed up face in my mind's eye. Then, just when I thought she would fuck off and let me finish my pint in peace, she surprised me again. "Can I buy you a drink?" I didn't have anything better to do, so I took receipt of another pint.

It turned out to be quite a session. Amanda was in the mood for getting pissed up and I rarely need any encouragement to indulge so we passed the afternoon on the balcony of the old Probe nightclub, knocking back Stellas and putting the world to rights.

"So did you ever get married?" I asked when we were both half-cut enough for the rules on personal questions not to apply. "I notice there's no ring on your finger."

"There's not one on yours either," she replied. "Why am I not surprised about that?"

I never wear the ring. I'm not trying to fool anyone. I certainly wasn't trying to con Manimal. "You tell me."

"Oh come on," she slurred. "You were never the marrying type. None of you were. Commitment-phobes, the lot of you. You could have knocked me down with a feather when Daniel actually committed to Karen after getting her pregnant. You were all out for what you could get and as men, you'll never really change."

"I'm guessing 'no' is the answer to my question then."

Amanda snorts into her pint. "Actually, I was Mrs. Amanda Jarvis for five years. I'm a divorcee, don't you know? Mr. Jarvis, the fucking bastard, cheated on me...which proves my point."

"No, that's just another bad personal experience which you use to reinforce your own stereotype," I countered. "You have a certain type, whether you consciously chase after them or not. You'll always go for blokes who will ultimately hurt you. Maybe it's because you want to believe that there's no good in men and find people who prove that."

"Bollocks."

"Suit yourself."

384

"I search for bastards who will hurt me to justify my belief in the worst of the male gender? Fuck off."

"I don't understand it either," I deadpanned. "You're such charming company."

Amanda balances on the edge of another tirade for a moment before her stern expression melts into genuine hilarious laughter. "Maybe you're right. But bastards tend to be great I bed," she added, her eyelids lowering. "Are you still a bastard, McKinley."

After I'd shagged her every which way and broken at least three pieces of hotel furniture in the process, I laid back in the bed and thought, yes - I am still a bastard. A stupid bastard. What demons had this drunken fuck-for-old-times-sake awoken? What would become of me now that the cage had been breached and the beast was loose? I'd almost made it. Then I cocked it all up on the very day I was cutting the final ties with the city which had laid temptation at my feet on a daily basis. Stupid, stupid bastard.

twelve

Three Lions

June 1996

Football. It's coming home, apparently. Although, I have to admit, it doesn't actually feel like it's ever been away. The surge of patriotic adrenaline that's currently running through the nation feels very much like the rush most of us have been on for the past eighteen months. It's just been turned up a few notches and now comes swathed in England white and the flag of St. George. Put the high of football together with the buzz coming from our music and you get a huge speedball that's got the whole country bug-eyed and euphoric. Plus it's hot. It's fucking hot. The heat combines with an atmosphere you can almost taste to make the city feel like a 24-hour, open-air nightclub. Everyone's out and everyone's up for it, day and night.

It couldn't be happening at a better time. I just want to forget about girls and relish this summer. We're the focus of the world for so many reasons and we're basking in more than just the heat from the sun. It's a global spotlight shining on this green and cool-as-fuck land. Our bands are back on top; we're setting standards and making news. Now we're hosting an international tournament that we could very well win. There's no time for what could have been. It's all about the here and now and it's happening so fast you just have to strap yourself in and go where it takes you. If you look back, the whiplash will break your neck. All eyes are looking forward. We're all on this crazy ride together and no-one knows where the brake is. More importantly, no-one cares. It's full speed ahead into the summer of '96.

The buzz is so full-on that none of us are willing to consider the very real possibility that this could be the last party. This may not be the part of proceedings when the host has abandoned the niceties and polite requests in favour of police intervention but it could well be the moment you make it to the house after a few beers at your local to find the farewell bash well underway. We're not being thrown out yet but it could only be a matter of time.

In real terms, Ellis and I *are* being thrown out. We signed on for benefits earlier in the week and have the rest of June to find a new place to live after our student status evaporated. We're now officially "ex-college" and therefore ineligible for the dubious home comforts of our decrepit digs. McKinley graduates in three weeks' time (– there must have been some pact with the Devil) and is likely to be just another vapour trail in the sky by the end of August. Rob is still treading the boards as part of Shaven Avon's bizarre Shakespearean extravaganza and, according to his last scrawled postcard from South Shields or somewhere equally exotic, he's considering signing on for a season as Pip in another company's production of Great Expectations (– they're probably called something crap like What the Dickens?). Anyway, this means our travelling thesp is unlikely to grace us with his increasingly theatrical presence until at least Christmas - and God knows where the hell any of us will be by then.

But Christmas seems like an age away under this relentless summer sun and clear blue sky and while reality certainly lies in wait for us like some sex offender in a darkened park, we'll continue to blissfully wander through this season of sunshine, until we can no longer postpone the brutal fucking we will most likely get when autumn comes calling.

I spot Ellis crushed up against the gates of the Castle just before opening time on Saturday morning, the result of drawing the short straw and being sent ahead to reserve our places for the opening match while I trawl the city in search of a new place to live. England kick-off the European Championships against Switzerland this afternoon and Bob the Bastard has set up a big screen TV in the beer garden. Seating will be limited which is why Ellis is surrounded by a large gang of shirtless skinheads, all sporting sunburns and distorted prison-style bulldog tattoos. They jostle impatiently like a pack of terriers before a hunt and bark excitedly as a burly figure looms out of the darkness of the pub and begins to slide latches and turn keys. Bob steps aside and Ellis is swept ahead of a red-skinned, testosterone-powered wave of raging thirst and patriotism as I wait for my moment in the vacuum left by the rampaging mass. As previously agreed back at HQ, Ellis makes for the viewing area while I casually head for the bar. It works with military precision; Ellis taking the little known route through the games room and outside via the staff exit beside the kitchen, while I order the beers from the food hatch where Kirsty the barmaid is hiding from the hordes. We're sat in a prime position in front of the screen with refreshment before you can say "two pints of Stella."

"So? How did it go?" asks Ellis after we toast our success and the hoped-for, nay expected, victory of our national team. "Find anything good?"

I lay a number of sweaty, crumpled pages in front of him on the table in the manner of a poker player with a losing hand. "Unless you don't mind living above an Indian take-away, beside the murder pub or so far out of the city we'll have a completely new postcode - no, not really." I take a welcome draught of ale and look on the bright side. "But it's early days, man. We have all month."

"Which take-away?"

"Does it matter? The place would continuously stink of madras."

"And that's worse than Calvin Road because..?" Ellis is entirely serious.

I wait for him to come to his senses. He doesn't. I relent. "It's the Passage on Cutter Street."

Ellis nods appreciatively. "They do a top korma in the Passage, geezer. We could do far worse."

"I'm not living above an Indian just so you can be closer to your favourite curry, okay? Not when they deliver for free. We'll keep looking."

"What about the Scotsman's house? Do you reckon he'd rent it out to us?"

"Are you expecting to come into a large amount of cash in the near future? It's a four-bedroom townhouse, geezer. We are newly unemployed...officially. And even if we combine our benefits with our cash-in-hand from the hotel, we'd still not have enough. Besides, his missus currently owns the gaff and I'm sure she'll want someone other than a couple of doleys squatting in there."

"We could still ask."

"Yeah, right. No fucking way." McKinley doesn't even bother getting into a discussion as to how Ellis expects to pay the rent on his house as he takes a 50 percent stake in my seat on his arrival at half-time. Balanced on one arse cheek, I join the charades by giving Ellis a told-you-so shrug. Ellis, however, is half-cut and euphoric after the first 45 minutes during which he contributed to the Castle's sky-rocketing sales of Artois and Alan Shearer gave England a 1-0 lead. He seems to think he has the Scotsman in a position where some subtle negotiation may swing things in his favour.

"Just think about all the hassle we'll help you avoid...All those agents' costs, all that searching for tenants, all that worry about if they're fucking your gaff up..."

"I won't be worrying about you fucking my gaff up because I know you would and besides, you won't be getting the chance...So dream on, wee man."

"Technically, it's not your house," Ellis retorts. "We could go straight to your missus?"

"Are you a fucking comedian now?" I can tell from McKinley's tone that he's getting pissed off.

"All I'm saying, man, is that it's a sweet deal...We'd do you proud."

McKinley sighs. "Okay, I'm going to give you my conditions...on behalf of the owner...and you can then tell me if you still think they're sweet or not." Ellis moves in closer with a look of expectation creeping across his slightly scarlet face. The Scotsman leans to meet him so he can be heard clearly over the latest chorus of 'Three Lions'. "You're going to shut the fuck up about renting my house, her house or anybody's fucking house that I may have a say over or I'm going to pour this pint over your head, and go home...In that order. I'm out for a drink, I hate fucking football and I'm Scottish. It's no problem for me to just get up and go. So are you going to drop it and let me be?" The burning intensity in McKinley's eyes gets magnified through his glasses until his stare becomes a laser beam trained on Ellis' face. Ellis backs up slightly and ponders the sudden yet obvious change in climate.

"I need a slash."

"Good boy. You know it makes sense." Ellis gets up and heads for the toilet. McKinley shakes his head at me, his eyes returning to their usual myopic state of calm. "Cheeky bastard."

"How was breakfast?" I ask. McKinley arrived straight from the morning shift at the hotel, via the Hartington's ever generous bar judging by the way he weaved his way through the increasingly vociferous England support.

"Fucking terrible as always. Just me, gay boy Dennis and those mental fucking waitresses," he sighs. "That reminds me," he says, perking up. "All the mad bastard's ramblings totally got in the way. The lovely Kate was on service this morning and was asking about you. She wanted to know if you were involved with anyone."

Hold on. Is this the same Kate who I have been lusting over for the past eighteen months - off and on, but mostly on - and who has been wholly unavailable due to the inconceivably long relationship she's been having with her incredibly inattentive childhood sweetheart? Is this the same Kate who has been the slim thread tethering me to hope through all the disastrous trysts and nightmarish shags? Is this the luminously unobtainable Kate who has starred in a franchise of masturbation fantasies ever since I first set eyes on her?

"Oh yeah?" I ask casually, after slapping some restraint into the narrator of my internal dialogue. "What did you tell her?"

"Well, I didn't tell her about the frenzied toilet shag which nearly resulted in fatherhood or the constant pining for the girl who always disappeared when things got good and who ultimately turned out to be like all the rest and broke your heart."

Touché. "Okay...so what *did* you say?"

"I told the truth...That you're a sad, lonely git who needs a good seeing to and who has a weakness for vacant blondes." He glances sideways at me as he draws on his pint, wondering if I'll take him seriously or not. The look of hope on my face persuades him to cut me some slack. "I told her that you wouldn't exactly slam the phone down on her if she gave you a call." He pauses to check I'm still with him. Why wouldn't I be? "So I gave her your number...and she said she'd call you."

The second half of the match goes on in front of my eyes but nothing except McKinley's news registers in my brain. What does this mean? As far as I know, Kate is still with her bloke. If she isn't, McKinley would certainly know and would have certainly told me. My pursuit of Kate, however sporadic it may have been, has hardly been a secret between us (or anyone, actually...I can be quite obvious when desperate). Besides, if she was single again, McKinley would have definitely resurrected the Proxy Fuck doctrine, given that Kate was the ultimate target in mind when that particularly notorious philosophy was conceived. Considering he hasn't dared bring that up again, I can safely say that Kate remains attached. So again - what does this mean?

As England start to labour against a Swiss team which seems to be unwilling to roll over and die as the script dictates, I wonder if I should just stop analysing this and everything else and just go for it. This is, after all, the chance that I've been wanting for the past year-and-a-half: a girl I like actually liking me. Plus she's a fit girl who actually likes me. A fit girl who actually likes me, who has a great body and has the potential to be wild in the sack. Okay, narrator, you win this time. The internal dialogue is spot on. I'll take the call and take the chance when it comes.

Switzerland score a late penalty. The match ends a draw. I choose not to stay and dissect the missed chances under the burst bubble of expectation. Instead I head home in the hope that my time of doing just that is about to be over.

Ellis is out watching Spain draw with Bulgaria the next day when Kate calls. She sounds a lot younger and more nervous on the phone than at any other time in the previous 18 months during which we've probably spoken to each other on at least five days out of seven.

"McKinley told me that you wanted to speak to me," I say after the initial uncomfortable greetings. "Is everything okay?" I try and sound like I'm concerned and caring rather than itching to get whatever needs to be said out of the way so I can finally get in her pants.

"Err...yeah...Umm...It's my birthday on the fifteenth." It's currently the ninth. Nothing like giving a bloke plenty of warning. "I'm thinking of having a party...and wondered if you wanted to come...you and McKinley...and Ellis."

"Yeah, that sounds cool. So how old are you going to be?" I've heard it's rude to ask a lady her age but I figure that's just a rule that applies to women who are getting on a bit and don't want to admit they're over-the-hill. Asking a youngster like Kate is like giving her a chance to take pride in reaching maturity. Plus I want to make sure I'm not going to end up in the nick if I end up sorting her out.

"It's quite a big one...It's my eighteenth," she proudly says. Nice. "So will you come?"

I cast an eye over at the calendar and after a second's appreciation of Kathy Lloyd's satin-clad crotch, I spot a huge red circle around the fifteenth. Almost pulling the phone off the wall, I strain to see what huge event the *Loaded* itinerary has in store for the boys: Scotland versus England. Ouch. Hang on...It's an afternoon kick-off. "We'll be there." I swear I hear a whispered 'yes' somewhere at the end of the phone line. I wait for my smile to pass in case it influences my tone. "So, why are you asking me...us...now? Won't we see each other at the hotel?" It seems that a short family holiday is going to act as a buffer between this slightly nervy conversation and the night we meet to celebrate Kate's coming of age. Part of me almost wants to sigh with relief but the rest is slightly aggrieved that there will be a six-day period of apprehension before the party. I know what having too much time to think normally means.

"You can bring someone," she says out of the blue. "Not just McKinley or Ellis...but someone...special."

"Okay," I reply, stopping myself from blurting out the painful truth that there isn't anyone and that I would really like to make that crystal clear in case you are preparing to leave your boyfriend or cheat on him with me, which I would also be okay with. "But I think it'll just be me and the boys."

"Six days? That's perfect, big man." Despite his hatred of "fitba", as he calls it, McKinley is showing willing again by accompanying me to a rather drab 1-1 draw between Denmark and Portugal. Ellis is on Steak Hammer duty. "If it was tomorrow night, you might go steaming in, all up for the cup and spoil it. Best to have a few days to get your tactics sorted."

Yeah but now I've got almost a week to play it out every possible way in my head. Six days is more than long enough to get cold feet. "Wouldn't it be better to just forget about tactics and go with the flow on the day itself? Too much planning can be a bad thing."

"Aye, you're not wrong there but as things have proved in the past, Danny Boy, no planning at all tends to lead to you fucking it up big time," the Scotsman adds sagely. "Just think about this - she's still with her fella, so do you go all out and tell her that you're mad for it or do you wait to see if she has a plan?" He raises his eyebrows. "Didn't think about that, did yer?"

"She knows I've got a thing for her. Everyone knows I've got a thing for her. You don't think she may be asking me along because she has a thing for *me*?"

"Right," McKinley says. "Because it's going to be that easy. Give it some thought, big man. If this is what you really want then make sure you have a plan - otherwise you could blow it."

All this talk of plans is doing my head in. What is a plan other than something that can go badly wrong or has to be adapted at a moment's notice as circumstances change? What's the point? Alright, I concede the Scotsman has one, a point that is. I had no plan for dealing with the aftermath of the Julia incident but that worked out fine...for me. (She was so overcome with shame that she quit her job which probably led to her being unable to support herself through the rest of her studies, ending up with her on the game down Allerton Square.) Then there was Psycho Faye the Sperm Stealer...but that was all McKinley's idea and perfect evidence of where having a plan will get you - essentially chopped up in wheelie bin filled with lime. Then there was Deepthroat Debbie, where the only plan there was to get her back to the house and take advantage of her...which I did, to a certain extent. Until she turned into that bird from *The Exorcist* on Hooch. It wasn't exactly Operation Market Garden but I concede that having an objective of sorts helped. It certainly helped Ellis (- and continues to help him if the awkward John Wayne gait he tends to have after an evening with the MC is anything to go by). But then I could never plan with Karen because I never knew where the fuck she was going to be and when. All in all, experience tells me having a sketchy idea may help out in times of need but having a plan more often or not blows up in your face.

"I'll have a think about it," I finally say, to keep the Scotsman sweet. "I'll definitely consider my options."

"Why don't you consider the option of getting me a pint before I die of thirst?" he asks, waving an empty glass in my face. "Consider that my consultancy fee."

Considering that this is the country's biggest celebration of football since the 1966 World Cup, it's unsurprising that McKinley eventually reaches his soccer saturation level and drops off the radar. Despite the euphoria which seems to roll through every street like a heat wave, and the fact that you can't walk anywhere in the city without seeing a football shirt or hearing the distant strains of Baddiel and Skinner, by the time I make it to the final whistle of Bulgaria's 1-0 win over Romania - a game which, in normal circumstances, would have been avoided like the clap - I'm about ready for a night off too. Ellis, however, is just getting started. He downs his pint and prepares to get us refills in preparation for the long-haul; an evening of Switzerland versus Holland and then probably speed and vodka chasers down Pulse. I hold my hand up just in time to stop him.

"I need a break, man. I'm going to see what McKinley's up to."

Ellis frowns. "But you're coming back, right?" Euro 96 has again injected a sense of confusion into the young man. Here he is, in the middle of the country's biggest sporting celebration in a generation, at the centre of the greatest explosion of abandon and hedonism in a decade, and he finds himself in a relationship with an impressively-muscled divorcee with a penchant for S&M. For a bloke who never had a real girlfriend until Sonique and who so badly wanted to throw himself heart and soul (with no strings attached) into being a Lad, this continues to come as quite a shock - especially at times like these. No one can really blame him for wanting to make the most of his play time. Sorry, but this time I'm going to have to disappoint him and leave to him to play with himself.

"You can save the table but I'm probably not going to make it."

"Geezer." Ellis looks deflated. "It's pound-a-pint night and the footie's on. It's Thursday, man. Thursday night's alright, right?"

"Mate, the football's always on. I need a breather. I'll see you at home."

The city hums with the day's fading warmth and humidity under a blanket of vibes; the clash of electrical charges, a metropolis alive with opportunity, fuelled by alcohol, cheap drugs and the promise of more to come. The suits are out in force as office blocks ejaculate the shirt and tie brigade out onto the pavement in search of crowded bars and beer gardens. Wives all over the city will be putting cling-film on pasta dishes and Shepherd's pie while their hubbies head straight from work to the pub for the next championship game. Just as likely the ladies will be out too, mixing with friends and catching up over alcopops and spritzers as their men folk indulge in tribal bingeing in sweaty hostelries. I weave through the noisy streets breathing in this very British summer. It's all light-hearted now, spirits are high, but these streets will turn mean as the night falls. England aren't playing until Saturday but patriotism isn't something many of these blokes keep in a box for special occasions. Give them a few hours in a crowded pub and their colours will soon be on show. Cut-price Euro piss and belligerent nationalism can be a volatile cocktail.

I cross Allerton Square on my way to the Scotsman's and smile to myself when I see that even some of the early evening prostitutes are getting into the spirit of things. One or two have skimpy market stall knock-off England shirts tied up under their sagging chests and a couple are squeezed into patriotic hot pants. Football's cumming home... Halfway across the square, I spot McKinley cutting across the opposite corner. He seems disinterested in the tarts which is a surprise...a worrying development, actually. A hag done up like Dolly Parton in *9 to 5* asks him if he's looking for business but he doesn't even stop to ask her if she does student discounts. He wanders on without acknowledging her and doesn't even react when she loudly mutters some abuse at his back. Something's not right. I stray off the path and cut across the dog shit minefield to intercept him.

"Oi, Jockstrap..."

McKinley stops and looks over as I take evasive action to avoid a fresh mountain of pit-bull faeces. His usually ghostly visage catches the dying sun and glints like porcelain. Seeing McKinley with a pale face isn't a rarity. The comedian Billy Connolly once said that while most people go on holiday to get a tan, the Scots go on holiday to get white. Even when he hasn't got that north-of-the-border blue tinge to his pallor, it is not unknown for McKinley to go a deathly shade after being stitched up with a large bong or when his exceedingly high tolerance for beer has been met and surpassed. But for the Scotsman to lose his colour due to an emotional response, that's a cause for concern. His gait seems sober and when I come face-to-face with him there's not a whiff of alcohol on his breath and his eyes don't have that tell-tale pinkish tinge that suggests a crafty smoke. And yet he's standing there before me with a face which would make Dracula look like he'd just spent three weeks in Tenerife. Alarm bells start ringing.

"Alright, big man?" He lacks conviction too.

"Jesus. Who died?" I kick myself immediately, wondering if someone actually has.

"No-one," he says. "At least...Not yet."

Five minutes later, still without explanation, we're sitting in the beer garden at the Potter's Wheel looking at the diverse cross-section of discarded litter floating by in the nearby canal. The Potter's has refused to put the football on at any time over the month of June which - given it's already notorious reputation for ultra-violence - is a wise move. As a result, it's a lot less crowded than the majority of bars in the city and the local headcases have seemingly relocated in a bid to get their jollies elsewhere. I sit there opposite McKinley, expecting terrible news. Maybe things finally got out of hand and we're going to have to bury a hooker in his back garden in the dead of night. Perhaps a dalliance with some bored housewife has led to her gangland husband putting a price on the Scotsman's head. Or maybe...

"My fucking brother's in town."

Nope. Didn't expect that one. "Your brother? Since when have you had a brother?" Apparently, he's always had one...Well, for the whole time we've known him and the 30-odd years before that. It's just that his existence has been quietly omitted from the truncated version of the life story McKinley has been telling us ever since he arrived in our lives. While I was not expecting the sibling revelation, I'm certainly not prepared for what happens next: the Scotsman opens up.

"I basically raised myself," he admits slowly and quietly. "My dad did one when we were little and my mother just went fucking mad after that. Total basket case. Two kids, no job, no bloke...no hope. My brother went nuts too, ending up in and out of borstals from the age of 14 so I lived with friends until I got my first hotel job. I moved into the staff quarters and never looked back...or went back." He takes three heavy chugs on his pint and finishes it in a trio of gulps. "I worked and worked, learning the ropes, paying my way...until I could support myself. That's when I went back to school, eventually ending up here and at the university."

I always had the suspicion that his upbringing had been tough. Some of the stories McKinley told in the context of crazed, drunken shenanigans were pretty over the top; people high on E jumping out of high-rise windows at parties, robbing paralytic strangers in the street, going out tripping with someone's mum - so we had an idea that his teenage years were a little more wild than most of ours. But these stories always came during those nights you sit around hammered, comparing experiences. It was piss-up poker; 'Running over a parked car while drunk' is topped by 'streaking naked through the city while on acid'. McKinley always held the winning hand. We never touched on the context of these stories, which now seems to be that, without parental control or guidance, McKinley went off-the-rails before eventually getting himself together and building a better life. His brother, however, apparently never got back to the straight and narrow.

"And he's here now?"

"Aye. Somehow heard about my graduation and suddenly wants to be the big brother I never had. Bastard...Another month and I would have been out of the country and he never would have found me."

I'm thinking that there must be some kind of brotherly affinity here somewhere. Both McKinley boys growing up in adversity, surviving in their own ways, different but the same. "Why would you never want him to find you?"

"Because he's a fucking psychopath," McKinley says. "He makes Begbie from *Trainspotting* look like Bungle off *Rainbow*."

Imagining the slightly camp yet affable six-foot bear suddenly turning nasty and glassing George the Hippo in the face before taking a pool cue to Zippy's head distracts me from the look of real dread that has crept over the Scotsman's sallow face. "And he's in town."

McKinley nods slowly. "He's asleep on my fucking sofa."

"So where has he been all this time?"

"No idea. Probably prison."

Okay...A recently released psychopathic Glaswegian turns up two days before England play Scotland. Things may very well take on a different hue in the near future. "So, is he dangerous? Do we need to be worried?"

"You don't have to be worried about anything, big man, because once he's had a kip and a feed, I'll give him some cash and stick him on a train," McKinley says, in a frighteningly stern tone that convinces me that nothing to the contrary will happen. "He's not staying."

I try to convince the Scotsman to come back for a smoke at Calvin Road before heading home and packing his brother off to God knows where but he refuses, preferring to grab the bull by the horns. He's full of surprises today. We stay for another pint as the sun finally starts to set and after a chaser of Dutch courage, McKinley takes a deep breath and heads home. I do the same in the opposite direction, half wondering if I should have gone with him. The image of the Begbie brother pulling a shiv quickly convinces me that I made the right choice and I quicken my step, putting more asphalt between myself and a rough stabbing. I get home to find Ellis, freshly showered, grimacing at me from the kitchen. Is he still pissed off? Actually, it's the literal opposite.

"There's a lunatic in McKinley's house, man. I went looking for you after I got bored at the pub. Fuck knows how he got in but when I rang the doorbell, this bloke appears in the upstairs window and starts pissing on me."

"That'll be McKinley's brother," I inform him.

"His brother?"

"Sit down, man. I'll fill you in."

We don't hear anything from McKinley until Saturday morning. After spending most of the Friday debating whether we should call the Old Bill, an ambulance or both (– never whether we should go round and look for ourselves), the phone rings at Calvin Road and a sleepy Ellis takes the call. A short conversation later and Ellis is passing on the latest info over coffee and burnt toast.

"Begbie's still here," he tells me. "Apparently he's taking off tomorrow, something about not being able to get a train to where he wants to go."

"I thought the train to anywhere–but–here leaves pretty regularly."

"McKinley had to strike a deal or he could have been here for longer. So he's here...and he's coming out with us tonight."

"To the game?" I'm surprised by how shrill my voice can get at times. I cough and lower the tone from frightened little girl to just above masculine. "He's coming to the Scotland game? Jesus..."

"McKinley takes full responsibility and Begbie has given his word that he'll behave."

"Well, that makes me feel a whole lot better." I'd woken up with a washing-machine stomach and news of Begbie's attendance has just poured a pint of bleach into the mix. Earlier this morning, I'd surfaced from an uneasy dream into a hour-long doze where thoughts of Kate's party, McKinley's potential murder and the coming clash of the old foes had crashed and barged into each other in a brain still reeling from an ill-advised real ale evening down the Stanley Arms. The Czech Republic's 2-1 victory over Italy had been so entertaining that I hadn't taken much notice of how many times Ellis had come back with pints of Mountaineer's Crevice (or something). So my head was already a little delicate before having aspects of reality jack-booting around in it. Now, as well as considering what will happen with Kate, what I want to happen with Kate, *if* I want anything to happen with Kate - I also have to think about what carnage we can expect at the Castle this evening when England take on the Jocks.

The Castle. Our local. While Ellis and I could be relocating to any number of suburbs in the next few weeks, we'd still like to stay as close to where we are now for the sole reason of having the Castle and the Hartington (business and pleasure) within respectable walking distance. If Begbie smashes the pub up and/or causes actual bodily harm to one of the locals, we can think about living pretty much anywhere else in future because Bob the Bastard will live up to his name and ban us - regardless of whether we are involved in the violence or not. He's that much of a bastard. We will be guilty by association. I put this to Ellis and we start considering a change of venue to a pub we won't mind getting barred from.

402

"What about the Lamb?" Ellis asks. "It'll have the game on and although it's handy for a quick one on the way to the Warehouse, I could live without it."

"Yeah, but we should avoid anywhere which is likely to get tasty at the drop of a glass." The Lamb is always a potential flashpoint pub. "No need to put temptation in Begbie's way. We should think of a pub we don't often go to, which is not full of townie tossers and which will be showing the game."

"The Trowel. I haven't been in there since Christmas."

Inspired. I fucking hate the Trowel. I happily agree. "Excellent. Let's go there. I'll give the McKinley brothers a call."

The ten minute walk to the Trowel is undertaken in complete silence. Before Thursday, this date had been the reason for much positive anticipation. Now there's more than a little dread. Ellis is alone with his own thoughts, no doubt still battling it out on some remote mental plain over whether he's a carefree Lad or an accidental boyfriend, but also nervously considering the coming few hours and whether he'll make a potentially fatal mistake by calling McKinley's brother 'Begbie' instead of Craig. I'm harbouring the same reservations but I'm also feeling the growing tangle of knots associated with tonight's party – should we escape the Trowel with our lives. Eighteen months of lusting could come surging out tonight and blow Kate's pretty brains out all over the headboard. It's what I've wanted to do for so long. So why is there a knot of doubt forming along the lines of whether I really want this? Have a word with yourself, Daniel. She's young, she's fit, she's blonde...but she's not...

"What are you having?" We're suddenly standing at the bar. Ellis is waving a twenty in my face and I'm far enough away from taking that final step on my last thought process to not care where it was leading.

"Stella. I'll get a table." The pub is about two-thirds full but most people are still loitering around the bar or at the tables in the main room having lunch. We're about two hours away from kick-off and while there are a few white shirts scattered around and a group of Scotland fans by the fruit machine, it's still pretty low-key. After claiming a table with a good view of the screen and taking receipt of a very delicious looking pint of cold lager, I excuse myself. On my way to the pisser I get a view of the beer garden and see the majority of those fans who'll be crowding around us later. Making the most of the warm early afternoon, about twenty or so England fans are boozing heavily in the sunshine while a large group of Jocks in orange wigs and Tam o'shanters are singing 'Scotland the Brave' while conquering the kiddies climbing frame. My stomach sinks and my bowels somersault.

On leaving the remarkably pristine bogs, I'm shocked to see McKinley sat beside Ellis at our table. He wasn't supposed to arrive until just before kick-off to keep his brother's alcohol level to an acceptable level, at least until the game was underway. I quickly scan the pub for someone who resembles a Scottish psychopath - I could take my pick - but I soon spot the one person who can only be Craig. Wiry in that ripped and muscular way that you can only get from bad prison food and hours contemplating your sins in the jail's gym, he stands at the bar in his Pringle v-neck and golf slacks necking a pint in one, just seconds after it has been handed to him. Three others sit on the bar. I'm hoping they're for us. Once the empty glass is finished with, Craig is passed another by the cautious bar man. He swallows a half-pint in one mouthful, belches his thanks and scoops up the remaining three and half pints and swaggers over. McKinley rattles off the introductions and then gets stuck into his pint. Never before has he looked so in need of a drink, and that's saying something.

"So are you boys fucking students as well?" Craig asks, draining the rest of his second.

"Not anymore, Craig. School's out forever," I say, throwing in a reference which I hope will endear me to the Alice Cooper–loving axe murderer. Sometimes doing your homework pays off.

"Aye, fucking Alice knew the score, big man. No need for any of that shite once you get older. What about you, bawbag?" he pokes Ellis in the ribs. "You a fucking schoolie an' all?" Ellis chokes on his beer but luckily coughs it back up into his pint rather than all over Craig's fetching argyle sweater. McKinley finishes his drink and gets up to go to the bar. "Don't mind if I do," says Craig, handing his brother an empty glass.

And so it goes on until just before three o'clock. Craig is polishing off three pints to every one the rest of us can manage. McKinley is barely saying a word, keeping his head down in an effort to survive the night and get his brother onto the train in the morning with the minimum of fuss. Ellis is getting plenty of stick but is soldiering on gamely despite nearing his own level of raucous inebriation. I'm trying to engage with Craig as much as possible, just to try and create an atmosphere which suggests that he's among friends – or at least not enemies. But as kick-off nears, and the rowdy Scots from the beer garden mix with the predominantly white-shirted hordes in the bar, the growing feeling is that battle lines are being drawn.

The two national anthems are bellowed out with gusto (Craig stands on his chair to conduct the Scottish choir) and despite emotions running high due to the occasion and the vast amount of booze that's been consumed, the first half is uneventful both in the pub and at Wembley. Maybe we'll get away without any blood being spilt and the day Begbie came to town will be remembered only for the hangovers that followed. But as predictable old pundits are likely to say when searching for a cliché: football is a game of two halves. It's when the second one gets underway that the combustible atmosphere hanging over the assembled crowd ignites like a burning fag-end tossed onto a puddle of petrol.

To start with it looks like it's all going to be Steve McManaman's fault. The Liverpool winger, who looked like he'd rather be somewhere else for most of the first 45 minutes, is on fire from the restart and soon whips an early shot just over the bar. It doesn't take long before his fancy footwork puts England on the attack again. White shirts dart everywhere around the penalty area pulling blue shirts out of position as McManaman feeds the ball to Gary Neville on the right...Neville hits a first-time looping cross...the ball evades two Scottish defenders but not Alan Shearer who stoops to head the ball past Andy Goram to put England 1-0 up! The Trowel erupts. The first half has lulled us into a false sense of security so Ellis and I are out of our seats in celebration, forgetting that Craig is about ten pints more pissed than us and about 100 times more psychotic. He sits there, fuming, barely keeping a lid on the volcanic rage which is bubbling inside him. He tries to douse the flames by necking his pint and then what's left of mine. He then gets up and storms through the crowd of singing Englishmen to get to the bar.

"Do you both like the way you look?" asks McKinley, leaning in to our beaming faces once we're re-seated. "Because if you do that again, I'm not going to be able to stop him from rearranging your features."

"Come on, man," I smile. "He's alright. It's just a football match. Besides, he's Scottish. He must be used to losing by now."

"Keep that up, big man, and you're not going to have a face for Kate to sit on."

Such is the depth of the crowd behind us that Craig doesn't make it back to the table, choosing to stay at the bar. The first evidence which suggests he's still with us comes when Andy Goram makes a great save from Terry Sheringham's almost point-blank header. The gutted "oohs" of the England fans die out and a clear Glaswegian voice rings out in the vacuum: "You fucking cunts!" McKinley holds his head in his hands.

That same voice rings out again above the cries of frustration minutes later when Tony Adams scythes down Gordon Durie to give

Scotland the chance to equalize from the penalty spot: "Adams, yer bag o'shite fucking cockney bastard! Geddin'!" A small part of me hopes Scotland scores as this would do much to take the sting out of Craig's rising anger - but David Seaman saves brilliantly from Gary McAllister and, as one, the England fans by the bar turn to Craig and mockingly shout "AHHH!!" at him. There's not even time for a punch to be thrown before the ball is down the other end of the pitch. Gascoigne latches onto it...he lobs it over Colin Hendry's head...and volleys it in for England's second! WHAT A GOAL!! Ten minutes to go - it's all over now.

No truer word said. A smash of glass at the back of the pub near the bar heralds the inevitable. A crowd surge knocks a few tables over and sends a couple of sunburnt Newcastle fans sprawling into McKinley's lap. In the space created by the spontaneous brawl, a yellow argyle Pringle sweater can be seen wrestling, not with a white-shirted adversary, but with two blokes in Celtic shirts. Craig has one of the Celtic geezers in a head lock, slicing his cheek open with a heavily sovereigned fist. The other looks like he's having the life throttled out of him between Craig's knees.

"Game well and truly fucking over," curses McKinley and after rolling the surprised Geordies off onto the floor he stands up and wades through the crowd to where his brother is now fighting the entire bar staff. Ellis and I take our cue and follow him out.

Out in the street, Craig is scarily aloof, as if he's waiting for a bus. His left eye is starting to close and his top lip is swollen and split. I suspect the blood on his left hand which has turned his rings crimson is the other bloke's, not his own. He listens calmly as McKinley talks to him. Ellis and I sit on the wall which rings the pub car park and watch the two brothers promise that they will never contact each other again. McKinley takes out his wallet, hands Craig a wad of cash and then flags down a taxi. Craig mutters something before getting in and being driven out of McKinley's life. Our Scotsman sighs and wanders over to where we sit in silence.

"I need a drink."

"Not in the Trowel, I'm guessing."

"No. Not in the Trowel. Nowhere where the fucking football is on either."

"So what was that all about?"

McKinley shakes his head. "Those Celtic fans...They called Gascoigne a fucking Hun. One thing my brother hates more than Sassenachs and that's Celtic fans slagging off Rangers..." He sighs. "So now I'm back to having no brother again, okay? Not a word. History." Ellis and I nod in agreement. "Now where were we on you two buying me a drink?"

After a soothing one in the Potter's Wheel (which is becoming a unexpected port in the storm this month), we leave McKinley to get his life and house back in order while we head across the city to Calvin Road to prepare for the party. Ellis and I both seem intent on letting the Begbie episode slide into folklore without feeling the need to discuss it in the here and now. Ellis has other things on his mind.

"Do you think it's okay that I didn't tell Monica about the party?" he asks as we make our way home. I didn't actually think about whether our collective invitation stretched to significant others. When Kate said that I could bring someone 'special' I was so wrapped up in the idea that she was digging for rivals that I didn't consider Ellis and Steak Hammer's situation. I consider it now.

"Kate didn't say anything about bringing anyone else so I suppose that means Monica wasn't invited...so you're in the clear." I don't sound at all convincing. I can find a number of ways to support my mate's decision but deep down I feel like he's asking for trouble by not telling her. Letting her know he's going and that it's a work-related invite is one thing, not telling her at all is another.

"But it's too late now, right? If I tell her now it'll be the same shit but a different reason." He kicks a discarded Coke can across the road in frustration. "This fucking R-word is too hard, geezer. This...*relationship*. How am I supposed to know how to do all this stuff? Women are way too complicated." I sense another of the Golden Couple's sporadic break-ups on the horizon. But this one could be different. Instead of Monica dumping Ellis because he can't commit, it could be Ellis ending it because he honestly can't handle it. Monica has been chucking him on and off for the last few months in a bid to get him to man up but I've always had the feeling that she never really wanted shot of him. It was shock therapy. Now it looks like it may have back fired. If Ellis walks, that will be that. I'm not convinced, however, that he really wants to end it.

"Listen, who's to say she'll ever know," I say. "And besides, why should it matter? You're Ellis. You have a life. You do your thing. This is part of that. This is not part of Ellis and Steak Hammer..."

"Oi..."

"Sorry, Ellis and Monica. The things you do together, that's the couple life. The reason you don't do everything together is so the stuff you do share is more important. What's she doing tonight anyway?"

"No idea."

"There you go. She could be going to a party. Or watching Patrick Swayze movies with Deepthroat Debbie. It doesn't matter. As long as she's not screwing someone else and you're not on the nob, then what's the big deal? You'll see her tomorrow or something, she'll ask what you've been up to, you'll say 'I went to Kate's birthday party with the lads' and it'll all be cool."

Ellis considers this. "Yeah...It's like a smaller version of the Glastonbury thing, right? I wanted to go and I went. It worked out okay." I don't remind him of what he already knows; that it was only okay after a fortnight of blazing rows and floods of tears. "It'll be fine," he adds, somewhat unconvincingly. "Anyway, tonight is about you and Kate, fella. Ready to give her a portion of older man for her birthday?" He grabs my shoulder in a vice-like grip and shakes me in that age-old display of male support. With all the sectarian violence, family drama and relationship counselling, I haven't really had a chance to think about the possibilities this evening may hold. Now I'm back on that train of thought, the knot of doubt twists again. What was it I was saying to myself before? She's young, she's fit, she's blonde...but she's not...

The party is in full swing by the time we eventually arrive. McKinley has been in attendance for a good 45 minutes before we roll in and has discovered a taste for the punch - which, he informs us, has been spiced up a little...by McKinley. We apologise for the delay but all is forgiven when Ellis hands the reason for our lateness over in a subtle handshake. McKinley's eyes widen and he turns quickly on his heel, heading for the downstairs bathroom with the wrap.

"That was the smaller one, right" I ask.

"Absolutely," Ellis assures me. "Even if he hoovers the lot, we'll be sorted for the night." He taps the breast pocket of his leather jacket. "It pays to be cautious, especially with that greedy bastard around."

"You made it!" A slightly slurred yet familiar voice cuts through the bad techno and excited chatter. Kate appears at my shoulder looking good enough to eat, have seconds and then take the rest home in a doggie bag. Her long blonde hair is freshly washed and loose, spraying out over her bare shoulders. The tight white vest she is wearing hugs her slim torso and tightly follows every curve. Her endless legs stretch out of the shortest pair of cut-off jeans hot pants I have ever seen. She

410

looks like she's just stepped off a Californian beach into my ultimate surf babe wet dream fantasy. Ellis is almost dribbling on his bowling shoes. I think words are required before the perving becomes awkward. I lean in and kiss her cheek, breathing in cinnamon shampoo and sun-warmed skin.

"Happy birthday," I whisper in her ear. I linger in her hair for a moment too long to be casual and I feel her gasp a little. I move back to a safe distance. "How was your holiday?" Unknown quantities of McKinley's special punch are already working their magic and Kate freely goes into one about how amazing the Devon coast was while completely missing the concept of small talk. It begins to sound like a story in real time, and as I'm waiting for a moment to politely head for the nearest alcoholic beverage, I see Ellis fade silently into the crowd, leaving me to nod, smile and check out her tits while she reminisces about some traffic jam they got caught in somewhere near Brighton...

When I eventually escape and find my errant friends, both are talking loudly and animatedly in the kitchen as McKinley transforms the family liquor cabinet into a range of powerful cocktails. Not willing to act on ceremony, I chop out a line of amphetamine sulphate on the breakfast counter in a bid to catch up.

"So Danny Boy, she's looking fucking lovely...and quite pissed. A perfect combination." The Scotsman hands me what could be loosely called a raspberry daiquiri and winks. "If you don't sort her out tonight, I will." I remind him of his reasons behind the notorious Proxy Fuck arrangement - that sex with beautiful girls would lead him to wanting more - and he replaces his lecherous grin with a look of mock deflation. "No fair, big man. Let an old pervert have his fun."

"Where's the boyfriend tonight?" asks Ellis, lighting up a Marlboro.

"Did you see the spotty twat sitting on the sofa playing the video game? That's him." McKinley tuts. "Like I said before: you know he's not fucking her right."

"Boys, I've only just started getting off my face," I smile. "It's summer, England are in the quarter-finals - sorry Jockstrap - and we're having it large. Let's just party and see where the evening takes us." We toast our dubiously concocted drinks and celebrate the moment.

Two hours and one severely depleted drinks cabinet later and Ellis has commandeered the stereo. A cheekily prepared Britpop mix has replaced the teenie dance rubbish and the majority of the guests are now cutting up the lawn in the back garden to a fine selection of tunes. The Scotsman, as predicted, has finished off his specially prepared wrap and is throwing angular shapes in the middle of a group of giggling 17-year old girls. If the speed probably wasn't telling him the same thing, he would undoubtedly consider himself to be in heaven. As I'm frugging along merrily to 'Bluetonic' by the Bluetones I catch sight of a tense scene in the living room between Kate and her boyfriend. Through the patio doors I can make out the flush of anger on her cheeks and the indifferent belligerence on his acne-pocked face. I've kept a casual eye on Kate all night and not once have I seen them interact until now; no kiss, no conversation, not even the slightest bit of eye contact. He's been sat on his fat arse ever since we got here and he hasn't paid a bit of attention to her. He just has eyes for Sonic the fucking Hedgehog. As 'Bluetonic' morphs into Shed Seven's 'Bully Boy' and the garden party goes into overdrive, Kate spits a final expletive in her boyfriend's face and storms out, heading for the front door. I flash a quick look at McKinley in the hope of getting the green light, one which would take full responsibility for what's about to happen out of my hands, but he's somewhere in the sweaty ether, gliding over the throng on a narcotic flying carpet with no attachment to reality whatsoever. It's all down to me then...I head for the alleyway between the houses, exiting in the front garden where Kate is sat on the low wall. I thought she would be crying but she's not - she's just sitting there, fuming. I approach with caution because she looks like she's about ready to kill someone.

"Is it safe?" I ask as I creep towards her, trying to inject a bit of tension-defusing humour.

"Would you treat me like that, Danny? If you were my boyfriend, would you ignore me?"

"I can't see how anyone can ignore you," I reply, taking a seat beside her, although with a blast range of a couple of feet between us. "I mean, have you seen you? You're pretty hard to ignore."

She seems fixated on her anger and doesn't tune into the compliments. "It's always like this. *He's* always like this. I can be laying there in my sexiest undies and he won't notice." Seriously? This is a teenage boy we're talking about here. Even if he was shy there should be some response to having someone like Kate lying spread-eagled in lingerie on your bed, begging for a shagging. There's definitely something wrong with the boy.

"He's just a kid, Kate. He'll wake up in a few years and spend the rest of his life kicking himself that he never noticed." I'll put money on that. Jesus...

She turns to look at me, her eyes still crazy and her ire still burning. "Will you fuck me?" She swings one of those willowy legs over the wall and straddles the brickwork. She fixes me with an intense, angry stare. "I need you to fuck me." I'm caught by how quickly I've been transported into McKinley's imagination and shocked to find that I'm no longer in my own. The reality of the situation I've fantasised about for over a year-and-a-half is a lot different from the vision that has been played out in my head a million times.

"Why?" I ask, which is a very different response from the James Bond-like 'but of course' I always imagined I'd say.

Kate looks confused. "Do you need a reason?"

"I need to know *your* reason," the rational person currently squatting in my head forces me to say. "I get the feeling that it's less about me and more about your boyfriend. If you want me to fuck you to get your bloke to take notice, then the answer is no."

Kate frowns at me. "You'd turn me down? After trying to get in my pants since the first day we met, you'd turn me down when I'm giving you what you want?"

"Yeah but it's not really what *you* want though, is it? It might have been until today but this is now something else." I get off the wall, both literally and metaphorically. I make my choice. "It's true, I always wanted you to ask me but not like this. If you want to get back at him in there, fine. Just dump him. Then he'll learn. But don't swap one situation for another. I wouldn't be any better for you. Sure, I'd fuck you but after that it wouldn't go where you need it to go." I kiss her cheek again but don't linger to breathe her in this time. "Happy birthday." Then I walk out of the garden and head home alone.

she's electric

Whether it's the narcotics running through his system or the urge to finally tell the full story, McKinley tears through his soliloquy at a rate of knots. The three of us sit there, gobsmacked. In all the years we've known him, he's never been so open - or said so many words in one go, to be honest. Even when we used to sit around, just the two of us and a lump of hash, and get seriously into a discussion, the Scotsman was always succinct. His advice was always tailored to my needs and any references to his own experiences were coded. Tonight, he's really driven the old McKinley out onto the open road and put his foot down.

Most of what he says doesn't come as a great surprise. We all knew to a certain extent that he had arrived in the city with a target and was committed to reaching it. It was one of the things I respected about him most. That and the fact that he appeared to have found true love and - blowjobs and furtive tugs aside - was honouring that the best he could. None of us knew that his struggle with fidelity had anything to do with fear. Real fear. Fear of losing himself and his future. He always said he would have his balls cut off if Brenda ever found out – which she would, and which is why he never had sex throughout his time with us here - but there was never any inclination that he was fighting a perceived addiction which he thought would destroy his life.

We sit blinking for a moment, both wired and surprised. McKinley downs his gin and tonic in one and slams the empty glass on the table, bringing us back to the reality of the Camel Club. I take a deep breath...

"You know that this fear of yours, that you have a sex addiction which will ruin your life, is all a bunch of bollocks, right?" I level a serious stare at him. "Unless you're just taking a deep breath and you're about to tell us about the millions of Indonesian hookers you've been through to keep you sated, I'm guessing Manimal is a one-off mistake."

"Only because after I got back to Brenda, I was wracked with guilt...and I thought I was about to blow my life apart."

"Did it lead to some superhuman shag fest?"

"No."

"Isn't that encouraging in itself? All this time you thought that having sex with random birds would make you as bad as your dad and brother and have the same effect on your family as they had on you. But it's not like that. The fact that you are still with Brenda and the boys and not festering in some brothel with your cock turning black means that you're just a bloke, not some possessed victim of some sex demon."

"It does sound a bit fucking melodramatic, man," adds Rob. "And I make a living from melodrama so I know what I'm talking about."

"Listen, I bet you didn't tell Brenda about all the girls you fondled in the Nineties, did you? Well this is just a version of that, only you shagged Manimal." I see a funny side to the situation for the first time and snort my amusement. "Mate, what were you thinking?"

"She's a top shag, big man," says McKinley, slightly defensively. "And she's alright when she's not being a fucking bitch."

"You told Ellis it meant something," interrupts Rob. "You didn't fall for her, did you?"

"Did I fuck. That was the wee man getting all black and white about it." He turns to Ellis. "See, man, you have to watch that if you're going to get hitched. It was the same when you had the whole phobia of commitment and relationships. You saw it in absolutes. It's much more complicated than that but you'll be in even deeper shit if you carry on thinking that one thing means the other. A commitment when you're barely out of your teens does not mean you're going to end up marrying the first bird you have sex with...except in your case, of course."

"You told him that as well?" Ellis splutters. I may have spilled the beans on Steak Hammer's penchant for tunnelling him out with a dildo all those years ago but I'm not guilty for revealing details of his late virginity loss.

"Wee man, it was just a guess," McKinley smiles. "It was hardly a long shot though. You've never exactly been one for putting it about."

Ellis frowns back at the Scotsman who seems to be slowly returning to his old self, another burden lifted. He ignores the latest slur and returns to the previous topic of conversation. "So what changed then? Why did shagging Manimal mean something if you weren't into her?"

"Like I said," McKinley replies, "I thought it meant that I was going to turn into a sex pest beyond control and lose my woman and kids because of it. I was shocked that I'd given in so easily with Manimal of all people and thought I'd not just hit the top of a slippery slope but fucking swan dived off the edge into shag oblivion."

"Maybe if it had been with a fit bird, you would have done," I muse.

"Aye, no doubt, big man. No doubt. As I said years ago, I couldn't just get a rub out from some top tart. I'd want more...which is why I got you to do it. So maybe shagging a pig like Amanda was the best thing I could have done. Hoorah for ugly birds!" He cheers and waves Shawna over for another credit card-busting round of spirits.

Ellis remains thoughtful and a little disapproving. "So what, you now stay with your woman out of guilt?"

McKinley turns a resigned face towards Ellis before addressing the issue in my direction. "Danny, do you remember when you just split up with your first bird...whatshername...Anna? We had a conversation about my arrangement and I told you that when it comes to messing around with other women when you're attached, you have to get it straight in your head...what it means. If you understand what you're doing and how it fits in the big plan, then you can justify it. Well, that's fine when you have a plan. I had a plan and getting involved with birds on more than a casual sucking and groping level would have fucked up that plan. That plan was getting out of the shit and building a life. That day, when I came back to sign the papers over on the house, my plan seemed complete. I had the wife, the kids, the job, the money, the international lifestyle... I was cutting the final ties by selling the house. But instead of feeling free, once I started talking to Manimal I realised that it scared the fucking life out of me. So I did something stupid..."

"Why didn't you just buy a sports car if you were having a mid-life crisis?" Rob asks, again without engaging his brain first. "I could have sold you one of mine."

"You don't drive," Ellis says. "You've got a chauffeur. Why do you own sports cars?"

"They're an investment, geezer," Rob says. "And anyway, this is about why McKinley didn't buy one, not about why I did."

The Scotsman gets things back on track. "Because, you big ponce, sticking your cock up the exhaust pipe of an MG is nowhere near as fun as screwing a lagered-up, sex-starved tart like it's your last shag on earth. Especially when the objective isn't to make you feel younger."

"Why did you do it then?" I ask.

"I think I needed to have a new plan, a new target. My whole life I've been working to get away from something. That day at the house I felt like I'd finally escaped but the thing is, as soon as I felt I'd got out, that I'd broken out of the cycle, I felt closer to the beginning than the end. I had everything to lose but nothing to gain. So I put it all at risk so I could have a new objective."

"Which was?"

"To spend my life making it up to my family, I suppose."

"But you'd battled and beaten all your demons to get that family in the first place," I added. "You'd won."

"You never win," McKinley says, his face now telling the story of his regret. "You just keep playing the game and hope to stay ahead."

Ellis looks disappointed in McKinley. "So now your life is about making amends."

"It's always about making amends...To yourself or somebody else, it doesn't matter. Another thing to remember when you're walking up the aisle, wee man."

Whether he knows it or not, McKinley's story has added a coat of conviction to the belief in what really matters which has been returning slowly since my conversations with Ellis outside the Passage to India and with Rob back at the Warehouse. There can be drastic consequences if you not only yearn for the past but believe it's better than the present to such an extent that you actually decide to return to it. You may be hoping to find something you feel your life is missing back there but you run the risk of losing the important things in the here and now at the same time. The result can be that you end up with nothing. Sometimes, you get more than you bargained for and then have to live with the consequences. You spend your life making amends.

thirteen

Don't Look Back in Anger

August 1996

The three months which have passed since I stormed out on Karen in Amsterdam have been among the most defining of recent times in terms of what it means for the country, its music, its culture and its people.

I, however, have barely noticed because when I haven't been high as a kite, drunk as a skunk or bellowing along to 'Three Lions', I've been churning over and over every little detail, every word and every gesture of that brief meeting, a chance encounter in a foreign bar which may turn out to be just as defining in my life as England winning Euro 96 would have been to the nation as a whole.

Given everything which has gone on over the past few weeks, you may be wondering why I keep going back to that coincidental event in May and why I have given it such high importance in the overall scheme of things. You are not alone - because I am currently standing beside you, equally incredulous, going "what the fuck?" Just three weeks ago, I was sitting on a garden wall next to a gorgeous young blonde who was asking me to have sex with her, actually telling me she needed me inside her firm, nubile, teenage body. Just three weeks ago, for some inexplicable reason, I essentially told that gorgeous young blonde "thanks, but no thanks" and turned my back on eighteen months of longing and God knows however many future months of sex with the girl who I once thought was the platinum nymphet of my dreams. At the time I based this inexplicable decision on the belief that she just wanted me to jump her to get back at her lazy, inattentive boyfriend; a situation which would normally inspire a response of "That's fine. Let's screw." But I caught a nasty case of morals out of nowhere and I have no idea why. The only reason I can come up with as I repeatedly slap myself for being such an incredibly stupid human being, is that three minute argument with Karen Anderson in a tacky pub in Amsterdam. And it makes absolutely no sense to me why.

I've turned the events of that day over in my head countless times since. That knot of doubt I had growing from the moment I woke up on June 15 had originally been tied in the immediate aftermath of the Amsterdam odyssey. Kate's enquiries into my personal life and her invitation to her birthday party had added new twists but the first knot had been pulled tight by Karen. This was the knot at the heart of that tangled ball - the nucleus of doubt that made me question whether a tryst with Kate would be such a good idea. I mean Kate was young, she was fit, she was blonde...but she wasn't Karen.

Often when life is twisting my melon, I turn to music for guidance. Sometimes there's a story I can relate to in a lyric, or a song which puts into words the underlying chaos in my head. Rarely does music provide definitive answers but it can often show you that you are not the first to be in a certain situation, which is sometimes enough to get you out of that particular hole. Knowing that you're just dealing with the crazy gamut of human emotions and not some alien dread which has come down to uniquely haunt you is all you need sometimes. However, while trying to find anything to help me understand what's happening in relation to the Karen situation, the best I've found so far is a lyric from 'Columbia' by Oasis:

There we were, now here we are

All is confusion; nothing's the same to me

I can't tell you the way I feel because the way I feel is oh so new to me

There we were.

Destiny had us happily crossing each other's paths from time to time. Every time our worlds collided, something changed in me, albeit slowly at first. After our first meeting I spent a week dreaming of Karen Anderson before my life slapped me awake and pushed me back into the same old routines. The impact of her body, her lips on mine soon faded into a warm, distant memory. At that time, it was impossible for me to even consider that she would be more than just one of many Thursday night snogs which is why, after recovering from that brief interlude in Fantasyland, I went upon my way with a small reminder of Karen Anderson filed away along with many others.

Meeting her again, almost a year after that first night, led to one of the most profound moments of my life so far. Seeing her again felt like the next day, not twelve months after the fact. While it seemed to me that no time had passed, it also felt as though years had gone by but years we had spent together. Staring up at those stars through the battered roof of that derelict bandstand, I not only felt a connection to the cosmos but also with the young woman lying beside me. It felt like a deep, ancient connection yet heart-bursting and new. When we kissed again it bore no relation to the time before. This was a moment shared away from the crowds and noise of a nightclub. It was less impulsive and fleeting than a snatched moment in a pub. It meant something. It planted something. Again, as before, she ran off at the end but this time I ran with her and the cryptic nature of her farewell was even more enticing:

Keep looking for me. She wanted to be found. She wanted me to find her.

Feeling as though I had been given a sign that this was meant to be, I would have begun the search immediately had it not been for Kelly and the baby scare. But for all the feelings that resurfaced during that time, and the new ones which came from agonizing over whether I was the father, that intensely stressful period brought clarity in its wake. Girls like Kelly are exciting and fun but come with the threat of consequence and recrimination. There had been far too many Kelly's. I needed to sort things out and find out what - who - I really wanted. Despite the emotional intensity which made it feel like a lot more, Karen and I had only really shared two brief encounters so I was more than a little surprised that when I found myself at the crossroads, I chose the path that I hoped would lead to a possible life with her. I decided that I would work towards being the man worthy of this incredible young woman. I wanted her level of openness, I wanted to feel as sure about myself as she did, I wanted the wisdom she seemed to possess in dealing with this crazy, ever-changing life. If I took the first steps towards these things, I was sure that she would lead me the rest of the way. She had already shown me so much in such a brief amount of time. What a life it would be to have years of that?

Now here we are.

I never expected to find Karen in Amsterdam. Why would I? This is a city built for the Lad even before the Lad by that name and definition even existed. It's a sleazy male amusement park; full of sex, drugs and alcohol-related rides and excitement. I was sure Karen Anderson didn't buy into any of that (although I was hoping that she wouldn't be totally against any of them if we ever got it together, especially the first). I thought Karen was above it all. That's why I decided to change my ways.

But seeing her there, more hung-over than I've ever seen any woman - and taking into consideration where I've met most of my conquests, that's saying something - after raging through the Dam in a typically Ladette manner, totally knocked me and my perception of her for six.

All is confusion; nothing's the same to me

It all seemed so clear cut before Amsterdam. I was the Lad and she was the lady. I was the one waking up bleary-eyed most mornings after yet another night spent in the pursuit of hedonistic excitement (although I must stress that I have never sought out any kind of establishment or situation where muscle-bound geezers would wave their plonkers in my face - so she has one up on me there). I was the one who could be seen lurching around the streets in a gang, encouraging all and sundry to 'get them out'. It was me who could be spotted in some dark corner of a seedy after-hours basement, inappropriately mauling semi-conscious members of the opposite sex. It was me who could be found in most places which served alcohol to a soundtrack of pounding British rock music.

Karen was supposed to be the one that flitted around the city's social scene, having a few drinks with her mates in a responsible manner before dancing the night away in one of the more upmarket nightspots while happily tipsy at best. She was the one who was supposed to adhere to her own rule of three G&Ts before getting a cab home and into bed for a reasonable hour due to work or study commitments the next day. She was the one who never let the hand stray inside the blouse or down the front of her knickers during passionate yet controlled fumbling with not-entirely strange men.

I was the one in need of saving.

She was the one who was supposed to save me.

It's all fucked up now.

I can't tell you the way I feel because the way I feel is oh so new to me.

What is this I'm feeling? It's something totally off my usual scale of emotions. The best I can do is break it down into barely digestible parts but, as a whole, there's no overall classification which will help me come to a solution as to how I should deal with this. I'm pissed off, first and foremost. Pissed off because I had struggled with a similar whirlwind of feelings after the Kelly fiasco to come to the conclusion that I wanted to be a better man for Karen, only to find out that I needn't have bothered. Pissed off because I was looking for the girl of my dreams and thought that I had found her but, in the end, she appears to be just the same as everyone else. Pissed off because she was larging it around Amsterdam without a care in the world while I was mincing over bridges in angst, wrestling with my conscience like some poofy toff in a period drama. Pissed off because...she out-Ladded me. Really? Hmm...That's a bit crap.

I'm also sad. The mad, drunken, cock-waving, shoe-puking part aside, Karen Anderson is still rather fucking great. But she isn't who I thought she was and that's sadly disappointing. Unless, that's how she really is and I was just expecting the impossible...which is possible...I suppose. In theory. I'm also sad that our paths might never cross again because I was stupid enough to throw destiny's generosity back in its face. (Actually, we can add this to the pissed-off column because I am actually quite fucking outrageously aggrieved that I stormed out of that bar and acted like a spoilt brat when I should have embraced yet another precious moment with her.) I'm also sad - and pissed off - that I may never get the chance to apologise for acting like that. I'm also sad and pissed off that I may never get the chance to tell Karen Anderson that I'm in love with her.

Hang on...

I'm *in love* with her?

I'm in love with her.

So that's what this is...Huh.

I'm lying on the sofa listening and wallowing to The Smiths' 'Heaven Knows I'm Miserable Now' on repeat when Ellis comes home from work with the Scotsman in tow.

"See what I mean?" says Ellis to McKinley, pointing at me, prone and maudlin on the couch. "It's your own fault, man. You blew out the blonde. Get over it and move on."

The Scotsman bats my legs off the sofa and sits next to me as Ellis disappears into the kitchen. "Fuck's sake, big man, it's been weeks now. Haven't you sorted yourself out yet?"

"Switch the album," shouts Ellis. "You'll get more sense out of him." McKinley leans over me and ejects the CD. Straining with the effort, he blindly grabs a random album from the heap and slaps it in. He's lucky with his choice. Ocean Colour Scene's *Moseley Shoals* starts up with the more life-affirming 'Riverboat Song'. I shake myself from my Morrissey-inspired depression and try on a fake, upbeat expression. McKinley looks towards the kitchen door to make sure Ellis is still preoccupied before slipping into his concerned guru mode.

"Usually I'd say you deserve to feel like this after passing up the chance to fuck Kate but I think I understand why you didn't do her," he confides. "I mean, I would have shagged her on the spot but then I'm not you. You're you...and you have quite a reputation for making arse-about-face decisions...so I s'pose I'll let you off."

426

"Kate wanted revenge and even though what she was offering was what I thought I wanted, I couldn't do it," I say, ignoring the iron insult hidden in a velvet compliment. "It wasn't morality. All I could think about was Karen. Kate was there and all I could think about was what it would do to my chances with Karen and how wrong I was to walk out on her."

"Look, this Karen bird was never ever going to be that vision in your head, man. No-one is just one thing and not the other and if the one thing you believe in is a fucking angelic goddess on a pedestal, you're always going to be disappointed. We're all light and dark, big man, light and dark. "

"I know that now. But I blew it. S'pose I got what I deserved." And heaven knows I'm miserable now.

"Why? Because you're such a bad man?" McKinley's most sarcastic tone is intended to make me feel like a tit. Mission accomplished. "Danny Boy, seems to me you've made your choice. You turned down Kate for this other bird. You've finally seen both sides of this Karen, and it's obvious to everyone - except you - that this whole package is what you want. Why else would you pass up the dream shag?"

"It is...she is...what I want...I think. But if that's who she is...who am I?"

A large fart and a satisfied groan from the kitchen suggests our quality time is about to end. McKinley slaps my knee. "You're the bloke who's supposed to keep looking."

Ellis wanders in and throws a can of Kronenberg to each of us before slumping into the armchair opposite. He cracks open his can and takes a long draught. He looks over at my suddenly more serene face and then at the Scotsman. "That's the first time in a fortnight that he hasn't frowned," Ellis says. "What did you say?"

"Not me, wee man. A bit of Ocean Colour Scene...that's all he needed."

"Oh yeah, that reminds me. I have good news and bad news" Ellis continues, missing the wry smiles exchanged between the Scotsman and I. "The good news is that the tickets for Knebworth arrived at my mum and dad's this morning. The bad news is...so did the phone bill. The three hours I spent waiting on the hotline almost cost as much as our four tickets put together. My dad's wig almost spontaneously combusted."

Knebworth. Of course. Sometime during my long dark night of the soul, Oasis announced that they would be playing the biggest shows of their career at Knebworth House in Hertfordshire this month. And when the going gets tough, the tough get tickets for a generation-defining musical event during which they can get off their tits and forget about all the shit in their lives. Thankfully, while I was trying to work out what I was feeling, my friends got their less self-absorbed arses into gear and sorted it out. Ellis camped out at his folks' to do battle against an estimated three million other hopefuls, all laying siege to the ticket hotline on the day they were released for sale. He got lucky. Countless others didn't. But, thanks to his determination, come next weekend - August 11th, Ellis, McKinley, Dennis the Menace (well, someone has to drive) and I will be part of a 125,000-strong crowd at the crowning moment of Britpop as the Burnage boys step up to claim the throne. Now if I can just work out who the hell I am, track down the girl of my dreams and tell her that I love her, I might even be able to enjoy it.

This latest planned odyssey is the best evidence yet of the new and improved Ellis. He's shown a rediscovered resilience and confidence since he broke up with Monica. In the aftermath of England's semi-final defeat to Germany on penalties (again), he went straight round to Steak Hammer's gaff and broke it off. It wasn't just an emotional reaction to being beaten by the Krauts AGAIN, it was like his Road to Damascus -

so he says. He apparently saw the light. England may have lost but it didn't mean that they would never play again. Despite the pain of defeat, the sun would rise the day after and life would go on. It wouldn't be the end but a new beginning. Leaving the MC would be like losing to Germany, he said, but qualification for the next tournament would begin in earnest directly afterwards. He would be like Terry Venables, he said, planning for the future with help from the experiences of the past. He told Monica this too - probably using the same analogy because she accused him of being high and pissed - which he was. But even when she came round to our new flat in the sober light of the following day, he eloquently and categorically stated his case again. He wasn't cold but he left no room for any misunderstandings. In fact, I've never seen him so sure about anything. Monica had no answer. His case was that water-tight. She left - and we haven't seen or heard anything from her since.

So while I've been loafing around under a cloud of self-pity, Ellis has been throwing himself into life again. Maybe he needed something huge to take his mind off what appears to be the final split. Whatever the reason, he's embraced the idea of Knebworth like a man possessed. Not only has he sorted the tickets but he was the one who cajoled Blur fanatic Dennis into driving us to Hertfordshire and back. He's a Lad reborn. It seems like everyone's finally coming off the fence and making a stand for what they want.

This includes the Scotsman. His graduation was celebrated in true Lad fashion but the festivities were tinged with more than a little sadness. A degree in one hand and a one-way ticket to Indonesia in the other, McKinley stood on the faithful, beer-stained bar at the Orchard and announced his departure. The majority of those in attendance - regulars who had born witness to almost three years of the Scotsman's antics in that very pub - raised their glasses in his honour...and then covered him in a ten-beer salute. It was a fitting and moving tribute. Now Knebworth will be our own private send-off. McKinley's flight departs from Heathrow three days after the concert. Within 48 hours he will be reunited with his woman and the life which was put on hold back in '94 will begin again. After all the opportunities he's had to stray and take a different path, the one which was always under his feet remains his chosen one. You've got to hand it to him.

Rob also continues to make a stand for what he wants - which means he still hasn't shown his face around these parts since he left in May. Despite our best efforts to get in touch with him - Ellis and I even paid a visit to his bastard dad in an attempt to discover an address or phone number - the wayward thespian remains elusive. After missing out on McKinley's graduation-leaving bash, Ellis tried to hunt him down to get him to come to Knebworth but it seems that this chapter of our lives will come to a close without Filthy Rob. He's off chasing after his new love - the adoration of crowds.

Now that college is over and the taxpayer is paying for the roof over our heads (not to mention contributing to the steady intake of drugs and alcohol), there are more and more opportunities to work at the hotel. As well as the usual kitchen shifts, Dennis has been mad keen to get me and Ellis working around the place during daylight hours. But with the last weeks of summer blazing away and the prospect of a new head chef taking over from McKinley in the coming days, I'm less enthused about showing up for work than ever before. Once McKinley leaves, the old Hartington really won't be the same. Ellis, the Scotsman and I have been the life and soul of that place for the past three years and once one of those goes, the body is surely on borrowed time. They may be able to execute a successful transplant once the Scotsman departs but chances are that this new heart will end up being rejected by the original organs. I'm not going to hang around to watch the Hartington flat-line so at the end of what turns out to be my final shift, I quit.

"Are you still going to be available for nights?" asks Dennis.

"Dennis, I haven't been available for days," I tell him. "I thought you may have started to get the message when I stopped showing up for those pointless gardening shifts you kept putting me on."

"I thought you were just struggling to get out of bed on time," he replies, slightly crestfallen. "I expected things to pick up once you got used to the new schedule."

"That's just it. I don't want to get used to the new schedule. I'm part of the old schedule. I don't want to be part of the new one. So I quit. Sorry."

Back at the flat with only the four bottles of champagne I stole from the wine cellar on my way out for company, I toast the end of a relatively short but fruitful career in the hospitality industry. Many a lesson was learned at the Hartington; how to make roses out of carrots and lilies out of tomatoes, how to make microwave dim sum look like freshly prepared Asian delicacies, how to successfully star in a no-budget porn flick. The last three years have been an education but now it's time to graduate. While most of the time it seemed like a distraction, the college course we attended concurrently to the shagging, drinking and drugging which revolved around the Hartington's incestuous circle actually paid off. Both Ellis and I may be dole moles at the moment, scavenging off the state, but we're educated layabouts. We have the diplomas to prove it. All of which is another reason why it's time to wave goodbye to the hotel business. The longer I stay on, the harder it would become to leave the comforting madness of the old Hartington. I could quite easily spend another three years bumming around, working cash-in-hand while claiming benefits. But then I would never have got the fear which is currently bubbling up inside me along with the knock-off champers; the fear that the real world has come knocking - and that it might now be time to get myself a proper job.

This, you see, is one of the cornerstones of the Masterplan. Now I've finally discovered that I'm in love with Karen, I want to complete the task I set myself in Amsterdam; to complete my journey away from the past and embrace a better future. It's like Luke Skywalker in *Return of the Jedi*. He ran out on his training, leaving Yoda all pissed off, to make the mistakes he needed to make. Only then did he realize that he needed to complete his training to ultimately get what he wanted and find out who he really was. That's me, right now. I'm Luke back on Dagobah, only this time I'm going to improve myself for my own gain as much as to win Karen's love and approval. I'm going to find the man that I want to be. Do or do not, there is no try.

Ellis comes home to find me triumphantly swaying around to the 'Theme from Star Wars' at full volume while brandishing a pint mug full of champagne in one hand and half a snooker cue in the other. He doesn't bat an eyelid; he just ducks my ersatz lightsaber and turns the volume down on the stereo. "Alright, Obi-wan, I take it you handed in your notice."

"Told them to stick their fucking job, I have, hmmm..." The inebriated Yoda impression raises a smile on my flat mate's face. "Ran off with four bottles of bubby, I did, yes..."

"So now what?" Ellis asks, grabbing an unopened bottle of champagne out of the sink of ice water before slumping on the sofa. "Are you really going to get a job...like a proper job?"

"Yes I am." I say with drunken conviction. "But not until after Knebworth. Nothing gets in the way of that, my son. Nothing. We're going to bring this summer to an end with a bang."

"Champagne supernova!" Ellis cracks open the next bottle of champers, sending the cork rocketing into a pile of dirty glasses, smashing at least three in the process.

Yoda shakes his head. "Control, control...you must learn control!"

432

Dennis has the arse when he arrives to pick us up at 9:00 am on the morning of the gig. He's overly courteous to Ellis but blanks me, lending weight to the belief that he sees my jumping ship as a personal insult. As Ellis makes the third call of the morning to the Scotsman's house to find out just where the fuck he may be on this most important of days, I choose my moment to clear the air.

"Are you pissed off that I've left the hotel?"

"The Hartington has stood for over 70 years, Daniel, and has seen many comings and goings. It will probably stand for another 70 and it certainly won't miss you."

"True...But you'll miss me, won't you?" I give him one of my cheekiest of smiles. "Go on, admit it." I search his glacial face for a hint of breaking ice.

"Get over yourself," he says, a hint of a smile flickering at the corners of his lips. "At least with you safely over here we won't have as much to worry about when we next do a stock take. Enjoy the bubbly, did you?"

"Err..." I drag nervously on my pre-journey reefer, searching my compromised mind for a story which will explain the empty bottles still littering the kitchen. Bloody Ellis, if I told him once...

"Oh don't bullshit me, Danny. Jesus. Consider it severance pay," he winks and everything is cool. "Anyway, where do you think the beer supplies for today's little adventure came from?" He takes the joint from my lips and laughs like a man possessed. "Where's the Scotsman?" He shouts. "Let's get this show on the road!"

McKinley eventually turns up an hour after he should have been here. Luckily we factored in the possibility of someone fucking up the plans so when he does roll in at ten, he actually arrives perfectly on time. "What would you prefer - me turning up here at nine with no gear or coming an hour late after scoring a fat bag of quality Columbian?" Nobody tells him about our contingency timing. Why should we? According to our designated driver - who has graciously promised to stay off the booze for the entire day ("Why drink and drive when you can take drugs and fly?") - the 90 minute drive to Knebworth will be a breeze through the mid-morning traffic. Even with expected hold-ups as we approach the site, we should still be there in good time to get into the spirit of things before the opening act. Everything is as it should be.

"Fucking knees-up Mother Brown?" moans co-pilot McKinley, his hands stinging from our driver's successful attempts at protecting the Saab's stereo. "It's Oasis today, didn't anyone tell you? Oh-ay-sis..." he enunciates, "Not fucking Bleurghh."

Dennis, eyes hidden behind sunglasses which even Elton John would consider too camp, snorts a self-satisfied laugh and puts his foot down to overtake a line of meandering traffic on the dual-carriageway west. At one with the two-lane blacktop and the wining cockerney strains of Damon Albarn, he is the lord of all he surveys. "This is part of the deal, Scotty," he mocks with the confidence which has been rising like lava since we instilled him with it over a year ago. "Didn't anyone tell *you*?"

The Scotsman cranes his neck round the headrest and fixes Ellis with a furrowed-brow stare. "What did you promise him?"

Ellis shifts uncomfortably under McKinley's glare. "It's an hour and a half tops, man. What's wrong with a bit of Blur for ninety minutes? We'll have all the 'Sis we could ever want in a few hours."

"What did you promise?" The Scotsman asks again as Alain Prost beside him weaves between competing drivers.

"I said he could play *The Great Escape* all the way there...on repeat." City dweller, successful fella, thought to himself, whoops I've got a lot of money.... "Come on, it's not that bad." Ellis defends himself as the muttered curses from the passenger seat turn and spew out onto the onrushing tarmac. "We all loved *Parklife*, right? It put the Brit into Britpop..." Lives in a house, a very big house in the country... "I like Blur," he continues, reassuring himself. "I don't see why it has to be about one and not the other. It's all good music, man."

"Fucking what?" McKinley turns again with such speed that he nearly gives himself whiplash.

"Remember the rules of the Saab," snaps Dennis. "No homophobia and no slagging off Damon."

"Shut up you big gay Albarn shagger." The Scotsman doesn't do rules unless they're his own. "Listen wee man," he continues, ignoring the offended mumbling beside him and directing his full attention at Ellis. "*Modern Life is Rubbish* is excellent. That started Britpop before there was even a word for it. Aye, I'll give you that *Parklife* has some top tunes on it but it's a bit fucking patchy though. But this..." He waggles a dismissive thumb behind him at the stereo. "Music hall Benny Hill fucking Chas'n'Dave pile o' shit. Sad bastards, man. They're over."

Ellis looks stunned. McKinley is very rarely as outspoken about his musical tastes as this. He likes what he likes, plays what he likes and usually just turns up his nose at what he doesn't like and gets on with dulling his senses with drugs and alcohol. "Come on Danny, you still like Blur, right? You're always cranking up 'Charmless Man'." I smile and nod. Ellis and McKinley wait for me to give more of an explanation. I don't.

"Why are you wearing a woolly hat?" The Scotsman asks after eyes and brain have combined to point out a glaring fashion anomaly which has gone unnoticed from the second we got in the car. Ellis also spots my strange attire for the first time. After analysing my headgear more closely for a second, he pulls the beanie off my head.

"Earphones?"

"Cheeky bastard!"

"That's not part of the deal. Everyone has to listen to Blur or I'm turning this car around."

"No you're not, Daisy, don't get in a state." McKinley soothes our driver's ire. "Have a spliff and chill the fuck out."

"How long have you had those on?" enquires Ellis.

"Ever since I saw that Dennis had brought just the one CD with him," I grin sheepishly.

"Show us what you've got then, come on." McKinley leans round and yanks the CD Walkman from inside my tracksuit top and flips it open. *What's the Story (Morning Glory)* spins angrily, removed untimely from its laser and brutally exposed to the air. "Nice one. Stick it on."

"I will pull over now and forcefully remove all those unwilling to listen to Blur before that CD goes on this stereo!" Dennis clenches the steering wheel in rising anger, his knuckles turning white.

"Keep your wig on, man. You own the fucking thing yourself. I've been in here with you while you were playing it." In a bid to make the sale, the Scotsman adopts the tone of a second-hand car dealer. "Look, you would have brought it along yourself if Ellis hadn't come to you with this deal. You know good music. You certainly don't buy into this whole Oasis-Blur divide bollocks...So let's just have a bit of variation eh? Be the bigger man here."

Dennis knows McKinley is full of shit and yet he can't help but be seduced. "Put it on then but we're skipping through 'Wonderwall'."

There's no argument there.

An hour later, under a low-level layer of ganja smog, the dying strains of 'Champagne Supernova' herald our arrival at the tail end of a slow, creeping traffic jam leading into the rolling parkland of Knebworth. Either side of the column of buses, vans and cars edging towards the site wander hundreds of similarly clad Oasis fans; gangs of officially t-shirted followers slouch past our open windows, monkey-walking their way towards history; Fred Perry accompanies Ben Sherman on the march towards immortality, floppy Kappa sunhats shield heads full of 'Shakermaker' and 'Slide Away' on the sun-beaten path to glory. Mad dogs and Oasis fans go out in the midday sun... It's an awe-inspiring sight. Liam Gallagher's voice, at once in competition with itself and in harmony, drifts through the Hertfordshire air, soaring from open windows in a mixture of songs and styles, blending his rock snarl with his heart-rending balladry. His nasal tones are joined by those of distant followers, joining in with anthems old and new, leaning into cars to accompany stereos or bellowing solos into the electric atmosphere of anticipation. The overarching sensation is one of belonging, of togetherness, of victory. The last two years have been building towards this moment. Britain is Great again. The Kingdom is United.

As if to accentuate the point, Dennis is moved to press play again and the wah-wah intro of 'Hello' begins to reverberate through the car. He turns the volume up as *Morning Glory's* opener rolls from the speakers, flowing out into the sunshine to become everything it was meant to be - a song for the people - and sparking cheers from the faithful passing us on their way to worship. Hello...hello...it's good to be back...it's good to be back...

A year ago, Oasis were staking their claim to be our leaders with that ramshackle, thrillingly arrogant set on Glastonbury's main stage. Now they are ready to step up and claim the throne after earning our support and loyalty through three years of life-changing music and attitude. Now as then, you can almost taste the energy created by the expectation; breathing in the excitement is like sticking a battery on your tongue. But unlike the summer of 95, this is all about one band. The other acts here today have supporting roles; they're making up the numbers on a festival bill. The power being created around us comes from one source.

We may be eager to see Cast or The Charlatans but it's nothing compared to the thrill running through 125,000 people today at the prospect of seeing Oasis crowned before our very eyes.

We sit with the doors of the Saab flung open, sipping icy beers that have been kept cool in the freezer bag thoughtfully provided by the Hartington House Hotel. Smoke from ambitiously rolled six-skinners drifts from the passenger and back seats, swirling in the air of chatter, laugher and song around us in the rolling acres. There's no need to rush. We just sit and absorb.

"You never answered the question, fella." Ellis' question comes out of the blue and in the middle of a rather stoned daydream. It creates a short fuse in my mind as I try and grab the thread of his enquiry as it drifts past in the breeze. Sorry. Gone blank again.

"Say that again, this time with some context."

"Blur. I asked you in the car whether you still liked Blur."

Weirdly, this creates a moment of panic. My eyes dart around our proximity in search of anyone who may have overheard Ellis and who may take offense. It's like saying fuck in church, or calling your bird by another girl's name. I hope it slips by unnoticed and doesn't create a shitstorm of grief. This paranoia is over in a flash as more analytical thoughts are stirred by the flighty THC as it finds another part of my brain to tickle. Why should it matter? The whole thing was media manipulation anyway. Okay, so in the heat of the hype, people really bought into it - us included - but it seems ridiculous now. That couple who the tabloids found, the bloke and his missus who were on the verge of splitting up because he liked Oasis and she was a Blur fan, I bet they're here today. He probably forgave her for microwaving his CDs as soon as the News of the World's cheque cleared. He probably still slips in a crafty one from behind when she's asleep in her *Parklife* t-shirt from time to time. So what if Blur scored a Number One with the heinous 'Country House' and the NME crowned them "Top Dogs" on the following week's cover - which only had the tell-tale cum stains missing to convince everyone that the result had made the editor shoot his load in joy. Look around us now - is this Blur preparing to play the biggest outdoor gigs in Britain EVER? Are a quarter of a million people going to sing along to 'Stereotypes' over the course of this historic weekend? No. While I wouldn't have considered coming here in a Blur t-shirt, it wouldn't have been because I was scared of getting beaten up. I would have been more concerned about being laughed out of Knebworth.

"Yeah, I still like Blur," I eventually say. "But I'm with McKinley. *The Great Escape* is pants."

"And 'Charmless Man'?"

"I'm being charitable, geezer," I answer, winking at the grinning Scotsman. "I think the album is shit but I have to support the best tune on it out of respect to their other work. It's not a patch on 'Starshaped', or 'Badhead'...or even 'Girls & Boys', which fucking grates after a while. But if I didn't play at least one song off *The Shite Escape*, I'd feel bad for them."

McKinley bursts out laughing. "I'm sure they appreciate the support, big man."

"I love the album. It's a masterpiece." A belligerent Dennis swings his pipe cleaner legs out of the driver's seat and pushes his emaciated self upright against the door frame.

"Big man, have you learnt nothing? Jesus, all the man hours we put in getting you a life and you come out with statements like that. I want my money back." The Scotsman takes this turn in the conversation to chop out some lines on the offending CD's cover, as if that's all it's good for.

"I was born...not made," drawls Den, obviously reaching his tolerance point for weed. His eyes bulge from red-rimmed sockets like eggs being pushed from a hen's arse. He tries to untangle his tongue from the cotton wool covering the roof of his mouth as he prepares to defend himself as vigorously as his incapacitated state will allow. "It was my destiny to be golden. You just happened to be there when it began."

"Right," McKinley agrees sarcastically, while hovering over a wide stripe of cocaine. "If we hadn't dragged you out, you'd still be in the Bat Cave. You'd be a fucking golden cellar dweller." He snorts the thick rail. "Aye, fucking 'mad fer it' in a basement."

"He's right, D," I add, taking the driver's seat next to McKinley in preparation for my own chemical boost. "You'd still be listening to Simply Red if we hadn't rescued you."

"I still listen to Simply Red."

This time I'm not the only one searching our immediate vicinity for possible signs of attack. Ellis is out of the car scanning the horizon like a parka-clad meerkat. "Keep it down, man. Someone might hear you."

"So what? I can listen to what I like. I can do what I want. I'm free to do whatever I like. I can be gay and love dick and no-one can stop me. The rules are - there are no rules."

"Err...There are actually," says the Scotsman, getting a belligerent rush from the charlie and strolling round the bonnet to meet Dennis head on. "Not listening to ginger bollocks Mick Hucknall is one of them."

"I've never seen these rules," Dennis struts Jagger-like on rubbery legs to meet the on-rushing Scotsman. "And if I had, I would have torn them up." He sticks his beak in McKinley's face, threatening to turn the banter into aggression.

"Settle down, big man..."

"Bollocks! I'll show you. There are no rules."

"What are you going to do?" Ellis looks slightly nervous.

"I'm going to be myself...I can't be no-one else..." Dennis flounces away from the confrontation while executing the most effeminate Gallagher impression ever.

"Supersonic. Nice one. Just don't get arrested, okay?" I look over at the Scotsman who raises his eyes to the heavens and shakes his head.

Ellis taps his watch. "We should make a move," he says. "Kula Shaker will be on soon."

Crispin Mills and his boys have come from nowhere with a brave mix of Hindu mysticism, Hendrix licks and just the right amount of Brit attitude to gate-crash the current party without getting their heads kicked in for being a bunch of foppish toffs. It's a big day for them with their debut album still a month away but a couple of swaggering top five singles have already endeared them to the masses. It helps that their combination of spaced-out weirdness and guitar-led aggression compliments the chemical (im)balance of the crowd.

Still surging with the ebbing high of the coke and mentally detached from most of reality due to the surprisingly strong weed, the four of us certainly get into the spirit of things. We're hanging off each other and transcending as if it was kicking out time down the Orchard - and we're not alone. There's a good few hours to go before Oasis take the stage but the site is almost full which gives the opening act a real boost. With just 30 minutes to fill, Kula Shaker go for broke with the balls-out attitude of 'Hey Dude', the Jimi-esque 'Grateful When You're Dead' and the accomplished rock stomp of 'Knight on the Town'. The crowd lap up every song, screaming for more as if these entitled psych-gurus are the ones we all paid our hard-earned cash to see. By the time 'Tattva' closes the set, the tens of thousands already in attendance are swaying and ascending in the hazy sunlight as if this is the day's closing hymn.

The crowd is still drifting on the last notes of dreamy psychedelic sitar when Dreadzone take the stage. Two musical worlds collide as the dying strains of Indian reverb hanging in the dusty haze merges with a swampy dub bass line that begins to ooze from the mammoth speakers. It certainly takes more than a few minutes before the mystic spell is broken and the dance vibe claims the crowd back from their Tantric trance. The samplers start bombing the audience with heavy bass and electronic drums and the trip switches in everyone's heads click from melodic, spiritual rock to full-on blissed-out rave mode. Soon our arms-aloft shuffling has been replaced with pumping fists and pounding feet as the afternoon shifts into a dancier gear. How fickle we all are. Lines of division have been drawn between bands of the same genre and bands of similar ilk from rival nations and yet here are almost 100,000 indie fans going nuts to a dance act. Five minutes ago, we were having a religious moment to a bunch of Ravi Shankars. Later today, things will no doubt get even tastier when a bunch of green-haired electro punks take the stage. We say we're either Oasis or Blur, we love Britpop and hate US rock, and yet stick a load of pills and powder inside us and it all just becomes music. That's how it should be - it just takes a bunch of drugs to break down these barriers to allow us to be honest.

Dreadzone are channelling the summer heat and laying down a druggy Goa vibe behind us as we join what looks to be an attempt to make it into the Guinness Book of Records for the longest and most frustrating queue for over-priced beers ever. McKinley leans out of the queue and squints at the distant pumps. He brings his hand up and fits the tiny barman in the space between forefinger and thumb. Cogs whirr and smoke begins to drift from his ears. "From my calculation, based on how small the barman looks from here, this queue is approximately six hundred miles long and it will take us just over three weeks to get a beer." With the afternoon sun relentlessly beating down on the flowerpot-hatted masses, the policy of stopping people bringing their own drinks in starts to feel like some act of torture perfected by the Viet Cong. It really starts to bite when my mind turns to the untouched

Grolsch in the back of Den's Saab. Even rancid, warm Grolsch would taste like heavenly nectar right now. The thought of beer makes me gulp hard in my desert-scorched throat. "Uh-oh." McKinley snaps back into line and tries to make himself invisible. "You'll never guess who's standing about ten people in front of us." From his reaction, I guess he's referring to someone we'd rather not see. Chances are it's a bird. Given the number of bad sexual experiences I've had in the last three years in which McKinley had a hand, my mind reels at the possibilities. "It's fucking Manimal," he whispers as if she's standing behind him.

Manimal? Amanda! Karen's flat-mate. She's here. Karen's here. She must be. "Is she on her own?" I ask, my mind already trying to access the reams of pre-prepared speeches.

"Aye. Looks like it."

I'm not having that. "There are about 125,000 people here right now and we end up in the beer queue ten people back from Manimal. Doesn't that tell you something?"

McKinley leans out of the queue again and sizes up Amanda with a grimace on his face. "Yeah, that it's a good job I didn't shag her. Minging. If she can turn up here, she can turn up anywhere. Imagine trying to explain that one." The Scotsman shivers in spite of the heat.

"Seriously, what are the chances?" I'm talking myself into a state of conviction. "They reckon that about three million people tried to get tickets for these gigs. Around 250,000 succeeded. Divide that by two and spread them over two days. We choose Sunday and manage to get the tickets. We get here and Manimal has had the same slice of luck. If that's possible, surely it's possible that Karen's here too."

"Danny, are you carrying the coke?" Ellis asks. "'Cause if you've hoovered it all before Oasis..."

"It's safe, don't worry. Anyway, there's something more powerful than chemicals at work here, geezers. The universe, man. Destiny."

"Destiny," says Ellis. "Destiny is going to help you find Karen here...today...in all these people. If she's actually here at all."

"Exactly."

"Danny?" Destiny calls. Karen stands just behind Ellis looking more amazing than ever. Her chestnut hair has been lightened by days under the summer sun and her skin glows with a healthy tan. Her eyes, initially hidden behind a giant pair of 2-Tone Jackie O shades, sparkle as she raises her glasses, propping them up in her hair. Her face takes on a quizzical expression and her eyes narrow as I struggle to grasp this opportunity Destiny has presented me with.

"Hey, Karen...I..." There's so much I want to say. I don't know where to start. Apologies, explanations, revelations, declarations. All the words charge from my brain towards my mouth at the same speed, crashing over my tongue in a huge, mangled pile-up. I take a breath as she continues staring at me in that expectant, although increasingly annoyed kinda way. I smile, gather myself and say..."Hi." Ellis and McKinley turn their backs to me, eyes front. They obviously understand that having an audience is not going to help me get a grip of the situation.

" Fancy seeing you here," she half-heartedly says while trying to look nonplussed.

"Right? It's weird that we keep meeting in the most unlikely places," I reply, hearing familiar phrases pass between us but with a new and not altogether pleasant tone.

"Yeah, very strange." Awkward pause. "Okay, have fun." And with that she brushes past me and makes her way to join Manimal in the queue. My mind is still reeling off the scripts I've spent the past few months preparing before I realise that Karen has left and isn't there to hear them. Hang on...

"Karen, wait up..." I jog out of the queue and catch her up. "What's the problem?"

She lowers her shades and strikes a 'fuck you' pose. "Sorry, no time. I've got loads of beer to drink before finding a dick show. I love getting pissed and having cocks waved in my face, don't I, Daniel?" The nearest eavesdropping lads in the queue cheer and mutter comments which would usually lead to me chucking beer over them and following through with raging fists but I'm too stunned. Karen spins on a heel and stomps off towards Amanda who's got an evil smile on her face. Karen's arse, usually a part of her body which gives positive signals when leaving, is telling me this conversation is well and truly over. I ignore the jeers from the lads who would, apparently, like to wave their plonkers in my bird's face and join Ellis and the Scotsman in the queue.

"That went well," McKinley deadpans. "Destiny must be well pleased it made all that effort."

My performance in the crowd for Cast is pretty poor by my usual standards. If this was a team event, I would have been substituted by the time the band launch into 'Sandstorm'. My heart just isn't in it, I'm not giving it 110 percent, I don't have anything in my locker, blah blah blah... John Motson would have ripped me to pieces on Mosh of the Day. I'm going through the motions while Ellis and McKinley throw themselves about in the potentially dangerous vicinity of a bunch of blokes who seem intent of beating each other to a pulp. I'm self-consciously bobbing on the spot behind the main scrum, mulling over the latest, weird encounter with Karen when a surge of positivism comes in from somewhere. After twisting my melon over *why* she's so pissed for most of the Cast set, I start focusing purely on the fact that she *is*. She's pissed off. It's six months since we saw each other in Amsterdam and yet what happened there is still affecting her. That can only mean that it meant something, that my reaction touched her. Okay, I admit that my reaction was more than a bit shit - I've come to terms with that and understand where it came from - but it was a reaction that she didn't like which means she cares. If I can find her and explain why I was so out of order in Amsterdam, maybe she'll see that I care too.

And I was out of order. At first, I thought it was just me convincing myself that I was so there would be conviction in my argument if and when I got the chance to explain things to Karen. But after thinking about it I realized that McKinley was right. We're all light and dark. Karen was never going to be the goddess I had created in mind. She didn't have to be. She just had to be herself. Just like me. Just like all of us. That's who The One is - the person who has the right balance of light and dark, the person who accepts your own combination of shades, the person who is just themselves when they're with you. How the fuck am I going to find her in this sea of people - and tell her that I finally get it?

McKinley staggers out of the bar-room brawl in front of me with blood pissing out of his nose all over his white Lacoste polo (- that's going to stain). His glasses are all bent and mangled round his face and he's mouthing something incoherent at me and pointing to the sidelines. I nod in agreement but hold him back from stomping out of the crowd in a vain attempt to locate the Third Musketeer. "He's fucking on one, let's go," shouts the Scotsman, spraying claret all over my Fred Perry. "He knows where to meet us." He nods towards safety and we leave Ellis to his fate.

Such is the attraction of ex-La John Power's latest Merseybeat combo that the queue for beer is tiny in comparison to earlier and I manage to get us a couple of pints with minimal effort as Cast inspire more blood-letting with a full-force rendition of 'Fine Time'. I slalom through a gaggle of teenage Manics fans in bikinis and stencilled body slogans to get to McKinley who's plugging his face period with a serviette from the nearby hamburger stall. "So what happened?"

446

"Fucking Ellis, that's what happened. There was this skinhead rolling around, off his tits on E, and pissing all these lads off. The next thing I know, I get a tap on the shoulder, turn round, and Ellis has his arm round the geezer, taking the piss and dancing it up. It's funny for about second until one of the pissed off lads throws a jab, misses both Ellis and matey, and lands a right hook on my snozz." McKinley frames his face as if to say... 'and this was the result'. He squints at me. "Where were you, anyway?"

"Having a revelatory moment, man," I answer, taking one of the Scotsman's jam rags and scrubbing what I can of his rhesus negative off my shirt. "What do you reckon is the best way of finding a needle in haystack?"

McKinley thinks for a moment, catches the slowly disappearing thread of my metaphor and smiles. He points towards the hamburger stand. "Ask the hungry pig," he smiles.

"And I should help you because..?" Amanda is half-cut and being even more of a bitch than she usually is when she's sober.

"Look, I know you have a problem with me...I don't know why...but..."

"You're only out for the shag, like all you lads. You're as bad as him over there." Manimal points at McKinley who stops dabbing at his nose long enough to offer a sarcastically coy wave in her direction. She gives him one of her most evil sneers along with the finger. "You're pathetic. You think us girls are just going to swoon over your bad behaviour and your bullshit and fall into bed with you. You expect everyone to think like you, that nothing should hold any deeper meaning, that it should all be about fucking and having a laugh. You make me sick."

"Is this all McKinley's fault?"

"Grow up, Daniel. I don't like you because I know what will happen if you do ever get into Karen's pants. You'll have a good time and she'll never see you again. Well, Karen's worth more than that and she deserves more than you...More than any of you put together, in fact. So give it up and fuck off." Manimal turns to storm off but I grab her arm before she can leave.

"Listen, you may have been right in the past but things have changed." I strengthen my grip on her arm as she tries to pull away. "I need to tell Karen that things are different. I don't give a shit if you believe me or not. It only matters that she believes me...and if she's as amazing as I think she is and as worth it as you say, then she'll be able to make the right decision for herself." Amanda stops struggling. "Ask her to meet me at the RAC tent just after the Manics come on. Please." Manimal pulls free of my grip, gives me an unreadable stare and disappears into the crowd. McKinley saunters over looking slightly guilty. "Okay, what did you do?"

It seems that on the fateful night in Pulse, the night Karen Anderson first got under my skin, McKinley and Manimal did more than just drunkenly snog. Usually when the Scotsman is on the prowl, he keeps his rules of engagement in mind: there will be no shagging and no involvement. This normally means that he finds the most drunken slapper around - one who will take the least work and offer the minimal amount of resistance - he'll utter some ancient spell and then cop off with her. If it takes more than a couple of minutes to get to the point where he has his hand up her blouse, then it's likely that his prospective conquest is either too sober or in need of too much convincing - at which point, he'll cut his losses and move on. It seems that Manimal was both sober and a hard sell that night. And yet, he didn't move on. He actually engaged her in conversation. Once in this trap, he couldn't help himself. He started making empty promises. "I just wanted to get my hands on her jugs," he admits as his explanation reaches its finale. "I was blinded by them. I couldn't think of anything other than chewing on her nipples...so I told her I really liked her. I even suggested a date."

A cranial connection short-fuses but it's not enough to cause a complete mental meltdown. When my back-up system cuts in, I ask: "Did you meet up with her then?"

"No way, man. When I sobered up the next day, I couldn't even remember what her name was let alone any of the stuff I told her. But she came round to the hotel a few times...Asking me out." He looks genuinely guilty now. "I told her the truth, that I was pissed and just wanted to feel her up. She wasn't best pleased."

"So she's got the arse with me...because of you?"

"Not entirely, big man...I think I was just one in a long line of blokes mesmerized by her jugs. They have voodoo qualities you know. Fucking scarily powerful, man, I'm telling you."

"And you didn't think about mentioning this in the, what, two years since this happened?"

"Danny Boy, this happens to me all the time," he soothes. "Manimal is just one of hundreds of birds I've conned to get my hands on a pair of tits. She's not alone in hearing the lines, man. And besides, the Karen situation has nothing to do with what Manimal thinks. Karen will do what she wants and fuck what her flat mate thinks. If she didn't, do you think all this drama would have gone on for this long? No way. She would have cut you loose long ago."

He's right - which suggests that I'm also right. Karen has her own mind and even Manimal's hatred of the male gender can't affect that. A huge cheer from the masses behind us signals the arrival of the Charlatans on stage. McKinley dabs the last of the dripping blood from the tip of his nose and follows me back into the crowd.

That feeling of inclusion I keep banging on about? Nothing so far has even come close to the cosmic bond which now binds us together as we humbly stand in front of The Charlatans. At any other time, these enduring legends would command our respect and loyalty. In these extraordinarily sad circumstances, they also deserve our support and sympathy. Barely three weeks since keyboardist Rob Collins was killed in a car crash, The Charlatans arrive at Knebworth to a massive outpouring of love. Steeling themselves in the face of such an empathic crowd, Tim Burgess and the boys play hard for their departed mate and honour him with a flawless performance. It's a hugely moving occasion as we join together to remember and pay tribute, not only to the missing member but to the rest of the band as they deliver a blistering show in the face of such adversity. The Charlatans are fucking rock. No question.

As the Charlies wrap up their emotional set, my mind cannot help but turn to those people who are important in our lives. Right now, for me, that means Karen. If Manimal has seen through her rage at the whole of Lad-kind and accepted that Karen can make her own decisions, then Ms Anderson could be making her way to the RAC tent at this very moment. I make plans to meet the Scotsman and Ellis (if McKinley can find him and if he's still alive) at this very location at the end of the Manics set and race off to make good on what could be Destiny's reprieve.

The Manic Street Preachers are already enduring some early abuse from the more partisan sections of the crowd when Karen eventually parts the waves of fans and makes her way over to where I've been sitting politely declining offers to sign up for full vehicle cover. She sits down in the plastic garden chair beside me in silence. I'm not sure where to start and a short uncomfortable silence passes between us. I'm about to put the racing thoughts in my head into some sort of order when Karen breaks the deadlock. "What do you want, Danny?"

"The chance to talk to you."

"No, I know that. I mean, what do you really want...from life?"

"If I told you, you'd probably run off again."

"Is it hard for you to talk about how you feel without joking about it?"

"I'm a bloke. That's what we're supposed to do."

"That's rubbish," she replies, somewhat testily. "That's what all this Lad crap is telling you. What are you afraid of? That having aspirations other than drinking ten pints a night might threaten your masculinity?"

Man, this woman is intense. "Okay..."

"You need to figure out what you want. Do you want to be that wonderful guy under the bandstand or do you want to be that self-absorbed wanker who made me feel like shit in Amsterdam? Sort it out. And if you can't, then leave me alone."

With that, she gets up and walks back into the crowd. I knew that Karen wasn't the kind of girl who would just melt into my arms but I didn't expect her to give me such a hard time. I mean, come on! Was I really that bad in Amsterdam? Did I tell her to her face that she was out of order, that her drunken, dick show-loving Ladette extravaganza had pissed me off on a major scale? Well, yes. Kinda. Maybe I should have waited until I was out of earshot and in the company of the boys before getting all that off my chest. Instead I gave her an earful right there in the pub. In hindsight, that wasn't your best day, Daniel.

She has every right to be pissed off with me. I judged her that day. I did exactly what everyone does to me and the boys the moment we step out of our homes. We're labelled by the way we look and the way we behave. That meant everything once - we actively sought out that judgment, it confirmed who we were, where we belonged. We didn't care then that people were making assumptions. We wanted those assumptions to be true: that we were Lads, that we were British, and that this was our time to rule. The difference with Karen is that I know the other side of her. I've seen beyond the assumptions. I may not know the complete picture yet but I've seen more than that one side which caused me to act like such a cock in Amsterdam. I've seen her passion for life, I've seen the self-belief she has. I've seen the huge desire she has to see the best in people and her expectations in all of us to be extraordinary. It strikes me then that she expected more from me, that she actually believed that the sensitive, honest and authentic side of me would win out. She wanted me to be passionate, to believe and to be extraordinary. She'd given me every chance to think about how I could find and express that part of me. Every time we met, I discovered more and by leaving me, she made me question what I'd found and what it meant. She expected me to continue evolving and yet when I was faced with a different test, when I had a drunken, messy version of Karen Anderson to deal with, I regressed. She wanted to show me enlightenment but instead I turned my back on her and returned to the dark ages.

"Hallo sir, do you own your own car?"

"Sorry, mate. Still don't have one." I know we all look the same around here but it's only been five minutes since you last asked me. Am I really that unremarkable? No, bollocks to that. I'm extraordinary. Karen Anderson thinks I'm a wonderful guy, she said so herself. (She also called me a self-absorbed wanker but we'll forget about that for now).

"Is there anything else I can help you with, sir?"

"No thanks, man. I need to do this on my own." And with that, I make a pledge to myself to large it like never before and ascend to a higher plane when Oasis arrive. I'll then be ready to give myself to Karen Anderson. "Light and dark, man. Light and dark." I leave the perplexed RAC geezer behind and go in search of the Lads and our places in history.

As the Manic Street Preachers launch into one of their last theatrically bombastic numbers, I navigate my way to the meeting spot and manage to locate McKinley who has a rather dishevelled Ellis in tow and a wild-eyed, open-shirted Dennis at his side.

"How did it go big man?"

"I'm not sure."

"You're making progress then."

Everything is building nicely for Oasis until Dennis succeeds is reaching a new level of waywardness after discovering that yes, he does like cocaine after all, and no, he won't be bothering to hide it. After sticking his hooked beak into the stash and then galloping off with a face like a powdered French duke with a hot poker in his britches, we're convinced that's the last we'll see of the mad bastard. None of us seem bothered over the huge amount of gear wasted on Dirty Den's visage (there's more in reserve) or the fact that we might have to hitchhike home because we're now starting to really have it. Night is falling and the Manics, after winning over most of their doubters, bid their farewells We're increasingly mad fer it as live music makes way for a recorded interlude for the last time before Oasis take the stage.

"Right, we need to be over there," I point, indicating a willingness to get into the reserved pit some 500 metres away from our current position.

"Our tickets don't get us in there, geezer." Ellis is currently lacking the can-do attitude which means he needs another hit. McKinley reads the signs and soon has a key tip up his nostril. Ellis wrinkles his nose frantically as the Scotsman and I try to stifle giggles. A few moments later, the necessary attitude adjustment has taken place. "So what's the plan? What's the blag? Had our passes stolen, have we?"

I slap his back. "Follow me."

Making your way through a large festival crowd takes equal parts determination, arrogance and dexterity. You shouldn't give a shit about stepping on anyone's toes or forcing a human obstacle to make way but you should always try and create your path with the minimum of contact. Of course you're going to have to brush past people and sometimes barge a little but the way you carry yourself - the arrogance of your progress - will get you through with the minimum of fuss. No-one is going to question you if you look like you have every right in the world to force your way to wherever you need to be. Polite people never get far in crowds. Self-belief is also at the heart of the blagging needed when you get to your destination.

"Alright, mate," I say to the youngest-looking steward I could find at the barrier separating the main crowd from the first pit. I try and walk straight past him into the reserved area.

The Steward blocks our progress. "I don't think so."

"Geezer, we just came out of there...to get beers, remember? We asked you if you wanted one."

"You don't have the right passes." The Steward says but the doubt has already shown itself on his face. He'll cave.

"But we just came out. We said, 'fella, want us to get you a beverage?' and you said you couldn't because you're working. It was like twenty minutes ago or something."

"Big man, we're right there," McKinley joins in and points frantically at a group of Lads and Ladettes about twenty metres in. "That's our lot there. See? Over there. That's us. We're there. That's where we should be. Know what I mean?"

The Steward becomes nervous at hearing the Scotsman's intentionally gruff accent and the fact that he's coming on like Rab C.

Nesbitt on PCP. Ellis stands behind us surveying the crowd with saucer-like eyes, chewing like a cow on amphetamines.

"Come on, man. The beers are getting cold, geezer and the band will be on soon." I beam at him encouragingly. The Steward's resolve collapses. Without a word he ushers us in, as much to get us out of his face than out of a belief for our story. "Nice one, fella. Just let us know if you want a beer, okay?"

With that, we're in.

The reserved area is still not hard against the stage - that area's reserved for the millions of celebrity liggers and even our level of blagging won't get us in there. Plus the security blokes down there make Steroid from the Orchard look like Quentin Crisp. But we have a great view of the stage from where we are and we're in a prime position for the imminent mosh.

I've been in a lot of big crowds before and have experienced euphoria on a grand scale on many occasions but when Oasis roll onto the stage tonight I feel like my heart will burst and my spirit will fly. The roar of the crowd rushes towards the band like a tsunami and the force batters me; it's behind me, beside me, inside me. I feel like I'm standing in the midst of a crushing wave, a barrier attempting to stand firm against the tidal surge. I fight for breath as my own screams mix with the voices of thousands gushing forwards. As the enticing, extended intro to 'Columbia' thuds out into the early evening air, all eyes turn to Liam as he stands impassive behind massive shades; surveying his subjects, embracing their mass adoration as if he's accepting a long overdue birth right. "Are you mad for it?" he yells. Too fucking right we are...

What a different message this song carries tonight. There we were, now here are... This is not about good turning to bad, this is about rising up from the depths and reaching the top. There we were - in the shit, in the dark, in the past; now here we are - living the dream, burning bright, writing the future. This is goodbye to the doldrums, an arrogant, straight middle-finger to the masters of our former lives. The chains are off. We're free.

We're not spared a moment to take stock or breath before an onslaught is meted out on us. In the space of a dozen songs, the full power of Oasis is unleashed with barely any respite, reminding us all why these five blokes are able to command an audience of some 250,000 people over one glorious weekend. 'Acquiesce' shoots the crowd through with an initial heady rush of adrenaline, getting the hearts racing for an amphetamine sprint through 'Hello' which has acres of breathless fans bouncing. After a brief surreal interlude during which Liam bizarrely riffs on crockery items, 'Some Might Say' chugs out of the monstrous PA and the whole crowd loses the plot, only for the insanity to reach greater heights when 'Roll With It' follows. We finally get a chance to gasp for air with the anthemic 'Slide Away' but our breath is better served belting out the words while swaying along. There'll be other opportunities for oxygen so why waste a chance to scream along with the Laddish love song?

I suddenly start regretting not taking a few welcome lungfuls when the massive 'Morning Glory' starts pounding out and the entire place kicks off. Everyone's having it in large way as the gig slides into a higher gear, sending a new energy flowing over the masses. The serious moshing really gets underway when the stomping 'Round Are Way' heralds the arrival of Party Oasis, a band which excels as much when it embraces its pop sensibilities as it does its rock heritage. Following that up with 'Cigarettes & Alcohol' is just cruel - the pit once more becoming a relentless surge of bodies as the glam celebration of all things Lad hits a primal nerve. We're facing spontaneous combustion in here so it's a prayer answered when we reach the mellower mid-section of the gig. Despite the fact that the string-laden ballad seems to deaden the electric vibe hanging over Knebworth, it's a Godsend to see Noel move his stool onto the stage and pick up his acoustic guitar for

'Whatever'. It gives the boys a chance to regroup. I scan the immediate vicinity in an attempt to locate the others. McKinley is just to my right, gurning away well within the boundaries of some bird's personal space, making her visibly uncomfortable. He pretending to be fixated on the stage but I know his attention is actually focused in the area in front of his groin. The girl tries to shuffle away from the penis which is currently poking her in the arse but there's nowhere for her to go except into the back of the bloke in front of her. She's trapped between a rocker and hard dick. Another result for gig perverts everywhere. I spot Ellis over to the left; he's about a foot taller than most of the people around him so it's not that difficult. His head sways from side to side on that elasticated neck of his before craning it over his shoulder to clock me. He starts making his way over, holding a crumpled packet of snouts out as an offering. I take a cigarette from him and accept a light. We smoke in silence, taking in the scene and welcoming the calmness within the storm. There's no sign of Dennis. He's lost in the destruction of the passing hurricane.

Back on stage, Liam dedicates 'Cast no Shadow' to Rob Collins - "Live forever mate" - and sombre reflection adds to the sense of sudden deflation settling over the increasingly lethargic audience as the high octane tunes continue to take a back seat. The song ends and drifts into the vibe vacuum created by the drop in mood and the crowd's ebbing energy. In a bid to rally the masses, the Gallaghers call for a "really fucking massive big fuck-off boo for Man United" - which everyone to a man responds to with venom, regardless if they're a football fan or not. Thankfully the inclusive feeling is back for 'Wonderwall', the mega-hit which polarizes opinion among fans. Is it too commercial and a bit shit or is it the anthem of the 90s? Regardless of where we all stand on the song's worth, there's no grumbling about its inclusion here tonight and the voices are once more back in unison after a period of downtime.

Despite not being the song's greatest fan, 'Wonderwall' stokes my own personal fire again. Then the genius of 'The Masterplan' completes my revival. Noel and Bonehead sit at either side of the stage armed with acoustic guitars, looking like two kids sent to defend their village from a rampaging army with only homemade catapults for company. Even the atmospheric harmonica can't dispel the feeling of vulnerability as the song begins. But when this anthem strums its way to its swirling chorus, we're Goliaths slayed by the Burnage David. What a fucking huge tune. There's no vulnerability here - only hope and resolve. This is the time to make the change "...*to make some sense of what you want to say.*" I wasn't ready before, not completely, but I am now - or as ready as I'm ever going to be. This is where I begin. This is the moment of truth. What matters now is how I choose to use it. This is much more than just standing on a bridge in Amsterdam trying to decide whether or not to be a lad or a man. This is more than just standing at a crossroads. "*There's four and twenty million doors, down life's endless corridor...*" My personal door is slightly ajar. There's no more fucking about. I need to burst through and claim what's mine or lose the opportunity forever. "*Please brother take a chance...*" This really is Destiny calling. "*...All we know is that we don't know what is gonna be...*" It could all go tits up or it could be the most phenomenal experience of my life...but if I don't go for it, I'll never know for sure. "*Please brother let it be...*" I look left and right at my closest friends. I can see them receiving the universal message, it's written all over their awestruck faces. Ellis and McKinley know that we are being sent off into a new dawn. Each of us, not just Ellis, McKinley and me but everyone here, is being prepared. "*And as they fall upon the shore...Tell them not to fear no more...*" This is the power of Oasis. Their songs talk to the everyman and give the mundane meaning.

Noel said it, we're all young and we're all making history. What happens today will live on. The world is changing. Tomorrow will be a brighter day because of what's happening here. All the shit which has come and gone will be forgotten and the slate will be wiped clean for the quarter of a million people standing here under the stars tonight. They'll wake up with new lives.

It makes so much sense that 'The Masterplan' is followed by 'Don't Look Back in Anger'. If 'The Masterplan' is the blueprint for a better life, then 'Don't Look Back in Anger' is the best advice anyone who's moving on can ever have. Fuck the past. There's no reason to look back in anger at what has gone before because the future has begun and it's a fucking blinding one. We've won and this is our victory party. The slog is over. We've dragged ourselves out of the mire to stand on the hilltops. We'll look out on the field of dreams tomorrow. "*Step outside, the summertime's in bloom...*"

Amsterdam has no meaning here. Kelly was never pregnant. Anna never existed. All the slags and anarchy were part of a nightmare which has faded from memory. There's no more looking back - only forward. Karen is my future. I've never been more sure of anything. I just have to convince her that she is.

"Mate, where's fucking Dennis? I haven't seen him since he legged it with a face full of coke," Ellis shouts - unnecessarily - down my ear during the pause between songs. Someone needs to lay off the Charles. "He better not have done one or we're fucked. Stranded." Ellis is grinding his teeth and moonwalking on the spot.

"Who gives a shit where he is?" I grin. "He knows where to meet us. He'll be there."

McKinley has his head furtively in his jacket as the band crank up in readiness of the next tune. A plume of pungent smoke soon billows out of his collar-cum-chimney, followed by a red face and watering eyes. "Danny Boy, the pipe...the pipe is calling..." With a crinkled smile he hands me the small clay device before hacking up a lung. I take the lighter and stoke the bowl, drawing hard on the flame to bring the grass back to life. Within seconds I'm coughing my guts up in the middle of a heaving scrum as Oasis launch into 'My Big Mouth'. It's a new one but the punky onslaught and Liam's insane delivery is enough to get the masses ebbing and flowing across the turf. Ellis forgets his concern over the whereabouts of our driver in a flash and disappears into the throng on spring coiled legs.

He's still missing in action during the next tune, another new one, and while I'm trying to catch a glimpse of where he's gone, I spot Karen and Amanda dancing on the periphery of the main action. It's definitely gettin' better, man...

"Big man, get on this..." The Scotsman leans into me and offers up a key tip of coke. I shake my head and cock a thumb towards where Karen is now swaying to the intro to 'Live Forever'. McKinley sees the determination in my face, nods his approval and takes the hit himself. He pats me on the back as I begin to make my way across the battle lines to where my future may lie.

Amanda clocks me first and I see her whisper into Karen's ear as I twist and turn my way through the masses of bodies separating us. I half expect Manimal to meet me halfway and block my path but instead she just turns back to watch the band. Karen doesn't even acknowledge me as I create a space beside her but it's obvious that my presence is unsettling her. Her dancing becomes a little less free and her body language suggests that she's slightly uncomfortable. I'm hardly Mr. Laidback. I'm half nodding along to the tune and half watching her out of the corner of my eye, thinking more about what the fuck I'm going to do next than appreciating the Oasis anthem of affirmation. I hadn't really thought this one through at all. Part of me wishes I'd taken the snifter from McKinley. At least I wouldn't feel so pathetically tongue tied. But I also know that it would have been too false and this is a moment I want to be in. I'm already fucked up enough. One more hit may have opened the arrogance floodgates and I don't want to blow it by coming over all Tony Montana on her. The song ends and Karen turns to me just as I'm about finished formulating my opening line.

"So, have you sorted yourself out then?" Karen asks as 124,998 pairs of arms stretch into the night sky. (Mine hang loose by my sides and hers are folded across her chest.) Sorted? I'm overly sorted, darlin'. I've been caning it all day in an attempt to feel as biblical as possible and now when it matters, all the gear combines to render my mind a pile of slush. I smile humbly at her, hoping to earn some breathing space. "Do you need some more time, Danny?" she asks sarcastically. "Because you've got about twenty minutes before the offer ends." With that she goes back to watching the show.

I know I want this. I know I want her. I'm in love with her. But where do I start? To make matters even more fucking complicated, Liam announces the arrival of John Squire on stage for 'Champagne Supernova'. John fucking Squire! One of my all-time heroes. Stone Roses haircut, casually open plaid shirt, jet black Les Paul. JOHN SQUIRE. I'm going to have the come up with the most important speech of my life, to win the heart of the girl of my dreams, while a British icon is let loose on one of my favourite band's most epic tunes at the biggest live gig of my life. Destiny is really making we work for this. Jesus...

'Supernova' soars and dips, building towards a finale which will no doubt go down in rock history as one of the defining of a generation. A moment when the crown is finally passed from the abdicating king to the crown princes. It's a moment full of symbolism - and a moment made for the big gesture. I seize my demons and force them down. They're strong but I go for broke.

"Look, Karen...In Amsterdam, that wasn't me," I shout in her ear as Squire begins the longest, most pleasurable wank in the history of self-indulgent guitar solos. "Well, it was me but I was pissed off. I mean, I was really happy to see you...I'm always really happy to see you because you make me feel amazing. But in Amsterdam, you didn't. You made me feel like every other girl has ever made me feel, like what goes on between us doesn't matter. I want it to matter to you…because it matters to me."

"I'm not sure anything really matters to you, Danny…not really," she shouts back. "Maybe the drinking, the birds, the drugs…maybe the music? Where would I fit in? Would you find a place for me in all this?"

"I'm not a Lad, Karen. I mean, I am but not a 'Lad' lad. This…This is me." I point theatrically to myself with the most honest face I can muster in the circumstances. On stage, Liam Gallagher whines out the closing words of 'Champagne Supernova' and the crowd around us erupts in euphoric celebration. My whole being aches to praise the moment along with my generation, to unleash my most basic instincts and roar my allegiance to our new leaders. But there's much more at stake in this moment than nailing my colours to the Oasis mast. Karen searches my face and the urge to go ballistic with the thousands surrounding us squirms beneath my features as she probes for honesty and sincerity. I look her square in the eyes as I fight down the dark half. "I'm not a Lad, Karen."

"Danny, you're drunk, probably high as well and at the biggest Oasis gig of all time. How are you not a lad with a capital L?" I stand before her, mouth agape. "I never wanted you to stop being *you*. This is you, and that's fine. I don't want you to change. But I know there's more to you than this. If you can't accept that then there's no way you're ready to share your life with anyone, let alone me."

Liam is reeling off some kind of incomprehensible 'thank you' speech ahead of the final song while Noel kicks off a low squall of feedback, heralding the arrival of 'I am the Walrus'. Squire has recovered from shooting his load all over 'Supernova' and looks to have wood again as he gives his axe a few long, preparatory strokes. I've got about ten minutes of extended Beatles tribute and guitar strangling to get my message across to Karen before she fades away into a quarter of a

462

million people. I grab her hand and start pulling her through the sea of faces around us. She soon gives up asking me what the hell I'm playing at and starts to follow willingly as Liam tells Knebworth that he's sitting on a cornflake, waiting for the van to come. We break from the main crowd and navigate our way through sporadic groups to get to the relative peace and quiet of a merchandise stand. "Okay, Danny, you now have my undivided attention," she says in a tone that is on the wrong side of pissy.

"Listen, I've been crazy about you since the moment you said my name in that toilet queue back in the Orchard. For almost two years I've been looking for you and until recently I had no idea why. You told me to keep searching for you, do you remember that? Well, I've been doing nothing else. Not only in the phone book and on the streets but in here." Again, I slap my chest but there's no theatre about this gesture. My body and mind seem relieved to be getting rid of all this pent up emotion and they're working purely on instinct. I'm letting it all out and I'm shocked to discover that it's easier than I ever thought it would be. "I found you inside me. That's where you've been all the time. Once I realized why I wanted to find you, it was easy...You're The One, Karen Anderson."

Karen's slightly grumpy face has been slowly relaxing ever since I started talking. Now she's glowing and the frown has been replaced by a coy smile. "Did you practice that?" she smirks.

"No way," I say with nervous relief in my voice. "That was as much a surprise to me as it probably was to you."

"How much of that was you and how much of it was what you're on?" She pokes me in the ribs with a playful finger but her face is a mixture of hope and trepidation.

"What the sober man has in his heart, the drunken man has on his lips." Smooth. Where the hell did that come from? It was a good line but it needs more to make it a great line. "It was all me, Karen. It's the truth. You make me want to be a better man. You make me want to be that bloke under the bandstand." The poking finger stops poking me and joins its siblings in grabbing the side of my trackie top. Karen searches my face again and this time there is no struggle in my face. She has my full attention. A kilometre away, Noel and Squire simultaneously abuse their guitars as the building cacophony of feedback rolls out over the field. The onslaught finally ends and the brothers bark out their farewells to the assembled loyal masses.

"I'm complicated, Danny. I do weird things for even weirder reasons. I'm flawed. I'm hopelessly romantic. I'm totally loyal and I demand the same level of loyalty from those close to me. I'm the best friend and the most passionate lover. I don't like bullshit and I'll walk away from anyone who doesn't treat me with the respect I deserve. When I love, I love with everything I have. If I'm crossed, the person who crosses me will be dead to me. Believe me - you'll never meet anyone like me." Karen finally takes a breath. "Do you think you can handle that? Can you handle the person I am?"

I pull her towards me and give her my answer. When I pull back from her lips, I try and read her reaction, hoping that this kiss is evidence enough that I can handle all that and more if it means I get to be with Karen Anderson. "So, are you going to run off again?"

Karen strengthens her grip on my top and smiles. "You know what? There's nowhere else I want to be right now." A million fireworks explode in the sky above Knebworth as a soft rain begins to fall. "I think you may have finally found me, Daniel. More importantly, I think I've finally found you."

fourteen

Ellis' Story

What a fantastic time to be young.

Imagine being so full of energy that you don't know where to be or what to do. Imagine having a head so full of plans and ideas that you can't sleep. Imagine suddenly finding the place and the moment which promises to make everything you ever dreamt of come true. It's hard to put into words what it felt like wake up from a life of family pressure and school to have this perfect storm of ambition and opportunity swirling around me. Until that moment, I'd just been gestating in a state of enforced education and social convention. I was finally born in 1994. I had been delivered into a world which was about to get a load of the real Ellis ...in a big way. That's what it felt like when I set my bags down in Calvin Road on my first morning on earth.

The timing was perfect. I'd been out of sixth form for a year and my mother's nagging had reached unbearable levels. Unlike most teenagers, I didn't blow up. I didn't shout back. I didn't fight or rage against the stifling oppression forced upon me under my parents' roof. I kept my head down and worked. I slaved every hour God sent for that year. I even managed to con some overtime out of the Lord towards then end, convincing Him that matricide was on the cards if he didn't somehow find a way to cram more hours into the day. I sliced ham, wired cheese, stacked shelves, froze my bollocks off in the meat lockers - anything Tesco's asked of me, I'd do. I was doing it for the money and the chance to stay away from the endless bitching.

Most former teenage layabouts will tell you in their later years that they can totally understand why their parents despaired of them in their most lethargic moments. In most cases, school ends and the layabout wants to do just that - lay about. Parents tend to forget how hard it is to attend school for eleven or twelve years with no choice in the matter. Teenagers don't see the logic of immediately signing up for another four or five years of that, however more relaxed college and university may be. They want to have a break. Parents don't see this. As soon as the layabout has been on the sofa for a few post-exam weeks, suddenly you're wasting your life. Looking back with hindsight, most of us will appreciate the fact that our parents crow-barred us off the couch and got our arses into gear - because it would have been so very easy to do fuck all forever if someone hadn't bullied you into getting a life.

Me? I understand this on behalf of those people who went through that. My own situation was pretty similar apart from one major difference. I wasn't a layabout. I had a plan. I was working my arse off in a supermarket to get to the point where I could have a life on my own terms. I may not have been spending my every waking hour in a college prospectus or researching possible future courses but I was out of the house every day at seven in the morning, paying my way. I barely crashed out on any piece of furniture other than my own bed. And yet, I got the same stream of motherly moaning as someone who had dropped school for a career in growing dreadlocks and eating Doritos in front of *Supermarket Sweep*.

My mother's concern was not that I was wasting my life - but that I was in danger of not following the one she and my dad had in mind for me. I suppose this amounted to same thing in their eyes. I had reassured

466

them that I had every intention of returning to education once I had raised enough cash to live comfortably while doing so - but in a place, if not a galaxy, far far away from them. This is what concerned my mother the most. She couldn't control me if I wasn't under her roof. She couldn't continue her slow indoctrination if I was miles out of earshot. The bitching and nagging was about me moving out and the fact that I would never be as successful as my brother Sean if I let the distractions of student living get in the way of my quest to live up to the standards that had been pinned to the wall ever since I followed him out of the womb.

As I previously said, I didn't snap or talk back when the nagging was in full flow. I barely said a word to my parents, actually. This is also a typical trait of the surly teenager and one I used to my own advantage. But it was fucking hard not to start a fight when the topic of living away from home was brought up. You see, Sean - who was six years my senior - may have gone on to be a very successful advertising executive at the tender age of 24 but he did so by getting the fuck out of the family pressure cooker as soon as he could. My mum's argument, therefore, that I would fail in life if I moved away from home while continuing my studies was not based on any bad experience Sean had but purely on the fact that she thought I personally wouldn't be able to cut it. It was her lack in faith of my ability to take responsibility for myself that drove her campaign. That hurt - even more so when she was eventually proved to be right.

I hadn't really excelled at school. I'd managed to get a few GCSE's and I stayed on for an extra year to get better grades in the subjects I needed to get into college. But it didn't really interest me. I had friends but people on the whole didn't live up to my expectations. These expectations came from my favoured source of reality: television. Television and cinema painted a life far more exciting than actual living could provide. The characters and situations on the screen were monstrous in comparison to the mousy humans around me in their daily drudgery. I socialised to a certain extent, mostly getting into low level mischief around the small town I was brought up in, but I was more engaged with the word I could access through the box. This preference for an alternate reality had not been lost on my parents and without them, left to my own devices, I may never have finished school with the bare minimum of results I finally achieved. The idea they had that I would drift and dream without constant badgering was born in those days when the glow from my TV would illuminate my bedroom long into night.

I think my parents thought that I would just spend my days in my student digs watching television, finally free from the constant demands to "turn that bloody thing off and go outside." But as I said, I wasn't a layabout. Television wasn't turning me into a vegetable - it was turning me into a supernova of ideas. This is something that I will always respect and love my brother for - even when he's being a self-righteous prick.

Before he was bestowed with the mission of bringing honour to the family name (a mantle that was forced on to me when he buggered off due to the pressure of it all), Sean was my best friend. He was more than that, actually. I'd go so far as to say that he was my guru, my teacher, my idol. By the time I started at the local high school, Sean had been gone a year but his legacy remained. The glow he left behind briefly bathed me in the same light - until all the teachers who thought the sun shone out of his arse realised that I was a completely different proposition. Until that light dimmed, I was Sean ...'s brother and so had that same gene of wondrousness somewhere inside me. That made my life just that little bit easier until I used up all that credit and started collecting debits under my own name. I was thankful for being his brother in that early phase. I had inherited a little slice of good fortune, something all first years finding their way at a big school would be lucky to have. Those older kids who'd looked up to Sean treated me well as if looking out for me somehow got them closer to him. That, as anyone will tell you, can be enough to keep you from the beatings and pranks that punctuate the early days at a new school.

His benevolence wasn't confined to proxy respect at school either. He set about giving me a parallel education at home, one which do more to form my personality and future than any provided by a salaried teacher.

First there was film. I loved television programmes but until Sean unlocked the world of cinema, I was just watching. When he began systematically introducing me to the classics of every genre, I started to absorb. Scorsese, Coppola, Truffaut, Hitchcock... The list of great directors seemed endless, their art fantastic, their quality unrivalled. I not only sat through hours of war, science fiction, drama and crime but I started to read everything I could get my hands on which gave me any insight into how this magic was created and what was going on in the minds of these geniuses. I had found another world to inhabit – one based in reality but armed with the eternal possibilities of fantasy. Sean would show me a new film almost every day and then we'd sit for hours discussing it. He would tell me stories surrounding the making of it, the stars and their related work. It wasn't long before I knew that this was what I wanted to do with my life and set about planning and dreaming my way towards it.

Second there was music. Sean had an eclectic taste which bucked the trend of following that latest scene or movement. He was a big Stone Roses fan and had bought into the Madchester vibe body and soul in the late 1980s. The first record he played me was the Roses debut album and the effect was immediate. It soared, it pined, it was both hugely uplifting and painfully vulnerable at the same time. It dragged emotions from me that I never knew existed. But his collection stretched further and wider than the E-soaked days of the Hacienda: from 60s psychedelia to 70s funk and disco through to 80s post-punk and the fledgling indie scene of early 90s Britain, I was given the opportunity to delve.

Just as it was with film, the listening experience for me had to be enhanced with the surrounding knowledge of the people who made this music and the times it was made in. His journey through the intertwined histories and influences led me to the Beatles and the Stones, the Byrds, the Doors and then onto James Brown, Curtis Mayfield and Marvin Gaye. Sean was again my guide and I lost count of the hours we sat motionless and thoughtful to Joy Division, amused and awed by the Smiths, and enthused and joyful with the Charlatans and Inspiral Carpets. Sean showed me the importance of music in defining who you are and where you come from. He told me that to give your personality the best chance of developing, you have to embrace music and let it take you to where your identity is waiting for you. Don't force it, he said. There is a place and time and music for everyone.

And then he left.

I won't lie and say that I didn't feel abandoned. In all honesty, I felt betrayed; tricked into believing my ally and benefactor would lead me all the way through the dark woods of adolescence, not leave me in its blackest heart to be fed on by wolves. Running out on me and leaving me with my mother and her crushing expectation felt just like that. I felt sacrificed as if Sean had pegged me out on some altar to avoid being carved up himself. I suppose in the early days after his departure I did hate him for that. But then the negative emotions turned into something else. My resentment galvanised me and filled me with the spirit of competition. I didn't want to punish Sean in any conventional way, like never speaking to him again or exhibiting only animosity towards him whenever we met. I wanted to kill all my birds with one fuck-off big stone: I'd shut my mother up and teach my brother a lesson by becoming someone in whose shadow they could only squint at in awe. My mother's expectations and my brother's achievements would not pale into insignificance; they would be incinerated by the blast from my all-surpassing greatness.

This was the attitude I arrived at Calvin Road with. In normal circumstances, this should have been dismissed as youthful naivety. But in Britain at the end of 1994, everyone was thinking like this. Everyone - nine-to-five office workers, rock stars, politicians - were all getting on a culturally charged ego trip. Something was about to kick-off and everyone wanted what they could get out of it, me included.

Many things came together at that time to feed my ego; an id which was ill-prepared for what the combination of such mental rushes would produce on the blank canvas of my personality. I was hoping for a detailed masterpiece. I got Jackson Pollock on coke.

Suddenly everybody was telling everyone else how great things could be and how we were the generation to make the change. Even though I'd read reams of material which suggested the doomed hippie movement of the 60's had thought the same way, the connection wasn't made. That was history, this was now.

No-one drove me on more than Danny in those early days. We'd bonded over music at college and even though he was a few years older and I was the course pup, we soon formed a powerful partnership which became a dominant double personality among our peers. Through the music which was fuelling the sense of a coming epiphany, we found ourselves at the cutting edge of what was happening and what would happen. We were the first to get into the bands who would later define the era, we dressed in fashion which was only just getting recognised as the new style and we radiated the carefree, reckless attitude which would become the default setting for everyone - boy and girl - over the next three years. We were so cool that even being friends with Rob couldn't affect our standing. In fact, we actually managed to make Rob cool - to a certain extent, the extent that an unwashed vagrant could be considered cool. Danny slipped into the role vacated by my brother with ease and with the shackles of home life removed from my wrists and ankles, his tutelage began to take me to all manner of places where I never thought I'd go.

Danny wasn't much of a druggie when we first moved in together. He'd been a regular pot smoker for a few years and his periods of experimentation with LSD and amphetamines had given him some enlightening experiences but no great taste for them at this time. But compared to me, he was Pablo Escobar. I would lose the ability of coherent speech after a four pack of Stellas. While Danny picked up where Sean had left off with my music education, he created an all new syllabus for me when drugs started to become readily available at Calvin Road. Soon my ego was not only being boosted by my newly acquired status as one of the cool kids but was being massively inflated by a steady intake of mind altering substances.

As the whirlwind of Britpop gathered strength and speed, and the growing hedonistic attitude attached to the music reintroduced the use of neglected drugs, the third part of the Unholy Trinity conspired to lead me entirely astray. Lad culture was tailor made for me. It was loud, arrogant and out of control. It gave me license to say what I wanted, to behave how I wanted, and have no one to answer to. Mixed with the promise of Britpop - which was gradually getting its can-do message out to the people, the surging rush of my new love of substances, Lad culture gave me the testosterone-fuelled drive to go out and become the massive success I already was in my own mind.

However.

I was a convert to everything by now. But while I had the Britpop belief, the artificial confidence which came from being constantly off my tits, and the Laddish carte blanche to rampage around demanding that life gave me what it owed, I was even further away from where I needed to be. Britpop had opened the door to my ego; it told me that everything was achievable, that I could be and do anything I wanted - but when it got mixed up with Lad culture, it - and everyone involved -

472

lost its way. I had all manner of explosive desires but I had no direction. I didn't see that I was being told to go out there and be all I could be - but there was no clear instruction as to how I was supposed to do it. I had my target - to eclipse my brother by becoming an acclaimed director - but the set of rough guidelines I'd been given were missing the pages which explained how this was supposed to happen if you'd followed the previous chapters about getting endlessly hammered.

I had bought into the hype so heavily that I thought it would all work out if I just larged it to the max. I believed all I had to do was pick up a camera and the finished product would be the 90s equivalent of a classic like Mean Streets. The belligerence wasn't just confined to the pubs and clubs we were then starting to hang out in with alarming regularity, it was evident in every aspect of my life, especially college. I was beginning to struggle because I thought I was a genius waiting to happen and that my visions would be recognised as such. When the lecturers slated my work as incomprehensible and muddled, I raged against them. They didn't know what they were talking about and couldn't recognise the new direction that my talent would take film. I didn't realise at the time that this was just the Lad talking.

I wasn't the only one who started to lose their way. While the hedonistic abandon and inflated sense of self were the main aspects of Lad which were steering me into a ditch, Danny had been sucked into a vortex filled with potential shags. Oh, he was off his face as much, if not more, than me and regularly betrayed his fabricated, unruffled exterior by getting very messy and obnoxious but the part of the new culture he seemed most drawn to was the focus on getting his end away. By this time, of course, McKinley was firmly attached to the gang as the fourth Musketeer (although he was far from a naïve d'Artagnan, more like the most wayward aspects of Athos, Porthos and Aramis rolled into one). The Scotsman was a lover of the wine, the women and the song but had his own weird code when it came to screwing around. As such, he became this weird sex guru - like a permanently aroused Yoda but with marginally better grammar - dispensing perverted wisdom and guiding Danny (and then subsequently me) down the path of casual fornication.

The Lad manifesto had a special place for women - and that place was on all-fours with their bare arses in the air, a stencil saying 'open for business' sprayed on a quivering cheek. As a convert looking for guidance in every aspect of this cultural explosion I found myself in, it didn't take long for sex to join the list of potential signposts to the greatness I was pursuing. Maybe adding random fucking to the agenda would take me to the required level. When I signed on for this latest of new experiences, McKinley was only too happy to welcome another member to his shag cult.

The realm of intercourse is a daunting one for any virgin but put the uninitiated into a situation where the opposite sex is in full ravenous pursuit of sexual emancipation and it's enough to shrivel the most willing but unused todger. Even though I was bursting out of my skin with (artificially constructed) ambition and confidence in most other areas of my life, I was still frightened to death of joining the age-old dance while also almost out of my mind with need. Thankfully - although in hindsight that may be pushing it a little far - Danny and the Scotsman were on hand to guide me.

The first blind date McKinley set up for us was a disaster but at least it was a disaster which ended due to the mental instability of the women involved, not because of any physical failure on the lads' part - by which I mean me. Perhaps that was why I agreed to go along with Danny on a second, again instigated by McKinley. That and the fact that my self-pleasuring endeavours at this point had almost forced me to wear a wrist support. God knows what would have happened had this one gone tits up. Maybe I would have spent my life getting my sex from prostitutes, afraid to enter into anything other than a financial transaction to get what I physically needed from a woman. Luckily, my date that night was Monica.

I'll admit it here and now: I was just after a shag. Any shag. I knew Monica as DJ Sonique from the Warehouse and as MC Steak Hammer from old school friends who took great pleasure in spreading her myth. I knew she wasn't my type. My type, as an 18-year-old Lad virgin, was whatever made my hand crank faster; usually that month's laminated unobtainable from *Loaded*'s latest bikini shoot. And these were never chunky, muscle-bound Jamaican birds. But I also knew that the Steak Hammer myth - if true - could lead to me getting royally fucked which in turn would usher in the age of Ellis the Shag Monster. I only needed to do it once for the pressure to be off forever. Monica would set me free.

Besides, she was only going on this date as wingman for her mate and it was clear to both of us that this arrangement was all about Debbie Does Danny. Even though blokes like me were probably not Monica's chosen quarry, as it turned out, she came with the attitude that if she was going to play chaperone to her friend, she may as well get some pleasure for herself out of the good deed. It must have been White Boy Day...

Danny and the Bastard Jock have made sure that the whole world knows about Big Vern and my slightly unconventional loss of virginity (two for the price of one), so retelling that part of the tale is unnecessary. What is important - and what has been left out of the version that has me being tunnelled out by a big plastic cock - is that we made a connection that night; a deep, powerful, spiritual and mental connection. I wasn't looking for it and I certainly wouldn't have been looking for it with someone like Monica but I found it all the same. When I realised what was going on, it shocked the life out of me. The feelings I had were wholly alien and they scared me shitless for the next three years until I made one of the worst decisions in my life out of sheer panic.

To the outside world (which at the time meant Danny and McKinley), my decision to end things with Monica in 1996 was all about reclaiming myself from a situation which I felt had stolen my personality. I justified dumping her by claiming my eyes had been taken off the prize by losing myself in this thing I thought was love. I ignored the fact that, since 1994 and moving to Calvin Road, I'd been careening off my chosen path while high and drunk. It pained me in moments of clarity to think that my mother had been right all along and that moving out to follow my dream would put that dream at risk. I had been my own worst enemy when left to my own devices but instead of blaming my slump on my own hedonistic tendencies, I lay the blame at Monica's doorstep. I chose to hold this 'thing' I could barely bring myself to call a relationship responsible for my waywardness. I didn't realise it at the time but Monica had actually been pushing me in the right direction. She was actually the person I needed to guide me out of the mess and back towards my target. By breaking up with her, I not only denied myself love but also my best chance of actually getting everything I ever wanted.

Britpop came to an end with a bitter hangover and acidic comedown while Lad culture eventually grew up. I was left in a vacuum again. Just as I had in the months before the best time of my life, I went to work. I would earn my corn and wait for the next tsunami of possibility and opportunity. During this time, I would blow numerous chances to make things happen and almost lose my best friend. Twelve years since deciding to bide my time for that next big thing to sweep me up towards greatness, I'm still waiting.

fifteen

Death of a Party

May 1997

Looking around McKinley's house some ten months after I last set foot in our former staging area I start to wonder why he was so against Ellis and I moving in. So Jerry and Melanie may be respectable, if being middle-aged, childless and gainfully employed fulfils all the necessary criteria of respectability, but they're still a couple of lazy bastards. McKinley always took a few days to catch up with dishes and laundry but he eventually got round to the menial tasks which make living within four walls bearable before botulism claimed both the house and his life. Jerry and Mel (or Melons as the Scotsman refers to the ample-chested one when she's out of earshot i.e. when he's on the phone from Jakarta) seem to think that if they allow everything to putrefy, eventually there won't be anything left in need of cleaning - including cutlery and plates. (They also seem to have a bottomless well of patience as well as a blind eye to fungus and mould.) All of which begins to explain why Ellis and I are round the house helping to prepare for an election party which isn't due to start for a good eight hours.

I'm pretty sure even we wouldn't have let the house turn into a scene from one of those educational nature programs where the dead mouse decomposes in superfast time. I've always been one of those who believe that the standard of your surroundings when you move in dictates how well you treat them while you're in residence. Take Calvin

Road for instance. Even before Mr. Sifter moved in with his tomcat ball sweat and tactical incontinence, there was always a strange whiff to the place, like rancid meat. Coupled with the apparently hastily repaired floorboards in the living room which bulged and sagged at will, we were beginning to wonder whether the previous tenants had been Fred and Rose West. Mushrooms which could have supported the caterpillar from Alice in Wonderland after a good few years of letting himself go would regularly appear in the bathroom while the kitchen constantly smelt of feet. As a result, neither Ellis nor I really gave a shit about the communal areas. As long as our bedrooms didn't stink of faeces or body parts, we could live with it.

Unfortunately the Scotsman didn't ever know about our philosophy regarding respect to housing. He just saw the state of the shithole we lived in and took it as read. As a result, we were never even given cursory consideration as tenants of his pad. He wasn't to know that we would have treated his house with a lot more respect than Jerry and Melons have because the place is a palace compared to anywhere either of us has lived before. It would have demanded our respect. Plus McKinley's bird would have had our balls on a silver platter if even a hint of man-stench had settled in the ceiling-to-floor velvet drapes.

But overlooked we were. Fair play. We were both on the dole and McKinley had spent enough time at Calvin Road to see how the pair of us had handled a shared house and had been witness, at disturbingly close quarters, to how hard we could party. Jerry and Mel - a curator at a local gallery and a counsellor at the Citizen's Advice Bureau - fitted the profile for the perfect tenants, well, perfectly. That is until McKinley packed his bags for Indonesia last August, leaving the keys to the kingdom in the trotters of Porky and Mrs. Pig.

Ellis and I knew the Pigs relatively well from various nights drinking after hours at the hotel. They were friends of Gerry the Boss and his grisly wife Angela. I'm sure McKinley thought that they were part of the same swinging circle the hotel owners were rumoured to be part of and secretly harboured ideas of getting involved in a purely supervisory capacity. In fact, having the potential for wild sex parties going on under his roof probably swung it for them (no pun intended). The Scotsman - no doubt nursing a throbbing bell-end while doing so - signed our base of operations over the day before he flew out of our lives.

With his triumphant return less than eight hours away, Ellis and I are back at the scene of many of our best nights with the Scotsman. Much to our disgust, however, we're elbow deep in dirty dishes, not knee deep in drugs and loose women.

"How the fuck did we get roped into this?" Ellis asks, using a chisel on the remnants of a concrete lasagne. "This is your fault."

He's not wrong. When I heard the Scotsman and his missus were heading back from South-east Asia for their first visit since leaving I volunteered to organise the festivities. I must admit that the idea of them returning to the UK on the day before the most important general election day in a generation and then turning up on the old manor in time to witness a predicted and much anticipated swing back to the left made me lose the plot a little. I not only volunteered my own services but press-ganged Ellis into service too. Not just that but I also decided we should throw a massive bash to welcome home the McKinleys and celebrate the potential return of Labour to power. I didn't think Jerry and Melanie would go for the idea of the party being held in their home, despite the persuasive fact that it would be taking place in their landlords' honour in the house they owned. In fact, they jumped at it. I can see why now.

"I know McKinley isn't getting here until six but I still don't think we're going to get this place cleared up in time," Ellis puffs, giving up on the lasagne and throwing the heavily scratched Pyrex dish into the bin. "Where's fucking Jerry? I thought he was going to lend a hand."

"He is," I reply, lugging the fourth bin liner of assorted crap through the kitchen to the backyard. "I sent him to pick up the drinks from Bob." Bob the Bastard at the Castle has agreed to provide the alcohol at trade prices as long as we collect it. Jerry, the only person we know with a car who isn't Dennis (I'll explain later...), was therefore dispatched to the pub. Ellis stares me out until realisation dawns. Oh... I forgot to mention that Jerry, as well as being an idle fucker, is also a borderline alcoholic. Shit. "I'll give Bob a call," I say as the full horror of a party with no alcohol and only a litany of pathetic excuses from a hammered Jerry for entertainment dawns on me. I'm pleading with Bob to stop serving Jerry and send him home immediately with our supplies when the front door bell goes. Ellis passes me in the hall muttering something about how 'this party better be fucking rocking' as he heads for the door. His pissy muttering turns to an upbeat exclamation of surprise as he opens the door to one of my special guests. After considerable effort I managed to book, for one night only, Filthy Rob.

"You never said we were expecting any celebrities," Ellis shouts from the front door, exhibiting more joy than I ever expected to hear from him on the occasion of finding Rob on the doorstep.

"It wouldn't be a surprise if I had, would it?" A year of distance has also made my heart grow fonder and I give the prodigal son a solid man-hug as he follows Ellis into the hallway. "I take it you didn't hitch-hike this time."

"You must be joking," Rob grins. "I can actually afford a bus ticket these days." He hesitates before segueing along a monetary train of thought. "Tony's not coming tonight is he?"

"Err..."

"Just don't tell him I'm a working actor. I'm still skint if he asks. I still owe him."

"Glad to see that some things don't change," I say, slapping his shoulder heartily. "Need I remind you that you still owe me?"

"And me." Ellis adds.

"So what's the deal with this place?" Rob asks, moving swiftly on. "It looks like you two have been living in it."

Ellis comes back from the kitchen with three cans of Carling, signalling that the housework can wait until after the excitement of our reunion makes way for the comforting routine of old friendships. "Cheeky bastard, it was always you who made our gaff such a mess."

"Me and Mr. Sifter...He's not here is he? That fucking moggy hated my guts."

A brief silence as a moment of solemnity is observed. "The old boy passed on," I say with a tinge of real sadness. "I went back to Calvin Road shortly after we moved out to get my footie boots from the shed and I found him dead in the corner. He didn't smell that different to when he was alive actually. I thought he was just having a kip."

"To Mr. Sifter" Ellis raises his can in a toast. "And the return of old friends."

The telephone rings. It's Bob. "Can one of you boys come to the pub? Jerry's over the limit and I'm not going to let him drive home. One of you is going to have to come and get him." Jerry's only been gone an hour. What a lush.

"Ellis? Bob wants you to go and pick Jerry up from the Castle. He's arseholed and can't drive home."

"Okay," he says without argument. "Anything's better than cleaning this place." He drains his can and punches Rob playfully on the arm. "You're still going to be here when I get back? No plans to run off and play Captain Hook or something?"

"Up yours. I'm a Shakespearean actor, I'll have you know," Rob mock boasts, puffing out his chest. "My Bottom was very well received."

"I bet it fucking was…" Ellis mutters as he heads for the door. "See you in an hour."

"Don't stay there and get pissed as well," I shout after him, feeling immediately like some old fish wife or foul-mouthed council estate mum. "I don't want to have to come up there and get both of you." Ellis mutters something inaudible which sounds like 'take yer valium, mother' as he slams the door behind him.

"You know he will," smirks Rob. Sadly I know he's right. I phone Bob at the Castle and get him to promise not to serve Ellis any alcohol. Bob gives me a mouthful for tying up his morning with pissheads and phone calls before agreeing to threaten Ellis with a lifetime ban if he doesn't leave immediately with Jerry and the alcohol after arriving at the pub. Sorted.

With an official tea-break called, Rob and I put our feet up in the living room. I ask Rob to fill me in on his adventures as a travelling thespian, knowing that we'll be lucky to get round to my news by the time Ellis gets back. If the little bastard thinks he's going to come back to find the house spotless, he's in for a shock. They'll be plenty of furry plates and rotten food for him when he returns.

Rob starts at the very beginning back in May last year when he disappeared shortly before we were all due to head for Amsterdam. After meeting with Aiden Craske, he packed his rucksack and headed back to Bangor where Shaven Avon were beginning rehearsals for their random acts of thespianism tour. Although not surprising that Rob had a modicum of acting talent, I am shocked and impressed that he managed to nail four main Shakespearean roles in as many weeks, learning the parts simultaneously. It was during this time, apparently, that he developed his new addiction.

"Suddenly I was at the centre of everything," he tells me, leaning towards me and fixing me with an intense stare from the opposite sofa. "I wasn't Filthy Rob or Rob the Nob, I was the Prince of Denmark, I was Don John...I was fucking Banquo, man!" He stands up and I half expect him to start reciting lines. To my surprise, he takes out a wrap from his back pocket and starts preparing a couple of lines on the mantelpiece above the fireplace. Jesus, who is this bloke!? "No-one knew about all the shit that had gone on before. It was ace!" He hoovers up a thick rail and offers me the other of equally generous girth. Now rushing on the charlie's immediate upward surge, Rob's on tour, telling me about how the applause of the crowd and the rush of live theatre became a habit. (He doesn't however, mention how or when his other habit kicked in). He rattles off verbatim quotes from the review sections of tiny local papers and starts anecdotes filled with backstage praise that never come to a conclusion. "And the birds, man. The birds are just mad for me. Top class women, not the dregs I had around here," he finishes his beer and sits down again. All this energy, all this utterly new and surprising information is blowing my mind. I can't tell him about our events of the last year if I tried. This new Rob demands that much attention. I can't tell him that Karen and I have been together now for over six months and things are going slowly but smoothly. I can't tell him that Ellis and Steak Hammer have been apart for nearly a year and that, even though his exterior suggests a Lad reborn, he misses her like hell. I can't tell him that we're both working men now, albeit in starter jobs - Ellis filing at the parole office, me working the local beat at the Daily. All this and more will have to wait because Rob is on a roll. "I can't explain it Danny because it doesn't really make any sense but when I'm playing other people, I'm as close to being myself as I've ever been. I'm a different person every night and it doesn't matter who I am, they love me for it."

Being loved. That's what we all really want. I'm hoping that it's getting that way with Karen. I know I love her because through all the stuff that happened from the first moment we met until the day we finally got it together, she was always in my head - somewhere. Thing is, I don't know if I'm being loved back. Nothing's been said. I've not said it to her because, you know, it's been six months and if she hasn't said it yet how am I going to know if it's going to go down well or not? This is why things are going slowly. There's a step approaching in the future that we're going to have to take. Or not. I'm ready. I'm not sure if Karen is which is why I think she's dragging her heels. "So is there a special someone out there in the crowds of groupies?" I ask, shaking the coke and paranoia out of my head and getting back into the mostly one-way conversation.

"There's been a couple but I'm always on the road," Rob says. "I can't give them what they want right now so I give them what I want and then move on." The look of granite confidence slips a little, a minor rockslide but a visible one all the same. "There's plenty of time for attachment. Right now, I wouldn't want to deny anybody the chance." The rocks settle again in a practised, craggy grin. I get the feeling that it gets used a lot in Rob's line of work. There's no chipping away at that one. Whatever's buried beneath is staying that way.

A hacking smokers cough echoes down the stairs, through the hallway and into the living room, causing a look of surprise to suddenly inhabit Rob's face. His frown asks the question. "It's Melanie," I reply. "Her ladyship is awake."

Once Melons has had at least four cups of strong coffee and has tried to get into Rob's pants at least twice ("I love actors...why have one man when you can have five at the same time?"), the lady of the house is deemed fit for duty. With another espresso in hand, she heads upstairs in an attempt to restore order to the chaos of the bedrooms. Five minutes later, Ellis returns with Jerry and the alcohol. Ellis is surprised, pissed off, and then eager for a hand-out when I tell him Rob has been getting his coke out for the boys.

"Bob was a right bastard today, even by his standards," Ellis says as he hovers over a freshly chopped line on a vinyl copy of *Electric Ladyland*. Hendrix would have approved. I grin to myself and Rob silently chuckles. "The git wouldn't give me a pint, said if I didn't get home with Jezza and the beers he'd ban me for life. Wanker." Jerry refuses a snifter in favour of another beer and after the crates have been unloaded from Porky's battered old Volvo, the four of us start on the home stretch of cleaning (minus Melons who has gone back to bed, presumably after clearing all the clothes off it). McKinley and missus are due in about five hours. Most hands, if not all, are at the pumps.

Just before six o'clock, the doorbell rings. It's the Scotsman - alone. For someone who's been living in a sub-tropical climate for the past ten months, he's not very tanned. He does have a slightly pink tinge to his face but that could be due to the fact that he's just walked from the local Sainsbury's carrying a rucksack and pulling two suitcases behind him. Not one for public displays of emotion, he raises a limp hand in response to our cheers and then slips into the McKinley mode we've been missing from our everyday lives. "Give us a hand with these cases, big man," he gasps. "And someone get us a beer, for fuck's sake. I'm parched." It's like he's never been away. Ellis and I take a suitcase each as McKinley eases himself out of the large backpack with a pained moan. Rob wanders in from the kitchen with a glass of amber lifesaver. "Fucking hell, where did he come from?" Rob bows theatrically and hands the beer to the Scotsman. "How's life treading the boards, darlin'? Gay yet?"

"Where's your missus?" I ask.

"We're here for a week but she feels the need to stock up on food from the supermarket. I'm on holiday, I tell her, so I'm not going to be making my own food. But no. She needs to go to Sainsbury's. So she takes the hire car and makes me fucking walk here."

Ellis looks at the luggage. "You've brought a lot of stuff...but I think you've forgotten something..." McKinley gives him one of those withering stares. "Your balls!"

"Yeah, yeah, yeah... I see you haven't got any funnier since I've been gone. Now you're not being taken up the arse by Steak Hammer every other night you should work on some new material." Ellis laughs in the spirit of things but there's no humour in it and a flash of pain flickers briefly in his eyes. I spot it. Nobody else does. They all think he's fine. "Apart from giving me a hernia, it's actually a Godsend. I wanted to talk to you lot before she got here, lay down a few ground rules."

We all know the situation. McKinley was basically on a very long lead while he and his missus were on opposite sides of the world. But on a lead he was. The chain wasn't strong enough to stop him fooling around to a certain degree but the threat of castration was such that he - to our knowledge at least - never humped any of the strays who came and went during the last three years. We all know the score so we all know what to say and what not to say. Even so...McKinley feels the need to get us all on the same page. We convene in the living room for the pre-match team talk. "This is how it is, boys," he says. "She doesn't know anything about the other birds, okay? So don't say anything about any of that. But she's not fucking stupid, okay, so don't paint me as some kind of saint or she'll know for sure that's something is up. The drugs are okay but let's tone it down a bit. We don't need to mention the cocaine and the acid. Or the speed....Or the ecstasy. The dope is okay. But no Class A's." The team agrees as one. Now let's get out there and give them a helluva game... The Scotsman hangs back as Ellis and Rob go about getting the house set up for the party. "So how you doing, Danny?"

"Good, man. Things are pretty sorted."

"How's it going with your woman?"

"Things are going well...We're taking it slow, you know...She's coming tonight actually."

"That's what I wanted to talk to you about," he says, conspiratorially. "You kept to the guidelines on guests, right? There won't be any skeletons or mad old bints in the closet for the missus to discover."

"None of the female guests this evening will have had any sexual contact with you whatsoever," I assure him. "Or are ever likely to."

"Nice. What about deviants?"

"Apart from those two in there and your good self the only high risk attendees will be Peruvian Tony and Dennis the Menace." The Scotsman grimaces. "It's cool, man. I had a word with Tony and he'll be on his best behaviour...which will still be fucking insane but he promised to keep his trap shut under pain of death. As for Dirty Den, I had to invite him as he was the only one who could get us any gear."

"I thought you'd be the man for that now, working in the media."

"Have a word...The only thing I could get from the old farts at the Daily is some beta-blockers or maybe a Lemsip. It's hardly Rolling Stone." McKinley laughs for the first time since he arrived. "But if you can't wait until Dennis turns up, Rob's got a wrap of charles in his pocket." McKinley's face is a picture of pleasant surprise. "I shit you not."

While he is no less agitated when his missus eventually turns up, it's clear to everyone who was there in the kitchen watching McKinley go to work on a good third of Rob's stash that his demeanour has much less to do with introducing his long-term partner to the lads. We all know her name's Brenda but it's hard not to address her as 'the missus' after almost three years of hearing her referred to as nothing but. We stand there like Victorian children being introduced to our new governess; all polite smiles and well-behaved handshakes, while behind the façade we're all dealing with the conflict of being off our tits at the same time. The fact that the three of us have all turned into various all-singing, all-dancing members of the Von Trapp family does nothing to ease the Scotsman's anxiety. If he is going to survive this night, we're going to have to change his medication.

Brenda seems nice, although a little scary. It's clear why McKinley is on edge and the governess reference is not all down to how we're presenting ourselves. She carries a slightly suspicious air that all experienced school teachers seem to exude. After years of being exposed to the full range of behavioural flaws small children can exhibit, it's the default setting for someone expecting mischief and deceit. She's right to be suspicious. We're a bunch of little bastards behind the running noses and innocent smiles. Ellis, however, immediately endears himself to our new governess by offering to bring the shopping in. "He's a catch," she says, beaming at McKinley. "Handsome with manners. She'll be a lucky girl who lands that one."

McKinley's outburst of hysterical laughter is two-thirds instinctive, one third narcotic. "Ellis?" he cries, wiping spittle and snot from his face. "Aye, he'll make someone a good wife one day."

After Brenda and McKinley have taken care of landlord-tenant business with Jerry and Melons (kids not allowed), the Scotsman's missus takes a bath and McKinley visibly relaxes. The first guests are expected in an hour and the staging area of days gone by is looking like its old self: the fridge bulges with bottles of continental beer, spirits line the breakfast counter next to a liquidizer primed for cocktail duty, and the silver cigar case has been dusted down in readiness for the evening's joints. Everything's primed for what could be an epic night.

"So you boys all voted then?" McKinley asks, reclining in the battered embrace of his favourite Chesterfield armchair.

"First thing," I reply. "Me and Ellis stopped off at the school on the way here this morning. Two votes for the future, mate. Fuck the Tories, let's have a bit of Tony!"

"He's Blair, he's there, he's every-fucking-where..." Ellis starts up a modified football chant which dies out as quickly as it started. We're buzzed but we're not quite there yet. Ellis doesn't seem to care. But in reality he does.

"Shit, I totally forgot." Rob looks panic-stricken, like the Filthy Rob of the past, a clueless sap lost in a sea of self-loathing. "Is it too late?"

"What did you think you were coming back for?" I ask him incredulously. "I even told you that it was an election party."

"Yeah, but I didn't know what election, did I? You didn't make it clear."

I hold my hands up. "Someone? Please?"

"You wanna lay off the marching powder, Olivier," McKinley grins. "Get yourself down the school sharpish. You've got about an hour. If the Tories stay in power and you don't get your cross down, we'll blame you for the next four years of right-wing fuck-ups."

"Who says I won't be voting for John Major anyway?" says Rob, grabbing his coat.

"I want proof of a Labour vote or you're not getting back in," McKinley shouts after him as Rob dashes out. "Welsh bastard will probably vote for Plaid Cymru."

"I don't think they have a candidate here," Ellis muses. He remains ignored.

"We're going to win, right? I mean, everything has been building up to this for the past three years. Britain needs a geezer prime minister, and Blair's a geezer. He's going to be the Britpop PM."

"Everything else has changed, " pipes up Ellis. "The government has to be next."

"I just want the fucking Tories out, man," say McKinley with conviction. "It's been way too long and they're dead on their feet. I have a feeling people have had enough. It's gonna change tonight. You'll see."

"Let's drink to that."

And we do. Everyone does. By nine the house is full. The TV in the living room has the BBC coverage on and the hardcore election observers are settled in for the night, getting mightily pissed as Peter Snow's computer graphics soar and explode with every gain and defeat. McKinley holds court in the kitchen where a fine soundtrack plays and tasty concoctions are created. The air is full of optimism, excitement and the Charlatans' *Tellin' Stories*. Cheers from the living room draw interested revellers to the news, returning with reports from around the country as Britpop socialists everywhere give the Tories a good kick in the bollocks. The hallway and reception room buzzes with conversation and laughter while the warm evening is enjoyed by a hardy group of party people lounging on rugs in the backyard under a cloudless darkening sky. I'm floating in more ways than one. Dennis arrived in all his provincial queen finery - pink shirt slashed to the navel, cock-hugging jeans - and started handing out Es and masses of weed. The pill I dropped an hour ago is sending alternate waves of euphoria and pulses of energy through me. Rolling with the chemical ebb and flow, I dip into all the various groups, feeling the togetherness, feeding off the positive vibes; I reconnect with Karen in the cocktail lounge (the kitchen) after losing myself for a moment in the jovial political banter of the screening room.

"Hello handsome, you look happy," she grins. Even if I wasn't on ecstasy I would still want to shag her right here and now, party guests be damned. She looks amazing. I love girls who can pull off those skin-tight oriental dresses and Karen is one of them. The satin hugs every petite curve and even if she hadn't already whispered the information into my ear on her arrival, I would be in no doubt that she isn't wearing any underwear. There's no visible panty line on this girl and this dress would surely show it. She looks like she was poured into it. Her hair has grown out a bit since Knebworth and the now shoulder length bob is hooked up in a clasp at the back of her head, leaving that amazing face and those dark almond eyes free of distractions.

"Karen Anderson, you're amazing. Everyone?" I holler above the music. "Karen is amazing. Just thought I'd tell you if you didn't already know." McKinley cracks up and pours a gin-based hangover-in-a-glass and hands it to me. Karen smiles with both mouth and eyes and plants a passionate yet soft kiss on my lips.

"I'm not Karen Anderson tonight," she whispers in my ear before taking a sip of my drink. "I'm Chu-Mi." I raise a Roger Moore eyebrow. "And if you come and find me a little later, you can chew me too." I'm not shaken but something definitely stirred. She lingers with a lascivious look and then sashays out of the kitchen. Man, that arse is a work of art.

"Big man!" McKinley is in my ear now. "Have you seen what's going on outside?" I follow him out through the back door and stand on the patio where a scene which would make Caligula blush is in full swing. "Over there, in the corner. That's Rob..."

And Faye the Sperm Stealer. "No way man. What's she doing here?"

"Don't worry, she's been 'away' if you know what I mean. Secure little hotel with wall-to-wall padding. She's had so much electroshock therapy she doesn't even know who she is let alone who you are." And yet there she is with her tongue down Rob's throat...and a fast working hand in his pants. "Do you reckon she's got a test tube down there as well?"

"Did you invite her?"

"Err...I invited..." McKinley points to the other darkened corner where Faye's mate Sheena is practically humping...

"Is that Ellis?! Jesus..."

McKinley is beside himself. "Wait, wait, wait...I've left the best...or most disturbing... to last. Can you see those two under the tree?" Two figures, one tall, the other short, are a shadowy blur of motion. "That's Dennis fucking Tony Peru! Excellent! Full on Roman orgy!"

The last days of conservatism. It's quite apt really.

All this sexual energy (and the MDMA) eventually gets the better of me - once I've managed to erase the image from my mind of a sweating Dennis bumming a Peruvian midget to within an inch of his life. I find Karen perched on the arm of a sofa watching the election show. I stand beside her casually, pretending to watch the TV, but my hand is in her hair, stroking the nape of her neck. I feel her shiver. She looks up at me. "Are you hungry?"

"Yeah, I could eat."

Two minutes later we're in the spare bedroom and Karen has her dress hitched up around her hips. She hoists herself up onto the window sill and, as I kneel in front of her, she puts one leg over my shoulder and pushes herself back. He grabs the back of my head and forces my face into her. After what seems like hours on my knees, Karen slides off the window sill and drags me to the bed. Huge cheers reverberate up from the living room as we fuck in pure celebration of the moment. I'm lost in this woman, unaware of where we are, only that we *are* - that we exist. Nothing else seems to as Karen demands more and more from me, urging me with breathless commands, and I thank the God of psychoactive drugs that I'm rocking on this phenomenal E tonight because otherwise I think I may have waved the white flag by now. The cheers from below are replaced by football-chant singing. As the election revelry reaches crescendo - so do we. We lay there gasping for air as the world changes around us.

Back downstairs and marginally more composed, we find out that conservative prick Michael Portillo has just lost his secure Enfield Southgate constituency to Labour's (hugely shocked) Stephen Twigg. The Tories are on the ropes and victory is Labour's for the taking. The highly inebriated crowd are singing: "You're going down with Portillo!" Karen and I look at each and burst out laughing.

I wake up alone in the bed Karen and I shook to breaking point mere hours ago feeling like someone has fire-bombed the inside of my head. A hot sickness swims between my temples and a chemically-erased void inhabits the space where my memory should be. I search the vacuum for any clues. There's a vague image of kissing Karen goodbye as the sun came up followed by a taxi pulling away from the front of the house. This scene slides into another where Rob is plying me with more of his endless supply of coke while McKinley makes milk and Benylin cocktails for breakfast. But I can't remember where I am or where I'm supposed to be. I have the vague recollection that I have a job and for a second I panic that I'm supposed to be there. Something somewhere assures me I wouldn't be so stupid as to not take the day off...after...the something big which seems to have happened.

After lying in a state of disabling amnesia for a few minutes more, I venture downstairs is search of anything which can help me find the missing pieces. I can't remember the hand grenade attack which must have happened sometime during the early hours of the morning but the evidence to suggest we were hit by a rogue IRA cell is everywhere. Bodies are strewn among the wreckage; glasses, cans, plates litter the ground between spread-eagled corpses in every room. I count at least fifteen victims, Rob and Ellis among them. Despite the carnage, most look quite peaceful and all seem to be still alive...just. One is even propped up with a newspaper open on her lap and a cup of steaming coffee in one hand.

"Good morning sunshine. Sleep well?" Brenda may have come across as a bit of a stiff on her arrival but recollections soon surface of McKinley's other half guzzling margueritas like they were fruit juice and cursing like a sailor on shore leave. At one point I think I even received a large reefer from her direction. I question these sketchy memories because the Brenda in front of me looks as though she may have gone for a run first before collecting the morning papers and making herself a healthy breakfast. That's not the kind of behaviour you'd expect from someone who was caning it with the best just a few hours before.

"Did you really go for a jog this morning?" I blink a couple of times to check that the Nike runners on the floor by her chair are actually there. After refocusing, I see she's dressed in a tracksuit - not one of those leisure outfits you wear when you're being a lazy bastard around the house but a full-on Linford Christie.

"Aye," she says, her Edinburgh brogue softer and rounder than McKinley's Glaswegian. "I find it's the best remedy for a night on the lash. It clears the mind. You should try it, Daniel." Just thinking about her running makes me want to throw up. I think I may actually die if I actually try and get above crawling speed.

"I think I'll pass." Or pass out. I sway in the doorway for a moment. "Is there coffee?"

"What you need my lad is a good hearty breakfast." She puts her paper down and leads me into the kitchen by the arm. She guides me onto a stool, steadies me from falling off it, and pours me a cup of coffee. "How do you like your eggs?"

Brenda's halfway through making a plate of scrambled eggs and bacon for me when she starts asking more in-depth questions. I suddenly get the feeling that the pork rashes are not the only things getting grilled

494

today. "So the girl you were with last night...Is that your woman? She's very pretty. McKinley says it's been a bit of a dramatic pursuit."

"Yeah..." I reply cautiously. I'm hoping that in the spirit of brotherhood the Scotsman has explained enough to satisfy Brenda's curiosity while keeping the sordid details at a minimum. "But it all seems to have worked out in the end." Conversation over? Not likely.

"So are you in love with her?"

I haven't even told Karen yet, although I had to tell McKinley how I feel about her. Considering he counselled me through the first few steps of this new experience from about seven thousand miles away - at his phone bill's expense, I may add - I thought it only fair and in my best interests that he should know the score. Now I have to work out if he told Brenda or not, or if she's testing me. Or I could just not give a toss about what's going through my inquisitor's head right now and hope she'll leave me alone. "Yeah..." Again with the unconvincing reply. "We haven't got to the stage of telling each other how we feel though." How are those eggs coming along? They aren't going to scramble themselves. Less talking, more cooking, woman. Please?

"You should tell her. She seems like an intelligent girl. If you show all the signs of being into her but can't verbally express what you're feeling then she may think you're an emotionally stunted, immature example of this stupid lad culture I keep hearing about and, you know, Daniel...that doesn't fly with intelligent, beautiful women."

She didn't take a breath. Not once. But it's me who's finding it hard to breathe. What the fuck? I thought I'd handled the hard part of this balancing act we all seem to have been struggling with for the past three years by actually finding a girl I like and wanting to stick with her while enjoying the freedoms of manhood. Now I have to get all warm and fluffy and tell her about my feelings or risk losing her? I need to sit down. Oh. I am sitting down. Maybe I need to lie down.

"Did anyone get the number of that bus that ran me over?" Ellis shuffles into the kitchen, takes a look at the eggs cooking on the stove, heaves, and reaches for my coffee. "If this is the new world then it feels a helluva lot like the last one." He takes a bar stool beside me and drains my coffee. "You look like shit, Danny. Do I look as bad as him?"

Brenda looks from one to the other and back again. "You both look the same as each other - in denial." Jesus. Is this ever going to stop? I'd leave but I currently don't have the strength. Ellis looks around the kitchen, perplexed as though he's just heard a voice from another dimension. He looks quizzically at me. I shake my head and almost lose consciousness through pain. "It's okay, you can say it: what the fuck am I going on about?" Ellis does his best goldfish impression as Brenda lets rip again. "Daniel here is in love with his woman but his belief that telling her so and letting her see the real person inside will make him less of a man and therefore unable to enjoy football, beer and pornography. You, on the other hand, you are running away from the same thing - which is commitment, by the way - by sticking your tongue down the neck of any poor sex-starved beast who'll let you and guzzling booze and drugs in an effort to dull the pain of losing the one woman who, contrary to what you may actually think, made you feel more of a man than any lads night out ever could."

The goldfish turns to me, face frozen in a mouth-open gape of puzzlement and shock. "She didn't take a breath. Not once."

"Impressive, isn't it?" I sigh, pinching the bridge of my nose.

"How much did McKinley tell you?"

"Just the basics," smiles Brenda, finally serving me breakfast. "The rest is obvious to anyone with eyes, a modicum of common sense...and a pair of tits. You boys seriously need to get to understanding women."

"What's all the noise?" Rob wanders in, hands in his pants, face smeared with what hopefully is the remnants of Faye's whorish lipstick.

Brenda, hands on hips, looks Rob up and down. "Don't even get me started on him."

"She said I'm hiding from who I am behind the masks that acting provides and that...all the women I choose..." Rob struggles to find his thread; such was Brenda's lengthy diagnosis of his failings.

I try and help him out. "She said he continues to make bad choices with women even though this new career gives him the illusion of self-confidence and ego when in fact...in fact it..."

"It's just another barrier put up to stop him from accepting how damaged he really is," Ellis concludes. "And the crazy women are the best evidence that underneath the mask he's still a little boy who's scared of his dad...or something. Did I get that right?"

McKinley reaches for his ice-cold glass of water and Resolve, drags it across the table towards him and presses it against his head - which is resting on the breakfast bar. He groans deeply but weakly. "Whose idea was it to get her started on all that?"

"HERS!" All three of us exclaim at the same time. McKinley groans louder and with more force. He struggles to get his head off the counter with a rubbery neck and forces down the hangover cure. He belches a gurgle, catching the Resolve, water and bile before it can become projectile and swallows painfully again.

"Actually, this is all your fault for giving her too much information," I say, accusingly.

"I bet you did it just to save your own arse," adds Rob.

"I think I'm going to fucking die." The Scotsman is struggling like never before.

"So is she always like this?" Ellis has been acting very perturbed since receiving his own analysis. I knew he was struggling with the break-up but I share a house with him. It's not easy to keep everything hidden when you live in such close proximity with someone. But Brenda has only just arrived in our lives - barely twelve hours ago - and yet she knows more about his situation than I do and obviously a lot more than Ellis is ready to admit to.

"Yes, she's always like this," McKinley sighs. "It's fucking grating, mainly because she's nearly always spot-on. She can see things a mile off which is why I never shagged around. She'd sense it. Now she's called you boys on the truth, she'll leave you alone. The ball's in your court." He gets up and retches. "I'm going back to bed."

With McKinley safely back under the covers, Brenda on a shopping spree somewhere in the city and Jezza and Melons nowhere to be found, we decide to escape the bombsite and see what a New Labour afternoon looks like. The three of us sit on a bench in the park watching children play and parents chat: smoke no evil, snort no evil, drink no evil - ever again. It's easy to be a wise monkey after the fact. Sheathed in the darkest of sunglasses and bathed by the warm May sunshine we look out onto a changing Britain; a Britain of vitality, creativity and hope. A country ready to embrace the can-do mentality; a nation ready to shine as a beacon of renewal. The clouds of conservatism have finally dissipated and we're left to bask in the warm glow of a sunny future. We are this country's talent and drive, the engine which will drive our new leaders towards achieving the dream.

"I have to puke." Ellis gets up and staggers to the nearby bin, hurling a gallon of poison onto the discarded McDonald's wrappers and beer cans. Rule Britannia.

"So this is New Labour country now," I say. "Here, Blair and everywhere."

"Is it really going to make a difference?" Ellis says, gingerly reclaiming his place in line. "I mean, aren't all these politicians just the same, deep down?"

"It has to be different," Rob chips in, making a statement of hope rather than conviction.

"It can't be any worse, can it?" I ask. The question hangs in the air, alone and unanswered. "Things can only get better." Silence settles over us as we consider the possibilities.

"I fucking hate that song," Ellis finally says. "Shit election tune." The other two not-so-wise monkeys nod silently in agreement.

It takes me almost 48 hours to feel human again and on the night of the second day, I feel well enough to go round to Karen's flat and apologise for anything I may have said or done while under the extremely mind-altering substances which were coursing through my body on election night. Amanda opens the door on her way out. She looks at me as if I'm wearing a shit-covered blanket, ringing a bell and groaning "unclean...unclean." I'm actually looking immaculate in a freshly washed and pressed Ben Sherman, equally spiffy blue jeans and my chin is free of stubble. So up yours, Manimal. I'm a fucking catch. "Evening Amanda, you're looking lovely as always."

"Karen?" She bellows over her shoulder, narrow eyes still squinting at me. "It's for you." Amanda doesn't move from the doorway but stands there like a nightclub bouncer who lives by a strict guest-list and dress code. If your name's not down, you're not coming in. Except it is down and I am coming in. And as for the trainers rule? I've got my desert boots on tonight so hah! Karen strolls to the door; no make-up, hair tied back, wearing the Supergrass t-shirt I've been missing for weeks and a pair of sloppy Adidas trackie bottoms. How does she do it? She looks like a goddess even when she's just rolled off the sofa after an afternoon of *Sunset Beach*. An enthusiastic arm bypasses security, takes my hand and drags me inside.

"Night, 'Manda. Have fun!" Amanda's grumbling can be heard trailing off down the stairs as Karen kicks the door shut behind us and leaps into my arms, wrapping her legs round my waist and planting a fast kiss on my lips. "Hello lover."

"Hi," I return the kiss, softer and longer this time. "I see Amanda's charm school classes are paying off."

"I've told you," Karen scolds, crushing my hips with those horse-riding thighs of hers. "She's just very protective of me."

"Trust me, you can look after yourself." She climbs down and shadow boxes in front of me for a moment before landing a surprisingly painful punch on my shoulder. "Oi! Are you starting something?"

Half an hour later after starting something and finishing it to both our satisfactions, we're sat on the sofa considering our options. "Okay, I've got *Mars Attacks!* the new *Crow* movie, which looks a bit shit actually, and *101 Dalmatians*."

"*101 Dalmatians*?"

"Yeah, you know, spotty dogs, that Cruella woman... fun for all the family?"

"I know what it is, I'm just surprised you rented it! Did you wear a disguise?"

"No," I reply, only slightly offended. "I thought I'd go for something dark, something light and something fluffy and cute. There's something for every mood. Besides, you like animals and I thought you might be into it."

"Danny Jones, I think you're growing," Karen says with amusement as she playfully rubs my thigh. "Gone are the days when the choice would be between Schwarzenegger, Tarantino and some Stephen King crap. And even though the choice of *101 Dalmatians* is a sign of true love, it's a bit sickly for me - I'll go with *Mars Attacks!*" She slides off the sofa and crawls towards the VCR. Usually this would give me great pleasure as I never get bored with seeing that backside raised to the heaven which created it but today, instead of giving thanks to the God of Arses, I'm seized by a freezing dread. My mind and soul are confronting each other like boxers before a fight and the nervous energy between them is paralyzing. Which will win and take control of my gob?

"I do...you know." The soul wins. The mind retreats to its corner and utters 'impulsive fool' as the mouth stumbles over the points decision.

"You do *what*?" God! Why don't people ever understand those cryptic messages you stammer out in potentially life-changing moments, you know, the ones which are designed to avoid actually saying the words? Why do people always force you to be clear and make sense? My mind is off its stool again, ready to seize the opportunity to change direction and avoid the coming humiliation and pain the soul so obviously wants to wallow in.

"Love you..." The mind throws in the towel and spits its gum shield into a bucket of bloody water. "I...love you." Karen turns round from leaning over the video and sits down hard, facing me with a look of utter surprise. She sits there on the floor for what seems like forever without saying a word. She's just staring at me...which isn't helping with the current state of discomfort and vulnerability I find myself in. Part of me - the guy who would have brought *Terminator*, *Reservoir Dogs* and *Pet Semetary* round for a romantic night in - wants to break the uncomfortable silence by pointing, laughing and saying "gotcha!" But that is the part which I'm trying to keep in check. That's the part which has been keeping those three little words deeply buried for the past eight months. That's the part which Angela said could be my downfall. "Karen?" I stop short of waving my hand in front of her face. "Did you hear what I said?" She blinks herself out of her own stare and crawls towards me with a look on her face I can't read. It could be one of those looks which try to soften the blow of the sentence which begins, 'You're a great bloke but...' Or it could be that kind of look which slowly melts into tears of joy. She kneels at my feet and puts her hands on my knees. On closer inspection, it looks increasingly like the pose of a woman who's about to tell you you're going too fast.

"When I first met you again, after all those years, I wasn't surprised you were a Lad. You always had that boyish mischief about you. It used to melt me when I was a little kid, dreaming of being your girlfriend and kissing you secretly behind the science block. When we met at the Orchard that night, you reminded me of how I used to feel at school but it also reminded me how much I'd changed. You hadn't changed, though. You were just...older. That was the main reason I left that first time."

"That and bloody Amanda..."

"It was good that I left," Karen continues. "If we had just gone for it, that would have been that. I wouldn't have wanted to see you again. You told me when we met at the Belly concert that you'd tried to find me, that you wanted to see me again. I didn't expect that from you and it surprised me. It also reminded me that I had been thinking about you a lot in the year between, but I didn't really know why - until we went to the bandstand. I saw that you were changing and that the reason I'd been thinking about you since that night in Pulse was that I felt a change in you then but didn't think it was enough. That's why I wanted you to keep looking for me because I thought that if you really wanted me, you'd keep searching. Then when we met in Amsterdam..."

"I've already explained why I reacted that like," I blurt out again, unnecessarily.

"I know...And even though you were a proper dick to me, I realised why you were being such a dick. Because you cared. When I first met you again, I didn't think you would ever care. I thought that I would just be another conquest. Knebworth proved to me that you wanted more than that...which is why we're together now."

"So..?"

Karen stands up and pulls me upright off the sofa. She stares up at me and smiles. "You're not the Danny I used to know," she whispers. "You're the Danny who rents *101 Dalmatians* just because I might like it."

Never underestimate the power of a Disney movie. Sometimes you don't even have to watch it.

There comes a period during most extensive nights on the town when the concept of time is suddenly forgotten. During these moments, you can change venue, skip between topics of conversation and imbibe inhuman amounts of alcohol without even knowing it. You enter a waking dream state in which only objects within touching distance can be trusted. Even the people in close proximity to you take on an ethereal quality while the world outside of your hazy perimeter slides past you in echoes and blurs. The voices of your friends, the custodians of your safety in these time-slip moments, are the only anchors you have to reality and even they can seem distant and alien. They slip in and out of hearing like broken messages piped in from the great beyond; at times strong enough to give you a fleeting sense of security, at others muffled to the point of incoherence, adding to the sporadic disconnection which fills you with pangs of panic.

We should all be able to handle these moments of sensory fluidity. None of us are strangers to being out of our gourds. But for most of us - Rob ironically being the exception these days - this feeling is not as common as it used to be and as such, as the booze continues to flow, the evening is threatening to head towards that dark place where nothing good can come of it.

Rob seems antsy after what must have been quite an in-depth discussion on relationships, commitment and the struggles which go with them. To me, the debate seems to have been over in flash. The table full of empty glasses tells a different story. As does Rob's demeanour. The actor obviously wants a change of pace and atmosphere. "Shawna, sweetheart, any chance that you could arrange for four of your loveliest ladies to come over and give us some personal attention?"

Our hostess nods agreeably. "Of course, sir. Do you have any specific requirements or desires?"

Rob looks round the table. Ellis is starting to look queasy again, the Scotsman's eyes seem to be drifting in and out of focus and I'm taking deep breaths in an attempt to keep the wormhole which is starting to open above my head from sucking me into space. It's obvious that the night's excesses are beginning to catch up with all of us - except Rob. "I think anyone who can bring these three back to life will be perfect," he smarms in his most seductive Roger Forester tone.

"Certainly, sir." With that, Shawna glides away from our VIP table in search of a quartet of lap dancers to fit the bill.

"If some tart gets on my lap, I think I'll spew," McKinley's honest appraisal of his own condition is welcome, if also a little surprising. Rarely, if ever, has he passed up the opportunity to have a pair of tits rubbed in his face. While he does look a little green around the gills, it's possible that his recent admission has filled his addled mind with the guilt that now keeps him on the straight and narrow. "I'll give it a miss."

"Yeah, I'm not into it either," I add. "I'm happy to watch the girls on stage but I'm not going to get a dance."

Rob's face is a picture of amused disbelief. "I never thought I'd live to see the day that you pair of dirty bastards would turn down some bump and grind. You know I'm paying, right?"

"It doesn't matter, man."

"Really?"

"Look, I'm a big fan of naked girls but it's strictly a case of look but don't touch these days," I admit. "And before you start banging on about me being under the thumb, this is my rule. Just because I prefer to keep the action between me and Karen these days doesn't make me a pussy, okay? It might come as a surprise but I actually get everything I need from my relationship." The words, untainted with dishonesty, certainly surprise me but soothe me at the same time, "Getting my hands on a stripper's tits isn't going to be any kind of improvement on what I can have at home." And that's the truth.

"But you're not going to tell her you were here though," grins Rob.

"Are you fucking mad? Karen would kill me - or worse!"

Rob turns to the increasingly pale Scotsman. "What's your excuse?"

McKinley comes back from a private moment battling his demons. "I just told you. I'm on the verge of spewing my ring." He takes a couple of quick, short breaths and steadies himself by gripping the arm of the sofa. "I'm fucking well off my tits, man. I might have to go and chuck up." All this time Ellis has remained silent, hoping that by sinking into the armchair he's in he'll become invisible. Not a chance.

"The groom has to have one though," says Rob. "If these two are anything to go by, you should get what you can before committing to a life of monogamy, especially as you've been living one of those for the past fucking thirty-odd years anyway."

"And when are you going stop arsing about and get yourself sorted out then?" After our conversation back at the Warehouse I know better than anyone that Rob's not as dismissive of relationships as he appears.

"Who knows? But until I can see the attraction of watching a beautiful, magical woman slowly turn into the nagging bitch I stay out of the house just to avoid, then I'll stay as I am." Rob's face lights up as four dancers who look like they just stepped out of a United Colours of Benetton advert slowly begin to ascend the steps and approach our table. "I'm not ready to stay together with one person long enough to find out what I don't like about them." The blonde, the redhead, the African and the Asian stand in front of us and smile sweetly. Each has a killer, toned body sheathed in the smallest of smalls; their chests heaving in tiny bikini tops and their puffy crotches barely covered by micro thongs. "My commitment," adds Rob, almost salivating as he eyes each girl in turn, "lasts about the length of a song these days." He kicks Ellis in the shin. "I'm presuming you'll take the Nubian queen."

Ellis attempts to sink further into his seat. Failing to disappear into the upholstery, he chooses instead to put a hand over his eyes. If there was a sandpit available, he'd be head first into it up to his neck. "Not for me, thanks."

"Come on, it's your stag do. I'm happy to take Blondie, Red and the little Oriental dish off your hands but four on one would be greedy, even for me."

"No thanks."

Rob sighs. "Are you boys sure? I mean, come on Danny - you and blondes? You're really all over that?" I give him a silent thumbs-up while the Scotsman continues to focus on his breathing. "Okay then...Ladies, I'm all yours." Rob gets unsteadily to his feet and links arms with Blondie and Red as the Asian girl leads them down the stairs towards the private rooms. The African girl lingers.

"Nice one, Ellis," she says as he finally reappears from behind his hand. "Mon would be proud." She winks at him and smiles.

"But I wasn't here, was I Lindsey?"

"I didn't see you," she replies, feigning innocence. She turns to me. "Are you sure you wouldn't like a little personal attention?"

"Lindsey, is it? Believe me darlin', that's a very tempting offer but I'm going to have to decline."

"Pity. You're a cute one," she smiles. Lindsey turns to Ellis again. "If I don't see you before, Ellis, I'll see you at the church." She turns back to me. "Make sure he gets back okay." With that, Lindsey's Amazonian body slinks away, the negligible satin barely covering what's left of her modesty crumpling suggestively as she does so.

Ellis answers the question written across my perplexed face. "She's one of Monica's best friends," he mumbles sheepishly. "And one of the bridesmaids."

"Stripper bridesmaids, eh?" I grin. This could be some wedding. Perhaps I'll convince Karen that she doesn't have to come after all. McKinley forces himself up from the sofa and almost topples head first across the table. I stand up quickly and catch him, stopping him crashing through the glass while getting my own massive head rush in the process. "Easy, big man. You nearly went there."

"I'll be alright," he slurs unconvincingly. "I just need to get some air."

"I'm pretty wasted too," adds Ellis. "I won't be far behind you."

"Alright, but don't wander off. We'll wait for the Ponce to cum in his pants and then we'll all leave together." With that, the Scotsman heads for the exit via every banister and steadying piece of furniture. The last five minutes of focus have helped to quell my own growing mental and physical unease and I'm pleased to report that the wormhole is now closed. I watch McKinley slalom his way out of the door and sit down again, relieved to be back in the right moment in time and space once again. Ellis also looks to have recovered. He still looks blitzed but no longer ready to keel over and die.

"Lindsey was right," I say, raising my glass in his direction. "Monica would be proud...well, as proud as any woman would be of her coked-up, alcoholic fiancé turning down a lap dance." He chuckles and clinks his own glass on mine as I toast him. "You should be proud of yourself too, y'know? To get this far and be this sure with one woman is no mean feat, man. I'd count this as a triumph. Actually, no. An unmitigated success over everything that ever stood in your way." I tip my glass to him once more before draining the last of its gin. "Heard anything from Sean about what he has planned as best man?"

Ellis leans forward. "I've sacked him." He downs his own drink and grimaces. "I came to the conclusion that he doesn't know who I really am, and certainly doesn't know who Monica is. My best man should be someone who knows us both and knows our story. I only asked Sean because I wanted him to play second fiddle to me for once. But I decided that I'm not going to play that game anymore. I'm not going to try and live a second rate version of his life. I'm going to live my own."

"When did you decide all this?"

"After our conversation outside the Indian," he smirks. "I phoned him from the Warehouse toilets. He wasn't best pleased. He was doing his taxes, struggling to balance the books." Ellis fixes me with a sincere stare. "I want you to be my best man, Danny. It should have been you from the start but you know how things have been. You know how they've always been. That's why it should be you." I'm speechless. My inability to reply prompts Ellis to ask me again. "Will you do it? Will you be my best man?"

"I'd be fucking honoured, geezer." I admit it. I'm filling up a little. "Should we hug?"

"Let's just drink to it, eh?" he grins. He waves over Shawna for what turns out to be the last time tonight. "Shawna, can we have a couple of your most expensive whiskies over here, please? On the rocks. And put it on the soap star's bill, will you? Cheers."

Once Rob has finished rolling around on a circular bed with his multicultural harem, he settles the extravagant bill and we swerve our way out of the Camel Club and into the chill of the early hours to find the Scotsman sitting on a nearby bench looking more like his old self. It seems that a hearty vomit and one last sneaky line of cocaine is all he needed to get back on a relatively even keel.

"Happy now?" I ask Rob as he rearranges his crotch area. "Satisfied?"

"You know...I just may be." An enigmatic expression settles on his face, prompting a curious one to take up residence on mine. "I got her number."

"Who? One of the strippers? Rob, what did we talk about earlier about breaking the cycle and getting new, healthier habits?"

"I am...at least, I hope so."

"Dating a stripper doesn't sound like the first step to redemption, man."

"I don't know, big man," adds the Scotsman. "Sounds alright to me."

"Don't encourage him."

"Look, she's not your regular stripper...she didn't even get her top off."

"Then she's a bit fucking crap," sniffs McKinley. "I'm changing my view. I'm with Danny. Knock it on the head, man."

"She's just doing this to get through medical school," sneers Rob. "She's going to be a doctor."

"Can't she just stack shelves like everyone else?" asks an increasingly pale imitation of Ellis.

"Which one was she anyway?" enquires McKinley.

"The Chinese one."

"Sweet and sour," smiles the Scotsman. "Lovely."

"I know what you're all thinking but something clicked, okay?" protests Rob. "She's a nice girl."

"Aye, a nice girl who rotates her arse over a dozen sweaty blokes a night," grins the Scotsman. "Definitely a keeper."

"Maybe she is," says Rob. "There was a connection."

I back down a little when I hear an authenticity in his voice. "Any sign of mental health problems?"

"She seemed pretty sane," smiles the Actor. "Plus she's never seen *Billionaire's Playground*."

"Always a bonus."

"Right, I have to go home." Ellis summons the last of his energy and hails a cab. "I'm very happy for you and your stripper-slash-doctor future wife. I'll hope you'll be very happy together." We all hug the man of the hour in turn and come to the agreement that it has indeed been a top night, even by our own quite high standards of larging. Ellis praises us for a strong showing on this his special night. I thank him quietly again for asking me to be his best man and pledge to do him proud - and with that he's gone, spirited away in one of Black Cat's finest to spend one of his few remaining nights as a bachelor retching in the toilet and sleeping fitfully. We watch the taxi turn the corner and stand swaying in silence for a moment.

The Scotsman ends the vigil "Nightcap anyone?"

"The hotel bar may still be open," I offer, attempting to read my watch. "Although it's getting on for four o'clock."

"It's worth a look," says Rob, flagging down another taxi.

"So you're going to slum it at our dive, are you?" I ask. "I thought you had a suite at the Kingsley."

"I do but it's such a soulless fucking monstrosity," he spits. "The Heighton has a better atmosphere and a better bar. And I want a real pint, not some tosspot cocktail with a sparkler and umbrella stuck in it."

"Right then," McKinley says, opening the cab door and giving instructions to our driver. "Big man, the Heighton Hotel if you please."

Luckily - depending on your perspective, of course - the Heighton's bar is still open and a handful of well-oiled punters are keeping the takings high and the bar staff on overtime. You've gotta love a bar which will only close when there's no-one left to serve. The Hartington was like that - which is why, on more than one occasion, McKinley and I went straight into cooking breakfast from the previous night's drinking without ever going home in between. It also probably contributed to Barry the Barman's lack of a life. There are always punters willing to drink whatever hour of the day or night, especially in hotels catering to travelling businessmen. The Heighton's red-eye customers have middle-aged sales tosser written all over them. They snort and guffaw together at one end of the bar like vulgar, over-paid warthogs dressed in pin-striped suits and sweat-drenched Oxford shirts, their ties askew and their crotches beginning to reek of the effects of premature holstering. They slur sexist jokes to each other under a cloud of body odour, piss drips and stale ale. Lad culture may have turned millions of young men into belligerent misogynists but for most of us it was just a phase. The swine which rooted through Britain's coffers in the 80s were never so lucky. Margaret Thatcher's free market capitalism turned a whole generation of Hooray Henry's into permanently heinous fuckwits obsessed with their false sense of privilege.

The fuckwits barely notice us as we sidle up to the bar and order three pints of Carlsberg from the barman who, in spite of having more customers who could potentially keep him up past sunrise, seems pleased to see us. After taking receipt of the beers, and extending an invitation to the barman to join us, we avoid any possible confrontation with the Quentins by adjourning to the snug. It seems only fair. The last thing the poor bloke behind the bar needs is a trio of wankered Lefties battling the Upper Class in some scene strangely reminiscent of England fans on tour. Rob belches wetly and catches some unannounced vomit with a fast hand. He scuttles off to the toilets as McKinley and I take a seat. Once quietly ensconced in the benevolent old Chesterfields, I decide I owe the Scotsman the explanation he's been after all night.

512

"Things have been shit at home for months," I say, out of the blue. "But it was all me. Life was getting on top of me and I started missing the old times; the freedom and lack of responsibility. I started wondering if I'd be better off without all the demands and expectations, just living for me, you know? I was blaming Karen and Leah for changing my life when I should have been thanking them every single day."

"What were you going to do?"

"I don't know. I was hoping this weekend would make it all clear again. I suppose I was hoping that, one way or another, a return to old shits and giggles would bring me to a decision."

"And has it?"

"I can't live like this full time again...and in all honesty, I don't want to," I admit. "It was fun back in the day but it was never a permanent state, was it? We were all just passing through. We all needed to be that way for all our different reasons but we were never going to be those people forever, were we?"

"Thank fuck," the Scotsman replies. "My liver is eternally grateful for that."

"I think it's necessary to be able to dip back in from time to time, to satisfy parts of our old selves that we still hold onto but that's connected to our friendship, not the rest of our lives," I muse, fatigue and inebriation making their last push for conquest. "It's healthy to have a certain balance. We're all light and dark, man. We're all light and dark."

"I'll drink to that," McKinley smiles. We toast as a pallid looking Rob weaves his way back into the snug. McKinley suddenly gets to his feet as if he's just been stung by a wasp. "Fuck me, I almost forgot. Stay here, I'll be right back." With that he stumbles his way towards the stairs without any further explanation.

513

"So you're coming back for the wedding then," I say, not really asking.

"Of course," Rob replies. "I know I've got a reputation for disappearing but this is Ellis' wedding. He'd never forgive me if I missed it. It's not like a dinner invitation or meeting for a pint. This could be the only wedding he ever has."

"I certainly hope so. After all it took to get him to agree to this one, I wouldn't hold out much hope of getting him up the aisle again if this one went tits up."

"Do you think it will?"

I ponder the possibility for a moment. The course of true love never runs smooth, as they say, but Ellis and Monica's has been more like the romantic version of competing in the Paris–Dakar rally in a 4x4 with shoddy suspension. Before tonight I was harbouring concerns that, even as they approach the finish line, there might be a flat tyre or blown gasket to worry about. However, spending the evening with Ellis – and broaching more than a few sensitive topics with him during it – has given me hope that they'll cross the chequered flag and enjoy the victory together for years to come. "I think the danger to the relationship was always Ellis' fear of failure," I eventually say. "He wasn't really afraid of commitment. He just thought that he'd be shit at it. For as long as we've known him, he's been aiming at the wrong targets but I don't think that's a problem anymore. He wants this and I think, for the first time, he's happy that he's not trying to outdo his brother or keep his mum sweet. This decision he's made is about him and Monica, no-one else."

Rob looks lost for a second, the familiar hollowness to the stare and sinking of the cheeks returns. Lost in painful thought, he looks like the kid I knew before he learnt how to hide the external indicators of the torment behind his eyes. "It really hits home how much I've missed, hearing the things I've heard tonight," he sighs before shaking his head

514

and pinching the bridge of his nose. The thrilling effects of tonight's excess are fading fast, leaving us both in an increasingly fuzzy daze. We're spiralling down into frazzled reflection, dragged into the depths of introspection by the undertow of a rapidly departing, speeding high. We're in the final phase now. Limits have been reached and soon fitful, chemical sleep will attempt to claim us. Rob momentarily loses his thread as his mind flickers on to standby mode in preparation for the complete loss of signal. A short forced-out breath and a widening of tired eyes and he's back. "How did they get back together anyway? I remember you told me they were a couple again but it was lost in the middle of some stream of information and I never got the details."

The fact that I have to fill in the blanks with Rob is nothing new. What is unusual is that what I am about to tell him came to me second-hand. Up to a certain point, everything relating to Ellis' life was relayed to me by the man himself. We lived together for over three years and while there was never some kind of weird, pseudo-lovers' pact to tell each other everything, we did share. The fact that we were imbibing large quantities of substances which have a tendency to make your jaws flap - among other effects - meant that we spent countless nights under the influence talking about what was going on in our lives. But we never talked about how Ellis and Monica got back together. We didn't talk about that because at the time, we weren't talking about anything. We weren't talking full-stop.

I didn't leave for Dublin solely because of Ellis but his behaviour, from my perspective anyway, certainly made it an easier decision to make. Karen and I were at one of the many crossroads couples reach the longer they stay together. In the early days we'd chosen the same path when faced with the signpost pointing in opposite directions to Casual and Serious - taking the latter, we also (somewhat painfully) made the decision to take the road to Stay Together when we could have made a wrong and headed to Break-Up. This time, after committing to routes which brought us closer together, we had to decide whether to Stay or Go. Karen's job was relocating her to Dublin and we were discussing the wisdom of staying together but living in two different cities when Ellis and I started going through our own parting of ways. It's all academic now but had the screenplay taken off, I may not have followed Karen to Dublin. Despite the commitment I had made to her, somewhere inside it felt as though my commitment to Ellis had been made a lot earlier and that I had more of an obligation to honour that one. If we'd been given the opportunity to make films or TV together, there's a good chance my life would be very different to how it is now. Maybe I'd be more like the Danny Jones who briefly reared his head in the toilets of the Warehouse earlier this evening. It's debatable whether I would be the Danny Jones with long-term partner, daughter and thoughts of more kids and commitment swirling around in his head. Given the state that Ellis and I would get into together, even in 1998 when we should have started to know better, it's pretty likely that we would have been like the fucked-up guests refusing to leave a party which had long since ended.

I was undecided at the time. Karen moving to Dublin and me staying here was less dramatic as, say, Karen moving to Washington and me staying here. It wouldn't have been such a strain on our relationship but either way it meant that I wouldn't see her every day, which was something I was very much in favour of back then. But I wanted more than just being a reporter on the local rag and I really believed that the script ideas Ellis and I were coming up with had the potential to be huge. It wasn't just his chance - it was mine too. So when he blew it, he blew it for the both of us. That's why I was so pissed off. I felt betrayed. Ellis had not only sabotaged himself but he'd given no thought to what his actions would have on me and my dreams. He knew what they were - we'd spoken about them enough times - and yet at that moment it appeared to me that my hopes and dreams didn't mean anything to him. I felt that he had totally disregarded them. He had totally disregarded me. That's when I decided that there was nothing to keep me here. After a week of non-communication between us - during which I quit my job at the Daily - he called me at Karen's. I stood beside my packed bags in her living room waiting for the apology that never came. These were the last words I said to him before a year of silence began: "I'm moving to Ireland. It's too fucked up here. I need a new start."

My weekly conversations with McKinley continued and it was through him that I kept up-to-date with what was happening with Ellis. What the Scotsman told me on numerous occasions took me to the brink of ending my feud with Ellis but even when I had the receiver pressed to my ear, I couldn't bring myself to dial his digits. As weeks turned to months, the news got worse but it got even harder to make the call.

According to McKinley, Ellis was wallowing alone in the flat we used share, drowning in self-loathing and Stella Artois. Their phone calls would follow a regular pattern: First, Ellis would mumble about everything being shit and how the city was dying around him, that the hope and expectation of our heyday had evaporated. This would bring him onto the topic of wasted chances and the stupidity of believing in false prophets. He'd slag off the government, call Tony Blair a lying cunt and then launch into a slurred tirade about how fucking self-righteous I was and how I'd abandoned him when he needed me most. He'd eventually calm down to end his speech with heartfelt admissions of loneliness and loss, contradicting himself by saying he didn't blame me for leaving after he'd fucked up so badly. McKinley would then give Ellis the guru treatment he always reserved for me. He'd talk him down and only hang up when he was sure that Ellis was holding onto a positive thought that he'd provided him with. This went on for about three months. One day McKinley called me at work. He never did that and I feared the worst.

"You'll never guess what," he said. "The wee man has only gone and got himself a bird." Thank fuck for that, I thought. Even though I knew

Ellis better than anyone and knew he wasn't stupid or weak enough to kill himself, he did have an addictive personality and one which could have inadvertently taken him down that road had he given in to it. Ellis finding a new girlfriend was the most positive news I'd heard from back home for a long time. "I'll give you three guesses who it is." I needed only one once it became clear that she was someone we knew. "Aye, spot on. Fucking Steak Hammer's back on the scene."

The story goes like this (in the Scotsman's words): "One night, the sad bastard gets fed up beating himself into a stupor over some fucking granny porn and decides to get pissed up somewhere else for a change. So he drags himself across the road to the Castle because his knob is too sore from all the wanking to go anywhere too far out of his way. He takes a seat at the bar, looking and smelling like fucking Steptoe no doubt, and starts chucking pints of Bishop's Ringpiece or some other nasty fucking ale down his neck. Right, so he's getting well toasty and being a miserable bastard as he is, he starts shouting the odds. He's getting on his fucking soapbox again about how the future was stolen from him or some other bollocks from the wee man repertoire of sad excuses and Bob starts getting well fucked off with him. The two of them are about to come to blows when out of the blue, Steak Hammer of all people swoops in. She calms the situation down and almost carries Ellis out of the pub. Anyway, he somehow manages to convince her not to take him back to the flat, presumably because of all the crispy Kleenex all over the floor, so she takes him back to hers. He then admits everything; why he broke up with her in 96, how he thought she was going to leave him anyway, how he was afraid to commit, how he was madly on love with her but was scared of love. Then he says that the screenplay fuck up brought it all home to him and that he fears making a success of himself because he thinks it may still not be good enough. Now, Steak Hammer's been here before so she knows that the wee man can ramble for fucking England when he's off his tits so she puts him to bed and hopes to get some sober sense out of him in the morning. To everyone's surprise - get on this - he repeats the whole things again when he's the closest he can be too human and they decide to give it another chance. And he's telling me all this on the phone sounding like a five-year old who's been promised a trip to the fucking zoo!"

"So how did you two make things right?" asks Rob, now taking receipt of a brandy from the flagging barman.

"Once he was sure that things with Monica were stable, he called up one day from Dublin airport and asked if I could pick him up. He just turned up. It was awkward but we managed to smooth things over enough to start again. We never really got into it. We just decided to leave it in the past. The first time we really talked about it was tonight, which is one of the reasons why I think things are going to work out between him and Monica. He's facing up to things."

"Just in case he needs some persuading," says McKinley sauntering back into the snug, "I got him a wedding gift which might swing the balance." The Scotsman chucks a plain brown carton into my lap. He indicates that I should open the box with a wave of the hand and devilish grin. I flip open the flap at one end and slide the contents out. A 12-inch long latex dildo attached to a leather harness flops out onto the low table between us, prompting an amused cheer from the Scotsman. The cock thuds on the glass and wobbles for a moment like a black phallic jelly. "Son of Big Vern!" he cries.

"Jesus Christ," I giggle. "I can't wait to see that displayed between the toaster and the espresso machine."

"I was trying to think of an appropriate gift," laughs McKinley. "But I couldn't so I thought of an inappropriate one. Top stuff. What all solid marriages are built on, a bit of strapadicktomy!"

"Another reason not to get married, eh Danny?" Rob picks up the cock and slaps it across his palm like a policeman's truncheon. "Now that's just fucking dangerous."

"That reminds me," says McKinley. "I've got something for you too." He hands me another package, this one the size and shape of a paperback. I give him a suspicious look before tearing off the subtle wrapping paper. It's a VHS cassette. "It's the only copy, big man, I swear. I never made another. It might get a bit fuzzy on the part when she's doing the reverse cowgirl but that tends to happen when you leave it on pause for a while."

The Rachel Tape. My one and only foray into the amateur porn business. I'm suddenly a bundle of conflicted emotions. This is a piece of history, a snapshot of a time when we were out of control and free. It's also an unflattering depiction of drug abuse and wanton, casual sex - not to mention evidence of exploitation and a huge betrayal of trust. It's also something which could seriously piss off my missus and something which could seriously disturb my child should she stumble across it thinking it's Barney the Dinosaur. Destroying it would remove all the potential crises not destroying it could bring about. And yet - if it is the only copy - it would be erasing part of our culture. I'm torn. This is a decision which demands serious consideration.

"It didn't improve with age, did it?"

McKinley and I sit on the bottom of our twin beds watching the last shaky moments of coitus on the small screen in the corner of the room. By a stroke of dubious luck the Heighton hasn't evolved to provide guests with DVD players and so the old VHS-TV combos still hang from the walls in even the most expensive suites. The two of us sit and pass a small joint to each other while Rob snores on the sofa, just like in the days when this film was made. From the stringy puddle of drool accumulating beside his cheek, it's safe to assume he won't be making it back to his swanky hotel tonight.

"I don't know, man," says McKinley. "It's like those old John Holmes movies. Okay they lack the production values of the new stuff and the birds are bit minging but it's still a bunch of tarts getting royally shagged, which is never bad. You have to appreciate it for what it is." On the screen, my younger self thrusts manfully to orgasm, buries himself deep in his drunken slut of a co-star and turns to the hidden camera. He gives a sweaty peace sign and the action pauses before flicking off to static. I appreciate what I've just seen for what it is - a document from ancient history - and before I call it a night, I decide to burn it.